RESCUE & REDEMPTION

RESCUE & REDEMPTION

SIMON GREEN

Copyright © 2023 Simon Green
Other books written by Simon Green:
Hit & Split
The Complete Idiot's Guide to Motorcycles, 4th Edition, *Alpha/Penguin*
Muscle Car Dream Garages, *MBI*
Garage, Life in the Offbeat Import Car Shop, *Parker House*
Books with photography by Simon Green:
Dave Perewitz, Chopper Master and King of Flames, *MBI*
Cafe Racer: the Motorcycle, *Parker House*
Techno-Chop; the New Breed of Chopper Builder, *MBI*
How to build a Pro Streetbike, *MBI*

All Rights Reserved. No part of this book/work may be reproduced, stored in a retrieval system, or transmitted in any form or by any means -whether electronic, mechanical, photocopy, recording, telepathy, chiseled in stone, spelled out with rigatoni pasta -or via any other worldly medium, without the prior written permission of the author.

This book is a work of fiction. Names, characters, businesses, governmental departments, places, events and incidents are creations of the author's imagination or used in a fictitious manner. Any resemblance to actual events or to persons, living, dead, or in spectral limbo is purely coincidental. Seriously.

For John 'Sonic" Cantlie

A GREY LIFE

1.

THE COMPUTER CHIMED its incoming call tone at the exact moment its built-in clock indicated 9:00:00. The smartly suited man waited as the seconds continued to change, shaking his head at the predictability of such anal military punctuality. He watched as the seconds ticked away, to 9:00:29, then 30, then 31; for no other reason than to deny the caller such an infuriatingly punctual start. As the display showed 9:00:45 he sighed, reluctantly clicked the green phone icon, and watched as the computer's display changed to show the head and shoulders of a man in a multi-terrain pattern camo uniform.

"Good morning, Captain Bowyer, to what do I owe the pleasure?" The suit worked to ensure his face showed no evidence of the aforementioned pleasure.

Bowyer was already having the day from hell, and instantly bristled at the suit's blatant insincerity. *So it's going to be that kind of call, is it?* His nostrils flared momentarily. "I don't know, Chalmers, I've been thinking about you and wanted to hear your voice. How are you feeling today sweetheart?"

The suit hadn't seen that one coming and squirmed visibly in his chair. "Very amusing, Captain Bowyer, but I've got a busy day, so how about we just get to the point?"

"Happily," spat back Bowyer. "What are you doing with Sergeant Miller? This farce has taken more than long enough and if you don't want him anymore, then Her Majesty's Armed Forces will happily take him back off your hands."

"Miller's on leave," growled the suit.

Bowyer had no prepared response for that one, Miller's last adventures on leave are what had caused this friction.

"Yes, Captain Bowyer. Leave." The suit continued, "Although we did consider keeping him under observation this time; just in case he caused any new horrors on his holidays."

The urge to retaliate was overwhelming but the Captain forced himself to focus on his primary objective and the reason for this scheduled call. "Look Chalmers, you've read the report and I've read the report; Sergeant Miller has been cleared of any impropriety."

The suited man sniggered, "Well, that may be what the report shows, but we both know that regardless of any rose-tinted spectacles used by those who came to that conclusion, Miller went off script and undertook an unsanctioned operation based on personal motivations…"

The Captain's anger overflowed. "Obviously that's your personal perspective, and presumably why you've got him in this endless holding pattern you're calling 'leave.' But the official record shows that Sergeant Miller came up with a plan, a bloody clever one it must be said, a plan which saw the despised diplomatic immunity runner returned to the UK, where justice has since been served. Miller did this without harming a soul or causing any further diplomatic strain between us and our closest allies. In fact, his actions relieved the tension caused by that diplomatic abuse."

"He… came up with a plan." Chalmers heavily emphasized the first word. "As a military man, surely you see the problem with that statement."

Captain Bowyer was quickly growing weary of the conversation. "Do I need to remind you of the document contained within the official file, where you lot at GCHQ sanctioned Miller's American op?"

Chalmers sneered at the Captain. Being pressured by his own superior into back-dating orders for Sergeant Miller's rogue adventure still didn't sit well with him.

Yes, Miller had brought back the subject, Madyson Lutz. But how had he really achieved it?

Lutz had certainly been no help in discovering the how. She wholeheartedly backed up Miller's bullshit version of events, with zero signs of coercion. How had he managed that?

And Chalmers had still been hung up on the 'how' when his boss-lady had made it clear to him that their world was driven by results, that Miller had delivered them, and therefore it was time for Chalmers to 'Bloody-well move on'.

Gallingly, she'd even implied that if Chalmers had maintained a less authoritative and more consultative approach with his operatives, then the Lutz recovery op might have actually been sanctioned ahead of time.

He glared at Captain Bowyer as he thought things through. Chalmers headed a whole team of operatives, and his expectation of loyalty, obedience, and transparency from them was absolute. Finally, he shook his head as he spoke, "Whatever you may have read, Miller has lost our trust." *Certainly mine.*

"Which takes us right back to where we began." Bowyer's volume increased as his annoyance level rose, his hands amplifying the irritation behind his words, "meaning, that if you don't need him -we do."

Chalmers continued to stare at Captain Bowyer through the webcam, uncharacteristically tongue tied. An ultimatum was certainly not what he anticipated when he agreed to this unwelcome conversation.

Captain Bowyer looked down at his computer keyboard, knowing he needed a less adversarial way to end things. "Look, Mr. Chalmers, I understand your perspective." He looked back up at the likeness displayed on his screen. "Really, I do. But Miller was held back by you, even after he requested permission to deploy with his old Regiment." In the absence of a quick response, Bowyer continued, "And since that refusal, your only concern seems to be rehashing that…" But what should he even call it? "…that recovery op in America."

Obviously, he needed to move beyond that contentious subject as quickly as possible. "However, my perspective is far simpler." Thoughts of which made the emotions truly surge; grief, culpability, and hopelessness, all horribly intertwined within.

Loath to the idea of exposing them to this man, Bowyer swallowed hard and turned his face away from the webcam. He took a moment to compose himself, deliberately controlling and steering his own thoughts back on track. *You're a Captain in the British Army, and this issue must be finally resolved.*

He turned back toward the screen, intent on his goal. "Look Chalmers," another deep breath, "I lost two of my lads last night." He closed his eyes momentarily, finding only unwelcome visuals in the darkness. "So, either accept the findings of the official report and put Miller back in the field, as one of yours, or admit that you no longer require his services."

The Captain's stress was verging on the unmanageable, the loss being compounded by an overwhelming belief that his most senior sergeant's presence would have changed the previous night's miserable outcome. But this man was intent on holding back Sergeant Miller. And for what?

Bowyer exhaled slowly, knowing that getting into a pissing match with Chalmers wasn't likely to achieve what was necessary, and forced an awkwardly polite smile. "Please Mr. Chalmers, there really is no third option." He then shrugged, almost apologetically, "Which is why you'll be receiving a formal request from my Regiment's Lieutenant Colonel."

Captain Bowyer's posture then straightened in order to conclude properly. "I'm forewarning you of this, merely as a professional courtesy."

Chalmers glare faded. He stared down at his desk, wondering. Maybe it was time to just discard Miller? Or, would that decision be viewed as further evidence of managerial failure? Unwilling to be forced into a rash decision, he looked back up at the Captain and remained noncommittal, "Understood, Captain Bowyer."

While the call had certainly given him something to think about, there were more pressing issues which demanded his immediate attention. "So, was there anything else, Captain Bowyer?"

Bowyer just shook his head in response.

Chalmers then added, with unexpected sincerity, "I am sorry to hear about your men," before ending the call without a farewell.

Captain Bowyer leant his head down into his hands and started to scratch at the sand that seemed to continually find its way into his scalp.

"Crap." he groaned.

He'd just threatened Chalmers with an official request from the Regiment's Commanding Officer. The only problem being that it was all a huge bluff. While Captain Bowyer's need truly was dire, his CO had no knowledge of an official request for the return of Sergeant Toby Miller.

2.

"THE CELLAR IS this way." The runner's shoes squealed to a halt at the top of a descending set of stairs. "Charlie, what the hell!" He looked back toward his colleague, confused.

Charlie smiled his infuriatingly cocky smile before taking off in the opposite direction at full speed, "But the roof is this way."

Danny spread his open hands in front of his torso, playfully questioning Charlie's sanity as he often did. But with Charlie already out of sight he had no audience to play to, so he dropped them back down to his side and hesitated, unsure of which direction he should choose.

A loud overhead whistling noise stole his attention, and before he could even look up, the resulting explosion rocked the floor beneath him, its accompanying boom drowning out all other sound. "Screw this shit!" Danny shook the dust from his hair as he turned heel and chose the downward direction.

Meanwhile, Charlie held on to the ascending stair rail to steady himself as the building shook from the blast. Then, as the tremors settled, he resumed his upward sprint.

Charlie reached a landing and found four doorways spread out before him: three stained wooden ones and a shinily painted, odd one out. Without pause, he shoved at the misfit with his shoulder, and the heavy metal door reluctantly swung outward. An intense wave of baked dry air instantly confirmed he'd located the route back outside.

Standing in the open doorway he could not only hear the beat of helicopter blades but feel the powerful pulses of air being forced downward, rhythmically tugging at the buttons of his sweat soaked shirt.

Charlie lifted his heavy camera and walked purposefully up the short three-step staircase onto the roof terrace, steadying the camera to smoothly capture the scene.

As he stepped onto the roof's flat surface, he angled his camera upward, capturing the grey belly of the huge gravity-defying craft hovering noisily above his head, then lowered the camera, pausing to frame the view of the rooftop of the building opposite.

Through the lens, he could see two men, both wearing keffiyehs. One was shabbily dressed and holding some kind of substantial weapon, the other wore smarter robes and was guiding him forwards from behind. Charlie panned his lens away from the two men in order to capture the remainder of the rooftop scene.

As another man came into view, Charlie paused to allow the camera's auto-focus to settle, and as it did, he realised the man's black rifle was pointed directly at him.

Charlie's muscles twitched involuntarily, causing him to blink and miss the moment when the hovering helicopter opened fire on Charlie's would-be killer. Charlie regained his own focus just in time to see the man's form savagely alter, as rapid fire shredded his torso.

With his heart rate now soaring, Charlie worked to maintain his composure, panning his camera back to the left as smoothly as the surging adrenaline would allow. As he tried to carefully re-frame the first pair of men, his muscles spasmed yet again, this time in reaction to some kind of rocket accelerating upwards from the long weapon of the first man. And before Charlie could even process the implications, an immense wave of energy from a rapidly growing fireball shoved him violently through the still-open steel door.

"Charlie! Oh Christ mate, no! Please, are you still with us?" Danny leant in close, to check if Charlie was still breathing.

Charlie's eyes opened gingerly, taking in Danny with a dazed expression.

Danny sighed with relief, "Are you good? Is everything still working?" He looked his cameraman up and down.

"Did you see that shit?" Charlie rejoined the land of the living at full volume, surprising the hell out of Danny, and taking his blood pressure up yet another notch.

"That was wild! Where were you, old man? Did you see it?" Charlie was already shuffling around, dragging his camera back toward him across the concrete floor. "Oh no, look at it, Danny. It's knackered." Black coloured parts were now missing from the rear of the housing, exposing the camera's sensitive innards.

"Charlie!" Danny yelled, "Forget the bloody camera. We need to go. Do you understand me? An American helicopter just crash landed in the street."

"Well duh? I just got it, right here." Charlie yelled as he proudly patted the camera, causing another part of the housing to fall off and tinkle down the short staircase.

There was no doubting his bravery, but at times he really wasn't all there. "What do you mean by 'I got it' Charlie?"

"The chap with the surface air missile, I got the whole thing." Charlie looked very pleased with himself, but still wasn't seeing the full picture.

Danny stared at him, waiting for the train to arrive at the station, so to speak.

And the train arrived with, "Ohhh no, what if they saw me filming? We need to go Danny."

"That's exactly what I've been saying, mate." Danny helped pull Charlie up off the floor, talking to him as he checked him over more thoroughly, "You've got no bloody eyebrows, just in case you were wondering."

"What?" Charlie's hands shot up to his face, "You're pulling my leg, right?"

Danny led him down the stairs, checking around each corner

as they arrived. "Well, let's put it like this; did you just feel your eyebrows, Charlie?"

Charlie wasn't really sure; it was all a little overwhelming. His hands returned to where his eyebrows had previously been and was genuinely shocked to find none.

"Oh no, what happened? That's not funny, Danny. Not cool."

Danny shook his head in disbelief. *So, the first time you felt for 'em, you didn't notice?*

They'd reached the ground floor. Danny stopped Charlie with an open hand as he cautiously peered around the next corner, whispering, "Well clearly, I didn't take your bleedin' eyebrows, did I? Do you think I carry around a pair of hair clippers -on the off-chance you'll get knocked out?"

"What? I can't bloody hear you Danny. Talk up, will you?"

Oh jeez, the blast noise. Danny looked all around, before raising his own voice cautiously, "Can you hear me Charlie? Are your ears ringing?"

"I can barely hear you, Danny. My ears are ringing." Charlie looked at Danny, visibly disappointed at having to spell it out for him, "Really badly." He gestured toward his ear in an unnecessarily patronising manner.

Danny took a deep breath, already annoyed that Charlie was okay, then turned back to him, "Your fringe; that's gone too, by the way."

Charlie's hands shot up again, this time deliberately feeling around in an attempt to locate the missing hair, "Oh my Lord, Danny, I've got no bloody hair."

"Charlie!" Danny growled, "Keep the bloody noise down will ya, you wanna get us both killed?"

"Sorry, Danny." Surprisingly, his volume had finally dropped, a fraction.

"You still have hair mate, just not at the front. It's like a reverse monk, or premature male pattern baldness." Danny signaled they should both run down the hallway to the rear street-level door, figuring that the front of the building would be far too risky to use in the midst of the chaos that he could already hear outside.

Danny then swung open the street-level door and nodded for Charlie to follow him, straight across to the empty alleyway ahead.

3.

THE TINY BLACK and white bird sat on the balcony railing, barely a foot in front of Toby, who couldn't help but be charmed by the fearless little creature.

'Chicka-duh-duh,' it proclaimed confidently.

"Same to you, mate." Toby smirked.

The bird hopped a foot to the left before repeating the call more forcibly, as if Toby were stupid for not understanding it the first time.

"Oh, I'm sorry, am I sitting in your chair?" Toby went to move, then realizing that any movement would only scare the bird off, he gently settled back into the seat. "You can have it back when I'm gone."

The bird repeated its statement for the third time.

"Chick a duh duh, to you too, mate." The smirk grew into a grin, "Is that all you got? Chick a duh duh?"

'Chicka-chicka-duh'. The tiny bird held Toby's stare.

"Oh, you're a proper little smart-arse, aren't you?" His grin grew further still, "I quite like you, you cheeky little bugger."

The bird unexpectedly darted away, faster than Toby's eyes could even track.

"Who are you talking to handsome?" asked the voice behind him.

Toby's smile formed fully as he turned to greet the speaker. "We all know I'm not handsome. So, you either need glasses, or more serious help."

"Whatever Toby Miller, you're my very own stud muffin," purred Mary-Ann.

"Says the hottest woman I ever met." Toby's grin just kept growing.

"And you're especially handsome when you smile." She leaned in and planted a lingering juicy one on his lips.

"Only smiling coz I'm happy," he winked.

"Me too, handsome." She sat on his lap and leant her head on his shoulder. Toby breathed in the smell of her freshly shampooed hair and a wave of some unrecognisable emotion ran through his body.

"So, let me guess, you were talking to a little two-tone bird?"

Toby ignored the strange sensation going on inside and chuckled; the bird was clearly a regular visitor to Mary-Ann's balcony. "Yeah, two-tone, like the old record label."

"Record label? I don't know it; you'll have to educate me."

"Happy to. And I'm gonna name my new mate, Ska."

"Scar?" she asked, "What a funny name."

He laughed, "It'll make sense, once your education's done."

Her body was warm and felt soothing pressed against his. "I'm so glad you used your vacation to visit me."

Vacation? For a second the word threw him, it seemed inaccurate, even inappropriate, triggering an unwelcome reminder of the farce his life had become. He forcibly set it to the side, not wanting anything to ruin whatever was happening between the two of them. "I can't believe my sugar-momma flew me here." The smile resumed its upward trajectory, "I'm still feeling guilty about sponging off you."

Mary-Ann pursed her lips and shook her head, "Don't! I already told you; I didn't pay either. It's the only perk of my shitty job."

He squinted in mock anger, "Go easy! I wouldn't even know you if it wasn't for that shitty job."

Her eyes widened playfully, "True dat, guvner!"

He chuckled, as her mock English accent was passably convincing.

Toby beamed as she gave him another kiss, then jumped up and headed back inside to get dressed for the day ahead.

4.

"CAN YOU EVEN comprehend how close that was?" Danny asked Charlie.

In typical Charlie style, he sneered and dismissed the words as those of an overprotective mother. "Oh relax, Danny, we're alive aren't we?"

Danny's nostrils flared.

Charlie gestured to their civilized surroundings, "They've got Wi-Fi and ceiling fans, and we have cold beers. Life, my man, is great." Unfortunately, Charlie's volume still hadn't fully returned to normal since the explosion's effect on his ears, which was a new concern for Danny.

Charlie was always inappropriately loud for his surroundings, it was who he was and usually inoffensive enough, but this newly amplified noise level was downright abrasive.

Danny looked up from his laptop, hissing, "Can you keep it down?"

Charlie's images were superb; he had a natural talent with a camera in hand, but most writers never partnered with him for more than a handful of assignments, and Danny was starting to understand why.

Charlie vaguely mimed toward his ears, grinned that same mischievous grin and lolled back over to the bar. "What's your name, good Sir?" Charlie directed the question to the man working behind the bar, who appeared quite immune to his charm.

The barman stared silently at the blue-eyed westerner, his own dark eyes only breaking their staring contest to study the areas of missing hair and raw patches of burnt skin on Charlie's face. Having taken in the fresh-looking damage, the barman resumed the battle of wills.

But Charlie was unaware they'd even been holding a contest, "Oh my God, yes! That's a funny story actually," as Charlie's volume raised yet another notch.

"Charlie!" Danny snapped angrily now.

Anything potentially blasphemous in this environment was a whole new level of insensitive. And the mere idea of bragging about where they'd just been was reckless, even by Charlie's dubious standards.

Charlie was a product of Britain's most elite schools, the type that turned out Government Ministers and Naval Admirals, and while he was undeniably skilled and fearless, he was verging on being what Danny's friends back home would describe as 'an educated idiot'.

"Charlie, just come back over here, and keep the volume down." Danny was trying to walk the line between keeping his own volume civilized while simultaneously using just enough to get Charlie back under control.

But Charlie wasn't accustomed to being ordered around, especially by people like Danny, working class people.

So, with two beers inside an empty stomach and the adrenaline wearing off, Charlie was just getting started. He boasted to the surly bartender, "We…" his arms waving like a medieval town crier, "just cheated death, my good man."

Meanwhile, Danny looked around at the bar's other patrons; all men, all heavily bearded, and all wearing the same soft, round, crumpled wool hats. The men sat and drank their tea and coffee quietly -unlike Charlie who continued to spew noise obliviously.

As Danny scanned the bar trying to gauge the mood of the other clientele, he watched in concern as three men in the farthest corner quickly stood up and shuffled their way toward the closest exit. Every one of them looked disapprovingly at Charlie's antics as they filed their way out through the doorway and onto the street outside.

A hard shudder ran through Danny as he looked back at their table and saw they'd abandoned their drinks.

As insensitive as Charlie may have been to his surroundings, Danny was acutely aware of his own, and his instincts told him that things had already gone too far.

Pins and needles started pulsing through his skin. He clicked 'send' on the short summary story he'd just written for his editor and closed the screen on his laptop. He continued to observe the other customers, wincing as two more men stood up and left. This time in more of a blatant hurry.

Danny exhaled slowly, shoved his laptop into his bag, then walked over to Charlie and took a strong hold of his cameraman's arm.

"We're going Charlie." Danny was trying to disguise the mounting sense of impending danger but had no idea if he was succeeding. "I just want to apologize for my friend's rudeness," he directed his words toward the barman.

Calling Charlie a friend was a stretch, but referring to him as a colleague seemed like an even worse option. Being seen as two foreign travelers was considerably safer than being known to be two western journalists. "He's had one too many, but he's harmless."

"Don't call me rude! Who the hell do you think you are, Danny-boy?" Charlie's focus instantly shifted from the barman to Danny.

"As I say, Sir, I'm sorry. We'll leave you in peace now." Danny persisted in his attempts to smooth things over, but the barman seemed to enjoy maintaining his attempt at an oppressive silence.

"Charlie!" Danny's sharp increase in volume betrayed his rising sense of panic.

"We're going," he added at a carefully lowered level as he tried to guide Charlie with gentle pressure.

But as Danny tried to steer Charlie away from the bar, Charlie stubbornly resisted.

Danny gripped onto, and pulled at Charlie's arm even harder. And then harder still. Until, without warning, Charlie swung around and punched him. The powerful, but poorly aimed blow, landed square on Danny's ear.

Danny staggered back, startled.

He put his hand up to his ear, smarting at the sudden pain, "Seriously?"

Charlie merely waved his hand in a flippant manner, and then adjusted it to defiantly flick Danny the V-symbol, Britain's equivalent of the middle finger.

This was too much.

"Screw you Charlie Duggan-Smythe." Danny shook his head in disbelief, "Just remember that I tried." He turned his back on Charlie and started toward the door, looking one by one at the faces of the remaining patrons.

Danny hesitated at the bar's last table, applying gentle pressure on his newly throbbing ear with one hand, while checking he'd got all his belongings with his other. The punched ear was already ringing, but the good one was filled with the clear sound of Charlie hurling vulgar abuse. Danny left him to suffer the consequences of his own belligerent actions.

Once outside, Danny paused at the road's edge, looking for either the driver, or the car they'd been dropped off in. Even though a clear agreement had been made for him to wait outside, the driver had apparently bailed, leaving the guys to their own devices.

Danny winced and tried to blank out the throbbing in his ear, and thought back to how they got here, wherever here was.

The locally hired driver had said it was the closest safe bar with Wi-Fi, so they happily jumped into his raggedy car and not given it a second thought.

Were we set up? Danny couldn't seem to think straight, and time certainly wasn't on his side.

But Charlie? He slumped, as even after that outburst leaving him there seemed unthinkable.

Danny pivoted his upper body slightly, looking back toward the bar, pained at the choice he'd been given, then refocused on the throbbing which was now spreading throughout his whole head.

Nu-uh. That's not loyalty or decency. Just stupidity.

Danny forced the doubt from his mind and focused on his own, sizeable, problems. He carefully studied the view further down the street, first to the left and then to the right. There were men of varying ages loitering here and there, veiled women looking out over balconies, and a tiny kid who darted across the street like a spooked cat. But there were no familiar faces to be seen. And, as he caught sight of one of the locals glaring back at him, the absence of friendly faces was becoming blindingly obvious too.

Danny redirected his gaze toward the comparative safety of the ground, pulled his computer bag into his side, tightened his grip on it and started walking in the direction they'd originally come from.

To what end, he didn't yet know.

As he walked, he started analyzing his options. For now, he just needed to get away from the discontented crowd that Charlie had created. Then he could find somewhere secluded enough to pause in safety, dig out the phone from inside his bag, and hopefully call someone to his rescue.

He came to an abrupt stop and swallowed hard; there were no obvious candidates for the task. He had friends everywhere. Everywhere, but here.

A ripple of panic ran through Danny's body. He fought it, resolved to keep his gaze averted and continued up the street -figuring he could only handle one massive problem at a time.

As Danny picked up his pace, he heard a distinct increase in volume from the direction he'd just come. He hesitated, still horribly conflicted at having left Charlie to stew.

While tilting his head backward in an attempt to interpret exactly what the new sounds were, his right knee snapped forward from underneath him. It took him a moment to realize it had been struck from behind. Being unexpectedly one legged, Danny's balance immediately failed him. And as he struggled to regain his footing, he was struck again, this time in the back of the head.

The violent blow sent him forwards much too quickly to protect himself from the fall; the weight of his own off-balance body propelled his face straight into the cobbled pavement.

Neurons instantaneously transmitted the pain signals throughout his entire self. Then as the massive shockwave of pain settled its focus into his facial area, he was kicked in the left side of his lower torso, restoring the all-encompassing wave of agony.

As Danny's brain attempted to unscramble the pain messages firing all around his body, his head was hauled up from the ground by somebody pulling on his hair. The world turned to black and his only awareness became that of searing pain, and the metallic salty taste of blood filling his mouth.

5.

TOBY LEANED HIS head backwards to get better access to his helmet strap, then threaded it back out of the double D-ring closure mechanism.

Mary-Ann had already managed to pull hers off her head and was grinning like a child, "That was freakin' awesome!"

As Toby's face reappeared, she could see his grin was almost as big as hers. Although truth be told, he was amping it up as a form of gratitude for her having organized the entertainment.

"Wow! Have you ever done that before?" She was positively gushing.

"Not since I was a kid." Toby grinned back. Even as a kid it hadn't been go-karting as such, more a case of night-time joyriding in stolen hatchbacks, but Toby figured the adrenaline rush must have been similar enough to count.

"I need an iced, you up for one?" she asked as they carried their karting gear back to the rental hut.

Toby was baffled, he had no idea what she was talking about. And as he tried to decipher the meaning on his own, he finally realised something that had been creeping up on him since they'd first met; he didn't have to work around her, he didn't have to know everything, nor think multiple moves ahead. She had no agenda whatsoever, so he could simply ask her, which he did, "Iced what?" Although as it came out, he felt strangely vulnerable.

"An iced coffee, ya silly goose."

An iced pack, to reduce soft tissue swelling? That had crossed his mind. An iced coffee? Not so much. "Dunno, sounds a bit weird. They any good?"

"Oh my God, Toby Miller, they're awesome."

Apparently, the word 'awesome' was currently America's favorite adjective. To hear the same word repeated from anyone else would have been abrasive, but from her mouth it was charming and infectious. "Alright. I'm up for it. Uh, it sounds awesome."

"Cool, coz I know just the place."

Nope. He had to rethink his thoughts on 'awesome.' 'Cool' was another contender. He continued mulling it over as they walked. 'Cute' had to be the third one. Ranking the three words would be hard, but they were definitely the top three adjectives he'd heard since arriving back in the US.

Mary-Ann took her handbag out of the locker, which he noticed she always referred to as her clutch instead of handbag, or even purse. He'd always thought it was the norm for Americans to call it a purse, which showed how much he knew.

As he considered things he'd never contemplated before, she took her phone out of her clutch, and returned Toby's too. On autopilot, he checked for any new contact, only to see a missed call from his former Commanding Officer.

He unlocked the screen and found a waiting text too, 'Miller let me know when u can talk.' Again, from his old CO.

Toby's walk slowed to a crawl, the carefree feeling that had carried him for days was evaporating rapidly and being replaced at an equal rate by an extremely unwelcome sense of tension.

Which Mary-Ann spotted instantly, "Oh no." She stopped dead. "What's wrong, hunny?"

The word 'honey' being used with such warmth and affection, fought the building tension. But it was a short-lived victory.

Toby already knew the fun was about to come to an end. He looked up from his phone at Mary-Ann's face, and the child-like disappointment on it pained him in a way he'd not experienced before.

Mary-Ann studied Toby's face. His smile had not only evaporated, but that slightly menacing look, which accompanied his professional life, had already returned.

She'd known that this bliss couldn't last forever, she'd just hoped for a little longer before reality intervened. The hardest part was the knowledge that these heavenly trysts were so hard to organize in the first place. The uncertainty of when she'd see him next was already at the forefront of her mind.

"Sorry." Toby felt ashamed, knowing everything was about to change, and that it was all on him.

Mary-Ann's lips curled upward unconvincingly, beneath heartbroken eyes. All she could manage was an unconvincing, "It's okay, hunny," accompanied by a lacklustre shrug.

6.

DANNY WOKE TO so much pain, he immediately wished he hadn't.

He opened his eyes to darkness, then felt off-balance as he became aware of bright light somewhere in his peripheral vision.

He blinked aggressively, trying to correct whatever was malfunctioning in his eyes, but the darkness remained, except for the hint of light creeping in from the wrong place. It took a moment to realise he was hooded, and that the light was coming in through the opening at the bottom.

Removing the hood was his first thought, but his arms were immobile, attached to something rigid behind his back. He shook at the loose hood, but in response his head pounded agonizingly; it felt as if his brain was beating in sync with his heart and pulsating against the insides of his skull. He re-closed his eyes and groaned out loud.

As the worst wave of pain subsided, he opened his eyes again, only to find the movement had made the hood slip even lower; the sliver of light had now disappeared too.

Gradually, his other senses came online. The smell was what hit him next.

Oh, good God, what is that? He fought the gag reflex, quickly realizing the stench was coming from the hood itself. He tried to move his feet, but they were immobile too. He swallowed, but the only taste present was still that of his blood, and the only smell was that foul… *What the hell was it?*

Danny gently shook his head from side to side, and as the reality of the situation became apparent, some of his emotions silently released themselves.

7.

"THANKS FOR GETTING back to me so quickly, Miller."

"No problem, Sir. I was tied up, I'm away." Toby felt intensely guilty. "On holiday," he clarified apologetically.

"I know, Sergeant." Bowyer didn't want to come at Miller like a sledgehammer, so he forced himself to ease his way in with some light chit-chat first, "How's your holiday going, then?"

Better than Toby had ever imagined possible didn't seem like the most sympathetic response to a British Army Officer currently deployed in Afghanistan. So, Toby went with an appropriately bland, "Fine, Sir. Thank you for asking."

"Oh Miller, you don't change, do you?" Bowyer couldn't help but chuckle at Sergeant Miller's standardized response.

"Um." Toby wasn't sure of the correct response for that one, so went with, "Only when required, Sir."

Bowyer felt truly uplifted to be back in touch with his most prized NCO. "We could really use you right now, Sergeant Miller. Seriously."

That knowledge had already pissed on Toby's bonfire, just moments before. "Yes, Sir." He slumped.

Toby didn't know what else to say, after all he was just a tiny part of the machine, a part that had no control over its own direction.

It was time for Captain Bowyer to get to the point. "So Miller, the Regiment has formally requested that you are returned to unit from that shadowy world you've been attached to."

Toby hesitated as he absorbed the information. His CO was talking about a 'return to unit', a decision which hinted at failure on the part of the returnee.

Toby winced, then nodded. "I understand, Sir," and he really did. He'd apparently been an unusually good soldier, and then an equally efficient operative for the other part of the British Government. But recently, he'd become a bench-warmer for them, and there was simply no way that could be allowed to continue.

"Of course, we don't know if they'll release you, but we gave them an ultimatum, you could say. It's not particularly good for anybody having you sitting around, letting those talents go to waste."

As Toby stared into space, he realised that he appreciated it, regardless of the negative implications. His new career was obviously done, and for him to make a request for any kind of change would be viewed as highly inappropriate, no matter how desperately it needed to be done.

"Thank you, Sir," he responded, with a smile that his CO would never see on a satellite phone call. Toby then asked the one question that had been on his mind, since initially leaving on his holidays.

"How are the boys, Sir?"

Bowyer sank into his chair, then took a deep breath to respond, "We lost Corp. Shaw yesterday, and one of the new lads, Private Moore." Bowyer found himself scratching at the damn sand in his hairline again.

Fuck. Toby winced, then dropped down on to a low stone wall, the closest thing that could support his body weight. He shook his head and squeezed his eyes shut tight.

Before moving from the Army to his new flexible role, Toby had been mentoring Corporal Shaw, and the corporal had become a superb soldier. Toby had expected Shaw to fill his shoes at some future point.

The kid, Private Moore, Toby barely knew. He felt immense guilt at that because whoever Moore was, he had a family at home, and they were about to learn they'd lost their son on his very first deployment. Toby winced -he should have bloody-well been there with the Regiment.

He swallowed hard; his eyes still held shut. "What happened, Sir?"

Bowyer shook his head; this was always the most soul-destroying part of the job. "Patrol. Two local Afghan National Army bods were on point, and we were ambushed. I have no doubt it was a trap, and of course neither of the ANAs can be located anymore."

Toby clenched his one free fist. Even from a distance he understood the dynamic. The Jihadi sleepers would have already thrown away their ANA uniforms -ones they'd only worn to deceive the unwanted British visitors.

"Regarding young Moore, he just didn't have the instincts in place yet," Bowyer continued, "so he hesitated when the first shots were fired."

Now Toby could feel the torment as if he'd been there.

"He took multiple hits, in rapid succession." Toby could hear the Captain's breathing falter.

"He looked like a rag doll, Miller. Then Corp Shaw…" Bowyer wanted to cry just reliving the scene, "went in to help the lad."

Toby could picture it. You go in to help, but you can't because it's too late before you've even processed the thought.

But to suppress that instinct? That drive? It's beyond most soldiers.

It wasn't even necessary for the Captain to finish; Toby spared him any further explanation, "I understand, Sir."

Bowyer nodded and recomposed himself, he knew Miller had been present during far too many comparable situations. "Of course you do, Sergeant Miller."

Toby squirmed. To think, he had just been swanning about, like a love-sick pup. He scowled at his own self-indulgent actions. "I should have been there, Sir."

"No, Miller. Do not second guess yourself. You asked to deploy with us, and we asked for you too, but we were both denied. So, what you've been doing was forced upon you, just as it was forced upon us."

Toby knew he was right. But it didn't bloody help.

Bowyer continued, "Now, Sergeant Miller, if our request is approved we'll want you back in action ASAP. I wanted you to have the whole picture right now, rather than getting taken by surprise."

"I understand, Sir. We should maintain close contact."

"Agreed, Miller. And do try and make the most of the remainder of your leave."

"Yes Sir," Toby replied unconvincingly, before ending the call.

How? Toby shook his head angrily.

Before his move into intelligence work, Toby had been the most senior and experienced Sergeant within his unit, and now, in his absence it was all going wrong. How was it possible to put that out of his mind? Maybe there were some who could set aside that sickening feeling of culpability, but Toby wasn't one of them.

He needed to make his apologies, and head straight back home; it was the only option. The hedonistic fun was over, and Toby needed to be ready and waiting when the orders telling him to 'return to unit' came through.

Toby stood up and shook his head again, it was time to break the news to Mary-Ann.

8.

DANNY HAD BEEN fading in and out of consciousness, for how long, he had no idea.

He hadn't eaten since the morning before they'd witnessed the helicopter get shot down, but hunger wasn't his issue. His light-headedness and inability to swallow the tiny amount of saliva he could create meant the need for fresh water was becoming dire.

Water would also allow him to finally clear his mouth of the nastiness that seemed to be breeding there. It had begun with his own blood, but the stench from the damn hood had pervaded his mouth too, in spite of his conscious attempts to prevent that from happening by breathing only through his nose.

He could hear voices in the distance, although he couldn't understand a word being spoken. "Help!" he croaked pitifully. "Water, please."

He didn't know what his intended purpose was for these people, but letting him die from dehydration wasn't their aim. There were other, much quicker ways to have already killed him. Instead, they'd chosen to keep him here, restrained but breathing. So, for now, he was required to live.

"Please, water." His volume was growing weaker, the opposite of what he needed.

Danny listened as the voices silenced, then took the opportunity to try again. "Water, please," he wheezed.

He was unsure if he heard someone approaching. He tilted

his head to better listen, but was struck in the back of the skull again. Every muscle contracted in shock, as the pain shot through his body all over again, his head feeling like it was expanding and contracting in sync with his heartbeat again.

The new arrival started shouting at him, but Danny couldn't understand a word. He was more intent on fighting the sense of panic which had arrived with the blow. Then, a second voice arrived and pulled the hood from Danny's head.

The sudden invasion of daylight was blinding; Danny squeezed his eyes closed, then gingerly squinted as his retinas worked to adjust.

Two men stood before him, both of a similar age, probably in their late twenties to early thirties. Both were bearded, although one wore his beard short, while the other was going for a full-on medieval look.

Danny wanted to study the men but found he could only manage the briefest moment of eye contact before averting his gaze, in fear of more callous punishment.

It was clear that the longer bearded of his captors was the one who'd just struck the back of his head. He carried an old fashioned AK47, a gun as ubiquitous in the area as the beards of the men who carried them. The wooden stock of the gun was undoubtedly what had just whacked him.

The man with the shorter beard held only a large water bottle. Danny's eyes quickly widened in anticipation, then Mister Bushy Beard raised his rifle and aimed his sights at Danny, making him flinch involuntarily.

Danny had always taken pride in his ability to remain composed and rational in similarly volatile situations. So what was going on with him now?

Danny tried to suppress the rising sense of panic, only to see the first man was simply covering Danny with his weapon, so that the second could provide him with the requested water. Danny pulled hard on his own arms, which were still bound.

The words, "But I can't hold it," spewed from his mouth. *What the hell, they know that.* He closed his eyes and wondered at his own stupidity.

As Danny reopened his eyes, it became even more obvious this wasn't going to be a take-the-bottle-yourself kind of situation, as the man had already started pouring the water in the general vicinity of Danny's lower face. Danny lunged forward and tried to catch as much as he could, gulping away at air and water simultaneously.

As the last drops of water exited the bottle, short beardy seemed to ask long beardy to do something, before walking from the room. Long beardy hesitated and then seeing that his colleague had left him alone, walked up and leaned in close to Danny's face.

Danny couldn't fake any bravery, or even kid himself that he was unaffected by the situation. The man absolutely terrified him.

Long beardy growled something ending with the word, "American," before walking over to the corner of the room, where Danny's prisoner hood had landed on the floor.

Long beardy then untied the front of his old-fashioned trousers and pulled them down, exposing an arse covered in coarse wavy black hair. Then the guy started to urinate on Danny's hood.

Danny fought to fight the rising emotions; panic, fear, repulsion, and utter hopelessness. And, as Danny worked fruitlessly to compose himself, long beardy fixed his trousers, gingerly lifted the hood off the floor and carried it back toward Danny.

Danny pulled his head as far away from the approaching man as he could manage, "Oh God no, NO!" He heard some angry sounding blah blah blah, then the word, "God," followed by more indecipherable crap, before the man slid the moist hood back over Danny's head; all the while, laughing at his own sadistic ingenuity.

9.

TOBY LOOKED UP at the sign welcoming him '…To the UK Border'.

He grimaced at the endless line of people, all waiting to be permitted entry to his homeland. There were no local police waiting to usher him to the front of the line, unlike the last time he'd arrived home.

As he cast his mind back to that previous reception, which had preceded news of a painful personal loss, he decided he'd rather wait in line from here to eternity, over reliving that hell. Maybe that was his earned destiny for the afterlife, waiting in line, for an eternity.

The gaudily dressed teenage girl in front of him took two steps forward, as had the hundred or so people before her.

Toby looked down at the space which had appeared in front of him and savoured the two small steps of his own. *One small step for me, one giant leap for mankind.* He squinted in doubt, *Is that what he said?*

The teenage girl turned and looked at him, sized him up, then turned away again. Toby raised his eyebrows, bemused, and then peered further ahead, toward the distant UK Border Control booths.

So, he was officially being 'Returned to Unit,' which was undeniably a step backward in life.

He didn't know what to make of it. In a way, this was exactly what he'd wanted, something that had just been drilled home by the feelings of culpability he'd experienced on hearing the news of his lost comrades.

He sighed.

On the other hand, if he was honest with himself, it was thoroughly demoralising. Because he'd blown it. Plain and simple.

And, there was no point in kidding himself, this was all on him. He'd been promoted to perform a secret role, one which only a handful of soldiers were invited to do, and then he'd lost his boss's trust by going rogue.

That it had been done out of sheer desperation, and only to bring his young nephew's killer to justice, hadn't been universally forgiven, regardless of the officially promised clean slate. Which reminded him, he needed to go and visit her in prison, maybe even take her some of those American Oreo cookies, as they seemed to cheer her up. At least as much as could be expected, given the circumstances.

He sighed again.

"It's so stoopid." The teenage girl had turned to face him and was waiting for some kind of acknowledgement. "If you're this slow, then you obviously gotta hire more people. I got fings to do."

She wasn't wrong, at least regarding the staff shortages, but he knew the counter point. "Yeah, but those extras would be doing nothing when it's quiet." Border Force officers were government employees too. "And that's not how our government works."

"Oh good, you're English, too, I couldn't tell. I mean you look English. Well, like a English rugby player. Maybe?" She squinted at him in thought. "Or MMA? Do you like Rugby? Or MMA?" The floodgates had apparently opened. "I mean, I don't. But you know, you look like…"

He interrupted her, "Like I play rugby or do MMA?"

"Right!" She'd clearly been vindicated by his response, as her speed had picked up even more. "You might like them. I mean, who knows? People like all sorts of weird tat, yeah? I mean, me, I don't like 'em, I think they're dead boring. I'd rather be on my phone than watching that crap. Me? I like football, I properly like football."

"Well…" she didn't even look sold on her own words, "I don't actually, not really. But my boyfriend does. He's dead hot, but he's a bit of a wanker." She nodded her disappointment in said boyfriend/wanker.

"Is his name Jay?" Toby asked, as her boy-toy sounded just like a local kid of that name.

"What?" She sneered, "Don't be stoopid, no. Why would his name be Jay?" A sharp intake of breath accompanied a realisation, "Oh shit! I'm sorry, I didn't mean to say you're stupid. Just that it was a stupid thing to say, is all. Know what I mean?"

Toby grinned at the cheeky little monkey.

"Or a boxer maybe?" She was studying Toby's face again, particularly his nose. "Yeah, a boxer." She scrunched up her own little button nose, "Maybe." her eyes widened unexpectedly, "Wait! I just said 'shit' at you. Oh, you must think I'm such a dick."

"No, not a dick. That's definitely not what I was thinking." Toby shrugged.

She narrowed her eyes suspiciously, "Are you having a dig?"

This girl was a real handful; Toby couldn't have asked for a better way to pass the time. He smiled at her sincerely and shook his head.

"Hmm." She didn't really look convinced. "Then what were you thinking? Go on, tell me." It was delivered more as an order than a request. She took another two steps forward into some newly created space as she waited on his response.

"Ooh, look at us. We are flying along now." Toby grinned as he took his own two steps, triggering a cackle of wicked sounding laughter from the girl. Then his grin faded as he answered her, "I was thinking that I really screwed up, and now I'm a bit buggered."

"Oh." She paused for thought, then got back to it at the same pace she'd used before. "Yeah, but come on, it can't be that bad. Can it? I mean chill mate, it's not like you killed no-one." She smirked, then suddenly looked concerned at the intensity of Toby's expression, "Is it?"

Toby found a smile for her and shook his head, "No. Not this time." *But it was close.*

"Ha!" She didn't look at all convinced. "Uh huh. This time. You're dead funny, you are. Hang on, wait a minute." She looked to be searching for words but couldn't quite find them. She smiled an awkwardly insincere smile and then turned around to look ahead again, seemingly done with their conversation.

"Hey kid, I'm just messing with you, it's Army humour." Toby smiled apologetically to the back of her head.

She turned straight back to him, "Oh you bloody had me there, you wanker. I was like, whoah… is he like? You know? But nah, I could see you're just being a stupid wanker." Then her smile morphed into a more serious expression.

"But Army? That's way worse than rugby, or MMA. I mean, no offence. But you know, really? Army? I mean, why would you do that?" She was shaking her head in disappointment at Toby's pitiful life choices. "That's." Pause. "Bad." She scrunched up her shiny sunburned face in deep thought. "Wait…hang on. I'm not a kid, ya wanker."

Toby laughed out loud again, "I'll let that one slide, Missy." He lowered his brows, wondering about her age. He studied the people ahead of her, who were clearly a separate group, meaning she was at least old enough to have flown alone.

Toby looked back at her and smiled again. "You know what? You're obviously right; you're not a kid, my bad. So, what's your name?"

"I'm Kayleigh and yes, I already know, it's a very pretty name. I've heard it all before, mate." She fluttered her fake eyelashes at him, then scrunched up her button nose and bared her teeth -to make it clear that the fluttering was just her messing with him.

"Well, it's nice to meet you, Kayleigh. I'm Toby, but most people call me Staffy."

She looked at him as if he'd farted. "Staffy? What kind of a stupid nickname's that?"

She'd made him laugh unexpectedly again. "The kind that got chosen for me." It was time to steer her off that subject. "So, how old are you, Kayleigh? Coz I know a…" apparently the word 'kid' was off-limits, so Toby searched to find a more acceptable replacement, "…a lad. Lives down the road from my sister, his name's Jay. If you ever get done with your current wanker, you guys would get on like a house on fire." He nodded, "I mean it."

"House on fire! Ain't that stupid? I mean who came up with that crap?" She studied him again, trying to decide if he was still messing with her, before finally remembering the first part of Toby's most recent sentence, "Is he hot?"

Toby laughed out loud, then laughed again even louder. He shook his head at the cheeky mite, "I think he's dead hot. I'd do him."

"Ha! You stupid wanker!" Then her expression turned deadly serious, "You got any photos?"

Toby chuckled again, as he unlocked his phone to find the appropriate social media page.

10.

DANNY TRIED USING the minuscule amount of visibility at the bottom of the damp stinking hood to guide his fast-moving feet. But by concentrating on that, he instantly slammed his left shoulder into something else. It felt like a door frame. He halved his speed and switched his focus to protecting himself from further frontal damage by holding his tied hands out in front while widening his bent elbows as much as possible. But long beardy was pulling him so hard, that his entire torso was twisting; meaning Danny's arms couldn't remain straight enough to prevent the next impact.

While trying to tug his right arm back in to a more central, protective position, Danny's left foot caught hold of something, and his balance went. Danny landed on his knees this time, rather than his face, but only because his captor was still pulling so hard that it had held him up.

Danny tried to get back to his feet, but even that was made impossible by long beardy's continual tugging. His eyes welled up and he clenched his jaw knowing there was no point asking for courtesy or sympathy, that much had been made crystal clear.

At that point, long beardy came to an unexpected stop, so Danny hurriedly raised himself back into an upright position.

Finally, back on two feet, he heard a vehicle door being opened, then Danny was shoved from behind. His shins slammed into something solid, and he landed hard, thankfully on his right side, as his throbbing face really couldn't take much more.

"Bonjour?" a new voice asked meekly.

Danny hesitated, and on hearing nothing else, whispered back, "English?"

Long beardy erupted, as had become his habit, and struck Danny in the waist. Presumably he'd struck the man who'd spoken in French too, judging by the nearby groaning. Then the door to the vehicle was slammed shut.

"He is a real charmer, that one," said the French accent.

Danny's face was burning, the open wounds from his original attack were not being helped by the constant abrasion of the coarse sackcloth hood, or long beardy's piss. Danny simply had no enthusiasm to reply, instead he tried to get comfortable on the vehicle's floor and brace himself for whatever was next.

"Out! Get out! Now!" Danny couldn't rationalise the out of context accent, it almost sounded like a Londoner speaking, but surely that couldn't be it.

Then he was pulled by the legs.

It took every ounce of restraint not to lash out and kick, but the certainty that he'd pay a far greater price in return successfully held him back. As gravity took his legs from him, hands slid under his arm pits and lifted his torso upright, then the hood was removed.

As before, Danny's eyes couldn't manage the sunlight, but regardless of the temporary blindness, it was a blessing, a mercy, because the revolting hood was gone. Danny gratefully swallowed deep lungfuls of clean hot air and allowed the stranger's hands to guide his walk, while his eyes gradually acclimatised.

Danny blinked repeatedly in an effort to help his eyes, which weren't focusing with their normal efficiency. What vision did arrive was blurry, but sufficient to see he was being led across a baked dirt surface, with various single-story buildings ahead, painted in various cheerful colours.

All Danny wanted was the ability to rub his eyes to hopefully restore their normality, but his hands were still bound, so he had no idea when that luxury might be permitted again.

The buildings ahead were laid out as if to create a courtyard, and the areas which would have previously been gaps between one building and the next were fenced in. As his focus improved, he could see the gaps were in fact double fenced. He tried to estimate the gap between the inner and outer fences, and to see what lay beyond them.

Danny was abruptly hauled to a stop and his attention switched from the perimeter to his more immediate surroundings. Two men held him from behind, both wearing keffiyehs, although there were others close by, one of whom was holding a large, professional looking camera.

Danny's legs were kicked from behind yet again, and he dropped, artificially held up so as to force him into a kneeling position.

It took a second for his brain to process the implications of the scene, and then as it came to him, he panicked, losing all remaining dignity in an instant. "No!" his voice pleaded with the men who supported his body weight, "No, please. Don't, you don't have to do this. Please!"

The man with the camera approached, studying him in a detached, emotionless manner and Danny started hyperventilating. All he could do was think back to the video footage he'd seen of other Western journalists, of them kneeling in the dirt, in orange jump suits, with bearded men holding them from behind. Of these captors bragging defiantly, before pulling out a huge blade and slicing the journalists open before the camera lens.

"No!" Danny was full-on squealing now, the shrill noise drowning out the underlying sobbing, "I just tell people what's happening, not whether it's right or wrong. I show your perspective too. I shouldn't die for that!"

The cameraman raised the device up to eye level, as he continued his approach. Danny looked up at the man to his left, "Please, no." Then to his right, "Please." He couldn't control his sobbing, which ironically had cleared the dirt from his eyes. Just in time to…

Then he noticed the back of the camera was broken.

It triggered a slight sense of recognition, which put the brakes on his pleading. Danny stared at the cameraman as if he'd seen a ghost.

The camera was familiar, but he couldn't think straight. Danny searched his memory for the details, the specifics, then refocused on the camera ahead of him, with his mouth wide open. All the while in silence.

His jaw dropped open wide. *It's Charlie's camera.*

Of that he had no doubt.

11.

"MA'AM," CALLED THE seated young woman in the middle of the expansive room.

"What have you got, Lydia?" A suited lady strode over to the younger woman's desk.

"A new video has been posted on the Zarqawi 'abdi splinter group's site. Look." Lydia pressed the play button and they both watched as a man of northern European looking ethnicity (typically referred to in-house using standard Identity Codes, as an 'I.C. 1 male') was shoved to his knees by two unidentifiable Keffiyeh wearing guards of either Arab or North African ethnicity (I.C. 6 males).

The ladies watched as the I.C.1 male in the video grew ever more frantic, begging for mercy and sobbing, then as the camera reached its closest point, the detained man's manner completely changed, as if in some state of confusion. As he stared at the camera, the video ended, and the by-now standard terrorist political narrative took over.

"When did that go live?" asked the suited woman.

Lydia rocked her head from side to side as her screen's display changed in search of the correct answer, "Two hours and thirty-seven minutes ago."

"Roughly," stated her elder.

Lydia turned to correct the confusion. "No, exactly. You see I looked at…" she paused and then it came to her, "Right, yes. You got me there, Ma'am."

Her elder was smirking, "Good work, Lydia. Can you send me the video link? Then find me the best image of his face, screen capture it, and mail that to me, too. As soon as?"

"Absolutely Ma'am." Lydia's fingers were already at work.

As her superior watched, Lydia quickly located the clearest image, while her superior added, "And while I'm here, can you run me off a good quality hard copy, too?"

"Yes, Ma'am," then as Lydia spoke, the image displayed on her screen doubled in size, and sharpened dramatically. Then, the printer stationed at Lydia's side whirred into life.

"May I?" the suited lady gestured toward Lydia's desk phone.

"Of course, Ma'am."

"Good morning, Lydia, how can I help?" asked a male voice on the other end.

"It's me actually, Martin. I'm just borrowing her line." The lady settled her bum on the edge of Lydia's desk.

"What have you got?" asked the man's voice.

"A development… Um?" She took a moment to consider the appropriate course of action, finally deciding, "You know what, I'm heading over to your office."

"Martin." The suited lady peered her head through Martin's doorway as she rapped her knuckles on the frame.

"Come in Debs, what's going on?"

Debbie entered his office and settled into the seat on the visitor's side of his desk. "A new video was just posted, by the Zarqawi 'abdi group. You know? The ones trying to carry on with glorious ISIS founder Al Zarqawi's work?"

Martin nodded a weary acknowledgement.

"An I.C.1 male, a journalist, looks to have been recently captured." Debbie placed the freshly printed screen grab onto Martin's desk.

"Wait, how do you know the subject is a journalist?" Martin asked, studying the unfamiliar face.

At GCHQ, everyone in the building was involved in British Governmental Security & Intelligence, but Debbie and Martin were both Departmental Chiefs, in similar areas of overseas information gathering.

Debbie frowned, "Because I already know the bloke's face, from news sites."

She pulled her chair in closer, to lean on Martin's desk, "His name is Daniel Ellington. Danny."

She shrugged. "Danny is a wordsmith. He can shoot the accompanying images, but prefers to team up with specialist photographers so he can concentrate on the writing side of things."

"Okay." Martin was intrigued; Debbie seemed to know more about the subject than would normally be the case for such a recent kidnapping.

"He used to work a lot with an Italian snapper, an Antonella Ferrara, until recently, when he teamed up with another Brit."

"The suspense is killing me." Martin replied, deadpan.

"His current snapper is a young man called Charlie Duggan-Smythe." Debbie sat back in her chair, having both pulled the pin, and dropped the grenade.

Martin's eyes moved around in thought. Everyone in their department was required to store hundreds of names away inside their heads, but making the connections sometimes took a moment, "Why do I know that name?" He figured it was quicker to just ask.

"Youngest son of Lord Duggan-Smythe."

"Oh, good God no." Martin slumped back into his chair.

"Daddy is something like nineteenth in line for the throne, meaning kiddo is probably more like a hundred and nineteenth, which of course doesn't count for much. But it's an illustration of his family's status."

"No no, hang on. Rewind. We've jumped too far ahead. This man," Martin fingered the photo, "is not young Duggan-Smythe? This is a Danny who? Refresh my memory."

"Danny Ellington, a regular London boy, not much to tell really." Debbie shrugged.

"No accompanying video of Duggan-Smythe then?" Martin looked slightly concerned.

Debbie shook her head decisively.

"So, Duggan-Smythe, the younger, may have been kidnapped too. But it's also possible he wasn't present during this Danny's kidnapping." Martin paused as he gathered his thoughts. "On the other hand, Duggan-Smythe might've been there, but behaved in a way that changed the outcome. Meaning he could be dead already, or he's being held as a more valuable hostage," Martin summarized.

Debbie nodded her answer.

The various ways in which things could potentially pan out were already flittering through his head. "Does Lord Duggan-Smythe know yet?" he asked.

"Highly unlikely." Her response was quick. "This was only uploaded two hours and…" Debbie waved her hand to signify an approximation, "forty-five minutes ago. And as you know, these sites aren't known to members of the general public."

Martin's eyes were still searching the room for something not contained within, "Well, the Lord should be informed." Martin shook his head in dread. "But first, we need to call a meeting of the other chiefs of department."

Martin stood up, for no reason other than to make a start on whatever needed to be done.

"Christ Debbie, this could get messy, very quickly." He winced as another thought hit him, "Very publicly, too, if we're not careful."

12.

TOBY WAS AT the Regimental barracks folding various uniform items, before squeezing them into his kit bag for deployment.

He'd already stopped by his flat where he'd unpacked and left most of his civvy clothing, which was destined to be useless for the foreseeable future.

He pulled a note pad out of a drawer, a tiny two-piece metal pen from his pocket, and started a list of things to do before deployment. Deployment had changed everything, it always did. Regular people made a big deal of going on holiday, holding their mail, watering the plants, and packing just a couple of weeks' worth of clothing.

Deployment meant packing, preparing, and holding things for months at a time, rather than weeks. You had to be a planner. Fortunately, the armed forces created people who took an appropriately organisational approach to every aspect of their lives.

Toby stared into space, his head overflowing with thoughts. He needed to add the various social obligations to his list, which meant visiting his mum, sister, and friends.

Although, most of those friends were already deployed in Afghanistan, so that made for a pretty short list.

He should also go and visit the driver who'd killed his nephew; it was complicated, but he felt duty bound to help her get through her prison sentence.

Maybe he could go grab a quick drink with the copper who'd

worked that case too; they'd stayed in touch and ended up getting on surprisingly well.

She was civilian Police, which put her half-way between him and regular people in terms of her mentality and approach to life. But halfway had turned out to make for a pretty good bond -certainly better than with regular Joe Public, who seemed to inhabit a totally different planet.

Finally, he should try and leave things on the right note with Mary-Ann.

His shoulders slumped, wondering if it would be better to end the relationship completely. Toby grimaced and shook his head as he thought it through.

Sure, their last meet-up had gone well, but ultimately, how could it ever amount to anything? They had four thousand miles of separation and would repeatedly face months without any in-person contact, the core element of maintaining any relationship's health.

The one thought which overrode the rest was that it wasn't right making her wait for him. He couldn't shake the feeling that if some other bloke came along, then she should be free to give that a go -instead of living on hold.

The idea of her stressing and worrying about him for months on end, without getting anything positive in return; it just didn't seem fair.

Worse than that, he didn't need the associated guilt hanging over his head and distracting his focus. Not where he was going.

Bollocks to it. He added that shitty task to his short to-do list.

13.

"ALL RIGHT, QUIET down everyone." Debbie was presenting this one, it had landed in her lap, after all. "This, is Danny Ellington, grew up in Croydon…"

"Poor bugger," somebody interjected.

Debbie gestured to lower the volume of the chuckles that came in response. "Yes, thank you, Harry."

A large monitor, which covered half the wall, showed Danny's passport image -as once the government had anything of yours, it was theirs forever.

"So, Danny here, is a South London boy who studied journalism right down the street from where he grew up. Worked the monthly magazines before that industry withered away, then made the sideways step into news."

She clicked over to another image of him, now dressed in standard war correspondent gear.

"Doesn't he look the part? He's got all the right kit," chimed in Harry again.

Debbie now filled the screen with the first frame of the video showing Danny as a hostage, his face still caked in dried blood, from what could only have been a savage beating. Maybe that would shut Harry up.

"And earlier today, he was broadcast online as having been taken by extremists from the Zarqawi 'abdi splinter group. For those who don't yet know them, they're relatively new, enough so that we don't know their command structure yet. Although we do know they are going against the tide by growing within the region, at a time when most other groups are fading away."

Silence, finally.

"As you can see, Mister Ellington seems to have already suffered some abuse at their hands." She then allowed the short video to play for the room.

As the video came to an end and paused itself, a new voice spoke up.

"It's always miserable to see another person added to our hostage list, but I'm assuming you've done just that, and his name is now on that list. So, I don't mean to question you too prematurely, but the reason we're all here for Mister Ellington is?" asked Chalmers, clad in a particularly sharp blue suit and pink gingham tie combo.

Debbie didn't particularly appreciate being hurried, but a quick look around the room confirmed that Chalmers held the highest position. Still, she knew her decision to call this meeting was more than sufficiently justified and so she answered him powerfully.

"Because he was working with Charlie Duggan-Smythe, youngest son of Lord Duggan-Smythe. Who moves in Her Majesty's circles."

Chalmers' eyes widened at that.

Debbie gestured to somebody waiting outside the meeting room's large glass entrance door, received a thumbs-up in response, and called out, "You can come in, Lydia."

Lydia entered as instructed, looked around the room at all the influential security heads, and retreated into the room's darkest corner before commencing.

"Okay, Charles Duggan-Smythe is the youngest son of Lord Rupert Duggan-Smythe. Charlie, as he goes by, initially looked like he'd be following Daddy's earlier career steps by joining the Army, but he couldn't hack Sandhurst Royal Military Academy." She clicked through various images on her tablet as she spoke, all of which were mirrored on the room's huge monitor.

"After dropping out of Sandhurst, he…" Lydia looked doubtfully at her superior, before realising she needed to just get to the point, no matter how poorly it reflected on the subject, "did a whole lot of nothing. He was a womanizer who frequented the pubs and clubs of the Royal Borough of Kensington and Chelsea, and bought his way into the right party-loving social circles."

She clicked to another image which was also clearly British Government supplied, although this time it was the Metropolitan Police who'd done the supplying.

"That is, until he was arrested with enough 'H' to be charged with 'Possession with Intent to Supply'. A highly regarded London law firm quickly stepped in, to ensure his release. But the damage was done in terms of relationships with his family. More specifically, with Lord Rupert himself, who's had almost nothing to do with the son since."

Chalmers knew of Duggan-Smythe already. Both generations.

"Charlie, as he likes to be called," Lydia felt decidedly uncomfortable referring to the young aristocrat in such a familiar way, and so felt obliged to continually add the disclaimer, "eventually found his way into photojournalism, where he seems to have found some level of comfortable fit. He has a reputation for being confident and risk-loving, but not necessarily considerate of the implications of his own actions."

"We know this as several other writers abruptly parted ways with Duggan-Smythe, before he started teaming up with Danny Ellington here." The screen had now returned to the opening shot of Danny.

"Thank you, Lydia, and great work, especially for such short notice." Debbie smiled as she gestured that Lydia should now leave, her exit accompanied by approving murmurs.

Debbie could finally ensure the validity of the meeting was proven, beyond any doubt. "Now we all understand why we are here; to consider the implications of Charles Duggan-Smythe falling into terrorist hands, as a hostage, and potentially a method of currency to be used against us. Either in trade, or some form of morbid public display."

Even Chalmers remained silent, deep in thought.

14.

"WELL, LOOK AT you Toby, you're looking very well." Lucy's smile was huge, sincere, and already overwhelming Toby.

He'd have growled, but he'd learned over the years that was the wrong thing to do. He smiled a horribly awkward smile, and tensed his muscles as he tolerated Lucy Bell's hug.

"It's nice to see you again." Her smile faded as she sat down, already taking stock of his mental state. She altered her voice to sound more masculine, "I think we should sit down and be quiet, while we drink a pint. No need to ruin it by talking, woman."

"I don't talk like that." At least he could growl now, considering he hadn't started it.

"And don't bloody touch me neither, you useless copper." Her eyes held his stare, waiting for some change.

"Okay fine," he stood back up. "Come here then." and Toby wrapped his arms around her, finally reciprocating her original hug.

"Thanks Toby, that's so much better." She smiled again, then tried wriggling out of his grip, "Alright Miller, that'll do. I don't wanna have to call HR on you."

"HR?" he growled again and sat back down. "Cheeky bloody plod."

"So how are you then?" she asked, setting aside his customary jab at her professional role.

"Fine thanks. You?" he answered robotically.

"Oh my God, Toby! How many times have we been through

this? I'm not your CO, you can answer me honestly. One day we're going to turn you into an actual human being, you know." She glared, then the act slipped, and she smirked at him.

He raised his arms slightly and dropped them quickly, in mock protest.

"Fine, I don't know how I'm doing. There. That was bloody honest. Happy?"

She already knew to ignore his constant attempts to turn up the level of conflict, and instead search for the underlying message. "Why?" She'd also learned to mirror his abrupt pattern of speech.

He sneered in silence as he thought it through.

Lucy had learned this was all part of the process in prying him back out of his tightly closed shell.

"Work." The growled word came out all alone, but she knew it was a promising beginning.

"The old work, or the new one?" she asked cryptically, knowing that for both of them, work was not typically for public consumption.

"Both," he grumbled. They were just a couple of minutes in, and he could sense their bond again, although he could only admit to it begrudgingly.

They were mates, good ones actually. It was an unlikely bond, as professionally there was an element of rivalry between their worlds. But they were mates nonetheless, so he forced himself to snap out of his instinctively private mode, "It's…" but then stopped short again.

"Are you having a glass of rosé, with a little brolly stuck through a cherry? Your usual?" she asked. And against his will, the tiniest of chuckles escaped.

"No! A bloody amber ale, woman," she added in a gruff, playful voice.

She was taking the piss out of him again, the cheeky copper. He was starting to remember why they got on so well.

"And two pints of stout for you?" He was the one grinning now.

"Piss off. I'll take a glass of Chianti, and you know it." She settled back into her chair.

Toby waved over at the bar, and then settled into his chair more comfortably too.

"And when have I ever called anyone, woman?" He shook his head at her, then set the verbal stab aside and got back to the appropriate subject, "Alright then. As you know, they backdated orders, you know, from that whole mess."

She knew exactly what he was talking about.

"But my superior, at the Ministry." He shook his head as a way of trying to share the tension which existed there now.

Again, she clearly understood. "So, no new…" What was even the right term for what he did? "operations then?"

He shook his head again, but she could sense that he'd finally settled back into normality with her, "Damn, I'm sorry, Toby. What's the official line then?"

"Not sure there is one. I'm just on leave." He rolled his eyes, and shrugged, he'd have added more if he knew how to better share his feelings.

"Yeah, but that can't go on forever. How long did they say your leave was for?"

"What can I get you?" asked the barman who'd just appeared at their side. Toby nodded to Lucy who ordered her wine, followed by Toby and his beloved amber ale.

"They didn't. That's the problem," Toby added as the barman headed away.

It wasn't the real problem though, so he had to share more, "It's even worse than just that. The Regiment is still in Afghanistan, and…" he leaned in close, to use less volume, "two of my unit just got," he exhaled very deliberately, closing his eyes for a second, "…killed."

Her eyes widened.

"In a bloody trap set by some shit-bag locals. So, I'm good for nothing back here, while my boys are dying over there. And it's all coz I'm not there to help 'em."

Lucy focused on his eyes and felt his pain, he looked close to tears.

He took another deep breath and his nostrils flared, "In my unit, I'm the most senior Sergeant, so it's my duty to…" He was getting fired up just thinking about it.

"Oh no, Toby. That's terrible. Can't you talk to your CO? Maybe he can exert some pressure for you?"

Toby was still leaned in close, "He did. Gave 'em an ultimatum, by the sound of it. So I came back here, just in case the suits release me from the Ministry. Then I'm ready to deploy."

Lucy was nodding her understanding, but she'd understood far more than he thought, "And you were on holiday, visiting the American woman, right? Mary-Ann, wasn't it?"

"Yeah," Toby replied defensively, then sat straight back into his chair with his arms folded.

"Uh huh." Lucy nodded at him.

"That's got nothing to do with anything," he grimaced defiantly.

She pointed at his face, "It obviously does. You wanna see your ugly mug in the mirror? I've got a compact in here somewhere." She started digging through her small handbag.

"In your clutch?" He was shaking his head in annoyance. Why did he like her again?

Lucy stared at him, hard. "Who the hell are you? And how do you even know the word, clutch?"

He chuckled, then growled over the top of it to regain control.

Yeah, that's why he liked her. "Fine, maybe that has got something to do with it."

Not a muscle moved in her face; any false move on her part could clam him up again.

She had no choice but to wait.

He leaned back in, "What's the point to it? I just don't see one anymore." He shook his hands quickly, in anger. Nobody ever got to see his emotions, save for his sister, so Lucy Bell was lucky to see this part of him. He sighed, knowing that was absolute crap, he was lucky that she cared enough to listen.

"She's in bloody Indianapolis, and I'm here. And it's not like you can get a bus there, or a taxi, it's ten fucking hours on a plane." He dropped his head into his hands and rubbed at his eyes, he was in danger of showing some very unwelcome real emotion.

"On top of that, I'm never here in England, and even when I am, I never know for how long. And…" The fast flow of words was quickly coming to an end. Toby looked down at the table and replied much more quietly, "And what if I don't come back?" his eyes glazed over again.

"From an op, or a deployment; it's all the same shit. Then she's gotta deal with that. And for what?" He couldn't even look Lucy in the face.

"She's gotta find someone better than me."

"Oh Toby." Lucy placed her hand on his. He automatically snatched his away, but she knew him too well to be insulted by it. "Oh mate, you're looking at it all wrong."

"What?" The defensive growl was back.

"Don't bloody growl at me, Miller. If I say you're looking at it wrong, then you're looking at it wrong."

The institutionalised part of Toby could only listen, obediently.

"That's not your choice, Miller, it's hers. And if you don't give her that choice, then you're not the man I thought you were." She meant it as a compliment.

Toby leant his torso even further forward and dropped his weary head into his hands.

"Oh!" The barman stopped his hands moving, just in time to avoid spilling beer on Toby's head, "Here's your wine, Madam, and your pint, Sir."

Toby looked slowly up at the man, with who-knows-what written on his face, but it was sufficient to make the barman sprint-walk away from their table.

15.

"SO DO WE know where, exactly, Danny Ellington was taken from?" asked Departmental Chief Martin.

Debbie had considered that question already, "Not yet, but my team are on it."

"But we do know that the group are based in this general area, here." A new speaker stood up to indicate an area on the map, now displayed on the room's primary monitor.

"Which is a problem," added Martin, "as that area's rampant with Jihadis, and their sympathisers."

"And why did you add that salient fact?" asked Chalmers.

"What do you mean?" asked Martin, not seeing any logic in Chalmers' interjection.

Up until now Chalmers had been lounging back in his chair, but the meeting was turning into a much longer session than anticipated and he wanted to bring things to a head. He sat up straight to answer, "Because we're all thinking the same thought, but not saying it."

The room settled into an uncomfortable silence, which Debbie chose to break, "Which is what, Mister Chalmers?"

Chalmers rolled his hands forward, then outward, in a camp theatric style. "What are we going to do about it?"

The room fell silent once more, so Chalmers continued, "Britons are kidnapped periodically. We do what we can, we monitor situations, we add them to a list. But ultimately, unless an unexpected opportunity falls into our lap, they remain captive."

He paused for dramatic effect, before garnishing it with, "For some time."

The room knew this to be true, so Chalmers took a step further, "Mister Ellington here, would normally be doomed to the same fate. To try and survive with some dignity, until an opportunity arose for a prisoner trade." Again, with the theatrical arm embellishment, "Or something of the like."

"But this time around he was taken with somebody…" Chalmers considered his words, "whose absence will be more keenly felt. A symbol of our country's identity, you could say. A figurehead, albeit one born into that future role, rather than earned."

He looked around the room, "But we all seem to be pussyfooting around, desperate to avoid being the first one to say what we are all undoubtedly thinking. Which is, should we try and get the young Duggan-Smythe back?"

Several people broke his eye contact to instead look for lint on their trousers, or check their fingernails for untidy lateral growth.

"More specifically I think, we are considering the ramifications for us all, if we do not." He took a long, deep breath, the only noise in the otherwise silent room.

"So," their non-participation could only signal confirmation, "are we agreed, that it's time to finally discuss what we've been thinking this whole time?"

The room murmured, ayed, and nodded its reluctant response.

"Wonderful," Chalmers was still leading, "so what are our options for doing that?"

Having been given a clear direction, the occupants of the room were slightly quicker to participate.

"One option is to trade, for one of theirs," an older man volunteered.

Chalmers felt obliged to offer the appropriate counter points because while the rest of the room had been slowly beating about the bush, he'd used his precious time to already think through every possible course of action.

"Firstly, they'll wonder why we want to trade for him specifically, when we don't typically engage in any prisoner trades. Therefore, we'd have to come up with a credible reason why, for him, we're making that highly unusual exception."

Chalmers was talking fast, as his points felt like repetition to him, having bounced around inside his head for the last half hour.

"Then, we would need a high-level trade to offer them, in exchange for this particular young journalist. At that point what will they do?" It was a rhetorical question, so he ploughed on, "They'll look much more carefully into why we want him."

At that point Chalmers realised that he was in danger of blundering through his counter points too quickly for the group, so worked to slow down the pace of his delivery. "Now, as we all know, they have people living under the radar here in the UK. So how long before someone here learns of his family connections, and shares that information?" Chalmers paused to allow them to think on that. "And when they do finally learn who young Duggan-Smythe is, they'll re-evaluate, and break endless promises while they consider their options. Etcetera."

Nobody could argue that counter point.

But Chalmers needed to quash the idea completely, so chose a suitably powerful closing point, "I'd argue that doing anything which makes him stand out as being of value to us, will make a death sentence for Charlie Duggan-Smythe, more likely, not less."

The room settled into nods and pensive expressions, then the next idea arrived, "We could send in some troops, a targeted hit, with air support." It was a new contributor.

"I'd love to do that," Chalmers nodded in agreement, "Really, I would. But we never know where they keep their detainees because they're continually moved. And even if we managed to pinpoint a current location, picture for yourselves a Regiment of Her Majesty's Armed Forces over there."

"They'd blend in about as effectively as a convoy of bullet-hole-ridden pickup trucks, driving through the rolling green hills of Worcestershire."

The room was considering the visual and so to hammer that point home just as firmly, he embellished further still. "Picture a bearded man at the wheel, wearing a keffiyeh, with other I.C. 6 males standing in the truck bed manning large calibre weapons. Now imagine that lot, driving past your local pub."

He widened his eyes playfully, "But they're incognito, remember?"

Expressions confirmed the visual had been sufficiently compelling.

"Look, I'm sorry, but this region is almost impossible to penetrate with any element of surprise."

A sense of despondency was permeating the air.

"And as we've learned, when they know we're coming, they'll either move the prisoners again -before we arrive," he winced at the follow up thought, "And ambush our troops, to huge losses."

"Or…" Chalmers leant onto the glass table to present the other equally undesirable option, "They'll accelerate their timescale and use our people as terrorist recruitment aids, by putting on a show. It starts off like a sports team portrait, with everyone nicely lined up. Until they start getting beheaded."

Everybody present was looking anywhere, except toward Chalmers.

"They're at least considerate enough to leave the decapitated bodies there, for us to bag up and bring home. So that their families can suffer a second wave of grief."

The occupants of the room were finally starting to absorb what a monstrous challenge they'd inherited. As most people sat back, thinking through alternatives, Debbie chimed in with, "You said, 'almost impossible to penetrate,' Mister Chalmers."

His mouth put on the show of a polite smile, "I did."

"Almost." Debbie reiterated.

He nodded in appreciation; she'd always had the quickest brain in the room.

"There might be a way." Although his awkward smile implied they might not like it.

16.

LORD RUPERT DUGGAN-SMYTHE was reading through the day's news, in paper form of course. He was happy to use the online version for updates whenever the day presented him with an appropriate pause, but starting the day with an old-fashioned newspaper was a ritual, and paired with a fresh pot of tea, a thoroughly enjoyable one.

The news contained within the pages, on the other hand, was seldom enjoyable. The Queen was apparently taking a step back from official duties, not stopping completely, just directing her diminishing energies to more specific tasks. *There will never be another like her*, he thought to himself. She was a better Monarch than anyone had dreamed possible, he felt privileged to have both lived, and served, during her reign.

On the other hand, Prime Ministers were dropping like flies, with one thrown out after another, humiliating the entire nation on the global stage. The economy was on the way down, fuel prices on the way up, interest rates on the floor, and young people were more concerned with vacuous personal whims than anything of real consequence.

With the exception of the minority who chose to serve their country in some productive way, which led him to thoughts of young Charles. As always.

For Charles to have followed the family tradition of applying to serve in Her Majesty's Armed Forces was a moment of pride for

Lord Rupert. One he would never forget. To then change his mind and leave, was also unforgettable. Sadly.

Surely it would have been better to have never applied in the first place.

Then to compound the issue, the boy had decided to follow the rest of the malingerers down that petty, self-indulgent rabbit hole. Essentially the boy was having fun, while achieving nothing.

But against the odds, it had actually managed to get worse still. The drug bust really was the final straw for Lord Rupert, that couldn't be denied, but that one shameful incident wasn't why he'd stopped talking to the boy. It was just the last, in a very long line of similar failures and poor choices.

The real problem was the cumulative effect. It was merely the straw; his back was the camel's.

The boy must understand that nobody in the family had ever expected instant success, or perfection, only for him to try his hardest at something, and ideally for him to do well. Eventually.

The eternal hope was for the boy to show a work ethic, the tiniest hint of maturity, and to find himself a fitting direction in life. Doesn't every father want to show off their children's successes? Just a little?

The Lord lowered his newspaper, to better cast his mind back.

Lady Fiona Duggan-Smythe had only recently interrupted his day with tales of young Charles' work appearing in the tabloids. Initially, the Lord had been more concerned with the fact that his wife and youngest son had kept the lines of communication open, behind his back. But…

He'd had work published?

Professionally?

The Lord had been all ears. It wasn't The Times yet, but still, what if one day it was? Imagine that; his son, taking photographs in conflict zones, for The Times. That would be true pride.

Such unexpected news had felt almost miraculous, considering what had gone on before.

If Charles really was making a go of this reporting work, then that was all Lord Rupert had ever been waiting for. The idea that the boy was finally working hard at something, earning some respect from his peers, and no longer soiling the family name with such humiliating narcissistic folly…

The Lord stared into space. How long had it been? A year? And a year of professional success raising the lad's sense of self-worth, too. Would the boy still look the same? Would he carry himself the same way?

Maybe the time had come to request more regular updates on how the boy's new career was playing out. Maybe Rupert could even stage-manage a way to accidentally run into young Charles, at some point in the near future. A happy accident, ostensibly.

He could even use the opportunity to spontaneously offer some positive reinforcement, to let the boy know that he was finally headed in the right direction, and that it had been noticed by the head of the family. Maybe young Charles was no longer intent on sullying their storied last name, maybe he was writing an exciting new chapter about their successes.

A small smile formed on Lord Rupert's face. Being estranged from his youngest had pained him, but that didn't make him a monster, just a man intolerant of stupidity, frivolity, and laziness.

The smile grew.

Now that he'd made the decision, the idea of seeing his boy was actually quite heartwarming.

But he could keep that to himself. For the moment.

17.

CHALMERS STILL HAD the room's undivided attention. It was time to make his proposal, and it was one he liked for so many reasons. He mulled it over one last time in his head, ensuring that he'd anticipated and covered all likely counterpoints at the best point in time, which was before they arose.

He straightened his posture and made a start, "We could insert an operative."

Eyebrows were raised and the questions started instantly, "But that would surely fall under the role of MI6?"

"No," Chalmers answered calmly, "Not necessarily. We have our own operatives in-house. And, if the appropriate Ministers found out that we'd handed this over to MI6, because we were out of our depth here at GCHQ? Well, would you like your name attached to that memo?"

Silence. Inevitably.

Then someone else remembered an objection which had come into their head prior to Chalmers' silencing of the MI6 fan. "But we don't know where he's being held captive. Or if he's being held captive. Realistically we don't even know if he's still alive."

"I know." Chalmers was still just as calm, "My idea has considered all of those points."

"Go on then, Mister Chalmers," Debbie interjected.

"Well, we send in one of my department's operatives. As another British journalist."

Various faces looked confused, then a few expressions quickly altered to one of surprise, shock, even horror, in Debbie's case, "To be kidnapped? Is that what you're proposing?"

Chalmers shrugged the affirmative.

"That's absolute madness. They could get beheaded too. You can't seriously propose we send in one of our own people to do that? Who would even agree to it?"

One of my operatives will be given very little choice, thought Chalmers to himself.

"No, no. That is… beyond reckless," echoed another voice.

It was time to elaborate before a mutiny took hold of the room, so Chalmers stepped in again. "We send in somebody who knows how to handle these things, and they will be taken captive, yes. But remember, we're not inserting an actual journalist. We're talking about dropping a mongoose into the snake pit, not a helpless little mouse."

"I don't want my name on that memo either, Mister Chalmers." Debbie was still not buying in to it.

"I'm with Debbie." Nor apparently was Martin.

Chalmers' frustration level was rising, "So you were willing to discuss sending in what? A hundred and fifty soldiers? Two? Because any less, and they'd be outgunned at every turn -with horrific loss of life an inevitability."

He shook his head at them in disbelief, "Yet you're unwilling to let somebody with a perfectly tailored skillset fly in under their radar? Which is not only lowering operational risk, it also lowers the loss of life potential to the bare minimum." He had to that let point be fully absorbed by the assembled heads.

"I find it highly amusing that two minutes ago, everyone seemed to be in agreement that the most unacceptable risk was that of Duggan-Smythe being paraded on the news by terrorists -either in complete form or as just a head. Another option, let's not forget, is that he is used to humiliate our nation, as the most valuable trade that any terrorist group has ever laid their hands on." He let that thought hang in the air too.

"And we're not talking about sending in minimally trained young soldiers, following orders they barely understand. In my department, we're talking about hardened undercover veterans, and we don't make any of our operatives do anything. If those operatives decide the risk assessment doesn't add up, we modify until it becomes acceptable. And if that cannot be done, then they don't go, and it's over to plan B. Which…" he sighed, "We don't appear to have."

"I really don't know about this." Debbie was gently rubbing at her forehead, gradually realising there might be no alternative.

"Look. My operators were pulled in from various different roles, and they all have specific uses. But the one thing they all have in common is that they stood out in those previous roles. Even in an environment of our best people, whether that be armed forces or law enforcement, they were all operating on a different level."

"And…" he smiled, "one in particular, lives for this stuff, solo work in high-risk situations." Chalmers looked around the room, gauging their reaction as he spoke. "He's resourceful and seemingly immune to the stresses that most people succumb to. Honestly, sometimes it feels like I can't hold him back!" He chuckled, both at his own joke and the idea that Captain Bowyer had only seen two options, when this was undoubtedly a third one. He really couldn't have planned a better solution for the Sergeant Miller problem, not with all the time in the world.

"Really, I'm sure he'd jump at the chance to undertake an operation of this kind."

And if he doesn't, that'll be the end of him within my department.

18.

TOBY HAD RE-ENTERED the Army base after his drink with Lucy, the annoyingly likable copper. He was making his way back to his tiny office, to check his emails before turning in for the night, when a familiarly abrupt noise indicated his phone had received a text.

Toby pulled out his phone, 'Miller. Report for duty. DC Chalmers.'

He squinted in confusion.

Instead of being summoned by one of the regular handlers for his out of uniform governmental duties, it was signed by the Departmental Chief, Mister Chalmers.

That was a first.

Toby stopped in his tracks, and re-read the text, half thinking he'd misunderstood it. But nope, the message was still from the most senior person in the department, ordering him to report for duty. He shook his head, mumbling, "What?" to himself.

So, after a month of having no direction, and no idea of what that even implied, Toby's old Commanding Officer from the Army had officially requested for his return. In response, Toby had flown home, stepped back into his old Army uniform, packed his kit bag, started getting his affairs in order, and now it was suddenly back to plain-clothed work? As if nothing had happened?

Had the Captain's ultimatum triggered this?

Toby tapped at the screen keys, 'At what time, Sir?' wondering how much sleep he'd get before immersing himself in whatever was coming next.

'Immediately,' snapped back the texted response.

Whoa, what? It was twenty to midnight. Toby sighed, knowing it was the nature of the work, then typed, 'Understood,' and headed back the way he'd just come, pondering the significance of the change in contact protocols.

19.

DANNY TRIED BLINKING the grogginess away. He rolled his stiff neck, still wincing in pain, then started taking in his surroundings.

"Any better, English?" asked the voice with the French accent.

"Uhh." Danny tried to create sound, using an uncooperative, desiccated mouth.

"Look, over by the door." The accented voice directed his attention to a water bottle which had been left in… where was he? Danny rubbed at the floor with his hands, it was hard packed, but not man made. He leant forward onto his knees and stretched out just far enough to take the water bottle, twisted off the cap and started gulping at it, emptying it within seconds.

"You need more?" asked the same voice.

Only then did Danny start to get a sense of place. He'd awoken on the floor, of a horse stall, or something similar. There was a barred door, through which the water bottle must have previously been placed. But where was the voice coming from?

"Up here."

A man was standing in what must have been the next stall. The lower part of the wall separating them was of concrete block construction. The upper, made from similar metal bars to the door, spaced about four inches apart. The Frenchman waved another bottle of water at him.

Danny started to raise himself, but his right knee wasn't ready for his weight, so Danny allowed himself to slump back down, "Yes, please."

The Frenchman gently threw the bottle toward Danny.

"Thanks." Danny caught, and then emptied the second bottle just as quickly as the first, before some sense of civility returned, "Oh no, I'm sorry. I didn't think."

"Hey, it's okay, they bring more. It's better here than before." The Frenchman looked at Danny with empty eyes. "Where were you? Before," he asked.

Danny grimaced, confused, "Before what?"

"Before here. Where did they have you? I've not seen you before."

It made no sense. Danny's head was pounding, in all honesty he just wanted to release his emotions in private; making this simple conversation a struggle. Danny swallowed, realising what a luxury swallowing was after the last couple of days, and then tried to generate a useful response for the kind stranger, "Umm, I was in a bar?" It wasn't nearly enough information, but it was all he'd really got to offer.

"Ah," his new neighbour nodded knowingly, "You were just taken."

Danny looked back up at the man, noticing his hair was shaggy and unkempt. The man was bearded too, but with light brown hair, unlike the black bearded men who'd been abusing him up until now. Danny scrunched his face in confusion, "Yes, just taken." Danny nodded gently. The significance of the man's hair and beard was creeping up on him, in a very unwelcome way.

"Of course," his neighbour nodded back. "That is why," the man stroked at his own facial hair.

Instinctively Danny touched his jowls, feeling more growth than he'd been expecting. "How long have I been?" Another wave of dizziness then swept over him.

"This is the second morning. Second one here." Danny could hear the voice reply, but Danny's eyes were heavy. He leant his arm back down onto the dirt and allowed his heavy eyelids to close, because right now he just needed more sleep.

20.

ON ARRIVAL TOBY had been given a lanyard with a digital entry card attached and escorted up to a floor he'd never seen before. Then he'd been told to wait outside a large glass-walled meeting room, in which he could see the rear view of his departmental chief, Chalmers, seated near to the head of a large rectangular glass table.

The excessive use of glass made the room look like a goldfish bowl. A tired looking lady in a well fitted, yet crumpled suit seemed to be leading the meeting, and noticing Toby waiting, gestured for him to enter, albeit with an obvious look of confusion on her face.

As Toby entered, the room's other occupants turned to see who the newcomer was. Most interestingly, Chalmers' eyes widened in apparent alarm.

"How can we help you?" She searched for the rank signifier on his uniform before adding, "Sergeant."

Toby had his game face on, and snapped his response in the expected manner, "I'm reporting for duty Ma'am, to Mister Chalmers." Toby directed his stern gaze toward the named man.

What the fuck, Miller? Chalmers was furious but worked to keep it contained. "Outside, Miller." Chalmers jumped to his feet and strode from the room.

Toby was at work and so hid his confusion, merely looking back toward the lady in charge of the room, offering her another appropriately formal, "Ma'am," before taking his exit.

"What the hell are you thinking, turning up here in uniform?"

Chalmers was pissed off and with his back turned on the glass room, was apparently happy to let it show.

Toby ground his teeth together, inhaled deeply through his nose and then responded, "I'm reporting for duty. Immediately. As ordered."

Chalmers' unprofessional and emotional manner, following nearly a month of forced leave, had triggered an irritation in Toby and so, against his better judgement he embellished further still, "I'd have changed out of uniform, if I'd been told to."

Toby continued to hold Chalmers' stare in his uniquely cold manner, "But I was only told to report for duty, immediately." He then paused again before reluctantly adding the obligatory punctuation mark, "Sir."

Up until now, Chalmers' personal interactions with Miller had been minimal, the man was little more than another asset on his list. But as Miller's irritation became more blatant, Chalmers' discomfort increased accordingly, until involuntarily, he averted his eyes. Instantly aware of how it had advertised his anxiousness, he chastised himself internally, pointed his finger at Miller, then crooked it to signify Toby should follow.

But before re-opening the goldfish bowl's door, he needed to reassert his superior status, so turned back to Toby and whispered, "Don't you dare contradict me in here. Or you're out, for good."

The intensity in Toby's glare remained as he paused one more time, before responding with an indifferent, "Sir."

21.

TOBY WATCHED AS Chalmers talked himself around in a huge circle, coming right back to where he'd begun, which was that Toby was not a serving member of Her Majesty's Armed Forces even though he'd arrived in the uniform of those Armed Forces.

But the words weren't what held Toby's attention, it was the reason behind them that interested him. Toby stared without emotion at Chalmers as he spoke, then allowed himself to study the other members of the room.

None of these people were low level, that much was obvious, although it seemed as if Chalmers held a slightly higher rank within the room than most. The leading lady was the possible exception. She was confident and leading the room rather than merely presenting to its occupants, which in the world of suits usually accompanied elevated status.

As Toby studied her, she looked over at him and simultaneously interrupted Chalmers, all while holding Toby's gaze, "I'm glad to hear that, Mister Chalmers." Toby flashed her a half smile and redirected his attention toward Chalmers.

The lady continued without pause, "Because just…" she consulted her watch, "Two hours ago, you pooh-poohed the idea of sending in soldiers, selling us instead on the superiority of one of your operatives." She looked back at Toby, who again held her gaze.

This time the lady looked away first, and continued making

her point to Chalmers, "So, you can imagine my surprise when a uniformed soldier arrives, who is apparently your operative!"

Two hours? Toby found that interesting. So how long had this meeting been going on? And what exactly was Chalmers promising that Toby could do? The whole thing was a fascinating mess.

"Okay, so let's run through this again." The lady he now knew to be Debbie looked exhausted as she sipped at a fresh coffee, one of a large batch which had just been delivered, "Now that your operative is present."

She took a deep breath and got to it, "Miller, wasn't it?"

There was that strong gaze again. Not many people had it, but she did. *Good for her*, Toby thought to himself. "Yes, Ma'am."

Debbie was losing interest in the specifics of how long this had been going on, so switched to a simpler starting point for Toby, "Earlier, we discovered a terrorist website, broadcasting new footage of a Briton, a journalist who was kidnapped very recently."

Toby sighed silently. In his work he knew how most of those situations played out -beheadings, or trades. Not the most promising start for an operation.

"Do feel free to interrupt if you have any questions I've not covered. And apologies, Sergeant Miller, but it's been a very long night, and I don't think any of us are at our best anymore."

"Ma'am." Toby replied again, smirking at the idea she'd addressed him by his rank, due to his uniform no doubt. Chalmers would probably be seething on the inside.

"And they've since uploaded this video." She let the recording play for Toby, although for everyone else it must have been the hundredth time that night.

"Wait. Can you stop it right there please, Ma'am?" Toby sat up straight and leaned forward in concentration. "What's that expression?" Toby pointed at the paused frame, which showed Danny Ellington's odd switch from a look of terror, to a calmer one. The switch had caught Toby's eye, the fact that it had happened in an instant made it that much more interesting.

Debbie was so exhausted that she'd become blind to the tiny detail. She now refocused on the forgotten moment, "I'm not sure." She picked up the phone in the middle of the table and quickly punched three keys, "Lydia? Oh, I'm glad you're still here. Could you come back in please?" Debbie replaced the handset and waited in silence, still studying the screen.

Toby stared at the same image, trying to place the expression. It was a familiar expression, but he couldn't quite put his finger on what it was.

"Ma'am."

Toby turned to see a younger woman hovering in the doorway.

"Yes, thank you Lydia. You were going to try and find out where the video was shot?" Debbie nodded toward the screen.

"Yes Ma'am, already done. It was quite straightforward actually." Lydia wirelessly reconnected her tablet to the large monitor in order to show everybody a map of the region. "It's an expensive camera you see, so it stores all of the IPTC Metadata, and the GPS co-ordinates for every still image, or video, it captures. And this particular video was shot, right here." Her pointer highlighted the spot, and then she zoomed in tighter on the map.

Recognition. That was the look on the hostage's face. Toby signaled to get the newcomer's attention and then gestured toward the screen, "Can you go back to the video please? To the frame where we'd paused it?"

Lydia dutifully looked at her superior, who nodded permission instantly, and the requested image reappeared just as quickly.

"That look," Toby nodded toward the screen, "It's recognition."

"My God! It is. I've been trying to place it too," Another attendee contributed.

Debbie's face scrunched in confusion, they were probably right, but, "But what did he recognise?" Although the question wasn't directed at anybody in particular.

Toby was still staring intently at the image, "His expression only changed when the camera got close. So, it's gotta be the cameraman, someone else close to them, or the camera itself." Toby nodded toward the image, "but look at the timing of when it happened."

Debbie walked right up to the huge screen, tilting her head in thought, "What do you think, Lyds?"

Lydia was studying a smaller version of the same image on the device in her hand, and took her time in replying, "From that close, if it were anybody but the camera operator, then Mister Ellington's eyes would appear to be looking slightly to the side of the lens. But he's looking right at the lens. Look at the white of his eyes, it's equilateral. And if we combine the direction of his stare, with that timing?"

Lydia looked back at the soldier in the room, "I think if it had been another person present, then he'd have recognised them earlier than he did."

Then she had another thought, "Unless of course, Danny is short sighted."

Lydia's fingers darted across the screen of her device once more. "Which he's not; there's no record of prescriptive lenses on the Driver and Vehicle Licensing Agency's record for Danny Ellington." Now she nodded toward Toby, "So I agree with him, I believe he recognised the camera itself."

Toby smirked again, as once the government had your information, there really were no secrets.

Lydia's focus however, returned to her device. "I can tell you more about the camera. It's a pro-bodied SLR, I've even got the serial number in front of me. But more relevant is the cost..."

She was moving pages and typing as she spoke, "Six and a half thousand pounds, just for the camera body." She exhaled audibly, "The specifics about the lens fitted are also embedded in the IPTC data. And the lens used for this video, is another nine hundred quid. So that's an expensive set-up, it's certainly not your standard terrorist rig."

"Okay. And what were they using for their previous videos?" Debbie asked.

Lydia chuckled, "Already searching for that, Ma'am."

Debbie smiled back, some progress and fresh coffee had certainly lifted the mood.

"Well, they don't use smart phones, I'd guess due to the always-on GPS coordinates. So up until now they've always used an old fashioned pocket-sized digital camera with a little over twelve mega-pixels, making it at least ten years old. Which means this is the first time they've ever used such an expensive piece of current-gen equipment. I guess they don't know about the embedded data in a modern pro camera body."

"It's Duggan-Smythe's camera then," Chalmers finally spoke.

"Who's Duggan-Smythe?" asked Toby, cautiously.

"Oh! Charles Duggan-Smythe, son of Lord Rupert Duggan-Smythe, who incidentally is also former Armed Forces, Miller. Although commissioned, of course."

And suddenly the pieces fell into place.

Toby had been struggling to understand what made this kidnap different enough to call in a specialist operative, and there it was; Daddy was a Lord of the Realm.

A Lord. A man with influence and reach. As if it had been necessary for Chalmers to embellish it any further with the former commissioned officer crap, it was clear enough, the Lord was superior to the lowly NCO rank of Sergeant, which was Toby's previous rank.

Or current?

Toby's current status still wasn't very clear. Not even to himself.

Toby allowed himself an internal, *Fuck you, Chalmers*, before deciding to have some fun with his spoken response, "So he's not any old Rupert, Sir. He's *the* Rupert." It was an in-joke; 'Rupert' being the standard derogatory nickname applied to all well-heeled British Officers by the men in the ranks. But would Chalmers get it?

Chalmers merely looked over at Toby and narrowed his eyes in confusion.

He's clearly never worn the uniform. Toby looked away, having learned something new about Chalmers.

In the meantime, Lydia had been cross checking the camera's serial number from the digital data contained within the image file it had created, then she'd looked it up in the manufacturer's warranty database. But before she could share, Debbie stepped back in with, "There's been an idea in discussion, where we send in an operative."

Lydia slumped, recognising that now wasn't the time to further prove her technical abilities.

What? Toby had more questions than answers. "To do, what?" he asked, gingerly.

Debbie turned her gaze to Chalmers. He'd come up with the crazy idea, it was only fitting he owned the damned thing.

"Ostensibly, as another journalist, Miller." Chalmers started.

Toby raised his eyebrows in surprise, then caught himself, only to realise that Debbie had already seen him let his poker face slip. So, he shot her a big smile, before erasing all trace from his face to ask Chalmers, "To what end, Sir? I only see insertion as a valid step in recovering the man from the video, whose name you've not yet mentioned."

"Oh yes, of course Miller. Danny Ellington is his name." Chalmers' insincere smile was quite nauseating.

"Okay, so as a recovery op for this Danny, I can see insertion as a potential starting point. To be further developed of course. But?" Were they really going to make him say it? "You seem more concerned with another man, who is not in this video. So, excuse my confusion, Sir." Toby shrugged in an unthreatening manner.

"Well, obviously we need to bring back young Duggan-Smythe too." The unconvincing smile was still plastered across Chalmers' face.

And what about all the other detainees you leave to rot? Is what

Toby wanted to ask, but clearly Chalmers was from the same world as the Duggan-Smythes, and they always looked after their own. You had to give them that.

Listening to this, without letting out a sigh, rolling his eyes, or shaking his head, was so very hard, but Toby held firm. "So what do we know about the status of the second subject?" Toby couldn't even bring himself to say the entitled new subject's name.

"Well, not too much as of yet, but with the right operative inserted, we'll certainly learn much more than we can from here."

Chalmers looked over at Toby with a confusingly cheerful expression, "And following the success of your last undercover op, which I feel bound to share with the room."

Oh no... Toby closed his eyes momentarily.

Chalmers looked away from Toby, then stood up and straightened his suit jacket, "This man, ladies and gentlemen, is the operative who just returned Madyson Lutz." Eyes widened around the room. "The woman who'd attempted to run from British justice under the umbrella of diplomatic immunity." Chalmers then had the cheek to lead the startled room into an embarrassingly awkward round of applause for Toby.

"Which is why I think it's fair to say that after your last operation Miller, what choice do we have but to use you?"

Toby was backed into a corner, with all eyes on him, struggling to maintain an unaffected expression. When all he wanted to do was groan at how incredibly effectively he'd been screwed over.

22.

DANNY OPENED HIS eyes, scanned his surroundings, and then closed them again in an attempt to block out the reality of his new situation.

He gently shook his head from side to side. So, it hadn't been some terrifying nightmare, this crap was real. With his eyes still held tightly closed, he ran it through his head again; the helicopter being shot down, Charlie's catching it on film, then the brat royally screwing things up in the bar afterwards.

To think, he'd been riddled with guilt at the idea of leaving Charlie behind. He exhaled. Not anymore, Charlie had caused all of this, and now Danny was the Western kidnappee.

Danny shook his head from side to side again, then grimaced at the mistake. It was still throbbing, although not quite as severely as before. Danny raised his right hand and searched the back of his head for what was causing the pain and flinched as he found not one, but two huge lumps, his hair matted in dried clumps of blood over the larger one.

He opened his eyes once more and looked straight over at the doorway to his cell, and there on the floor was a new bottle of water. Danny shuffled over on his knees, wincing in pain as his weight rested on the right one. He picked up the bottle and shuffled back to his cell's rear wall, using it as a backrest.

He took a deep breath as he unscrewed the lid, then gulped down about half the bottle, forcing himself to stop before fully emptying it. Then Danny raised the bottle and leant his head forward. He located the dried blood with his left hand and used it to guide his right, slowly pouring water over the wound. "Shit, fuck, piss!" He hissed involuntarily as the fluid stabbed at the raw, open wound.

Danny's left hand very gently rubbed the water into his matted hair, wincing in pain the whole time. Then he poured some more, hissing through his teeth while trying to fight the agonising sensations it continued to trigger.

Enough. He worked on calming his breathing as he put the lid back on the bottle, which he tossed aside. Then he rested his head into his hands and worked on slowing his breathing down.

As the water he'd just poured onto his head warmed to match that of his body temperature, the sharp pain sensations dulled back down to a more manageable throb. Danny opened his eyes again and looked at his surroundings, shaking his head once more at what he saw.

Still, there existed some childlike instinct, making him want to cry, but it was time to finally fight that. He'd lived through the first part, so there was still hope. Possibly.

Danny took stock; he was a hostage and it was time to start thinking rationally, so what did he know about other hostages? A few managed to escape, but very few. Some were traded back, but only when offered up by terrorists who had someone they needed back badly enough themselves. The British Government weren't known for hostage exchanges, unless they were in equally dire need -although some trades did happen in secret, meaning that was another slight possibility. The tears welled again; Danny knew in his heart there was no reason to make him worthy of a complex, and risky, prisoner exchange.

So, what else was there? There was the other thing, the one they all knew about but tried to banish from their thoughts.

That one really made his eyes well up, but again, he had to fight it. He'd watched some of the beheadings, he'd even known two of the previous victims and he'd been shocked at how calmly they'd carried themselves at the very end. *How did they manage that?* It didn't matter, that was a thought he could postpone, for now.

What else was there? Danny struggled. *Come on man, what else happens?* He didn't know, and that was the final possibility. There was a tiny percentage of hostages who were taken, and held, and then even years later -nobody knew if they were still alive, or dead & buried in a foreign land.

The stark reality of his new situation was horrific. He continued to fight the tears welling in his eyes, and just about managed to contain them. Danny blotted at the small amount of evidence that had already escaped, then sat back against the concrete block wall and started to think it all through again.

23.

THREE HOURS AFTER Toby's arrival, the goldfish bowl team had agreed to a short break. All of the room's occupants had left, presumably to be anywhere other than that room. But Toby had nowhere else to go, no nearby office, no sanctuary. So, he'd made himself a cup of tea and sat back down inside the bowl, alone.

"Sergeant Miller?" the voice had come from the young woman, the tech savvy one.

She seemed shy, sweet even, Toby smiled sincerely and answered her with a simple "Hey. How you doing?"

Lydia hovered in the doorway, looking somewhat torn, but didn't seem ready to vocalise whatever the cause was.

"Feel free to sit, don't stand on ceremony for me," he offered.

Lydia maintained the silence, but also didn't make to leave the room. Toby looked at her and noticed that she couldn't look him in the eye. So it was guilt, he'd seen this before. The girl knew that he was being sent off, to do something more dangerous than she could comprehend, and she felt partly responsible for her role in him being sent there.

"It's what I do," he offered, pre-emptively.

Now Lydia looked him straight in the eye, before having further doubts and peering back into the sparsely lit open-plan area that surrounded the brightly illuminated goldfish bowl.

Her eyes scanned the desks that littered the outer area. There was nobody around, but she still felt exposed, so she cautiously entered the room which was usually reserved for people way above her pay grade, and leant on a section of glass wall closer to Toby.

Lydia went to talk, then quickly closed her mouth again. She was fighting her conscience, but it was pitted against concern for talking out of place, she needed to keep her job after all.

"Do you need to borrow some money?" Toby picked a suitably inane route, "I've only got about sixty quid on me, but you can have it. We can find a cash machine if it's worse than that."

Lydia laughed; it was a beautiful, song-bird type sound.

"Or is it my tea? Coz you can have it, I'll make another."

The laughing abruptly stopped, and she looked close to tears, suddenly spitting out, "You don't have to go you know. Even he said that."

He? Toby thought to himself, realising she could only mean Chalmers. Funny really, as Toby had got the impression he did have to go, or he was done. For good. Still, that was a choice, of sorts.

But she didn't know that and telling her certainly wouldn't help, so Toby looked down at the table trying to find another route.

Lydia lowered her voice to almost a whisper, "This is suicide." She looked close to tears, "and I don't want any part in sending you off like this."

Oh no, this wasn't good for either of them. Toby patted the cushion of the seat next to his, and Lydia slumped into it without pause.

Where to start? Toby took a breath, then took a shot, "Look, Lydia, wasn't it?"

She nodded gently.

"First, please don't call me Sergeant Miller. Chalmers was right. I was Army, but not anymore, so Sergeant is kind of pointless." He couldn't help but hear his own words. *I was Army*. That seemed to be an early decision regarding his dilemma.

"Toby," he nodded at her in a fatherlike manner, "That's best. Right?"

"Toby," she repeated.

"There you go, that was easy. You pronounced it quite well. Not perfect," he wiggled his hand to and fro, "but quite well." He shot her an easy grin, which she mirrored back at him, then he adjusted himself in his seat. "So, forgetting about me, for now. What do you think is gonna happen to Danny Ellington, alone over there?"

The answer to that couldn't be rushed, Lydia looked down at the table in deep thought, then her expression soured, "Prisoner exchange? Long term captive," she sighed, "Or public beheading."

She was an expert at her job, whether that meant searching, hacking, locating, or digging up old secrets. If it involved her keyboard, then it was within her comfort zone. This, was categorically not within her comfort zone.

"Exactly." Toby knew Danny's likely fate, and she knew it too. "Or I take a bit of a risk and go help him." He was underselling it, but there was truth in the simplicity, as is so often the case.

Toby took a deep breath as they both absorbed that unwelcome reality, "And the best thing for me, would be some help."

Lydia quickly looked back up at him. Toby noticed it and saw it as confirmation of that being exactly what they both needed. "Because the more help I get, and the better that help is, the more we lower the risk."

"Okay," she nodded. He needed the type of help she could provide; that knowledge lifted her spirits.

"These situations are always risky, so I work at lowering it. I've been sitting here thinking about that, especially about the camera, the one that might belong to the Rupert's kid."

She cut him off, "Oh, it did, there's no doubt. I ran the serial number, and the manufacturer's warranty is registered in Charles Duggan-Smythe's name." She was reassuringly confident when it involved her work, Toby could already see that.

"Good, so they probably have both these guys then. Ellington's already been paraded as proof, and Duggan-Smythe's camera points to him being captive too. But he's not being held alongside Danny Ellington, or Ellington wouldn't have looked at the camera like that. You know? The surprise?"

Lydia nodded energetically, that all made sense as a hypothesis.

But Toby was just getting started, "And Ellington was still wearing civvies, not an orange jumpsuit. So that's evidence of a period where he keeps his normal clothes before they change him."

"I'd noticed that too," said a voice in the doorway. Lydia and Toby looked over to see Debbie had joined them.

"Ma'am." Toby stood up to greet her appropriately.

"You can sit down, Miller, and we're already well beyond Ma'am. Debbie will do fine."

"He's Toby," Lydia couldn't hold herself back, at which Toby could only chuckle.

Debbie smiled at the pair of them, "So what are you thinking then, Toby?"

Toby was still arranging those pieces inside his head, and paused long enough to answer clearly, "I'll be alone, that's obvious," he shrugged. "But it's worse than that, I'll have no gear and no weapon, coz they'll take everything off me. They'll strip me naked at some point."

Lydia looked down at the table uncomfortably, which Debbie didn't miss.

"And when I'm there I can't source any new gear, which is a unique problem that goes with being a prisoner. Because any competent captors won't let me steal anything useful, they'll be vigilant about that. So, if I go in with nothing, I'll be stuck with nothing. That's what's really been bothering me."

"But..." he hesitated as Debbie took a seat alongside them, "If I've got that first day, with my own clothes. You know? And I'm thinking about how they seem to like these nice cameras too, enough to keep them onsite."

The ladies were both starting to see the direction forming.

He continued, "It's tricky." Understatement of the year. "I can only do so much alone. I'm captive, I have no kit and there will be multiple unfriendlies. Depending on the size of the detainee camp, let's say five, ten, twenty? More? Who knows? Too many for one bloke in his undies though."

Lydia winced and Debbie nodded at his thought process, "So you need help." It wasn't a question.

"Oh yeah!" Toby's eyes widened and he smirked, "I'll need a rapid response unit, a way of telling them where I am, and even more importantly -when they need to initiate. Does all that make sense?"

"Yes, absolutely. So, what can we send you with?"

"Well, what can I take, that I can hide in my clothing, and footwear?" Toby tilted his head and added, "Or in a camera, that's close by?" he scowled, "But probably not close enough to actually use."

24.

"MY LORD? SIR, I do sincerely apologise, but…" The man in two-piece pyjamas whispered as loudly as he dared, and then turned on the overhead room light.

After several years in the Army, Lord Duggan-Smythe had retained the ability to wake quickly, and rolled toward the edge of his bed to deal with the unwelcome intrusion.

"Do turn that infernal light off, Woodcock. Must we wake the Lady too?" The Lord swung his legs off the bed and strode toward his butler.

Woodcock did as told, then lowered his voice further still, "As I say my Lord, I do apologise, but it's a man from the government and he's insisting that I wake you, saying it is a matter of the utmost urgency." Woodcock winced uncomfortably, as he handed over the phone.

"Out!" The Lord gestured they should leave the room, noticing the Lady of the house had started stirring now too.

"Who is this?" Lord Rupert barked into the phone, as he strode along the long corridor.

"My name is Hugo Chalmers, Lord Duggan-Smythe. We've met at various social occasions, I'm a departmental chief at GCHQ, I do apologise for the early…"

"Early? What in blazes is so important at…" The Lord looked at the time and substituted the specifics with a guttural growl.

Chalmers was suddenly feeling rather out of his depth, not an experience he was accustomed too. He reminded himself the Lord had previously commanded an Artillery Regiment and got straight to the point, as would surely be required by such a man, "Your son, Charles. He appears to have been taken hostage whilst working on assignment. On the border of Syria and Iraq."

The wind went from Lord Duggan-Smythe's sails, his pace slowed to a crawl and then he stopped completely.

Charles. He'd finally shown some signs of hope, and now. Now, of all times, this?

The Lord felt his balance go off slightly, so leant against the corridor wall. He took the phone from his ear and worked on composing himself for the caller who'd just triggered this unwelcome wave of emotion, which seemed to be affecting his breathing.

The Lord's plan to accidentally-on-purpose bump into his son; why hadn't he put it into action before? He'd taken it for granted, that's why. Postpone it until tomorrow, next week, or the week after. The complacent belief there'd always be another later.

But there was no later, not anymore, he'd just run out of laters, and it had happened in an instant. The Lord's breathing became even more laboured. It was as if his lungs were disobeying his orders.

Lord Rupert cast his mind back to the boy's younger face, always cheeky, always full of life, always trouble.

"No." He moaned, as his breathing worsened further and suddenly his side seized, as if all of his muscles had contracted simultaneously. A vicious wave of pain struck through him like a violent clap of thunder. Lord Rupert wailed and clutched at his left side, wheezed, and dropped the phone as his hand seized, joining in with the bodily mutiny.

"No. Woodcock, help." The words came out chopped and barely decipherable. His lungs were failing him too, then his ability to remain upright, completely vacated his body, and his vision blurred.

"Oh, my Lord! Lord Rupert, no." Woodcock felt a rising sense of panic as he ran the couple of steps to his employer's side. He tried catching the Lord's weight as he dropped, only succeeding in lowering him to the floor a little more gradually. Woodcock leant the Lord onto his side in the recovery position, snatched the phone up off the floor and yelled at the man on the other end of the line, "You! Whoever you are, call an ambulance, immediately! Lord Rupert has collapsed."

Woodcock then tossed the phone and turned his head to summon more of the house help, "The Lord has collapsed. Wake up, everyone." He summoned all the volume his lungs and vocal cords could create. "Now!" he boomed.

Woodcock fought the rising panic, wrestling back control in order to manage the situation and help the Lord, a man who'd become more than a mere employer. The ideal butler relationship should last a lifetime, and in those situations, you inevitably grew to admire, love, and respect your employer.

Woodcock could hear new noises coming from within the house, so leaned in to listen for breathing, hearing only the faintest noises from his boss, "Don't worry my Lord, help is on its way." He squeezed the Lord's hand, supportively.

Then turned away again, to bellow down the corridor, "Someone help us, please. For God's sake, help!"

25.

DANNY TOOK A long deep breath of the hot acrid air and summoned some inner strength. He didn't know what his fate was, there was simply no way of knowing that. But he'd finally resolved to at least do whatever lay in his power to increase his chances of survival.

He unscrewed the cap from the morning's water bottle and knocked back the remainder of its warm contents. He was appreciative of the fresh water, but needed much, much more of it. The thought of which made him have a go at finally standing up.

Knowing his right leg was the painful one, he put his weight onto his left, and for extra support also grabbed at the upper part of the concrete block wall. Once he'd hauled himself upright, he put some pressure onto his right leg; it wasn't good, but he could probably move around on it, slowly. Getting up was apparently going to be the worst part of the process.

Danny cautiously took the couple of steps over to the side with his new French neighbour, and leant his weight onto the wall, before grabbing the bars that separated their cells. The first thing he noticed was that the bars felt very old and irregular in shape, and that they were solid, rather than hollow. Although, what difference did it make? His self-proclaimed ability to cope under duress hadn't been sufficiently tested, until now, and it was starting to look like a chronic case of wishful thinking.

So, whether the separating bars were made from cast iron, or painted balsa wood, didn't change much. He'd discovered he wasn't the coper he'd always imagined himself to be, and certainly not up to the stresses of anything as foolhardy as an escape attempt.

He peered into the next cell to see the Frenchman already looking back up at him, "You're looking better," the man greeted him with a slightly more forced smile than usual.

Danny nodded, "I wanted to thank you. You know, for the water. And the support."

The Frenchman looked away from Danny and shrugged, "Well, we only have each other."

That was a depressing thought, Danny stared into space while absorbing the implications. It was also becoming apparent that his new neighbour was in a far less positive frame of mind than on their previous encounters. He decided to move on; to finally try and give something back, "I'm Danny, by the way."

"Yannick." His neighbour looked back up at him.

"It's nice to meet you, Yannick." Danny finally managed to summon a quick smile for his new companion, the shock of which was infectious.

"I haven't seen one of those for a while," was the response, although the Frenchman's own smile faded rather too quickly.

"For how long?" Danny asked, "I suppose I mean, how long have you been, um? Held?"

Yannick raised his eyebrows, and thought hard, finally shaking his head. He couldn't even answer without some help, meaning his answer was another question, "What is the date?"

Realistically, Danny didn't know that for sure either, but having a much closer approximation than Yannick, he shared what he could.

Yannick closed his eyes despondently, having finally realised the duration of his own captivity, "Enough time for a nouveau-nee. A baby."

Danny's eyes widened in surprise, then he reminded himself to snap back into the more constructive mode he was now committed to using. "Okay, but?" Danny had so many questions and didn't know where to start, although for now he appeared to have nothing but time, and so went right back to the beginning, "How did you get taken? Are you a journalist, too?"

Then Danny leaned in closer and asked a more pressing question in a lowered voice, "I know what it was like getting here, but how do they usually treat us?"

Yannick leaned forwards, having heard voices approaching, and as he recognised one of them, he gestured quickly toward Danny and whispered, "Sit back down and ferme la bouche. No mouth, or you'll see how that one treats us."

26.

THE LAST OF the departmental chiefs had re-entered the goldfish bowl. Debbie scanned the room, noticing one absentee, "Does anyone know where Chalmers went?"

"He was on the phone but took off toward the lifts. Looked in a hurry," responded a colleague as she settled back into her seat.

Debbie considered waiting, but only momentarily, "Fine. He can catch up later."

She stood up and returned to her position at the side of the large screen, "So people, I just spent some time talking with Toby, and now we all have some brainstorming to do. To ensure operational success."

Debbie didn't handle operatives, had never even met one until now, and as soon as the words came out, she realised how effectively she'd just showcased her lack of relevant experience.

"Let me rewind." She slowed down, nodded her apology to Toby, and resumed in a manner more natural to her, "Sergeant Miller, who has asked us to call him Toby, is acutely aware of what a dangerous situation we're putting him in. So, what we're looking at, is minimising as much of that risk as possible. Because all of us here, want everyone over there, to make it home safely."

Toby raised his hand, to get the room's attention. "I appreciate the sentiment, but you can never ensure operational success. Especially at the planning stage."

He shrugged, almost apologetically, before continuing, "Usually you get where you're going, to find the variables have already changed, and plans have been altered accordingly. Then you make a start, but immediately something else goes wrong, forcing you to adapt on the spot. So, like I say, at the planning stage, we can only accomplish so much. But if we can set things up right now so that I'm best equipped to cope when things go wonky donkey, then we're off to a good start."

Debbie winced at Toby's blunt summary of operational realities, then took over again. "Okay then, in summary, what we have so far is the likelihood that both British journos have been taken, although with no indication that at the time of the video they were, or are now, together. That's problem number one, but let's come back to that."

People started typing and scratching notes in response.

"And we seem to have been steered into a situation," *By Chalmers,* she thought to herself, "Where we have to attempt recovery of both captured men."

"Now, Toby," her focus steered toward him, "Prior to your arrival, we'd discussed the idea of this being a military rescue operation; and considering your experience and knowledge of such operations, I'd be very interested in your thoughts on that possibility."

With Chalmers absent, Debbie was particularly interested to see if the soldier's response would align with the previously drawn conclusions.

Toby decided to remain seated while he shared his thoughts with the room. "I should start by saying that operational planning is typically led by the relevant Regiment's Commanding Officer, or equivalent, for smaller or larger units of men. And I don't mean to exclude when I state 'men', Ma'am."

"I understand Toby, it's standard terminology." Debbie nodded for him to plough on.

"But they always plan these things with their most senior NCOs." He shrugged, "People like me. So, while strictly speaking, you should be asking this question of a CO, or an OiC, I'll give you an informal idea of how they'd respond, based on previous experience."

Toby paused to consider the logical series of events when deploying a company (or more) of men for a rescue operation like this. And none of the scenarios played out well.

As he thought it through, his head started to shake at the inevitable results, "I'd need to give it a lot more thought Ma'am. Sorry, I mean Debbie. But I can already see a lot of problems."

Toby had no reason to disguise his internal reaction, so allowed his face to betray the concerns he could feel within. "Firstly, we know where Danny Ellington is right now, but not where he'll be in a week. And if the terrorists move him before we get there, then our men will be sitting ducks. All for nothing." Toby looked down at the table, momentarily distracted by thoughts of how he'd ended up in this bizarre situation.

This was an undercover task, but of a type he wasn't sure had ever been done before. Typically, undercover work involved gaining trust in order to infiltrate, meaning going in as somebody on-side. Whereas he was looking at going undercover, as a perceived enemy.

In itself, that was a lot to take in, without even considering the element of choice. And whether he actually had any.

He'd always known his previous operation had the potential to derail his career, but the official post-action report had concluded by praising his actions. So, he'd naively thought he'd dodged the consequences.

But the forced leave, and now this? It was undeniable evidence that not everybody had agreed with the officially given pat on the back. Toby was finally starting to see that somebody in a position of power was ready to bury him. Both figuratively and, it seemed, literally.

The room's occupants were waiting on him, and he knew it. But an unwelcome awareness was also creeping up on him, that whatever came out of his mouth next, might be life changing.

His previous comment wasn't yet irreversible. He could still backtrack and lie about the validity of the military rescue operation, selling the room on its merits, which would allow him to step away from the operation himself.

But there were no merits to the military rescue option, and selfishly creating an exit for himself would only force another group of soldiers into a shitty situation. His own Regiment were already stuck in a comparably bad spot. So, what kind of worthless human would that make him?

He shook his head at the thought, then looked up to see that Debbie was studying him, intently.

But he had to think, and she had to wait. So, what else was there? What other options could he come up with?

The problem was that he hadn't got anything else.

"Toby?" Debbie could sense the soldier's inner turmoil.

"Just a moment, Ma'am." And so he'd lie for what? In order to dodge consequences? There'd been far too much of that going around recently.

Consequences. Surprisingly the memory which came to mind wasn't Madyson Lutz's attempt to run from them. Instead, it was the moment when she'd bravely faced Toby's family, graveside. Specifically, the way she'd sobbed as she told them how she'd willingly trade her own life for young Luke's, if it were only possible.

And suddenly he knew it was time for him to take the same approach. If this were a suicide mission, then so be it. He'd be offering his life, in exchange for the little peace he'd already managed to give his own family when he'd previously forced Lutz's return.

Toby actually felt the tension ease, in spite of what he knew must follow. "What was I saying?" He finally looked up at Debbie, fully committed to what must come next. "Apologies Ma'am, it's just a lot to consider." He shot her a warm smile.

"I understand," although Debbie sensed he'd been distracted by much more than just operational specifics, so steered him back on course with, "You were explaining the risks of a military rescue operation."

He nodded, "Yes ma'am, right." *Just get on with it, man.* "Whereas an inserted operative would be taken to join the nearest group of hostages, wherever that may be. Which is a considerable advantage of solo insertion."

His mind was already working quickly again, "Returning to the previous discussion of a military rescue though, just for the sake of thoroughness. Even if Danny Ellington's captors stayed put long enough for a unit to make a coordinated approach, I still see problems with making a clean approach."

Toby played out the military scenario internally, his simulation based on years of uniformed experience. "Some of the Jihadis will be tied-up in the firefight with our boys, while others will head straight for the prisoners. And whether they move those prisoners, or kill them, depends on whether they think they've got a clean exit, or not."

"What I'm saying is that if our boys do a solid job of pinning the Jihadis down, then the detainees will pay with their lives. And if our boys don't contain the situation perfectly, then the detainees will vanish, right in the middle of the firefight, leaving us with…" *Fuck all,* probably wasn't the appropriate terminology.

He paused to run it through his head again, "It's a no-win situation, Ma'am. Personally, I don't see it being a valid option. Fatalities will be too high, for both soldiers and hostages."

"Actually Toby, that's extremely useful confirmation, so thank you."

He nodded toward Debbie, then added another nod for the others present.

"Which brings us back to you Toby, meaning the idea of inserting you alone, as a journalist. This also raises questions, such as where do we place you? To ensure you attract the right attention?"

"It is a much lower risk operation this way, just to be clear." Toby felt duty bound to confirm.

"Not for you, it's not." Debbie was quick to point out.

"Uh," He groaned. "There's far less risk for Ellington and

Duggan-Smythe though, which is the priority here. I'll find a way." And as Toby looked around the room, he found himself trying to recognise a new expression, one mirrored on several faces. It was strangely reminiscent of how the day had started.

"You are very brave, Sergeant Miller." Debbie was the one to break the silence first.

Toby looked quite disgusted at her comment. "No, Ma'am." He needed to steer the subject away from that misconception as quickly as possible. "Stupid though? Likely. Although I do have a serious concern, Ma'am. If I'm trying to pose as a journalist, then shouldn't I know something about being a journalist?"

Debbie's eyes searched the air around her in thought. In her exhausted state she'd assumed a camera and an accent would be enough. But his concern was valid, although easily remedied. "I think we can arrange some help with that. One moment." Debbie typed a quick message to Lydia, then refocused her attention on the people present.

"Now let's say you've been taken." She'd been focused on Toby up until now, but it was vital that everyone else became involved, so she altered her direction to include the other attendees. "As Toby has pointed out, he's likely to be stripped of all possessions quite quickly. But in the video from earlier," Debbie consulted her watch, "correction, yesterday, Danny Ellington was not yet wearing the dreaded orange-coloured overalls."

"So, let's assume that we have a short window, where Toby retains a few basic personal items, such as clothing and footwear. Let's also assume that his camera is kept by the Zarqawi 'abdi group, as has happened here."

"The big question is this; within those few items, can we supply him with a means of sending out a location confirmation signal? So that we can send in a quick response force, to extract everyone."

Her terminology showed her lack of relevant experience, but her intelligence and humanity mattered far more to Toby, so he pretended not to have noticed, and kept the forward momentum.

"If we can stash some kind of weapon too, that'd be really good for me." He raised the palm of his hand to preemptively pause any potential interruptions. "But another couple of things first. We have to assume I'm gonna take a beating, similar to Danny's. And I don't think the appropriate rapid response unit should be uniformed or arrive in Land Rovers. Whoever they are, they've got to blend in much better than we usually do."

The room fell silent, as everyone considered potential solutions.

"We've put a one-piece blade inside the heel and shank area of a boot before, kind of a pared down Fairbairn-Sykes knife. That'd give you a basic weapon," contributed a blonde-haired man.

"Absolutely, I'll take it." Toby nodded his appreciation enthusiastically. "But I have to look as civvy as possible, so let's avoid boots. To be honest, if I were a kidnaper, I'd hold my hostages with nothing more than the socks on their feet. Coz being stripped of your footwear slows you down, it gives you a nasty feeling of vulnerability and a reluctance to try and leg it. So, let's assume they'll look at it in a similar way. Normal civvy trainers are far less likely to attract their attention than a big pair of boots."

"Yeah, got it. Consider it done," replied the blonde man as he noted the appropriate comment. "We've stitched steel garotte wire inside a shirt collar before now too."

"What about inside the camera strap? so I'm not putting all my eggs in the same basket." Toby flashed a cheeky grin at the room, "And if you can hide an MP5 in my socks, that'd be great."

Debbie smiled as a wave of sadness simultaneously washed over her. She didn't quite understand how somebody so personable and even endearing, could so willingly dive into a situation like this; the empathy for what lay ahead was becoming an unwelcome distraction.

Debbie composed herself by looking down at the floor, then resumed, "We also…"

"Or gas!" Toby interrupted, suddenly sitting upright in his chair, "A little CS gas could be really useful in an enclosed environment like a cell block. Oh, apologies, Ma'am." He looked from her back toward the same blonde man, hoping for something encouraging from him in response.

"Uhh, I don't know, but I like what you're thinking. Leave it with me." The man went back to his shopping list of Toby's needs.

"Well," Debbie nodded at Toby, "This is getting a little less terrifying. Sorry Sergeant Miller, but…"

"It's terrifying for you? I'm crapping myself!" Toby smirked and winked at her.

Debbie was aware that her personal perceptions about risk were out of sync with the general population -who seemed to grow more risk-averse with every passing day. But his attitude toward risk was on a different level entirely. She tried smiling back at him but failed and merely ended up looking like she'd been sucking on a lemon.

Toby laughed out loud at her piss-poor poker face, then had to work at looking suitably restrained and professional again.

Debbie swallowed hard and recomposed herself. "Thank you, Toby, I think we're all glad of some positivity at this point!"

She paused for a moment as she speed-read a new message on her device's screen. "We'll also need to know if we can make a GPS beacon fit inside a professional camera body. Otherwise, Sergeant Miller here will be facing a very long wait for his rapid response unit." She'd picked up on Toby's gentle correction of her terminology.

"We've got so much more to cover, but I do have to interrupt the flow momentarily." She returned her focus to Toby. "Toby, Mister Chalmers just let me know he's got you in for something called 'Detainee Survival Training'. A quick refresher course apparently, before you head out."

She sighed uncomfortably, "And he needs you to leave immediately."

27.

LADY FIONA DUGGAN-SMYTHE ran down the wide hospital corridor, chasing the trolley which carried her husband. He was still alive, although she could only tell that because if he weren't then all of these doctors and nurses would be panicking, and they were not.

They weren't in the slightest bit panicked actually, they were noticeably calm and professional. She finally took her eyes off her husband to truly appreciate the people who were helping him to maintain his tenuous grip on this world.

That they weren't paid enough was the first thing which came to mind.

At that point, the lead person of the people convoy pushed open a new set of swinging double-doors, allowed the trolley pushers through, before stepping right in front of Lady Duggan-Smythe, blocking her route, "I'm sorry, but you can't go any further."

"But…" she scowled instinctively.

"I'm sorry," he interrupted her instantly, "but, there are no 'buts'. You need to let us get on with our jobs, so that we can do everything possible for your husband. And as soon as we have any news, we'll come and find you." The man made a point of holding her stare, before thanking her, turning, and closing the doors in her face.

Lady Duggan-Smythe hovered outside the doorway, shocked. People didn't say 'No' to her, and they certainly didn't issue orders, but… reluctantly she had to admit that it made sense. Rupert needed their full attention, not her distracting them. She turned away from the doorway, finally taking stock of all that had happened. It had been such a blur; she was totally disorientated. She looked at her wrist to check the time, but she'd left her watch on the bedside table, exactly where it lived every night.

Her phone -she felt for her handbag, also at home. And of course, her mobile phone was in her handbag. What a disaster. They'd left in such a hurry she had absolutely nothing. She looked left and right for a clock, and found none, but could see a vending machine off in the distance which might signify an area worthy of a wall-mounted timepiece. She took off toward the machine.

So, what had actually happened? She was assuming Rupert had a heart attack, or a stroke, but nobody had offered any real information yet. What did an aneurism look like?

She arrived at the vending machine area, where a large digital clock displayed 03:39. It was the early hours of the morning and she could distinctly remember a phone call. Also, that Woodcock was being annoyingly loud, and that Rupert had chastised him for it.

That was an unusual occurrence in itself, as Woodcock was a good man. They were her husband's words, not hers, but she was inclined to agree.

But Woodcock? Where on earth was the man? Her mind was skipping from one thing to another. She'd ridden in the ambulance with Rupert, but Woodcock had been following on, in one of the family cars. So, he must be in the hospital too, all she had to do was find him.

She looked around, finally taking in the scale of the hospital and felt her emotions sink even further.

28.

TOBY HAD RETURNED his ID card, exited the doughnut shaped building where Chalmers worked, and was faced with a drive to the Hereford countryside for some refresher training.

He turned the key in his car's ignition, unlocked his phone and searched for the quickest route there. He already knew what they did in Hereford, and who worked there.

Going there, for the training he'd been scheduled for... he shook his head. This would be about as much fun as the op itself. And what would the training involve? He didn't even want to think about it.

The journey was to be an hour, so not a particularly long drive, but how long would the training last? His instincts told him that lightning-fast was the way they should be approaching this entire operation. But sending him on a training course was the opposite of that, even one organized on such short notice. Courses could last days, weeks even. Time was not on his side, and yet here he was driving to sleepy Herefordshire, in the middle of the damn night.

He accelerated out onto the public road, running it all through his head. Chalmers had really backed him into a corner, then disappeared and left him to it. Toby couldn't help but return to thoughts of his own options -at least the journey would allow him some more time to do that.

Toby obeyed the phone's navigation app and hung a right at a green traffic light.

He needed to find time to let everyone know he was deploying, then hissed at the mere thought. This wasn't really deploying, this was? What could you even call it? 'Suicide' was what one of the intelligence ladies called it, now the word had crept into his vocabulary too.

There was another option that he hadn't yet considered. He could return to his unit, turn his back on his current role and let somebody else go undercover, he'd just have to go against etiquette and formally request a return to regular army duties.

That would be an irreversible decision though, so he had to be one hundred percent certain before committing to that, and he was a long way from it.

All of which meant his current options were to deploy in uniform to Afghanistan, or deploy in civvies to somewhere in Syria or Iraq. Some other soldiers would say there was a third option; request discharge and return to 'normal' life, meaning the civilian world. But he shuddered at the thought of that, twitching the steering wheel inadvertently as he did so.

Risk terrified most people, but normal life terrified Toby. What would he do? More importantly, who would he be?

A nobody, nothing, an outcast. He wasn't cut out for normal life.

The same two ladies back at the doughnut building thought he was brave, but the idea was more ridiculous than he could even verbalise.

As a kid Toby's normal life had been an ever-worsening series of decisions: fist fights, joyriding in nicked cars, receiving stolen goods, selling stolen goods, more car theft, more fights. More boredom than he could handle, girls looking at him like he repulsed them, his Mum looking at him with disgust, him looking at his own reflection and feeling shame, even self-hatred. He hated his face, his hair, his clothes, his decisions, the way he only knew they were such bad decisions after the fact. He even hated that on the few occasions where he'd recognised a bad decision coming, he hadn't even cared enough to stop himself. He hated every part of his good for nothing teenage years, including his friends.

Those teenaged mates were the only ones who'd not looked down on him back then, but that's only because they were right down there with him. There's really no one to look down on when you're already at the bottom, so the only team spirit they'd had was to ensure that none of the others would ever dare try elevating or bettering themselves. Their friendships were cemented in needling the rest of society, and no, never again would he return to that.

He shook it off, because that wasn't completely true, one person had always seen something worthwhile in him. His sister had always had his back, even during his lowest periods.

But rather than getting hung up on obsessing in the rear-view, he needed to focus on the fact that he'd become a different person. Now he looked in the mirror every morning and saw a strong man, one with a sense of purpose. Someone who'd taken a shitty set of personality traits and, with an unbelievable amount of luck, had fallen into a role where those traits actually served some useful purpose.

The self-loathing had turned into self-esteem, and finally, other people had grown to respect him too.

So, he wasn't brave, he was simply using the only strengths he'd ever had, in the only positive way they could be used. He was cheating a shitty destiny.

A return to normal life would be the ultimate loss. How long before that shitty destiny caught up with him again? It was unthinkable. The op was a far better option.

'Turn left in one hundred metres.'

What? He snapped himself out of his own thoughts.

Crap! Here? He swung the wheel hard, squealing the tyres and counter-steering the slide, but his shady past had made him quite the skilled driver, so he maintained control without too much drama.

What a great set of options. He thought to himself as he re-used those old joyriding skills.

Brave though? If only they knew. He shook his head in disgust yet again just as a white van pulled out, right in front of him, leaving him barely enough room to stop without slamming into the back of it.

"You fucking idiot! There's not even anyone behind me." He snarled, more as a vent for his own anger than an attack on the other driver. Then headlights blinded him from the rear too.

The confusion came first. *Why would you…? The roads are bloody deserted.*

Then his brain chose a different route. *Oh no, what if…?*

But a man had already pulled on the handle of his driver's door, which was locked from the inside. And as Toby finally started thinking straight, his window shattered, the lock plunger was pulled up by a gloved hand, and his door was swung open. All in an instant.

Toby looked ahead, pinned in by the white van. Behind, pinned in by the other vehicle. Both were big vehicles which towered over his little hatchback, so ramming them to make an exit simply wasn't an option. Shutting the people out of his car was no longer an option either.

In desperation, Toby turned the ignition off, took his keys out of the barrel and inserted the long ignition key blade between two fingers, with the metal blade projecting outward. He balled the other keys up into his palm and swung a hard punch, landing the key blade straight into the man's face. The man squealed in pain and stepped back, with his hands now holding his face. Toby pressed the seatbelt release and leapt from his seat, but he was tackled to the floor after just three steps. Then Toby felt a punch to his own head, his arms were yanked up behind his back, his mouth was smothered, and his world turned to black.

29.

LADY DUGGAN-SMYTHE FELT like her heart had dropped from her chest as the double doors finally swung back open. Her emotions had already made her feel light-headed but she'd been raised to always maintain her composure, so fought the various unwelcome feelings.

"Don't worry." The white coated surgeon instantly reassured her, "The surgery went very well, and he's made it through the worst of it."

"Oh my…" *He's alive.* Her lungs purged all their air in one go, her knees buckled slightly and then Woodcock appeared from nowhere, to ensure she kept her balance. She had questions, but needed a moment to compose herself, before constructively connecting any words together.

The surgeon watched to make sure she wasn't at the same risk as her husband had been, figuring his status report could wait until she seemed more settled.

"How are you feeling, my Lady? Would you like me to find you a seat for a moment?" enquired Woodcock.

"Oh, I'm quite fine Woodcock, please don't fuss." With the verbal put-down her perfect posture was restored, and she continued, "Thank you." Then, "Doctor?" implying he should supply her with his surname.

"Khan." Dr. Khan had a genuine smile.

"Please Doctor Khan, I don't think you can ever know how

sincere my thanks are for what you've done." She reciprocated the smile with equal sincerity.

"Well, there's quite a large team of us in there, so…"

"Then my heartfelt thanks are for all involved," she interrupted. "Now, please Doctor Khan, if you'd be kind enough to explain to me what on earth just happened?" She'd already participated in as much polite chit-chat as she could currently manage.

He adjusted his expression, "Your husband had a myocardial infarction, a heart attack. But he's out of the woods. Currently, he is sedated, and what this will mean moving forwards is going to be a much more in-depth discussion. But I can fore-warn you there will need to be recovery time, diet changes and absolutely no unnecessary stress."

Woodcock looked especially concerned at the last demand.

"As I say, for now the signs are promising, and I think we caught something quite early, that with time, might have become much worse. A couple of years from now, a similar trigger might have had a very different result. But before I head back in, I'm curious about something; did he wake up from his sleep feeling chest pain? Or was he awoken by it?"

"I don't actually know." Lady Duggan-Smythe looked over at Woodcock, "Woodcock?"

Woodcock's eyes widened, "I only know that there was a call from a gentleman in government." He looked acutely embarrassed at not having a better answer.

"Well? What else do you know? There must be more than that." The Lady didn't look, or sound, remotely amused.

Shrugging was always inappropriate for a butler, but it's exactly what he wanted to do. He squirmed slightly before replying, "Only that the gentleman caller's name was Mister Chalmers, and the news appeared to be unwelcome, and then the Lord, well, he…"

30.

DANNY WAS AWOKEN by shouting; he opened his eyes to the familiar faces of beardy short and beardy long, although their roles had been reversed, as this time beardy short was pointing an old AK rifle at him.

Beardy long yelled something unintelligible and then beardy short finally spoke, "Get up, now! Stand up."

Danny pulled himself to his feet, starting with his left leg, and using the wall as an aid -exactly as he'd done before. As soon as he was on his feet, longy started pulling at his arm, dragging him from the cell.

Danny took a deep breath and put his energies into calming himself, he finally wore no hood so could see his route and simply allowed longy to pull him wherever he needed to go. He had no desire to receive any further injuries.

They arrived in a sunlit area, partially obscured from camp view by blankets strung up on laundry lines.

Their small group had passed other people on their way, most were captors, but some prisoners seemed to roam freely too, which confused Danny. As Danny stood outside taking in his new surroundings, another man approached. He had a different manner about him, his beard was trimmed with precision, he wore cleaner clothes than anyone else, and walked with confidence; authority even.

Danny squinted in thought, realising that when he'd been

filmed after arrival, this had been the man directing the whole event.

The presumed leader came to a stop, looked Danny up and down, then spoke to beardy long who tried to remove Danny's shirt. Instinctively Danny resisted, but quickly reconsidered the idea and allowed the shirt to be hauled up over his head. Inevitably beardy long then reached down to Danny's cargo trousers, but that was a step too far and Danny cautiously pushed him away.

Without hesitation, longy punched Danny, the blow landing on his jawline. As Danny closed his eyes and soaked up this newest batch of pain, somebody else started yelling.

Danny opened his eyes to realise the yelling was not directed at him, but at longy, and that it was coming from the assumed camp boss. Having made his point, the man looked back at Danny, "This water is for bathing. Not drinking." He pointed to several differently coloured plastic buckets, all lined up against the wall of the building behind the blanket screen.

Danny nodded, still too traumatised to risk words.

"And your clothes are too dirty. There will be new, clean clothes for you to wear."

Danny exhaled slowly. It was clearly time for his orange overalls.

His clothes, the clothes he'd previously bought according to his own tastes and needs, were about to be taken from him. They were to be replaced by something over which he had no control, and as a writer he could only shudder at the symbolism of this pivotal moment. It would be a turning point in his news story, a story he now seemed very unlikely to ever write.

Danny nodded at the leader and fought the sense of despair welling inside.

And as he removed his trousers to wash down his battered and bruised body, he thought to himself, *From temporary to permanent, and from hope to hopeless.*

31.

TOBY WOKE SLOWLY.

He stayed perfectly still as he worked to erase the grogginess before daring to appear awake. He could remember the basics of what had happened and so already had some sense of where he must be. He gently twisted his wrists to find they were bound, as expected. Then did the same with his ankles, to find the same result.

He had no idea if he was alone or being observed by one (or more) of his captors, and at this point had no intention of alerting anybody to the fact that he was conscious. Not until he'd beaten the lingering effects of whatever he'd been drugged with.

For now, the smart option was to replay what had happened, inside his head.

So, what had happened?

He'd been boxed in, very skillfully he had to admit, by two vehicles who'd been waiting along his route. The route was the most obvious one from Cheltenham to Hereford, where he'd been ordered to attend a detainee training course. He rolled his eyes; *So, the training's already started.*

This was always destined to be a bad course, but he'd already skipped too far ahead.

Rewind.

He'd been boxed in, and then what? Whatever they'd used on him certainly wasn't helping his memory. Boxed in, then…? They'd smashed his car window. *What the hell? Who's gonna pay for that? Not cool at all.*

Then the worst part came back, he'd punched somebody in the face using his ignition key as an improvised weapon. *Oh no.* Toby scrunched his face up in shame. He really shouldn't have done that, that was a totally disproportionate response and some poor bugger would forever carry a nasty facial scar from it.

He couldn't help himself and sat straight up, suddenly driven to undo some of the damage, "Lads, I'm really sorry, I didn't mean to properly hurt anyone, I honestly didn't know we'd started."

Toby was hooded and turned his head from side to side, trying to pick up on any small noises, or even feet that might be visible within his limited field of vision at the base of the hood. But nothing.

Then a door opened, and he could hear somebody enter, which helped slightly, as now he at least knew he was in a closed room. "Honestly, I'm sorry mate. I didn't know." Toby felt utterly ashamed.

"You didn't know?" spoke a voice, distorted by some kind of voice modulator. "You didn't know she was protected by diplomatic immunity? Or didn't know there'd be a price to pay, for you overstepping your position?"

The voice had an American accent.

Toby felt a wave of heat shoot through his skin, then sweat started forming on its surface. Disorientation came first, then awareness of the need to override it with clear thought. *It couldn't be more consequences for the last op, could it?* Toby swallowed hard, as the sweat continued to form in a moist layer on his face and in his armpits. Suddenly a training course seemed like a much better option.

"How stupid are you? You thought a nobody like you could force our hand in such a delicate political situation?"

Completely disorientated, that's what he was. The drugs obviously weren't helping, but Toby suddenly didn't know his arse from his elbow, and couldn't seem to fight it. He'd sat up far too quickly and now he was in the thick of it, and still not free of the sedatives lingering in his system.

But he had to think.

The woman from the last op was married to a CIA guy. *But that bloke's career was killed by the scandal.* Toby just needed a little more time, more clarity, then he'd be able to cope just fine.

"You thought you'd run from consequences, just like Mrs. Lutz did. And now you're facing them, just like Mrs. Lutz did. How could it end any other way?"

No, this can't be happening. He aggressively shook his head, trying to dislodge the hood and at least look his captor in the eye, but it wouldn't move. *Think.* Mister Jeff Lutz, the husband, was probably serving out some crappy posting in an even crappier location, but maybe that was too narrow a focus?

What if Toby's actions had been as embarrassing for the organisation as they had been for the man? *No! This is fucked up.* Toby scrunched up his face, now glad of the privacy offered by the hood.

It really is the CIA. And they found out it was me who... How could they though? He'd covered his tracks so very well in the States.

Then it hit him; it didn't matter how careful he'd been. Because he couldn't cover up his family connection with the victim. It was that simple fact, that's what had led them to him.

So, it was the CIA; they'd got him, and they'd done it so very well. The implications were becoming horribly obvious to Toby, so screw the feelings of guilt at scarring someone, and lose the niceynicey training related behaviour, he had to play this shit for real.

Clam up, for now that was his only option.

"Cat cut your tongue?" asked the voice.

32.

THE INTELLIGENCE TEAM had broken up to allow everybody to get some rest. Debbie had grabbed a couple of hours sleep after setting an alarm to make sure her two hours didn't turn into ten. But the respite was short lived; there was far too much to do.

"What are we not seeing?" She was exhausted, but acutely aware that whatever suffering she was experiencing right now would pale in comparison to what their undercover operative would soon be subjected to. Basically, she was forcing herself to work, to increase Toby's chances of survival when it all became his turn.

Martin was struggling too; tiredness just didn't give you the mental acuity you needed. He had a list in front of him and started working his way down it, again. But when he reached the line which showed Toby as having infiltrated successfully, he had a horrible thought.

Debbie spotted the change in him, "What is it?"

Martin was slow to respond, unsure of his conclusions in his current frazzled state. "So, he's done it, he's in, and they think they've just grabbed another hapless western journo."

"Yeah?" Debbie didn't yet see what he did.

"So, what do they do next?" he asked her.

She shrugged, "Uh, they put him in a cell, or room, or animal stall? Maybe they move him around a couple of times? But he's a captive, so he's undercover, as planned."

Martin was already shaking his head, "No. We missed something."

She was too tired for a game of now-it's-your-turn, so just waited.

"They bloody film him and put it online, that's what they do."

She threw her hands up into her hair, "Oh no, for God's sake…"

Debbie looked down at her desk, utterly disappointed in herself. She stared down at her own list wondering what else she'd missed, and her eyes started feeling heavy again. She snapped herself out of it, sat back up and admitted, "I can't even think straight, I need…"

Time? Sleep? Neither were valid options.

33.

"YOU KNOW WHAT blows me away?" asked the American voice, "You're cruising around in uniform when you're a damn spook. You don't deserve to wear that uniform; you don't have the right. That's messed up. Our guys don't play those games."

Toby's mouth snarled as he went to fight back, but he caught himself. He let the air escape slowly and reclosed his mouth. *You're not getting a rise out of me.*

"In World War 2, if a soldier was working behind enemy lines out of uniform, then he wasn't protected by the Geneva convention, so they shot him as a spy. You're no better, you should be shot too. You're a fake, a piece of garbage."

That's not the history Toby had been taught. Maybe it was just another attempt to engage him in this attempt at conversation?

"So, Madyson Lutz, what was she to you? A schoolboy crush?" Toby's arm was suddenly prodded, he didn't flinch, as he'd been expecting much worse the whole time.

"Well, she was protected by the US Government. That's why she got flown home and that's why we shielded her from being extradited by you guys. We had her back. But whatdya think? You think your government will have your back now? After what you did?"

Doubt that. I was about to get my shot at redemption, but that's all gone thanks to you. I'll probably get added to some list of missing Britons, one of those long-term unknowns. Ironic really. But whatever happens to me, I'll take it on the chin. It's not like I ever thought I was gonna retire comfortably to slippers and tall bloody tales. This was always gonna be my world, until my luck ran out. I chose it, I love it, and I'm okay with that. So, do your worst, mate.

"Are you asleep in there?" Toby's hood was suddenly yanked rearward, "Or just dumb?"

Asleep. It's your droning voice, it's sending me to sleep. You'd send anyone to sleep, your missus must get sick of your bloody voice. Or your husband, it makes no odds to me. I pity them, either way.

"If you were a real soldier, then you'd have to go through the whole name, rank, and number thing. So, are you real? Or just a fake, coz I think you're a fake. You don't even have a number, do ya?"

Nine, nine, nine. That's how you call the old bill in England. Sixty-nine, that's the fun one -if you get lucky enough. Five-seven-nine, -oh-five-seven-nine; that one's for City Pizza, better known as Shitty Pizza, coz they're so fucking terrible. Toby laughed out loud at his inner monologue.

Then he got sucker punched in the gut. Without hesitation, Toby snapped his head forward in an attempt at a head butt, barely scuffing the perpetrator's arm.

"Oh, do you have it all wrong? You don't get to fight back, you only get to sit there, and take it."

Yeah, I have to take all your endless talking. Toby couldn't fight back physically, but that didn't mean he couldn't throw some frustration back at the interrogator, so he broke all the rules and went down his own, unconventional route. "Mmm," he started humming.

"What?" the voice sounded totally baffled.

"Mmm," Toby continued.

"What the hell do you think you're doing?" The voice was already angry, meaning Toby was on the right track.

Toby started tapping his foot, getting a rhythm going to sing along to, "Some die of drinking water, and some of drinking beer."

Another blow, this time to his upper back, but screw them, he was just getting going, "Some die of constipation, and some of diarrhea." His shoulders were going now too, then he choked as his air was taken from him. The hood was suddenly soaking wet, and he instantly felt suffocation. Toby couldn't make a sound, nor take a breath; he squirmed in pain, forced his eyes shut hoping to ride it out, while clenching his hands into fists so hard it made them hurt.

Then everything changed. The hood was yanked back, cold light blinded him, and air suddenly became available. He snatched at it and narrowed his eyes as they struggled to adjust to the harsh fluorescent light.

"You cannot waterboard him, we do have some bloody rules we've got to follow."

That's not an American accent. Toby's eyes still couldn't handle the harsh light.

"But he knew already. The wanker was just messing with me."

Neither is that one. Toby was disorientated, all over again.

"Training aborted." Toby heard a sigh, "Did you even stop to think about the consequences of pouring water on his head, Corporal?"

"I'm sorry, Sarge. You remember what he did to my face though, right?"

Toby shook his head, relieved beyond words, "You bastards, you totally had me going!"

"Yeah, you piece of garbage." The Lance Corporal was now taking another turn with the voice changer, "Yee-haw, ride 'em cowboy. Oh wait, I've got a good one." The accent remained, but the cadence changed, "I did not have relations with that woman." The speaker was laughing at his own jokes, "I love this thing. Can it do a Russian one too?"

"Lance Corporal!" shouted the Sergeant, aiming to silence him.

Toby's eyes finally managed to focus on the two men.

"Sergeant Miller," the Sergeant nodded kindly at Toby, "Let's get you un-tied, shall we?"

"Thank you," Toby nodded to the Sergeant, then looked up at the Lance Corporal, seeing a much younger man with a medical dressing taped to his cheek, "Honestly mate, I am sorry. If I'd known…"

"Miller!" the Sergeant interrupted him sternly, "We've done these snatch exercises many times, and so far, nobody's managed to do any real damage back. Now, I know that you've run your own courses too, so you already know this is a two-way learning opportunity, which means your response speed is gonna have to be looked at."

The Sergeant looked over at his Lance Corporal, "Bottom line is, the lance-jack here should have been more prepared for your speed, which means that he's got a hell of a lot to learn."

Lance Corporal Pole scrunched his face in disappointment. After having his cheek pierced with a car key, he was now looking at a dressing down in the exercise debrief? What a great way to start his probation period with the Regiment. It was clearly time to start taking things more seriously.

Pole took the couple of steps toward Toby and offered his hand to help Toby back to his feet. Toby needed no help, but it was a gesture, an unspoken agreement to set aside their bad start. Toby grasped his hand around the lance-jack's wrist, and Pole gave him a hearty pull up from his chair.

"Feel free to take a swing at me, Lance Corporal. I'm sure the Sergeant here can look the other way for a moment," Toby nodded his permission.

The Sergeant chuckled and turned his back as suggested, but Pole just shook his head and grinned, "You're all right, Sarge. I wouldn't want to mess up your face before you go undercover."

The sergeant turned back, chuckling, "All right boys, if we're all done flirting, let's go and find the boss. I understand that you already know each other, Miller. From way back."

34.

"OH, MY DARLING, I am so very relieved to see you." Lord Rupert squeezed his wife's hand, his teary eyes plain to see.

Lady Duggan-Smythe had never seen such an open display of emotion from her husband, although she'd hoped for it, for decades. "You're glad? I thought I'd lost you. Oh Rupert, the whole thing was terrifying, truly terrifying." She squeezed his hand back, then stopped and released it in an instant, "Oh! I'm sorry my dear."

He chuckled, very gently, "It was my heart Fi, not my hand."

"I know, but…" she didn't want to hurt him, which she couldn't really say. To imply he was now fragile wouldn't be a healthy way to start this life adjustment, the one she'd been told was so very necessary for his longevity. "I'm sorry, my darling" she repeated.

"As am I." his smile held firm.

He was done taking things for granted; he was a lucky man and it had taken an unwelcome taste of finality to make him truly appreciate just how lucky he was. He'd lived a wonderful life up until now, with very few regrets, but he'd always been chasing something new, and right now, his attitude was a total reversal. All he could think about was appreciating what he'd already got.

"Oh Roo-roo, what happened? I still don't understand, we were sleeping and the next thing I know, we're in here. The whole thing was a hellish whirlwind."

Lord Rupert winced at the memory.

Lady Duggan-Smythe panicked as she saw him flinch, and

expecting a re-run of the terror unleashed upon them in the early morning hours, jumped to her feet and screamed for a doctor.

Lord Rupert exhaled in a slow, controlled manner, "Do please sit down, Fiona. I'm fine."

Lady Fiona wasn't buying it and remained on her feet, with her attention alternately switching between her husband and the door.

"Fi, will you please sit down. We need to talk."

This sounded very ominous, Lady Fiona dropped into the bedside chair.

"Darling, there was a phone call, in the middle of the night." The Lord started gingerly.

"Woodcock mentioned a government call, but the man knew nothing more, which was extremely frustrating." Lady Fi winced, realising her typical overly emotional delivery of news would need to be altered to help her husband maintain a steady emotional state of his own.

The Lord smiled a patient smile, "Woodcock doesn't know any more than that. Nor does he need to."

"What's wrong?!" The nurse's shoes squeaked as she came to an abrupt stop just inside their doorway, her confusion apparent as the patient looked okay to her.

"I'm sorry nurse, it was a misunderstanding. I am fine, I assure you." The Lord appreciated her fast arrival, whereas before this blessed morning, he'd have probably been irritated at the intrusion and dismissed her abruptly. Possibly even rudely.

She studied him, suspiciously, "Well, as long as you're alright. But press that big button by the side of your bed if you feel off in any way. Okay?"

"You have my word, nurse." and Rupert smiled a kind, sincere smile. Lady Fiona liked this new husband of hers.

"So, Fi, our Charles is in a spot of bother." No, that was the wrong lead-in. "Well, Charlie's always in a spot of bother, but this one probably isn't of his own doing."

Fiona's heart started racing. Whatever this news was, it had traumatised her husband sufficiently to trigger…

She winced, "Please Rupert, just tell me."

He raised his hand as a request for patience, "My dear, this is exactly the sort of stress I've been warned to avoid."

Lady Fiona raised her hand to her temple, and her tears started welling. She knew she had to help Rupert stay calm, or the consequences were unthinkable.

Lord Rupert picked up the plastic cup from his bedside table, wetted his mouth, swallowed, then continued, "He was working on assignment, in the Middle East, and looks to have been taken as some kind of hostage."

Lord Rupert now made a point of looking down at the bedding to avoid the stress of seeing his wife's reaction to such distressing news.

He was intent on taking the Doctor's advice; he wasn't ready to be done with this life yet. He finally wanted to enjoy it for what it already was, rather than what it might be.

Making a point of continually looking down, and away from his wife's inevitable suffering, he continued, "I'm not ready to go yet, Fi. I am not leaving this earth, not with this divide in our family. This upset between Charles and myself -I've been a fool. My disappointment in him has become a habit, pure and simple. And that is over. No matter what it takes, no matter what it costs, and no matter the obstacles, I am bringing our boy home."

35.

"PRIVATE MILLER!" BELLOWED a Warrant Officer enthusiastically, as Toby entered the room.

"Not a Private anymore." Toby tapped at his Sergeant's rank markings, grinning in response as he took his seat next to the middle-aged WO.

"Funny that, considering I thought you weren't even in the Army anymore, Sergeant Miller?"

Toby's grin was childlike, "Good point, Sir…"

"Well, I have been getting updates on your career progression, Miller. Or is it Staffy? I understand that's what you go by now, lad."

Toby couldn't stop grinning.

"Did you overdo it on the sedatives, Sergeant Ross? Staffy Miller here doesn't seem to be able to wipe that ridiculous smile off his face."

"No Sir, I'd say we had the opposite problem. The sedatives didn't stop Sar'nt Miller from putting up an unexpectedly good fight, even tied to a chair he had another go at Pole's face." Ross nodded toward Pole.

The WO looked over to see the young soldier holding a fresh dressing to his damaged cheek.

"Aye, well, it looks like you underestimated your target, Corporal Pole, which is not good enough. Not here." The WO shook his head, exaggerating his disappointment to hammer home the point.

"So, have I got this right? Miller here, gets waterboarded after you smash his car window, while you get a sexy new scar on your face? A scar that I'm sure you'll make good use of the next time you go out on the pull?"

Neither Pole nor Toby knew quite what to do with that comment.

"Well that hardly seems fair, does it? I think that Sergeant Miller deserves your thanks." The WO's expression made it clear that he was not joking.

"No Sir, it's not fair, Sir." Pole worked hard to hide his discomfort, "Thank you, Sergeant Miller," the Corporal nodded dutifully.

Getting caught in the middle of a sarcastic dressing-down wasn't Toby's idea of fun. And stuck between a superior who demanded respect, and a subordinate who he'd just scarred for life, it took him a moment to conjure up the appropriate response. "Apology accepted, Corporal Pole, you can thank me properly another time, over some beers. And I'll be buying."

The Lance Corporal beamed back a cheeky smile and nodded his agreement.

Very nicely done Miller, you're still a sharp little bugger, aren't you? The WO allowed a sly grin to flicker across his face, before resuming, "This was just an exercise, but in the field that resistance could have been the difference between operational success and failure; or life and death. For you I mean, Corporal."

"Yes, Sir. I won't make that mistake again, Sir," snapped back a much more solder-like Lance Corporal Pole.

The WO sat in silence for a moment before continuing, "Even back in basic training, I could see that underestimating young Miller here would be a foolish mistake. So…"

He sat up straight for the assembled men, "I suppose it's logical to go straight from that remark into the snatch debrief. Firstly, Miller, you appear to have put up an unexpectedly determined fight."

"Thank you, Sir," Toby replied proudly.

"It wasn't a damn compliment Miller. I know all about your next op, where you're going, what you're doing there, and why you're doing it. Charlie Duggan-Smythe may be little more than an overgrown child, but daddy's still got some serious clout in Her Majesty's Forces. So, Miller, for the sake of this op, can you remind me; what is your stated occupation?"

Toby squirmed as he finally grasped the significance, "A journalist, Sir. A news photographer."

"Exactly. And how many artsy-fartsy photographers can be expected to fight back like that, against a squad of hardened Regiment boys?"

"Bollocks." Toby sighed in disappointment at himself, then panicked at his inappropriate language, "Oh, excuse me, Sir. It just came out."

"Och, I'm no bloody Rupert, Miller, as you well know. Therefore, my ears are not fragile, Rupert ears, they're dirty old NCO ears. Bollocks indeed! That would have been the end of you right there."

Toby nodded, as the WO rolled his eyes in disappointment, "Zarqawi 'abdi lift a journo who immediately sets to beating the shite out of half their men? Game over, I'd say. Which confirms our decision to invite you down here for some quick refresher training. Don't you agree, Sergeant Miller?"

Toby's shoulders slumped, "Yes, Sir. I do, Sir." And he did.

36.

THE FEELINGS OF self-doubt were worsening. After the epically disastrous phone call to Lord Duggan-Smythe, Chalmers had bailed on the second phase of the operational meeting between the various GCHQ departmental heads. That in itself was a huge problem, but a lower ranking problem than feeling wholly responsible for someone's heart attack.

That the heart attack was had by a Lord of the Realm, the head of one of Britain's most prestigious and influential families, amplified the associated stress. Further still, that this particular Lord was a chair on the funding committee for all of the relevant intelligence departments (Chalmers' department included) made the situation unthinkable.

What had he been thinking -calling the Lord personally? And with that news?

That he'd been awake for twenty-two hours straight, with a new day about to start, certainly hadn't helped his decision-making abilities. But still? You couldn't take those pieces and assemble them more clumsily. *What a cretinous mistake.*

Chalmers stood just inside the main entrance to the hospital, trying to figure out how he could rectify the damage he'd caused. But who was he kidding? There was no undoing what he'd done.

No, no, no. He was so angry with himself, disgusted even. He'd allowed his previous interactions with Lord Duggan-Smythe to alter his typically calculated approach to these situations.

But why? Those interactions were minimal, inconsequential. So much so, he suspected the Lord wouldn't even remember them. But of course, Chalmers remembered them; the man was a Lord, and that right there was his mistake.

You idiot, he chastised himself again. He'd believed this was his route up to the heady heights inhabited by Lords, Dukes, Barons, and the others who really ran the country. But instead of graciously accepting Lord Rupert's hand in help up that last step, he'd pulled Lord Rupert off the edge -nearly to his doom. On top of that, he'd managed to pull this beautifully choreographed stunt with everyone else watching.

He was ruined. There was no way around it, he'd royally screwed up -and that was to be his only contribution to the world of the blue-blooded.

Chalmers shook his head in disgust at his own catastrophic decision making. He couldn't even busy himself in his work and wait for it all to blow over, because an apology wasn't a consideration to be mulled over, it was mandatory.

It was time to finally get on with it, so he entered the hospital to ask where he could find Lord Rupert Duggan-Smythe, a distant relative of Her Majesty the Queen, one who'd barely survived a stress-induced, or should that be Chalmers-induced, heart attack.

37.

WARRANT OFFICER MCCORD opened the door to a large training/briefing room, then held the door open for Toby to follow him in, as Toby did for Lance Corporal Pole, and then Sergeant Ross behind him.

The room was filled to about half capacity with uniformed men; Toby's quick estimation was approximately twenty soldiers.

"Gentleman." The WO nodded as he took up his position at the front of the room.

"Sir," various voices responded.

Pole continued into the room to take a seat amongst the other men. Toby followed Pole toward the main seating area until he heard the WO's voice, "No Miller, you're needed here up front."

"Sir." Toby responded, turning to take his place alongside the WO, then took stock of the various faces assembled before them.

"Gents, this is Sergeant Toby Miller."

"Sarge," the same varied voices greeted Toby, who nodded back.

"Miller and I, we go way back. I had the pleasure of raising my voice at him, repeatedly, during his formative days as a recruit at Pirbright. But he turned out all right in the end, as you can see." The WO kept his pauses short, as there was a lot to cover, and time was not on their side.

"After exemplary service in his regiment, he was singled out for a lateral move. But not into elite forces like you gents. Instead, he was chosen to perform non-uniformed duties, for one of our intelligence services."

Heads were nodded in appreciation, and some eyebrows were raised. "He's in uniform today, as he's just coming to the end of a short period assisting his old regiment."

Toby sincerely appreciated the WO's abridged version of the otherwise complex story.

"All right then, Miller here is about to embark on an operation in our favourite desert, for which we will be his rapid response unit. It is a high-risk op, hence the request for our supporting role, rather than trusting it to whoever's already in-country."

Toby's smile grew as he listened to the WO. That's why he was really here? He was going to have the Regiment as his rapid response unit? He certainly hadn't expected it, but he couldn't have asked for more. Just knowing they'd have his back raised his confidence immeasurably.

"Two Britons have been taken by Zarqawi 'abdi, a splinter group which was formed with the intention, in their own words, of continuing the glorious work of ISIS founder Al Zarqawi. Who is, sadly, no longer with us."

The room filled with laughter.

"One of these Britons is a high-value individual, and the primary focus of this recovery operation. But are we going to leave the other, to rot away in some nasty little hot box?"

"Yeah, right!" said one voice, as chuckles echoed around the room.

"In that hole?" added another.

"Corp Pole can give him a piggy-back out of there!" contributed a third, to more laddish laughter.

"Yes, thank you." The WO held the speaker's stare long enough to make his point, then pushed on, "Of course we're not, because that is not how we do things."

"Sergeant Miller here has been given his own set of operational objectives. And to fulfill them, it has been decided that he should operate in an undercover role, as that offers the highest probability of operational success."

"Undercover?" asked a man in the front row, unable to hide his surprise, "Surely any undercover role would take time? You've got to get situated, win the trust of…" the man looked down at his own notes, "The trust of Zarqawi 'abdi, and surely your ethnicity will make that a hard, if not impossible, sell?"

The man's comments were directed toward Toby, but he was skillfully avoiding any pauses that could allow Toby to participate. "And considering that we're already assembled here as rapid response, time is clearly pressing. So, excuse my confusion." He folded his arms, seemingly done for the moment.

"I think it's over to you, Sergeant Miller," the Warrant Officer nodded at Toby, who moved centre-front to respond.

"This is not undercover, in the traditional sense." Toby looked the man up and down, adding "Sir." on seeing his two embroidered rank pips.

"I'll be traveling as a journalist, with the aim of being kidnapped at the earliest possible opportunity."

There were more than a few sharp intakes of breath within the room.

"Well, that is certainly audacious, Sergeant," nodded the Lieutenant.

"It's downright naughty!" added the Corporal who'd suggested the piggy-back ride.

"As you mentioned Sir, time is pressing. Our current information is that the secondary objective is being held here." Toby turned to face the map already displayed on the room's wall and indicated the location previously supplied to him by Lydia, "and this method is the fastest way to get me inserted."

"Once embedded, I aim to find out as quickly as possible from the secondary, if the primary is also being held at this location."

"And if he's not?" asked the officer.

The answer to that question hadn't yet been discussed, but Toby already had the seeds of a plan. "Well, Zarqawi 'abdi is a relatively new terrorist organisation, with only numbers in the low hundreds. And hostage camps are always relative to the size of the group they serve." He could tell he'd already earned the room's undivided attention.

"In the heyday of ISIS, there were detainee camps everywhere, as we all know. And their prisoners were moved repeatedly, even exchanged within groups who had differing political aspirations. You could say that hostages were a form of currency, and there was active trade all around the country."

The seated officer nodded his understanding.

"However, considering the size of this bunch, we're looking at one hostage camp, minimum, and three camps, max. They really don't have the infrastructure to manage anything more."

"I understand." The officer nodded once more but was still waiting to hear an answer to his question.

"So, if the primary is being held within this location," Toby gestured at the map without looking, "then your services will be required to help us all get out. Whereas if he's not in situ, then it will be up to me to determine the location of the other camp, or camps, from those present within this first camp."

The lieutenant sat in thought for a moment before cautiously responding with, "And dare I ask how you'll do that?"

"I have a way, which won't involve torture or bodily harm, if that's your concern. It won't get anyone in trouble." Toby's rules of engagement differed from the other men in the room, but he was being truthful.

The officer remained silent, finally deciding it was probably better to not linger on that subject. The next matter which required clarification was, "And how will you ensure you're kidnapped? I know it's hardly up there on anyone's wish-list, but plenty of journalists can go for years without managing it."

"I know, Sir. I've got that covered too." Toby's confidence was reassuring, but the officer still studied him, in deep thought.

As the lieutenant continued to consider the variables, the WO stepped in with a question of his own. "And what if you're all moved? Because we only have this location."

Before Toby could even answer, the WO added another question, "And how will you communicate your needs with us?"

"That's where the desk jockeys at GCHQ come in. I've already given them a wish list, and hopefully when I see them next, they'll have it all ready and waiting for me."

"Hopefully, indeed." The lieutenant made no attempt to disguise his uncertainty about Toby and the recklessness of the entire plan.

38.

CHALMERS STOOD UNSEEN outside Lord Rupert's room, fully aware he was postponing the inevitable.

His procrastination had initially started as a means of perfecting a plan of action inside his head, but it eventually turned into procrastination, for procrastination's sake.

Recognising that, Chalmers straightened his posture and yesterday's tie, then turned and took the final couple of paces to stand within the room's doorway, knocking on the doorframe for permission to enter.

Chalmers' view was poor, the curtain affixed to his side of the bed was drawn and the only thing he could see was half of somebody seated in a chair, on the opposite side of the room.

That somebody leaned into view to see where the noise had come from. "Can I help you?" asked Lady Duggan-Smythe, staring coldly at the person responsible for the unwelcome interruption.

Chalmers swallowed hard before replying, "My name is Chalmers, I'd..." he stopped talking, as he'd planned on saying 'I need to speak to Lord Rupert'. But that approach suddenly seemed rather heavy handed and presumptuous, and doubt was taking hold of him. He needed to ask, rather than state, and certainly not demand.

But before he could alter his approach, Lady Duggan-Smythe was raising her voice at him, "Go away Mister Chalmers, I won't have any more stress caused by you. Give your information to our man Woodcock and leave." She paused to take a deep breath, before trebling her volume, "Woodcock!"

Chalmers could suddenly feel his heart beating in his temples. He took a breath and tried to find an approach that would allow him to make his apology, while carrying out some kind of effective bridge repair.

"Fi." Chalmers could barely hear the male voice. "Bring him in," it added gently.

Lord Rupert had noticed some involuntary rise in stress on hearing the visitor's name. But he'd calmed himself, as was to be his new way. He'd also quickly seen opportunity in the man's visit, although it would be better to only reveal that at the appropriate time.

Rupert's years had given him wisdom, and experience had taught him which methods to use, in which situations. For this one he chose silence, accompanied by a regal stare. It never failed to create an ever-increasing sense of self-doubt in those on the receiving end, and the longer the stare, the higher the anxiety level.

Chalmers cautiously entered the Lord's hospital room, and realised there was only one seat, which was already occupied by a dignified looking lady; presumably, the Lady.

Standing was clearly his only option, so he stood at the end of the bed, feeling somewhat juvenile, and started his apology, "My Lord, my name is Hugo Chalmers." *'My Lord?' followed by 'My name?' In my first sentence?* At least he hadn't continued with 'my apologies'.

Chalmers raised his hand to his pulsating temple, then tried to set the distracting thoughts aside. "We spoke last night, as I'm sure you remember." He flinched at that too, but was it visible? Things were getting worse; the Lord was hardly likely to have forgotten the call that triggered his heart attack.

We are not amused. Thought the Lord, his face mirroring the historic phrase.

Chalmers knew he was required to remind Lord Rupert of the

point to the late-night call, at which point he started visibly perspiring, "It regarded your son, Charles."

The Lord was apparently still not amused.

Chalmers considered removing the silk pocket square from his jacket pocket to blot away the perspiration rapidly oozing from his forehead, but knew that would only shine a spotlight on his sudden bout of sweating. His armpits were warming as he waited, but he had no idea of how much information Lord Rupert had absorbed during the night's chaos, and so had no choice but to plough on, "Your son, Charles, was taken as a hostage yesterday."

Chalmers suddenly realised that the Lord's lack of movement made him look like an exhibit from Madam Tussaud's wax museum.

Or was it even worse? *Did he just die on me?*

Don't be ridiculous, the man is still sitting up unsupported. It really was time for him to get to the meat of the matter, "And I cannot apologise enough for the stress caused by that call, my Lord. So, if there is anything I can do?"

Still with the waxwork expression.

Chalmers was officially beaten, "I will leave my contact information with your man." Chalmers took a business card from his pocket.

Woodcock, who'd appeared from nowhere, yet again, thrust his hand in front of Chalmers. Then the hand disappeared, as did the man, almost as quickly.

Meanwhile, Lord Rupert who had continued to hold Chalmers' stare, knew the appropriate time had finally come. "I believe we've met before."

Chalmers felt the relief wash over him, like a cooling wave, "We have my Lord…"

But Lord Rupert instantly silenced him with a raised hand. "You can share some information with me, more specific information."

In his current state, Chalmers didn't grasp the significance quickly enough, "I'm sorry, I don't understand."

The Lord exhaled very slowly, holding Chalmers' gaze the whole time, then elaborated, "You asked if there was anything you could do, and I am telling you there is. You can share every single pertinent piece of information regarding my son's abduction. Is that clear enough for you?"

Chalmers felt a sinking sensation in the pit of his stomach, "Um, yes. Of course, my Lord."

39.

"SO, WE HOLD, locally, until you're able to trigger the GPS beacon. Which will confirm your exact location?" asked Lieutenant Linton.

"Correct, Sir," replied Toby.

"At which point we move in." the Lieutenant stated.

"No, Sir." Toby shook his head. "I'll only send the GPS beacon to confirm my location, and that I'm ready and waiting for a dawn breach. We all know that the last hour of darkness is the best time for that because they'll be at their most tired and therefore their least able to perform."

"Well, we can definitely agree on that point, Sergeant," which seemed to imply they couldn't agree on many other things.

"If I know that you'll be coming in during those last moments of the darkness, I'll do whatever I can to minimise any surprises coming at you from inside the building," Toby added.

Lieutenant Linton was nodding and looking a little more confident.

Toby continued, "If both captives are in the same location, then we get out of there asap. And if the primary isn't there,"

This is what the Lieutenant had been waiting for.

"Then we'll have no choice but to move the first batch of captives to safety. And once I've confirmed the next location, we'll have to revert to more typical military tactics, meaning you'll be lead, Sir. Obviously, I cannot insert as a captive twice."

Lieutenant Linton widened his eyes in reaction, "Oh dear," he nodded as he thought it through, "If we're hitting a second camp, that's going to be a whole different kettle of fish."

Toby already knew that. "Yes Sir, it will. Unfortunately."

40.

JUST HOURS AFTER his initial arrival in Hereford, Toby had already been flown by Gazelle helicopter back to his own barracks where he'd packed the few civilian clothes he had on hand. Most of his regular clothes were back at his own flat, where he'd only just left them. But landing a whirlybird in a civilian neighborhood simply wasn't an option, so he was destined to travel light.

He figured it didn't matter, after all, he'd be set up with his own set of orange overalls soon enough.

From there, the same helicopter had ferried him back to GCHQ, where he'd waved his goodbyes to three members of his new rapid response unit.

As he travelled back up to the same meeting room from the previous night, he realised how big an operation this was becoming. That the cost of helicopter transport had been viewed as acceptable, for just one person, on home soil, was both shocking and confirmation of Toby's gut feeling that this operation needed to be run at speed. It also seemed to be evidence of Lord Duggan-Smythe's status, and reach, within the British establishment.

Which made Toby switch thoughts to how much responsibility was being heaped on his shoulders.

As he mulled over these thoughts, his phone started vibrating in silent mode. He took it out of his pocket and saw 'Mary-Ann' on the display, with an accompanying picture he'd not added himself.

"That phone shouldn't be in here." His escort did not look

impressed and threw Toby what must have been his most powerful and intimidating stare.

"But it's my Mum. If I can't talk to her, then you've gotta tell her." He angled the phone's screen away from the security guard, who suddenly looked completely out of his depth. "Please mate, I ain't doing it, she'll kill me. I'm meant to call her every morning at the same time, and this morning I didn't check in. Oh my God, this is bad," Toby winced as if terrified at the prospect.

Then Toby took a moment before hitting 'Reject', followed by 'Power Off'.

The trouble maker in him wasn't yet ready to stop, "What have you made me do?" he said to his escort, who by now couldn't even look him in the eye.

Ping. The elevator announced their arrival on the appropriate floor. Toby left his bewildered escort and headed toward the goldfish bowl alone.

How did she manage to add her photo to my phone? She'd looked so happy, and so incredibly beautiful in the photo, which made it the most unwelcome distraction imaginable. "Bollocks!" he hissed to himself as he opened the doors to the glass meeting room.

"Toby." Debbie greeted him with some welcome sincerity.

"Miller." Chalmers' greeting was less sincere, less enthusiastic too.

Having a personal relationship that was capable of distracting him from his work was something completely new for Toby, which meant he had no practised method of setting it aside.

"Debbie." Toby nodded to her, trying to get himself back into the required frame of mind, then added a sterile, "Sir," to Chalmers.

Yup, that was more like it.

"I think you'll be happy with what we've managed to rustle up for you, Toby." Debbie smiled, so Toby returned the gesture, then studied the other occupants of the room. There were some familiar faces from the night before, some absentees, and one addition.

"Oh yes, and this is Antonella Ferrara," Debbie pointed her

introduction. "Antonella has kindly agreed to help you learn some rudimentary journalism skills."

"Piacere," said the heavily tattooed Italian lady who seemed to be looking at Toby with an expression of disappointment.

Toby had no idea what she'd said, or what the odd look was about, so just responded with a cautious, "Uh huh. You, too."

"Antonella used to work with Danny Ellington, so she can offer the additional benefit of some very useful personal and professional knowledge."

"Good, appreciate it." Toby nodded. Anything would help. Anything except the stink eye.

"You're back earlier than anticipated, which is beneficial, obviously." Debbie seemed like she was fishing for more information, but Toby wasn't sure if sharing more than she already knew was appropriate for the situation.

The people he'd just left were the most secretive regiment in the armed forces, they were notorious for it. And considering they'd previously stated that Toby's visit was for some kind of detainee refresher training, then that was the official line, and he would be required to stick to it.

It had quickly become apparent that while they'd started him off with a rapid (and relevant) refresher exercise, the main reason for his visit to Hereford had been to meet his highly skilled rapid response team, and to ensure they were all on the same page before their separate arrivals in-country.

"So, Antonella, what will you require from Toby?" asked Debbie.

In response, the same disgusted look reappeared on the Italian lady's face.

Now Toby glared, he didn't mean to, but some people triggered it against his wishes, "What? What's your problem?"

To growl at a woman was at odds with how he'd been raised, which was to always be respectful to women in particular. It was probably the only old-fashioned societal expectation the young

Toby had ever adhered to. But the world was equal now, and she'd started it.

"Ma che cazzo. Look at him. Does he look like a photographer?"

She had a point. Toby did not look like your average photographer. The room sat back in their chairs and absorbed the potential ramifications of Toby looking like, well, Toby.

Debbie had cleared the goldfish bowl so that Toby and Antonella Ferrara could cover the basics of Toby's impending cover.

"This," Antonella banged a large camera down onto the glass meeting table, almost hard enough to shatter it, "is a professional DSLR. If it were not professional, I could not treat it like that. It is strong enough you could hit somebody with it, in the head."

Is she for real? Toby knew he needed more time before writing her off completely, but his patience for patronising strangers was limited.

"Here, is the power switch. On, this way. Off, the opposite way."

This wasn't even funny; it was how long before he had to depart? And ideally, depart with some new knowledge inside his head.

There was enough time to mess with her back, but only a little, so he set straight to it, "Sorry, which way for on, again?" he asked, faking wide-eyed confusion.

Her nostrils flared, "Ma che cazzo. Come questo, like this." She repeated the action for the hopelessly slow learner.

Toby yanked the camera from her hands and responded in a rapid-fire manner, "On, off. Manual mode, aperture priority mode, shutter speed priority mode." His fingers flew around the camera, indicating the controls that matched the spoken words.

"Exposure compensation bracketing. Then we have flash on and off, presumably it can trigger multiple slave flash units." He didn't even pause to let his point settle, instead making it even harder, "I can drive a car, ride a motorcycle, drive an articulated lorry, fly a fixed wing aircraft, fly a rotary wing aircraft. I even know the basics of driving a bloody Challenger tank." The wooden picnic bench he'd run over was evidence to the contrary, but she didn't need to know about that embarrassing episode.

"So, don't waste my time unless you've got something useful to show me." Now the point could be left to settle.

Antonella looked down at the table, realizing her undeniable guilt at labelling him so quickly.

She knew an apology was due, but still couldn't quite shake her disbelief that he could be more than just some dumb soldier. Why had she made such a strong assumption? Her silence lengthened as she considered the answer -it was because he looked like a dumb soldier; obedient and fearless, but dull witted and damaged. It was more than just labelling though; it was inarguable logic -because who else would volunteer for this insanity?

"Look Kay, I don't have the time for this crap." Toby stood up from the table.

Her first reaction was guilt at driving him away, her second was confusion, "Ma, who is Kay?"

"Kay Catso, that's your name, right?" Toby knew nothing of her language, but enough of people to know she'd been insulting him; so, he'd replicated the sound of her words to use the underlying insult against her. But would she admit fault?

"Stronzo," she muttered under her breath.

"What's that then? Your middle name?" Toby shot straight back. Her response wasn't quick enough, so he ended with, "Enjoy your journey home," shook his head with a guttural growl and headed straight for the door.

"No, scusi, mi dispiace, I am sorry," her cocky, impatient manner was finally replaced with shame, "Please."

But Toby was irritated now, his plate was overflowing and his patience exhausted. "What? You done with the snarky attitude? Do you have anything useful for me? Are you gonna finally lose that chip from your shoulder?"

"What is this shoulder chip?"

Toby rolled his eyes, "It's what you've got." He waited, "So?" he boomed, probably too loudly.

Antonella, or Kay depending on your perspective, finally responded honestly, "It's just Danny, caro Danny, he is a sweet man, lui e gentile. He is a dear friend, and he has probably saved my life, when we 'ave work together before. So, I do this for him."

"And what exactly do you think I'm doing?" Toby was still torqued up.

"You? You will get him killed with this…" she ended with the now familiar look of disgust.

"No." Toby strode back to the table and waved the big camera angrily at her, "This is why he got taken, so if he gets killed, this will be the cause of it, not me. I'm his only bloody hope."

41.

CHALMERS HAD TYPED Lord Rupert's personal mobile phone number into his own. The idea of pressing the green button to call such a prestigious member of the aristocracy should have been exhilarating, but instead he could only feel conflicted. He sighed and pressed it nonetheless.

Just two rings in, a voice answered, "Mr. Chalmers?" It was a lady's voice, again presumably the Lady's voice.

"Yes. Am I speaking to Lady Duggan-Smythe?" He didn't dare address the speaker incorrectly, so felt duty-bound to ask for clarification.

"You are, Mister Chalmers. I'm vetting all of Rupert's calls for him, although I do know that he's been waiting, quite impatiently I must add, for you to finally respond. Before I pass you over, must I remind you of my expectations?"

"No, Lady Fiona. I understand and I'll make sure to cause Lord Rupert no additional stress." Chalmers felt like a reprimanded child. These interactions were clearly doomed to forever refer back to that first night.

"Thank you, Mister Chalmers, I'm handing you over now." The line went quiet, crackled slightly, and then a new voice replaced Lady Fiona's. "Mister Chalmers, what do you have for me?"

So, he wasn't even going to fake some kind of businesslike mutual respect?

For a moment, Chalmers' instincts told him to hang up and

end the call. His conscience would be clear, he could put it all behind him, and get on with life. He rested his head into his left hand and tightly closed his eyes, trying to consider every possible outcome.

By ending the call, he'd have avoided sharing privileged information (protected under the Official Secrets Act) with somebody from outside his department. But it wasn't that straightforward. Lord Rupert wasn't an outsider, strictly speaking, he was chair of the funding committee for every department.

But would that be a valid excuse for Chalmers' actions if he were pulled in front of a disciplinary committee? No, was the answer; because in his elevated world, blame, much like shit, rolled downhill.

"I'm waiting, Mister Chalmers."

I don't care, wait. By hanging up, Chalmers would have ended the possibility of being disciplined for sharing classified information. But he'd have also made a formidable enemy over something which would certainly be perceived as a willful act of defiance.

Even worse than that, he'd have starved this powerful man of the information he so desperately required in order to play some part in saving the life of his own son.

Therefore, Chalmers could hang up and trust everything to the op he'd bullied Miller into taking. Or, he could let Miller's op play out, while simultaneously allowing the Lord to take his own shot at getting his son back. Two routes to success, rather than one.

He came back to the fact that Lord Rupert wasn't an outsider. That would have to be the core of his defence, if it ever came to it.

"I have your son's current location, my Lord." It had just come out, almost on its own. There was a sense of relief, but Chalmers felt a sick uneasiness in the pit of his stomach too. He'd just crossed a blurry line, and he knew it.

42.

"MA'AM?" LYDIA WAS hovering in the doorway to her boss's office.

"Come in Lydia, what have you got?" Debbie gestured to the appropriate seat.

"I've been trying to consider everything that could have an effect on this current operation." Lydia plopped her bum down into the appropriate spot.

Debbie had never worked directly with an operative. In the past she'd received all relevant operational updates via their handler -one of Chalmers' subordinates. But Debbie's team members were always one step further removed from the actual human being taking the risks.

So, it was natural that they'd all feel personally invested in this one, much more so than for any previous ops. But that personal knowledge also had the potential to make them too emotionally invested, which was presumably why the system had been designed in such a way.

A quick nod to Lydia signaled Debbie was in the same place.

"Part of which meant looking into Danny's emails."

"To what end?" asked Debbie.

"To make sure that whoever takes Danny's news stories doesn't run his disappearance for their next headline."

"Ohh… Good call Lydia. How did that one slip through the net?" A second missed complication within such a short amount of time, didn't bode well.

"Well, it didn't Ma'am." Lydia smiled in pride, at which Debbie could only laugh.

"So," Lydia continued, "the last story he sent in was dated one day before the hostage video was released."

Debbie nodded, "Let's hope it's not his last story."

Lydia was obviously uncomfortable at the thought, her silence continued for long enough that Debbie gave her a verbal nudge, "What's on your mind, Lyds?"

"The soldier, Toby. I mean," she sighed uncomfortably, "do you think everything will go to plan?"

"According to Sergeant Miller, that seems quite unlikely, as I'm sure you remember. Although he seems as ready to adapt as anyone I've ever met." It was a better answer than to admit that operations periodically went to shit.

Debbie had been involved in previous missions where the undercover personnel had been killed, and wherever possible those remains were brought home for burial. She also knew that operatives were periodically captured overseas, but in this particular case, capture was the actual plan, which still made her head spin.

Truthfully, the nightmare scenario for her was Toby being discovered for what he really was. To be held over there, as a known intelligence services operator would be a horrific fate.

Although, none of this seemed remotely helpful in terms of motivating her subordinate.

So instead of answering Lydia's question in the most literal way, she addressed what for her, would be the most reassuring aspect, "By the end of the day, I hope to have ministerial approval for DNS tampering, packet filtering, even temporary IP blocking, while this operation is still live. That way, we can suppress anything that shares Danny's status as kidnappee, and therefore Miller's, too. We will control everything that is within our control, and we'll have to put our faith in Toby's abilities."

And pray for a little luck.

43.

LADY FIONA DUGGAN-SMYTHE sat watching her husband sleep in his hospital bed. She'd never seen him nap so much, presumably it was a result of all the medications, or the arduous operation, or… she shuddered at the thought. Or… the heart attack itself.

As a couple, they weren't new to challenges, they'd overcome some real horrors during their years together, but they'd always overcome those challenges by working together. One's strength would compensate for the other's weakness, with the roles continually reversing. They really were the ultimate team.

But there'd never been anything like this; two life threatening events happening simultaneously. And she couldn't even draw on her team-mate because half of her team, was… she shuddered again.

How was she meant to cope with this, alone?

Fiona elongated her neck, correcting her posture as she'd been taught to do whenever the weakness crept in, but against her will the tears started streaming, silently. She studied Rupert, watching his chest rise and fall gently, then switched her focus to the numbers on the monitoring machine. He was still here, and everything was how it should be, at least in the eyes of those who understood those numbers, but nothing was resolved; this was just a pause.

Rupert may not have died that night, but his mortality was more real than ever before, and his life expectancy moving forwards, was never more uncertain. She lowered her head into her hands and started shaking, continually wiping at the tears which came at an ever-faster rate.

But that was only the half of it. Literally, the half of it. There was Charles too.

She sunk further still, and her breathing became snatched, audibly so. She looked back at Rupert who wriggled, as if aware of her noise.

Oh no. She snatched her phone off his bedside table and ran into the small bathroom, carefully closing the door with the handle held downward to avoid even the click of the latch.

She flicked on the light switch and squinted under the harsh fluorescent lighting, looking at herself in the mirror, seeing an older looking lady than normal. Vanity had no business bringing her down any further, so she lowered the lid onto the toilet seat and sat down, back to the mirror.

Now what? Get a grip and return to her bedside spot?

But she wasn't ready for that yet, she'd only just turned her mind to Charles's problems, and they deserved her attention just as much as Rupert's did. The issue was that she didn't really understand Charles's situation. He'd been taken prisoner, no, 'hostage' was the word used. In the middle east, but where, specifically? She strained in thought.

Syria and Iraq, that's what had been said, which made little sense as they were two different countries. She snatched at her phone, unlocked it, and opened the world wide web thingy. Charles had shown her how to use it; he was very knowledgeable regarding modern technology.

So where was the little box she needed to write inside? *Ah, there; it's tiny. Now, where are the little letters? Okay,* s, *then* y, *then* r, *then… What on earth is a 'Syrian Hamster'? No, stop; don't search for that.*

The backwards button, start again. *It's doing it again! So ignore it, but how? Space, yes! There we go,* Syria hostages, *another space,* journalists, *enter.*

Oh dear, they look like prisoners of war. Her breathing worsened. *So? Oh, here's a good one,* 'Latest News, Videos.' *Let's click on that one.*

A video started playing with a well-spoken reporter wearing a protective vest of some kind, explaining about the latest people taken hostage, the whole thing filmed in some rubble filled streets. *Oh, okay. This is a different man, wearing an all-in-one set of orange overalls. Oh dear, the poor man; you bullies, let him stand up. Making him kneel like this doesn't make you superior…*

Fiona's mouth opened as one of the men behind him moved a big knife into view… "Ohh!" she snatched at the closest soft object, a hand towel, and shoved it straight into her mouth as she watched in disbelief.

As the orange suited hostage dropped to the ground she started squealing, the sound partially stifled by the towel. Fiona threw her phone to the other side of the bathroom and pushed the towel harder into her mouth, still squealing in horror at what she'd just witnessed.

ROCKIN' THE ORANGE

44.

TOBY HELD HIS phone, studying the contact page for Mary-Ann. How she'd managed the page modification didn't concern him anymore, it was the picture itself which held his attention.

"Call her; obviously, you want to." Antonella was peering over nosily at his display.

Toby sighed silently and hit the home button. His annoying companion didn't deserve to see Mary-Ann's page.

"Or, are you scared to call her?" Antonella pursed her lips.

"What's wrong with you?" Toby asked, stunned at her endless jabs. "Firstly, nobody's managed to bait me since I was twelve. And secondly, do you get off on being annoying?"

Antonella slumped and looked genuinely upset. Apparently, there was a human in there after all.

She quickly readjusted her position, straightened up and turned away from his screen. "Maybe you're not scared, but you have looked at that photo since we left Inghilterra. So, what do you want to call it? If the word is not scared?"

He rolled his eyes. Her assessment of his time management wasn't even true; he'd spent most of the journey listening to her endless jabs about how he looked like he was going to attack people rather than take their photos. How he needed to grow out his hair on top and get more lift on it so he wouldn't look, 'So uniform, so…' but she'd only finished that sentence with the same-old look of disgust.

She'd continued her review of his failings with an explanation of how he should never be clean-shaven again. Ever. Because a scruff is much more manly, more unconventional. Followed by an explanation of how his t-shirts weren't fitted enough; after all, he was quite muscular so he should choose them to show that part of his body better.

None of it made sense to him; look less military, but show your muscles off more? So instead he'd zoned out completely, which is when he'd started staring at Mary-Ann's image; the only image of her that he had.

"I don't want to call it anything," he finally responded.

Maybe he'd been wrong about normal life. He'd just spent some time off, away from work. That was normal life, and that hadn't been empty and distressing. He'd actually enjoyed it. It was a new kind of normal life, unlike anything he'd known before.

"You want some hand cream?" Antonella offered him a tube.

"Why would I…" he tailed off in disbelief.

"It is very dry. Ma dai, I try to be nice," she scowled.

"My God! Well, could you stop?" he growled back.

She flinched in response, "You shouldn't say that. Don't joke about Dio, about God. Not here." She paused, then added, "Or where we are going."

"Now that's actually useful information for me, isn't it? That's what I need. So, they won't like me talking about God?" he asked her.

"Of course not, they are true believers."

Good. That might be a useful pressure point.

45.

"I THINK YOU should take some exercise today; I'll give you a shoulder to lean on." It was Yannick making the offer.

Danny knew he was right but was still feeling debilitatingly traumatised by everything he'd been through, and this room, his cell, felt like a safe haven from what surrounded him.

Yannick could see the Englishman was tumbling down an introspective rabbit hole, and that threat from inside concerned him just as much as the one out there. He'd seen others retreat into their shells like this, and they'd never properly come back out again.

It was obvious to him that English Danny would have been very likable before this, probably somebody who'd have helped you in your time of need, somebody sweet, and caring. But those people could never handle this. They became a danger to themselves, even to those around them. Yannick really had to break the cycle while it could still be broken.

"You thanked me before, for the support," he reminded Danny.

Danny looked up. Yannick's support had indeed been uplifting, and it had come right when he needed it the most. Danny straightened his back against the horse stall wall, but remained silent.

"Now, would you please come for a walk with me?" asked Yannick.

An uneasiness filled Danny. To go outside was inviting more abuse from long beardy, but he owed the Frenchman, so he pulled himself to his feet; the dread still manifesting itself as silence.

"Good. Thank you, Danny. They should be coming around soon, then we'll enjoy some fresh air and sunlight together."

Danny closed his eyes and shook his head from side to side, very gently. Nothing about this was going to be enjoyable.

"Hey Khalid, how are you this morning?" Yannick managed a genuine smile for one of their captors. Danny was stunned when the man smiled back and reciprocated the greeting. The interaction made him feel off balance.

Danny's upper right arm was draped across Yannick's shoulders, his forearm hooked around his neck, using the Frenchman as a makeshift crutch.

"Let's rest a while, here in the sun." The words were for Danny this time. "You okay to stand for a moment?"

Danny nodded, allowing Yannick to release himself. Yannick then looked to a different guard for permission before walking to the edge of the courtyard and taking two empty plastic water buckets, which he carried back toward Danny.

"Chaises de plaige. I think you say deckchairs in English?" Yannick smiled a broad warm smile, upturned the huge buckets, and set them down on the floor. "We have no parasol today, but we'll make do."

Danny took hold of Yannick to lower himself onto the bucket stool, then closed his eyes to better feel the warming rays of the sun.

"Not bad, right?" Yannick nudged Danny playfully with an elbow. "It's all about the little things."

With his eyes still closed, Danny could feel some small change within himself. Since his arrival, he'd been feeling continually more terrified at the idea of impending execution, apprehensive of immediate beatings and hollow at the hopelessness of it all. The tension within his body had been continually mounting, and as a result, his muscles had reached a point where they were permanently contracted. But sitting on that blue bucket, with a hairy Frenchman at his side and the sun on his face, there was a tiny hint of reversal.

He didn't even want to open his eyes; the feeling was so welcome. It was as if pins and needles were running through his body, but they were working some kind of magic as they did so.

"This, is what we do." Yannick had closed his eyes too.

The new friends sat in silence, as various guards went about their business. Some patrolled the edge of the courtyard chatting to each other in a similarly easy going way, some looked up at the sun and enjoyed its warming rays too, a couple of laughs were even heard in the distance.

And the two men who'd had circumstances thrust friendship upon them, continued to soak it all up.

"You know, I found it hard too, in the beginning." Yannick broke the silence. "Okay, maybe that's an understatement." He laughed at himself, and Danny couldn't help but smile too.

"But it changed. Very slowly, I admit! But…" Yannick let out another chuckle, while Danny's smile faded.

"As the time passes, those things you knew before, they become more distant in your memory. The things, the stuff especially. You know? The things, the cars and the gadgets; I don't know why I ever cared about them." Yannick's smile had gone now too. "Really though, for the life of me, I can't understand what I was thinking."

Danny was captivated by the words, yet painfully aware of how far he was from that point.

"The only thing I miss, is ma femme, my beautiful, caring, funny and smart, wife."

Danny's eyes were still closed which helped him notice when Yannick's breathing faltered slightly. He opened his eyes and turned to his friend, now putting his arm around Yannick's shoulder to offer support, rather than continually take it.

46.

THE ROYAL AIR Force helicopter had been given permission to land at Milan's Linate airport, the mid-way point between the UK and Syria. They'd stood underneath its spinning rotors, fighting to stay still under the turbulence as their bags were handed to them by the crew.

They continued to fight the powerful downdraft as they walked toward the closest building, and before Toby and Antonella had even reached the doors, the huge whirlybird was already defying gravity and climbing to make its noisy exit.

"Vieni qui," Antonella beckoned to Toby. "Come here," she translated for him as she opened a door.

"Buongiorno," a sole uniformed man greeted the couple. "Passaporti."

"Ecco," Antonella handed him her passport. Toby already had his to hand, as some foreign language words needed no translation.

The man accepted Toby's, which of course, wasn't Toby's; rather a new identity. "Good morning, signore Baker." Apparently, the suits at GCHQ had taken Toby's traditional last name, Miller, being the old term for somebody working in a grain mill, and turned him into a baker, somebody who cooked the resulting products. "Hmm, pasticceria. Ho fame."

Antonella laughed out loud; Toby could only look from him, to her, then back again.

"He said baker, then pastry shop, then I'm hungry!" She'd

apparently thought the joke was priceless. Toby, however, couldn't help but fixate on how the man wasn't clean shaven.

He also noticed the bloke had his top button undone, his tie had been pulled loose and a packet of cigarettes sat in the middle of his desk, but the man smiled sincerely at Toby, which put Toby at ease. "I hope you enjoy Italy, Mister Baker."

The man's infectious smile simply had to be returned, which Toby did, adding, "I hope so too mate, thank you." And with that the couple were free to move on.

'Antonella Ferrara' was handwritten in thick black marker on a large piece of brown cardboard, which looked like it had recently existed as a box. The man holding the former box, which now shared the name of Toby's companion, was about Toby's height, Toby's build, and Toby's age. But the man was dark haired, the top was styled to give the hair some lift, he was unshaven, and his t-shirt was considerably tighter than Toby had ever felt comfortable wearing.

Antonella strode toward the man, "Sono io, la Ferrara. Parli inglese?"

"Si cara," he smiled at Antonella, "English, no problem."

"We have to get to Malpensa, veloce, for another flight." A civilian connecting flight had been chosen to ensure their arrival in Syria would be suitably unobtrusive. "But if we could make a stop, for a brioche and a coffee on the way?"

"Certo cara, I have a place." The smile was unchanged, but what really surprised Toby was that when the man turned to him, for the second time Toby was greeted with the same genuine warmth, "Signore."

"How's it going?" Toby couldn't help but offer it back.

"Now that…" for some reason Antonella was smirking at Toby, "Is more like it. You don't look like you want to kill 'im. Keep it up."

She turned her back on Toby, gave the man her bag, and the pair of them sauntered away slowly, while talking in Italian at a hundred miles per hour.

From the leftmost lane of the Autostrada, Toby's Italian doppelganger floored the accelerator and steered his way across four lanes of traffic. It had been performed with impressive skill, and a natural, blasé manner. The driver then steered the car right, one last time, then floored the go-pedal again to take the exit. Antonella was talking fast the whole time, seemingly un-phased by the man's intense driving.

The funniest part was that at their current speed, braking was the only sane option -and the only way to avoid power sliding the car through the traffic lights, just a short distance ahead.

Yet, they'd accelerated instead.

Some repressed part of Toby was absolutely loving the whole thing, especially the car itself, and he couldn't stop himself from laughing out loud. The driver heard the laugh, looked in the mirror at Toby, then surprised him by turning to face Toby momentarily, all while maintaining the completely inappropriate speed.

Having checked out his backseat passenger's unexpected reaction, the man progressively applied the brakes, and fought the car's hefty slide as he sailed through the red light, then came to an abrupt stop -right outside a chic looking cafe bar.

"Siamo qui." He pressed a button on the car's modified dashboard which illuminated a blue light mounted to the windscreen, then realised that while the foreigner would probably figure it out, a translation would be more proper, "We are here." After which, the driver carefully straightened his slim-fitting tee-shirt, pulled on his door handle, and stepped out of the car.

While still speed-talking with Antonella, the driver opened Toby's door from the outside and then the Italian pair ambled toward the bar, as if they had the whole day to kill.

Toby didn't know what to make of any of it. Barely any living being could have moved that car, from point A to point B, any faster than that police driver. The helicopter from earlier would have worked to keep up.

But now they were walking as slowly as possible, and the contradiction was just delicious.

"Buongiorno capo," the barman greeted Toby's driver.

"Ciao Marco," he turned to Antonella and asked, "Cappuccino?" Then asked the same of Toby.

"Can I get a tea?" Toby asked.

"No." The driver didn't even bother to disguise his disappointment in Toby's ridiculous response, and turned straight back to the barman, "Tre cappuccini per favore, Marco." He pivoted his head toward Toby and smiled again, "three cappuccinos, please." Then he leaned on the bar in a relaxed manner which was yet again totally at odds with the velocity of their inbound journey.

For the second time in as many minutes, Toby laughed out loud. The man nodded toward Toby, and squinted, as a form of question.

Toby couldn't suppress the grin, "Are we gonna drive like that to the next airport?" he asked. The antisocial teenage joyrider within him was apparently resurfacing.

The plain clothed policeman looked confused, not being aware of having driven in any particularly noteworthy way, meaning he could only respond with another question. "Why? You want more fast? Or more slow?"

"So, these are normal cop cars here?" Toby asked the Italian plod.

"Si, of course; maybe not for local Vigili, but for the real police, yes." The man grinned cheekily, "Italian police cars are better, no?"

Toby couldn't be bothered playing it coy, something about this place encouraged openness, "Oh yeah. They really are."

"You wanna try?" the Italian cop asked, deadpan, while shaking the keys at Toby.

"You serious?" Toby already had his hand out, and without pause the cop dropped them playfully into the palm of his hand.

Just as quickly, Antonella relocated herself to the rear door and the cop to the passenger side. The whole act caught Toby by surprise, yet again.

Most of Toby's life had been in uniform, and now he wore plain clothes, just like this guy. But earning the right to move up was a slow process, just as it must have been for this cop. So, Toby knew that there was no way in hell this guy should be allowing him to drive his unmarked police Alfa. Yet he was, and quite happily, which implied a complete lack of order.

But the two Italians had instantly taken their new places in the car without a single word being spoken, which implied a natural order existed.

He laughed, not understanding any of it, then started the car, realising that while he didn't get it -he definitely liked it.

'Live every day like it's your last.' Some of the Regiment lads were in danger of wearing the phrase out, but in that moment, Toby felt like he had the right. He smiled, brought the revs up, dumped the clutch and took off -leaving two long black marks on the road, right outside the pretty little Italian cafe.

47.

"THAT MAN, THERE." Danny didn't want to ruin this unexpectedly calming moment by attracting the attention of the approaching man. He was still living in permanent fear of consequences.

Yannick's eyes darted about, searching for the appropriate person, "Yes, Mister Ebeid. He's in charge here."

Danny had already gathered that. "He was there when I arrived." Danny thought back, "Which means he was there for you too, coz we were in the same car, right?"

"Right. But I already knew who he was." Yannick responded in a subdued tone. "He will probably come over and talk to us, so be polite. Act as if this is all normal."

Normal? Danny laughed involuntarily but it was born of disbelief, nothing positive.

In an instant, the tension returned, and Danny's breathing became snatchy. Danny squeezed his fingers into a tight fist, his nails bending under the force of his own grip. He couldn't handle this, he just wasn't ready, coming outside had been a terrible idea.

Danny looked over at the man briefly, instantly regretting it as the tension continued on up to brand new heights.

He was spiraling, and he knew it. The camp boss terrified him enough to affect his breathing and heart rate, and those bodily changes played with the mind, which initiated another cycle. He had to regain control of his breathing, so he inhaled and exhaled more carefully, counting his breaths in and out.

Danny held his eyes closed and fought for more control. The presence of the man led to thoughts of the purpose of the camp, and therefore to Danny's presence within it, which led to the visual of how it ended for most western prisoners. And that finality was the obvious trigger for Danny's panic. It was all raw emotion, and he had to find some rational.

Even analysing that thought process had made his eyes well up and triggered trembling in his hands, but he had to keep fighting it. He opened his eyes and blotted them with the fabric of his overalls, then stared down at the dirt floor.

Having rationalised the why, and calmed himself slightly, he started to doubt that core assumption on which everything was based. Not all hostages were executed, and not all groups were extremist, which meant not every camp was death row. Danny looked up, intent on studying this camp, his camp, with fresh eyes, only to see the camp boss standing right in front of him, which made him flinch -noticeably.

"Good morning, Yannick." The man's tone was incongruously light, which triggered a new bout of anxiety. Emotion was constantly overrunning reason.

"Good morning, Mister Ebeid," Yannick replied, nodding his greeting enthusiastically too.

"It is a beautiful day, isn't it?" The camp boss smiled warmly at Yannick.

Danny really couldn't handle this; it was a farce to role-play at being civilised, while presiding over this, even if this camp were more moderate than some.

"And you, our new arrival. How are you today? Your wounds are healing well, I hope?"

Danny ground his teeth together in disbelief, his eyes welled up again. *My wounds? The ones you inflicted? Maybe not your hands, but in your name.* He couldn't, wouldn't, look up at the man. With his eyes welling all over again, Danny forced himself to lock them down onto the dirt floor. But then Yannick elbowed him in the ribs, and not playfully like before.

'Be polite, as if this is all normal.' That's what Yannick had told him, but this was so far from normal it hurt. Danny knew he risked offending the camp boss, that Yannick had earned his trust, and that his advice must have come from experience.

Danny swallowed hard, took a breath, then did as he must, "They are healing, yes."

But Danny only had so much to give and stared down at the dirt floor the whole time. He knew his teary eyes would advertise just how much he struggled, and for him, that was a private matter. Even worse was the idea that by looking up at the man, an even more unwelcome and humiliating reaction would spew forth, involuntarily. No, the floor was where his gaze would remain.

"I think I hear south London in that accent. Am I right? I think I am."

Danny could have sobbed, it would have been the most natural thing to do, it's certainly what he wanted to do. He inhaled deeply again, constantly working at keeping his composure, "Croydon."

"Ahh! I knew I was right." The man's arms stretched outward, as if in some gesture of victory, unseen by Danny whose gaze didn't falter.

"I studied in London, in Holborn, do you know the Charing Cross Road? You must know the Charing Cross Road in Holborn?"

The man had picked up a hint of an English accent, but the location names were horribly mis-pronounced. Danny nodded at the dirt, wanting it all to end.

"I love London!" the man bellowed.

Then why do you treat Londoners like this?

"Yes," replied Danny. "I do too," as he lowered his head to hide the first real tear, which seemed to have escaped despite his best efforts.

48.

"GOOD MORNING, LUCAS. Thanks for finding the time to talk to me so quickly."

"Oh Rupert, don't be daft, I always have time for you. How's life?"

"Not well." Lord Rupert looked across at Lady Fiona, who was still holding vigil at his bedside, although her mood had deteriorated dramatically (and mysteriously) since his last nap.

"Oh." That wasn't the expected response. Lucas closed the file on his desk, realising he needed to give Lord Rupert his undivided attention. "What's going on?"

The stress seemed to be a separate living entity within the Lord's body, one over which he apparently had no immediate control. He was quickly learning how to compose himself, but only after the fact. He hadn't yet figured out how to stop the initial rising wave from bulldozing him in the first place.

Suitably composed, the Lord finally replied, "Sorry Lucas, let me explain. I had heart surgery last night."

Lucas's jaw dropped.

"Unplanned heart surgery. So, if I'm slower to respond than usual, it's only because I'm under strict instructions to take it easy." Lady Fi was staring daggers at her husband.

"Oh my God, I'm so sorry to hear that, Rupert. But I'm relieved to hear you sound so well after such horrible news." Lucas was truly flabbergasted. He'd always thought of Lord Rupert as indestructible, but the reality was that the years were creeping up on them both.

"The news worsens, I'm afraid." Lord Rupert was continually working at maintaining an inner peace.

Worsens? Lucas Montague didn't even how to respond to that.

"Young Charles was kidnapped, you see. He was working in the Middle East; he's a news photographer now. Can you believe that? How long has it been?"

Lucas was suddenly glad to be sitting. He was Charlie boy's Godfather, and now he felt utterly ashamed at having let so much time pass since their last contact. Although instead of responding, he started working the problem in his head, exactly as they would have done when they'd served together all those years ago.

"At this point, I assume you're already thinking through the options?" asked Lord Rupert.

"Of course I am, Rupert," replied Lucas with a hardness evident in his tone. "Unlike your heart attack, for which I can't offer any useful help, I can assist with a kidnapped son. In fact, Rupert, I'll give you my word right now that the people who took your son will be made to regret ever having laid their eyes upon young Charles."

"Which is exactly what I hoped you would say." Lord Rupert nodded reassuringly at Lady Fi, who closed her eyes as she exhaled audibly.

"What are the specifics?" asked Lucas, with confidence inspiring determination.

"Well, I've managed to gain GPS coordinates for the hostage camp where all western detainees are being kept. It's on the border of Syria and Iraq, I'm afraid." Rupert winced at the unwelcome complication.

But Lucas couldn't have cared less if the coordinates put Charles right inside the local Iraqi Army barracks; in a personal situation like this, he'd hand pick his very best team of private military contractors and they would be instructed to operate without constraint.

"You've lifted my spirits enormously Lucas. We both know from our years of service, that even with my connections, it could take weeks for our government to come up with a suitable plan, gain approval, allocate appropriate troop numbers, position them in the local area, and finally initiate."

And there it was again, a sudden increase in tension, instantly noticeable within his core. The Lord worked at suppressing the rising stress, "Which might be too late for my boy."

49.

TOBY STEPPED OUTSIDE into the type of dry heat he'd only ever encountered in the Middle East. He instinctively took a step back into the shade to wait for Antonella, but it didn't help much. Clearly it was time to get back into the habit of walking very slowly, at least when circumstances allowed it.

"Eccomi. Here I am," said Antonella.

Toby turned to where the voice had come from, then searched elsewhere, before coming back to the slim veiled woman whose arms were fully covered.

"Ma dai! What?" asked the same voice, with a horribly familiar accusatory tone.

"So, it is you then." He rolled his eyes.

"Che ca…" she stopped herself, "You were more nice in Italy."

"So were you, Kay. Are we gonna get to work?"

The veiled woman's eyes turned to slits which glared menacingly at Toby. But instead of being drawn in, he looked away to properly study his new surroundings.

She'd prepped him well enough, hopefully. Toby now felt able to pass as a photojournalist, not only in the sense of knowing how to use the gear, but also in terms of how he handled himself. This meant that unlike other ops, where Toby would typically get into the mindset of putting up walls and being totally operationally focused, he had to do the other thing, where you fake being someone else; in this case someone far less threatening, as Kay Catso had drummed into him. Repeatedly.

It went against the grain, but it was finally time to lighten his manner -as ordered. So, standing there at the side of the taxi rank, Toby worked on smiling, smiling about nothing in particular.

Antonella laughed out loud, then struggled to stop laughing for long enough to say, "Whatever that is, don't do it. Just stop." She composed herself while considering how to help him achieve the light manner that he was so spectacularly failing at.

"Think of Mary-Ann," is what she finally came up with.

Toby's brows furrowed, and the increased intensity of his stare was the exact opposite of what she'd been hoping for.

"Ma dai, now I see it." Antonella's playfulness had instantly disappeared, "You love her, don't you." The eyes visible above the veil intently studied Toby. "I mean, really love her." She brought her hands up to cover her veiled mouth.

What? Toby winced in confusion.

"But look at that face!" she continued. "I'm sorry, really. E vero amore, I didn't know." Antonella then stepped in close and slid her arm through his, the way an elderly couple would link together to take an evening stroll.

And yet again, Toby didn't get it. To start with, there was what she'd said. He couldn't let those words enter his head, so resolutely set that problem to the side. But even without her unsolicited and utterly insane input, she'd successfully filled his head with Mary-Ann, making him long for her. And she'd done it at the worst possible time.

Having disorientated him so very effectively, Antonella had then gone on to link arms with him, as if she were his girl. But it didn't feel sexual, or even remotely flirtatious, somehow it only felt supportive. What was it with Italians?

"Really Toby, I am sorry, I didn't think you… You," she emphasised sarcastically, "were even capable, and it's beautiful."

He really didn't understand her. Yet it felt as if she understood him; well enough for it to feel like an unwelcome intrusion inside of him. He was infuriatingly lost for words.

"You should call her before you have to give up your phone." She squeezed his arm gently with hers as she spoke.

"No!" In contrast, those words had come out effortlessly enough.

"Okay!" She wasn't buying it but was willing to let it go. At least, nearly willing to let it go, "Then you should call her when you are done."

Toby hadn't moved a muscle since she'd linked arms with him, and still didn't feel like moving. But he did like the idea of talking to Mary-Ann after the op, as presumptuous as the idea was.

The battered old taxi pulled up on the side of the busy street. Toby paid the fare, and they retrieved their luggage from the back. The driver helped them with the lifting, thanked them for the tip with an extremely enthusiastic nod, then got back into his car. But Toby wasn't focused on the driver, his eyes were studying Antonella.

Back in the UK, she'd quickly labelled him as an insensitive lug, whereas in reality, his ability to read people's emotional changes was at least as good as hers. The details on which they both focused may have differed somewhat, but she'd read him wrong, which was only on his mind because he was witnessing an obvious increase in her tension levels, presumably caused by their new surroundings.

"What do you want to do now?" Antonella asked him, nervously checking that her veil was covering her face appropriately.

Toby thought of Mary-Ann, smiled a natural smile, then responded in a surprisingly light manner, "Let's get a drink inside the hotel."

Antonella nodded approvingly and led the way inside. They located the bar, found a tall table, and left their bags on the floor at their feet.

"So, this is it, Dayr az Zawr." Seeing Toby's eyes widen, she westernised her pronunciation, "or Deir ez-Zor; a border town of sorts, with Syrian Arab forces to the south and west, and Kurdish forces to the northeast." Antonella was leaned in close, talking as quietly as was possible.

"It's also the last city before you reach the Iraqi border to the south." She lifted her veil back up over her nose, as it had slipped whilst talking. "If you want to get kidnapped, this is a good place for it."

Toby's plan was a little more focused than that. "Okay. You should probably go now, Kay." He hoped his pet-name would lighten the mood for her. In reaction he witnessed a brief moment of lightness, but anxiety quickly overcame it.

"No, I don't want to go, not until I know you're all right." She was still leaned in uncomfortably close.

Toby exhaled, "When you say, 'all right,' I assume you mean kidnapped? Which means we've got a problem, coz I won't have you near me when that happens."

"Ma bello cazzo, the people you're searching for hate Americans, and they hate English. I am neither. I can however, blend in, as long as I don't have to talk for too long. Eventually, they hear my accent," she felt bound to clarify.

"And caro, they kidnap men, not women," she wiggled her head, "Almost always."

Toby chuckled. Her attempt to persuade him that she should stay to watch his back was sweet, appreciated even. But never going to happen. "Nowhere near good enough for me." He shook his head at her, "And it's not up for debate. So, here's what we're gonna do…" he smiled warmly.

"We'll share a tea, coz you're not getting one of those creamy cappuccinos in here, as good as it was." Even veiled, he could see the smile form in her eyes.

"It really was, I think that was the best coffee I've ever drunk. I might even have to reconsider what I drink from now on."

Her hands were rested on the bar room table, so Toby reached in and wrapped his hands around them, driven to reciprocate the unexpected warmth she'd just shown him, "Then I'd like you to point me in the worst possible direction."

She grimaced and snatched her hands free.

Toby sighed, but his focus remained, "I'll stay on foot, and wander until I find what I'm looking for. I did notice a lot of destroyed buildings on our way in but the area looked uninhabited, and I need the worst inhabited one. Anything bombed out and deserted is gonna be useless, there's got to be people around."

She closed her eyes and shook her head.

"Look, signora Catso," He briefly saw evidence in her eyes of the same fleeting smile, "From the beginning it was always gonna end like this. So, I'm sorry, but it really is time for you to go. You need to let me go and do what I came here to do."

Her averted eyes were all that he could see, and they sure weren't smiling anymore. She shook her head quickly, apparently unwilling to look back up at him.

There's the guilt again. Toby could see that she was caught up in the reality of the goodbye, of the dread that it might be his last, and she was focused on how instrumental she'd been in making it happen. But he needed to get on with the job, and deal with whatever that entailed. Coping under duress was his comfort zone -as little sense as that would make to her.

As the silence elongated, Toby decided on a different approach, one that would properly close the discussion. He gently placed his hand on her jaw, and raised it delicately, until her eyes finally met his again. "What do you want me to say to Danny for you?"

Kay stood up from her stool, walked around to his side of the table and gave him a gentle, but heartfelt hug, "Tell him, kisses and hugs. Baci e abbracci."

As she held him, he could feel her trembling. He needed this to end, so he repeated the words inside his head, before taking a shot at trying them out loud, "Baci e abbracci?"

"Perfetto, mio cazzo." Antonella released him and stepped back.

"All right." Toby stood up straight. "I've got the right dorky clothes on, with loads of pockets. I've got a backpack with a computer and my camera." He reeled off the checklist, as if for a superior. "It's a professional camera you know, perfect for smacking people in the 'ead." He flashed her a cheeky smile. "But my phone is for you," he handed it to her, "coz I don't want these bastards having anything real of mine."

Her eyes saddened again.

"And do me a favour, Kay, take this overnight bag with you. I ain't gonna need it."

50.

TOBY STROLLED DOWN the street, camera in hand, smiling at people left and right as he navigated his way through the rubble and the rubbish, "Are you Zarqawi 'abdi?"

"No? Not gonna reply?" he shrugged. "Well, that's rude innit."

He looked to the next person, "What about you? Are you Zarqawi 'abdi?"

The hatred emanating from the locals was obvious, and it was intense. Yet he was still walking down their street, and being a pain in their arse, unchallenged.

Back in Hereford, his rapid response team's CO had pointed out that most journalists could go for years without getting kidnapped, and of course the officer had been quite right. So, Toby had needed to put himself into a situation which triggered an immediate response. For Danny and Charlie, days or weeks in captivity could be disastrous, even fatal; let alone months or years.

He'd had very little time to think since being 'assigned' to this operation, but it hadn't taken long for him to realise that surgical precision wasn't the right approach, which is why he'd gone instead with blunt instrument. And this was as blunt as he could come up with, but only time would tell if it was blunt enough.

His ambitious plan was to be in captivity by nightfall, which is why he'd already dumped the redundant overnight bag and restricted himself to just the journalist's backpack.

"Is anyone here Zarqawi 'abdi?" he called out to no-one in particular.

Frustrated at the lack of immediate engagement, Toby raised the camera from his side, unclipped the lens cap, and slipped it into his back pocket. He looked around, noticing that everyone seemed to be cautiously avoiding him rather than honing in on him. As he locked in on the next bearded local, the man jogged across the obstacle strewn street just to get away from him.

Toby growled his frustration. *Fine, I'll take it up another notch.*

He slung the camera's strap over his head, raised the heavy body up to chin height and walked straight up to the next local man, "Excuse me, are you Zarqawi 'abdi? I wanna interview them for the British press."

Toby matched the man's increasing pace as he waited for a reaction, and on getting nothing, raised the camera the last few inches and took an uncomfortably close photograph of the man's face. Then he carried on toward the next one.

Any man of his race, spewing those words, while blundering through an area known for being sympathetic to anti-western terrorist groups was guaranteed a reaction. But really; how long was it going to take?

He locked in on the next local man, and sped toward him feeling like the worst breed of used car salesman, "Are you Zarqawi 'abdi?"

Having reached the end of the long street, the one Antonella had told him was the most dangerous inhabited street in town, he'd achieved nothing. At least nothing tangible.

Apparently, kidnappers were like London taxi cabs; there were none around when you needed one.

Hold the press, could this be my cab? A small group of men had appeared from a side street and were striding purposefully toward Toby; all were bearded, all the right age, and all looked extremely emotional, so he'd got the job done in…?

He put his hand to his back pocket for his phone, feeling instead the lens cap. *Oh yeah, no phone. But I should probably put that lens cap back on.* He'd hoped to calculate exactly how long it had taken for his blunt instrument approach to succeed, but now he would only ever know an approximation.

With the lens cap in place, it was time to prepare himself for the next bit. He studied the incoming threat, seeing there were five approaching from the front; he turned slowly to scan his perimeter and found another three coming in from the rear, spread out wide. Even if he'd planned on fighting or evading, they'd made it very hard for him.

But he had to play by Antonella's rules, and she was quite right, he couldn't be him, it wouldn't be credible. So British journalist it was, "Are you Zarqawi 'abdi?" he asked one more time, before his leg was kicked in from behind.

Toby took the hit, snatched the camera in close to his torso and fell in a way that would protect the machine from impact. A few more kicks came at him, so he called out in an appropriately panicked manner, "Wait, I just want to interview you. British press!"

Toby allowed himself to vocalise the pain loudly, rather than internalizing it as he'd usually do. Then his head was covered with a nasty smelling bag, and he was lifted from the ground. He whimpered continually as they carried him, and reinforced his position, "You don't understand, let me go, I just wanna interview you."

51.

"I DON'T KNOW where to start." Debbie stood at the head of the long glass table once again. "Your operative, I suppose; that's as good a place as any."

Chalmers intertwined his fingers and then slowly placed his hands on the edge of the table. He observed Debbie as she spoke with a familiar expression set upon his face. What that expression was, Debbie had no idea. Only that it irked her somewhere deep inside.

"We've had confirmation from Antonella Ferrara, Danny Ellington's former photographer, that they've successfully located themselves in the city closest to the location where Danny Ellington was filmed, and hopefully, still located. Antonella was apparently able to ensure the operative entered the most dangerous part of that city, Deir ez-Zor. So now, our operative is officially operating solo, in one of the most hostile places on earth. And for clarity, this also means we no longer have any way to contact our inserted operative. Clear?"

The other occupants indicated their understanding. Chalmers rolled his eyes and took a breath. *So now she's referring to him as 'our' operative.* Previously all assignment of ownership had been attributed to Chalmers' department solely. She was already too invested for his liking, he shook his head at her, openly.

Debbie's dislike of the man was growing by the minute.

"Meanwhile, I was just denied ministerial approval for my

request to temporarily block UK access to any and all websites related to the terrorist group Zarqawi 'abdi, as apparently they have no record of this operation even existing."

Chalmers leaned forward and opened his mouth.

"No!" she snapped, "My ears bloody hurt from the abuse I just took. But it gets even worse." She was glaring furiously at Hugo Chalmers.

"As this operation does not yet officially exist, we cannot deploy UK troops in support of our operative. Therefore, Sergeant Miller has no rapid reaction unit to call upon."

Debbie had been fighting hard to maintain some professionalism. It had been so much harder for her to climb to the level she'd reached because she wasn't one of the boys, the back-slapping herd. She'd lived with the schoolboy jabs about being too soft, too emotional, and too nurturing for the job. But emotion right now was appropriate, so she let it fly and it all headed straight at Chalmers. "Therefore, Miller is alone and unsupported, in the worst imaginable place, and we can't even instruct him to pull out."

She looked at her watch. "Depending on how efficient he is," and he'd come across as very efficient to her, "he's looking at being kidnapped imminently! And once he's been kidnapped, they won't waste any time in filming him and exposing him on their propaganda site, which true believers all around the world will see. But remember, this is a site we cannot tamper with because your operation hasn't even been approved!"

"And..." the fury was evident in her voice now, "he's been issued with a nifty camera containing a hidden GPS beacon which he can trigger to call in help..." She took a lungful of air to fuel even more volume, "which doesn't bloody exist!"

Again, Chalmers went to talk, but again she cut him off. "What the fuck is wrong with you, Chalmers? Are you looking to get him killed? Is there another plan that I don't know about?"

Chalmers had decided that rather than attempt a timely response, he should wait until she'd finally finished with her emotional rant. He sat with his hands in the same position and maintained the same calm manner. As the pause elongated, he finally spoke, "May I?"

Even that came out sarcastically. Debbie glowered at him but offered nothing in response.

"In my department, we are not deploying armed forces, only solo operatives, therefore we are not bound by Parliamentary approval. My department operates under a separate remit which does not concern you. I also don't answer to you, Ms. Peters."

Debbie flared her nostrils and opened her mouth, but Chalmers now raised his hand to stop her, "No," he ensured he spoke without emotion, "I think it's fair that I take my turn now, without interruption."

He paused, enjoying her visible rise in emotion, "Yes, our operative is in country, but he is highly unlikely to be taken hostage quickly. And I already have the documents prepared requesting deployment permission for the rapid response unit."

"Approval is typically fast," he shrugged, "taking a few days, at most. And in the meantime, the appropriate rapid response unit has already been fully briefed and flown out to the closest Forward Operating Base. So, I really see no reason for these histrionics."

And considering that Miller's speciality seems to be operating without prior approval, a few days alone should serve as a good reminder of the importance in being a team player.

52.

TOBY WAS STAYING as quiet and still, as possible. Unthreatening, even pitiable, was his objective.

He'd been carried, presumably by the men who'd ganged up on him in the street, but he'd not been taken very far.

The most likely explanation was that he'd been abrasive enough to piss off the locals, and that some of the ones more sympathetic to the Zarqawi 'abdi cause had decided they'd had enough, and jumped him.

But they didn't seem to be the kidnapers he'd been hoping for, otherwise he'd have already started the longer journey to a detainee camp. And throughout the ordeal he'd concentrated enough on their movements to know that he wasn't very far from where he'd made a spectacle of himself -a few hundred feet at most.

But maybe he was wrong about them? Maybe those locals were real Zarqawi 'abdi members who only moved their prisoners at night?

He mulled it over, deciding that scenario was the less likely one -mainly because the place seemed lawless enough for them to be able to carry some dumb westerner around in broad daylight. In which case Toby was being held, waiting for some true believers to collect him from these amateur locals.

He'd never been in a situation quite like this one before: firstly, he'd made no attempt to fight back on the street; secondly, instead of suppressing any response that could have been viewed as evidence of weakness in him (therefore something for them to exploit later) he'd been amplifying his reaction to what pain he'd felt. And finally, here he was waiting like a helpless child instead of plotting his way out of the situation.

Well, this was certainly going to get old quickly. *How long will it take?*

Maybe it was a good time to grab some shut eye.

As a kid, Toby had only known one kind of sleep -deep and oblivious. He'd regularly slept through bedside alarms, his mum yelling, and his big sister prodding and poking him for her own entertainment. Once, he'd even rolled off his bed, making the lights shake in the living room below, and still slept through the whole thing.

When he'd joined the Army, it had quickly become apparent that would no longer be acceptable. You were expected to be as ready for action at 4am, as you were at 4pm. So, his body had been forced to adapt, and adapt it had.

Now his body automatically switched to whatever sleep mode was appropriate for the situation. At Mary-Ann's he'd slept like a child, much to her amusement. But here, he was destined to catnap until (or if) he finally returned home again.

What had woken him from this catnap was the sound of talking. He closed his eyes inside the hood and forced all unwelcome thoughts of normal life from his mind.

The voices were talking in one of the Aramaic languages, but he had no idea which. One of the issues which always hampered westerners working in the region was the quantity of languages in use, with further variations (in the form of regional dialects) thrown in, just to confuse the matter further.

It meant there were very few people who could be enlisted to help communicate with locals, and it was almost impossible to enlist someone who could still follow the conversation when the locals switched tongues to intentionally exclude the translator.

Toby grimaced, already knowing this was going to be one of those times that language would be redundant.

The noise level increased dramatically as a door was opened, and then the emotion and volume behind the primary voice intensified. It was what he'd expected; if somebody shouts, you feel intimidated, and if you feel intimidated, you retreat from the source of intimidation -a natural response.

But it's an approach that didn't work on Toby, defiance was more his style, the thought of which snapped him back into the here and now. Because for now, he had to appear suitably intimidated, "No, please don't hurt me, I only want to write your story. Please!" *Would one more 'please' be plausible? Or transparent...*

Then the hood was yanked from his head. It caught underneath his chin on the way up and tugged his head backward. But Toby forced it back down just as quickly, and snapped his eye lids shut so his retinas could adjust to the dramatic increase in light.

Whack.

A powerful punch landed on his jaw, the unexpected force stunning him momentarily. He scrunched his face in genuine pain and even with his eyes shut, stars started to pulse in his vison. *That wasn't very fucking fair, was it?*

Journalist, he reminded himself. "Argh," he wheezed, with his head averted from the punch's original direction, "Stop. Please." He added some groaning, easily done with the painful shockwave still travelling his head.

Toby swallowed hard, flared his nostrils, and opened his eyes just enough to memorise the face of the coward who'd sucker punched him. The Staffy Miller glare unintentionally surfaced, but Toby caught it, corrected it, and flinched convincingly, before turning away from the man's stare completely. The man continued to yell, all while barely an inch in front of Toby's averted face.

When Toby had gone through his Army basic training, Warrant Officer McCord (who back then had been a Sergeant) had pulled that stuff on the recruits all day, every day. The thought helped him to shut out the here and now. It had been a really nice surprise to see McCord again, and he was a Warrant Officer now -with the Regiment, no less. He'd done very well for himself.

The volume outside of Toby's head then increased further still, but the man's brief moment of dominance had already passed. *Sorry, I was somewhere else for a second, what were you saying?*

The situation was still fundamentally unchanged, so Toby kept his head averted and waited for it to blow over. The guy's breath stunk though. *Did you bail on your oral hygiene when you started growing that beard? That shit's rank, mate.*

"I cannot decide if you're really stupid, or really brave."

I'm trying to decide that myself, but it's not looking good.

The journey had gone as expected; he'd been shoved violently into the back of a vehicle, to amplify the feeling of helplessness and dread at what might follow.

They'd kept him blindfolded with the intentionally disgusting hood, to ensure locational security for their camp and tap into a captee's primal fear of both darkness and disease, but also to trigger the panic which came from disorientation and the lack of control over your surroundings.

After that, he'd been carried from the vehicle by multiple captors, an obvious tactic employed to make the subject feel both isolated from any allies and hopelessly outnumbered by adversaries.

And finally, he'd been shoved to his knees and held steady by two people, to instill fear of an immediate beheading.

He'd mentally coped with all of it, except for the fear of imminent beheading. It was disturbingly real, and the only thing he'd encountered so far that screamed out for immediate action. Toby needed to present his argument, and it needed to be powerful enough to get straight under the man's skin.

"I think that's a matter of perspective." Toby tried to present a calm, reasoned demeanour, but with some underlying fear, as they'd surely expect from him. "Which you should be able to relate to."

Camp boss Mister Ebeid seemed amused by the new prisoner's unexpected response and looked at his guards, laughing and with his hands, encouraging them to join in, "And what do you assume I relate to?"

The man's English was good, right down to the crisp British accent. Toby wondered where he'd been schooled, somewhere back home no doubt. It helped the situation though, as it removed the need for Toby to overly simplify his own word choice.

"Well surely you want to be seen as more than just another angry terrorist? You must know how anyone in your position is judged in the west." Toby shook his head, making sure to exaggerate the lingering pain.

He pretended to fight through the discomfort, then went on, "I'd have thought you'd see the benefit of being the first local leader with a wide audience. Coz if people can see how you've been wronged, they'll sympathise with you. They might even become receptive to your cause."

Throughout Toby's inbound journey he'd been working on key points to use during this anticipated conversation, and his closing argument had always been the lure of more followers for the terrorist's cause. But the man was too smart to dangle such a blatant carrot, and his language too advanced to require such a blunt statement. Toby had faith that the boss would already be drawing that conclusion without need for any clumsy additions. Toby looked at the laughing camp guards, then chose to tie things up by throwing a calculated barb instead, "Isn't that what you already have here? But on a very small scale."

The laughing abruptly stopped, "You understand nothing of what I believe in, or of my scale."

Toby shrugged apologetically, then offered the irresistible solution, "Which I came here to fix."

"But your offer is idiotic! Because my plans don't involve you, or anyone else, ever leaving." Ebeid snapped back angrily.

The words were undoubtedly problematic, but the display of

unchecked emotion was evidence that Toby was successfully getting under the man's skin.

Antonella had been the inspiration for his next words, "If that's what God wills, then who am I to question it?"

Toby was instantly struck in the back of his skull, as a flurry of noise erupted around him.

"Stop!" The camp boss hadn't exactly rushed to bring an end to the abuse, but he had at least stopped it. "It is true, none of us should question Allah's will. Maybe this," he gestured toward Toby's pitiful figure, "is his will." Mister Ebeid looked at the ground in thought and then beckoned to a guard carrying a large camera. The man was given an order in whatever dialect was in use at the camp, then as Ebeid strode away deep in thought, the newcomer raised the camera to film a video of Toby.

Toby slumped convincingly and tilted his head low enough to make his face barely visible to the camera lens.

Only when the man was done, did Toby look back up to see that the camera in use wasn't his own, but a different professional camera body. One with some damage to the rear of its bulky housing.

53.

LIEUTENANT LINTON HAD called the men together in response to an unexpected operational update over the satellite phone. "All right lads, I've just been told we're on hold. This means that even if we receive location confirmation from our undercover, we cannot go in."

The occupants of the large tent started looking around at each other, all thinking similar thoughts. Linton knew there was no point in explaining the why, as it really didn't matter to a squadron of men itching to go.

So, before the barrage of tangentially related questions could arrive, he was already continuing, "But that doesn't mean we're going to sit on our hands because once we're freed up to get on with our jobs, which I don't think will take long, I expect us to be ready." The men visibly settled.

"And for now, I expect four volunteers for intelligence gathering. Our current orders did not specifically prohibit that, which I have interpreted as clear permission."

As chuckles filled the tent, every hand was raised, as expected. Guys like this would choose anything over sitting in a temporary operating base, alone with their thoughts, apprehensions, and doubts.

"Okay, so Peters, Llewellyn and Baranwal," the lieutenant pointed as he named the volunteers, "you three are up." He'd picked an appropriate mix of abilities, experience, and rank within the three selected soldiers, but still needed to round things out with somebody different, "and Pole, you can tag along and learn something new. Sound good?"

"Yes, Sir!" Pole replied, a little too eagerly.

"When you realise what you're in for, that smile will disappear, I'm sure," chipped in Sergeant Ross from the back of the tent. Knowing laughs filled the air. "This will be a 'hard routine', do you know what that is yet, Pole?"

"Yes, Sarge, quiet as church mice!" Pole snapped back confidently.

"Oh Pole, you'll wish you were a church mouse; you'll need to be a lot quieter than that. There will be no talking, no sneezing, no blowing your nose, no scratching your arse, and no smells, which means your arse will need to be on its very best behaviour too." More laughing. "It also means no cooking, so you won't need a hexamine stove, or even tea bags. Understood?"

"Sarge." Pole's smile had already faded somewhat.

The lieutenant rolled a wheeled board to centre front, onto which was pinned a large satellite map of the compound and its surrounding area -the one located using the GPS coordinates from Charlie Duggan-Smythe's high-tech camera.

"So, all of you. Best spots to dig in? For these four gentlemen?" Linton looked around the room for responses.

"There's a patch of undergrowth there, Sir. They could make a dugout behind it, the foliage will work in their favour." The speaker pointed toward a blurry smudge on the photographic image.

"Far too close to their camp," responded Sergeant Ross. "As it is, we'll need to drop them off when the light's gone. Which is at? Time of local sunset, anyone?"

"About 20:00 Sarge," responded another voice.

"Correct. Therefore, we can only drop these boys off at… let's say 21:00 or 21:30, but how far out? A mile from the terrorist camp? Two?" The Sergeant was leading and simultaneously educating the room.

"At least, Sarge. Noise travels a long way with such open land. And we don't know how far out this lot are gonna patrol," added yet another of the soldiers.

"Exactly. So, we'll drive our boys in just as it's getting dark. I already noticed an old red van inside the compound with local plates on it, it looked nice and inconspicuous, so we'll borrow that. We'll drop the lads three miles out, then they've got to yomp that last stretch, at what? Four or five miles an hour?"

The previous respondent hissed disapprovingly through his teeth, "More like three miles per hour, Sarge. Their bergens are gonna be heavy. They're gonna need to carry a few days' worth of water."

"Good point, Corporal, so let's say they're in situ by 22:30. No, 23:00 don't ever underestimate, coz it'll screw you. Always overdo it. Then they've got to dig themselves a nice trench before the sun comes up."

The room nodded their understanding.

"Which is at 05:00 So, by five a.m. there can be no noise coming from you lot, and you'll need to be invisible to anyone scanning the horizon. With all that considered, will that patch of undergrowth still work for our needs?"

"No, Sarge," replied multiple voices.

"Let's have another look then. Back to the map."

54.

TOBY HAD GOT through his own hostage video without too much drama and was still wearing the clothes he'd changed into after de-boarding the plane earlier that day. He'd since been escorted to his new accommodation by the huge bully with the long beard.

Mr. Halitosis really shouldn't have motivated him like that. Survival was never the motivator it should have been, it was more of an instinct really -one that was consistently overruled by the need to come out on top, to complete the objective. Revenge however -that drove Toby on a much more conscious level. And as irrational as he knew it to be, he was now nastily motivated by that shitty sucker punch.

He sighed and looked around the room.

It had evidently been an animal stall until recently, and Toby was pleasantly surprised to see it featured an old, stained mattress laid on the dirt floor, although the room contained absolutely nothing else.

So, the set up wasn't great, but he'd had much worse. Many times on exercise, he'd slept in the open air in full combat kit, laid underneath a bivvy, which was essentially a water resistant sheet suspended a few inches above you, usually by sticks you'd picked up off the floor. You laid on the hard ground underneath this bivvy and got whatever sleep you could.

By the time the sun came up you were typically wide awake and relieved just to stand up again. Which is not to say you were well rested.

If his new room's mattress was an unexpected luxury, then the dirt floor was a dream come true. He'd imagined having to stash his smuggled gear in between stones in a wall, having dug at any weak cement joints all night long. But instead, he could just scratch out a small hole in the ground in a fraction of the time, then bury his stuff invisibly.

He just couldn't do it yet, which left him in a familiar position; alone, with time on his hands and a dire need to adapt to what was going on around him. Otherwise, he'd have no hope of ever getting home.

So, what had he got so far?

The first meet with the Zarqawi 'abdi camp boss had gone very well; after the expected opening salvo where the guy asserted his authority with some mockery and a show of strength, there had been a momentary flash of genuine interest in what Toby had been selling.

Now Toby had to make the man unable to resist the idea of broadcasting his political ideology to the wider world. The man needed to be so focused on his message that he wasn't properly focusing on the messenger.

The man's most likely reservations would involve the uncertainty of what Toby, this new journalist, would actually write about him. But Toby had that part all figured out.

What Toby hadn't quite figured out yet was how to ensure it was all done with his own camera; let alone if that camera was on site or if it had already gone AWOL.

He grimaced at the thought, then stopped himself -it was too early to be worrying about something like that.

Toby had been sitting cross legged on the dirt floor with his back leant against the exterior wall. He'd been facing the entrance door to his cell, but with his eyes closed the whole time.

He'd spent probably three or four hours this way, and as a result he'd been left alone. He'd spent the time fluctuating between situation analysis and cat napping -knowing his energies were best saved for the night hours.

Toby finally took a long, relaxed breath and opened his eyes. The room and the walkway immediately outside it were in total darkness. He looked up toward the bars which separated his cell from his neighbour's and saw no movement.

Toby slowly raised himself to his feet and took a look into the next stall. There was another man in the cell, but he was already sleeping, and by the sound of his breathing, he was sleeping soundly. Something about the sound of his breathing made Toby wonder if that man would notice if he rolled off his own bed, or whether that had been a problem unique to Toby.

Toby now had time to take stock of the rest of his cell. The back wall was built from concrete blocks, so he looked up and down trying to find some aperture within the wall, but in the darkness, found none. For now, he had no idea if the wall was of single block construction, or double. But he'd be able to take a better look at that in the daylight, therefore he set that thought aside.

His next realisation was that he was just one cell from the end of the building, yet the wall between him and that last room had no opening, unlike the barred opening between him and his new neighbour. Maybe the last room was a miscellaneous storage area rather than another animal stall? Again, he needed daylight to know for sure.

Toby walked to the front of the cell and peered through the openings between the bars. He gave the door a quick tug and then walked along the wall of iron bars trying to locate a weak point. Having failed to find anything promising, he reached his hand through the gap between the two bars closest to the door mechanism and ran his fingertips around the lock area to get a feel for how secure it was. Then he stepped back and moved toward the rearmost wall again, specifically to where it formed the corner between him and his sleeping neighbour.

Toby squatted down and rubbed at the floor with his hands, deciding it felt good enough to make a start. But before doing anything that might make a noise, he sat still for a minute or two with his eyes closed, so that no other stimuli could distract him from the sounds he was searching for. There were clearly people awake in the camp, but nothing close by.

Toby now sat down against the back wall and stretched his legs out in front of him. He raised his left leg slightly, then positioned the toe box of the shoe on his right foot under the protruding edge of the heel of his left one. He pushed and wriggled it as hard as possible. The trainers had already been opened up prior to his trip, and the team back in England must have been careful not to close them too tightly, because the heel and the upper separated fairly easily.

Instead of dismantling that first shoe, he now repeated the action for the other shoe. With both trainer soles split open, he pulled his knees back into his chest and removed the trainers from his feet.

After pausing to listen one more time, Toby peeled back the heel of his left shoe even further, fully exposing the void within, and started pulling at the handle of the very slim knife contained inside the sole.

As he rotated the knife to inspect it in the darkness, he could see it was double edged, made from some kind of hard composite material, with a knurled hilt. It was only about five, maybe six inches in length overall, so tiny, but better than what any of the other prisoners had. He set it down on the floor, digging again in the foil-lined rubber sole, to see if anything else was contained within the void of the shoe.

As he scratched at the shoe's innards in the darkness, he felt a small piece of coarse textile material. Tugging it out from the tiny foot-arch area was a real struggle, but he finally worked it free to find it was a long piece of double-sided Velcro.

Nice. It must have been included as a primitive way of attaching the blade to his forearm or calf, which he could use to hide the knife under his clothing.

Toby set the left shoe and its contents down on the dirt floor and repeated the tug of war with the sole of his right, eventually finding a small, unmarked metal cylinder with a narrow neck, and a very similar, but even smaller, second one.

Huh? He studied the two tubes in the darkness. One was hopefully CS gas, as requested. But the other? All that had been given to him by Antonella was a bag, and the note 'As requested'.

He looked at what he had: a simple blade, some incapacitating gas, and two destroyed trainers, both with foil lined innards now visible in their partially detached soles. Then it came to him, *Glue*.

He worked with smart people. Folks who knew that their undercover could hardly get up in the morning and walk around the camp with trainers looking like that, so they'd given him a method of restoring the shoes to their normal state.

Toby nodded approvingly, now the only problem was picking the one which would repair his shoes, rather than have him choking for air in the darkness.

He sighed, picked up the knife and set the blade on the neck of the smallest tube, then had a cautious thought. Toby pulled his shirt up to cover his mouth and nose before snapping the end off the smallest cylinder with his knife, then turned away quickly with his eyes closed and waited. *One and two, and three, and four, and… nothing.*

So, it was glue, probably. That it wasn't the CS gas was a huge relief.

Toby allowed himself another minute to listen out for sounds, then squeezed some of the maybe glue onto the first sole, gripping it tightly, hoping it would set. After a minute, he released his grip and gently pulled at what he'd just compressed, finding the sole was indeed firmly reattached.

Then he squeezed the remainder of the glue on to the second shoe, placing the empty tube inside it, before sealing it back up with firm pressure.

Now he just had to dig a small hidy-hole for the stiletto knife and the gas canister, so that tomorrow he could be stripped and reclothed in his new orange overalls.

55.

THE UNIFORMED DRIVER of the old red van wore a helmet fitted with night vision goggles. He drove without headlights and set his speed appropriately for the range of the sight-aids.

While traversing no man's land at night, the decision had been made to go dark. While the vehicle's engine could, in theory, be heard within a certain range, the lack of lighting meant that the vehicle's exact position and whether it was moving or stationary, would be much harder to gauge for anybody without similar night vision capabilities.

"Coming up on drop point one." The van slowed to a stop, the rear doors opened, and Lance Corporals Peters and Llewellyn jumped from the back and rapidly disappeared into the darkness. The rear door was pulled closed quietly and the van accelerated away gently, creating only the minimum possible amount of noise.

"Thirty seconds guys," said the driver to Pole and Corporal Baranwal after steering a hard left down a smaller track.

After the stated time, the driver braked, bringing the van to a complete stop, "And go."

In response, Baranwal opened the door, Pole jumped clear then held the door for his Corporal to follow. Leaving nobody else in the back of the van, Pole closed the rear door carefully and quietly. In response, the van disappeared into the darkness.

Baranwal set his hand down onto Pole's left shoulder, faced him and silently gestured the direction they were heading, then released his grip and started his run. Pole took a deep breath and set off after his unexpectedly quick superior.

At this pace, and in the dark, Pole's own breathing noises sounded deafening. He'd tried dialing it down, but with his heavily laden pack flailing on his back, his helmet and goggles bouncing on his head, and both hands tied-up in carrying his rifle, the real surprise was that his breathing didn't sound even worse. All of the brutal fitness training that had become part of daily life in such an elite regiment was clearly in anticipation of this.

Keeping up with Baranwal was no joke, but Pole had worked to maintain a gap of just a few feet, constantly worrying about running into the back of the Corporal. As a preventative measure, he'd been scanning his left flank before correcting his constantly varying distance from Baranwal, then checking over to his right for anything potentially hostile, and so on, all the while feeling a little out of his depth.

But now he stopped in response to a raised flat hand from the Corporal. He let out a sigh of relief at not having ploughed into Baranwal from behind.

Baranwal looked to the left himself, then back at Pole, before gesturing they should alter their course slightly, then took off like a greyhound. Pole resumed his scanning of the surrounding area as he worked to keep up again.

They'd entered a flat plain with various trees, all low and wide in their shape. The idea had been that the trees would break the shape of the horizon, making the two soldiers very hard to spot. The trees would also offer some shade during the day, and roots aside, they would make for easier digging than most of the rocky local terrain. In their operational planning meeting they'd picked a particularly wide tree, which had a clean line of sight toward the camp, and Baranwal's slowing pace implied he'd found it.

A flat hand was once more raised by the Corporal, who turned around to ensure Pole was still with him and understood his command. On receiving Pole's breathless confirmation, Baranwal indicated toward the position of the Zarqawi 'abdi camp, which didn't look like much in the darkness. Then Baranwal rested his rifle on the tree trunk, slid himself out of his heavily laden bergen and helmet, detached his small entrenching tool from the side of his pack, and indicated it was Pole's turn.

Pole repeated the Corporal's actions and the two men started digging, as fast as could be done in silence.

56.

TOBY WAS SITTING on the dirt with his back leant against the rear wall of his cell, waiting for the sun to come up on his second day in captivity. The increase in ambient light implied the sunrise wasn't far off.

If everything went to plan, this would be the exact time of day when his rapid response unit would arrive, after being electronically summoned, as planned. Which led him to only one thought.

The camera.

What else could he think about?

'Anything' was the answer, because getting hung up one thing currently out of your control was poor use of your time. So, Toby set it to the side where it could wait, accompanied by various other uncertainties.

Day one had gone very well, all things considered. He'd been taken hostage very quickly, and then relocated from the city to the camp -all during the same day. He'd taken a beating, but only of the ideal level, meaning he'd been hurt but received no serious damage. Toby had been worrying about things like broken bones, or open wounds which would eventually fester, but all he'd received was a few punches and a thorough kicking. So, he was hurting, but not incapacitated.

During that first day he'd even managed to plant the seeds, which would give life to his plan, in the mind of the camp boss.

So, pat on the back for Toby.

But, he hadn't seen his camera yet, his beacon for help. That was a problem.

Pat on the back withdrawn.

"What were you doing last night?" the voice came from somewhere above.

Toby looked up to see a bearded man peering down at him through the bars of the neighbouring cell. In response, Toby cupped his hands around his genitals and tugged them up and down a couple of times.

The man didn't laugh. Toby rolled his eyes, *you've obviously been here too long*. "I was seeing how deep I could dig," he lied.

The man stared at Toby, trying to get a read on him. He certainly couldn't remember being this at-peace after his first night as a hostage, in fact he'd sobbed; he'd done it as quietly as he could manage, but he'd sobbed nonetheless.

"There's no digging your way out of here, not with your bare hands." The man shook his head in disbelief, then chose to add more, "And even if you could, we're in the middle of nowhere. There are guards everywhere, they come and go with no pattern, and they're all armed."

But the man apparently still wasn't done chastising Toby, "And even if you could get past the camp guards, the next people you'd run into would just bring you back. For hundreds of miles, it's always the same -they all hate us."

"Well, thanks for that." Toby smiled up at him. "That helps my morale."

Toby's neighbour shook his head at the new fool, moved away from the bars, and disappeared from sight.

Pole and Baranwal had just put the finishing touches on their trench, they were dug in and already sheltering under a tightly strung section of appropriately colored scrim netting, with only just enough room for their foreheads to peer out through the gap.

Baranwal had clearly done this before; he'd got them set up

before the daylight had arrived, as planned. What the plan hadn't allowed for was the uncooperatively hard and rocky ground which surrounded the tree.

So instead of standing, the two soldiers were only dug in to a depth that would force them to kneel throughout their entire first day. At least that's what Pole had assumed. Hopefully they'd resume digging later, until their trench was deep enough to be somewhat comfortable for the three full days and nights they were scheduled to spend inside it. Only time would tell, as church mice don't get to ask questions.

The Nepalese born soldier tapped Pole on the shoulder, pointed at him in silence, then made a sleeping gesture by placing his flat hands together and raising them up to his cheek before resting his head onto them. Finally, Baranwal pointed at Pole again, to hammer home the point. Pole nodded, settled himself into a corner and closed his eyes, feeling both exhausted and distressingly demoralised.

Noises indicated the camp was coming to life, but Toby remained in the same position with his eyes closed, waiting for the inevitable morning greeting.

It came in the form of, "Up, up!" from the long bearded halitosis bully, who was accompanied by a younger looking guard with a shorter beard.

"Toilet?" Toby finally opened his eyes.

The long bearded guard handed his patinated old rifle to the younger one, who nervously set its sights on Toby, then the bigger bully took some keys from his jacket pocket and unlocked Toby's cell door. The man yelled at Toby, using some kind of Aramaic variation.

"Don't understand you," Toby responded, "but I do need the toilet."

The younger guard lifted his head up from the weapon's sights to listen to Toby, as the bully continued to yell who-knows-what.

"Go right here," the younger guard screeched, trying to make the translation heard over his infuriatingly loud partner.

It was just another mind game and Toby knew it. There was no allocated place to take a leak or a dump within his cell, and to do so would create a disease-ridden camp within days. The guards didn't want that any more than the inmates did. So, the bully's game was clear; make the new prisoners go inside their cell to both humiliate and demoralise them. Presumably, some poor bugger would then have to clean it up once the cell was empty.

To Toby, that indicated he was about to be taken from his cell. It also implied that the tall bully had all-but-no English language, while the AK carrying younger guard had a decent working knowledge, so Toby stared at the big bully and distilled it down to something even he'd understand, "Need, to, shit." Then he redirected his attention toward the younger guard, "If I write a story about your group which explains your religious and political beliefs, it will humanise your boss, and the rest of you by association. So, do you think that story should include you two making me shit on the floor of my own pig-pen? Right next to where I sleep?"

The men argued, with the bully making the lion's share of the noise, as expected. Without any warning he lashed out, high-kicking Toby in the side of the head, then went straight back to yelling at the younger guard while stabbing a finger into his chest. The most infuriating part was that they'd both stopped paying attention to Toby -it was as good as an invitation.

As he watched the distracted men bicker, Toby's head pounded, but his nostrils flared in anger, and he bared his teeth. This was the second time that Stilton breath had done that, and the second time that Toby had let him get away with it. Toby imagined swinging his right leg straight up into sewer-breath's testicles, rolling to the side to use the big man's torso as a shield, and then using the strength in both of his legs to thrust the long bearded bully straight back into the short bearded one. The brief moment of chaos would enable Toby to seize the younger man's AK. He'd be jogging out into the courtyard within seconds, armed, and focusing only on shot accuracy. But…

He couldn't do that.

Not yet.

Toby calmed his breathing, telling himself the time would come, soon enough. In the meantime, he resolved to alter his behaviour around these two. The pathetic whimpering act was over, at least as far as the bigger bully was concerned. He looked up at acid breath and spoke calmly, "Every time you do that, I'll share it with your boss. I'll make him understand how impossible it is to write anything constructive about Zarqawi 'abdi when the group's leader can't even control his own people." And he glared in true Staffy Miller fashion.

The guards' argument intensified further, then the bigger bully grabbed Toby by his shirt, hauled him to his feet and dragged him from his cell.

Toby worked hard to keep up, all the while clenching his arse muscles uncomfortably, *I really do have to bloody go.*

57.

TOBY HAD BEEN allowed to do what he needed to do, but only with the stall door left propped open. These petty power games were an abject failure at intimidating him, and therefore redundant. But he had to assume they were also perversely rewarding for the perpetrators.

So many times throughout history, it had played out the same way. Order had turned to chaos, for whatever reason, then some believed themselves no longer bound by society's rules and their truly repugnant inner-self surfaced. Once normality resumed, a restored society set to investigating what had just happened and ultimately deciding who should be held responsible. A complete denial of their actions always followed, the ultimate display of the cowards they truly were inside.

While mulling over these distant thoughts, he'd been dragged again, this time from the toilet block to another area. This one was located outside and consisted of several water buckets lined up against a wall, with a rudimentary privacy screen made from old sheets and towels.

What hadn't happened was more physical abuse from the bully, which seemed to be evidence that Toby's new approach was appropriate, at least for now.

"Clean yourself with this water," ordered the younger short bearded man, shouting the command in the same authoratative manner as his elder companion, although far less convincingly.

Toby removed his shirt, his trainers, socks, then jeans. He left his underwear on, then started washing himself. As he rubbed the water onto his body, he couldn't help but think, *this is why you don't get inked-up with your Regiment's insignia.*

Once complete, he removed his underwear and wrung all the remaining water from them, keeping his back turned on the guard the whole time. Then Toby climbed back in his damp briefs, before turning around to face the armed young guard.

The long bearded bully threw a set of orange overalls at Toby, plus some flimsy canvas plimsolls, then gestured toward an open courtyard where a handful of other prisoners roamed and sat.

Toby headed in the direction he'd been steered toward, knowing he had to pick his battles, that this one wasn't worth fighting, and well… what else was there to do?

As he walked, he studied the other prisoners; it seemed like you could calculate their time spent here by the length of their facial hair. That thought made him scan the small crowd more quickly, looking for the shortest beard.

Sitting on an upturned bucket was a man with an unshaven appearance, rather than a full beard. The man had some colorful bruising on his face and looked over at Toby. Realising that Toby was already studying him, the man looked away in panic.So, he'd found Danny Ellington. But the guy was clearly traumatised, which was problematic because Toby had planned on approaching him, introducing himself, and trying to learn more about Charlie Duggan-Smythe's location, or fate. But now he had doubts about the idea.

There hadn't been time prior to Toby's departure to consider Danny's mental state, and suddenly it seemed like everything hung on it. Toby stared down at the floor thinking it through.

He was no stranger to post traumatic stress, many of the soldiers in his regiment had suffered its effects. But this wasn't post-trauma, this was mid-trauma. Did that change anything?

Toby shut his eyes and groaned; he knew that PTSD was

volatile, unpredictable in its manifestations. He also knew that Danny was smart, so if Toby wandered over now, already knowing his name, then Danny would quickly figure out that Toby didn't belong, and there was a risk that Danny might feel threatened by Toby's out-of-place presence, rather than uplifted by it.

Maybe he could introduce himself as a fellow British journalist in order to better assess Danny's mental state, before opening up?

No, because Danny knew the crowd, the whole journalist scene, and Toby wasn't a member. He'd still be a suspicious newcomer to Danny. Even more so, having been caught in a lie.

It all required more thought, so Toby steered himself to a quiet corner and found his own bucket to sit on.

Danny Ellington appeared to have made a friend.

Toby had been studying the various captives and specifically Danny's interactions with them, which were non-existent -save for the one bearded man.

Maybe Toby could approach Danny's new friend, rather than Danny directly? His friend seemed to have settled into camp life by befriending the guards well enough for some simple social interactions. It was a smart move, minimising the physical abuse, and buying some trust. All of which implied a calm, reasoned demeanor, one which Danny did not appear to currently possess.

Toby's thoughts were interrupted as shouting erupted across the camp, quickly spreading from one guard to another. Toby could feel a dramatic change in the atmosphere, his gut feeling was that something bad was about to happen, the news of which was adrenalizing the guards with the knock-on effect of terrifying the other prisoners.

Toby watched as one of those prisoners, who'd been strolling alone, quickly joined the closest group, and as that group merged with another -the subconscious belief being that safety lay with the crowd.

Toby stayed put on his upturned bucket. He was a prisoner and had to behave as such, but running scared to join the rest of them wasn't in his DNA, and even for perception's sake he didn't feel it necessary considering how distracted everyone was. Anyway, he was the new guy, everyone knew he had no friends to run to.

Toby studied the scene, seeing that several of the prisoners were looking back toward their cellblock building, so Toby scanned the various guards, then looked over toward the building too.

The first person to walk out was the camp boss, followed by a couple of guards, then by the long bearded bully pulling somebody in orange overalls. Finally, four more guards, including the younger short bearded English speaker from earlier.

Toby looked back toward the main group of prisoners, studying their panicked emotions. Something was about to play out, it terrified them, and Toby had a good idea of what that meant. He checked to see if he was being observed, before turning away to carefully scan the countryside surrounding the camp.

There were very few places where he could see the horizon, due to the camp buildings and the various parked pickup trucks favoured by the terrorist group. But there was a visible patch of land in the distance, one with various low trees that would offer shade and a clean line of sight into the camp.

Toby had a decent understanding of how the Regiment did their work and couldn't help but wonder if they already had eyes on the camp. He avoided his gaze remaining in any one place for too long and slowly brought his head back around to the spectacle playing out in front of him.

The camp boss came to a stop in the middle of the prisoners' exercise area. The camp guards then formed a perimeter, unslung their weapons from their shoulders and held them with both hands. It had the rhythm of a practised, familiar routine.

Toby exhaled slowly.

One of the guards took up a position about twenty feet into front of the boss, turned to face him, and unslung Charlie Duggan-Smythe's old camera from his shoulder. Then the bully dragged the orange suited prisoner to stand next to the camp boss. The prisoner finally raised his head, and Toby instantly recognised the man's face as that of his new neighbour.

Toby closed his eyes and looked down at the floor. His breathing started to run away from him in reaction to the adrenaline running through his veins, but Toby had to control it. Adrenaline existed to give your body an edge in dangerous situations, but this time, the adrenaline was redundant, because Toby couldn't do a thing. Toby looked back up and exhaled deliberately.

After being dragged out with his head held low, Toby's neighbour seemed to have consciously altered his posture, now standing up rigid with his head held high.

His neighbour's face showed no emotion, he was in complete control. In spite of the emotions that must have been boiling up inside him, he was a lesson in restraint. Toby gently nodded his head in admiration as his eyes welled up, he suddenly felt intense guilt at not having made more effort in the early hours of the morning.

Toby continued to watch as the camp boss started playing to the camera, spewing his extremist political drivel, simultaneously the long bearded bully took up a position immediately behind Toby's neighbour. The two camp guards who'd been holding his arms now forced Toby's neighbour down onto his knees and as the prisoner raised his chin contemptuously, the bully positioned his hands either side of the man's head.

One of the bully's hands moved toward the man's unkempt hair and grabbed a handful to prevent the head from moving, and the other, which had drawn a long knife, moved towards the man's neck. Toby looked back over to the patch of land with the trees, wondering, then looked down at the floor directly in front of him as chaotic noise erupted around the camp.

Corporal Baranwal kicked at Pole with his foot, not aggressively, just enough to make him stir. Pole hadn't been sleeping soundly, you never did in these situations, so he roused quickly.

Baranwal pointed toward the camp insistently, then lowered his eyes back down to his rifle's long range optic.

Pole raised himself from the floor, grunting ever so slightly at the stiffness in his aching knees, Baranwal turned to him, stared daggers, then went straight back to his rifle sight.

Pole closed his eyes in shame at making the forbidden sound, grabbed his own weapon and pointed it toward the camp.

Both soldiers watched through their scopes as a group of Zarqawi 'abdi guards brought a prisoner out into the sunny exercise area. They continued to take it in as the filming started, and finally as the poor prisoner's throat was sliced by a dark bearded man who towered over everyone else. The noise in the camp was audible, even at such a distance.

Pole took his eyes from his sight and stared into space, having never seen anything comparable in person, but Baranwal tapped him and indicated with his own weapon that Pole should resume his observation, then tapped him again even harder and made a show of looking down at his own right hand directed dead ahead, before clearly and deliberately altering the angle of his hand, by just a few degrees.

Pole looked back through his optic, panned to the right as directed, and saw a familiar face sitting on an upturned bucket.

So, Sergeant Miller had successfully infiltrated. Already.

Pole touched at the stab wound on his cheek absent mindedly.

58.

"DO YOU AGREE that we use different ways to make our point? Depending on the situation, or the audience?" Toby had taken the calculated risk of approaching the camp boss, uninvited. "We might communicate with a son in one way, but it's different for your daughter, or wife. Be honest, would you use the same approach with a smart learner, as you would for a dumb subordinate?" Toby looked at the long-bearded bully as he added the last option.

The camp boss shook his head, he had no idea what the new guy was talking about, and this really wasn't the time. He gestured wearily for his guards to move Toby out of his way. "Do you want to be next?"

Toby had to ignore the threat, so continued undeterred, "But you? You only communicate with the West in this way." Toby pointed down at his neighbour's lifeless body, just as a pair of guards seized his arms.

But Toby persisted, "Don't you see, you could change everything? Be the first to have a mouthpiece in the West, the first of your kind able to present their perspective, without any filter." Toby was being pulled backwards by the guards, but resisted gently, knowing he wasn't going to get a better opportunity to make his point. Everybody was at their most emotional after that show, meaning they were at their most receptive too.

"Can you imagine a news story that doesn't demonise you?" It was a hard balance, resisting the guards enough to prevent them from removing him, without appearing too physically capable.

"Demon?" Ebeid exploded. "I'm not the demon here! You invade my country; I fight our invaders bravely and fiercely, and I am the demon? I…" He leaned in close to Toby and snarled, "I do Allah's work!" The boss was furious. It was working.

"Okay, so you just told me that and it's compelling. I see how strongly you believe it, but I'm just one Westerner, and based on the video you just shot, do you think that's what others will see?" Toby nodded to the pitiful prone form of his neighbour again, a man he'd ignorantly snubbed during their only social interaction.

Camp boss Ebeid shook his tightly clenched fist at Toby, "I can't trust you people. Whether it's weapons or words, your intent is always the same. You are all the same."

"Of course you can't trust me!" Toby raised his volume to match that of the camp boss, and felt the grip on his arms intensify dramatically, "I can't trust you either, we both know that. Which shapes how we have to do things."

Having made his point, Toby knew it was time to take a breath and lower his volume, "But you can trust me more than most, after all, I came to you." Pause. "Has that ever happened before?"

The leader held Toby's gaze in silence.

"Why else would I take such a risk?" He paused again, allowing a little more of the tension to subside before adding, "I'm trying to do something that's never been done before." Which was true enough.

The boss sighed, and gestured for his men to release Toby, "Go on." He looked deeply into Toby's eyes. "What do you mean? Because to voluntarily do something so stupid, you must have thought about it very carefully. So how can this possibly work?"

Oh my God, did he just bite? Have I done it? Toby didn't dare assume it quite yet. "I interview you. You get to say whatever you want; you tell the world everything you want them to hear. I write your words, on my computer. And I take photos, with my camera." He carefully emphasised which camera he needed to use. "You can wear Keffiyeh to cover your faces if you like. But we need to show people that you're real human beings, with a valid point of view -one they've never considered before."

The boss was too busy listening to participate.

"Then I create the story. A big, honest story, and I give it to you, all of it. I also give you the press email addresses you'll need to send it to, and then you send it; not me." He paused to make that point settle. "You send what we both agreed on, knowing there's been no alterations done after the fact."

The boss couldn't take his eyes off Toby, so it was time to remove all remaining doubt. "You're an educated man," *Why did people never notice when they were being buttered up?*

"Think about public opinion in America during the Vietnam War. Think about the power of words in the western press." There was no way Ebeid would be able to dismiss that one.

"It's your story; I'm just the writer." Toby held the man's stare, but with no hint of his usual threatening demeanor.

The camp boss looked down at the floor in thought, as his guards looked on, seemingly as eager to hear the response as Toby. Ebeid nodded as he finally started his response, "My story. Without being twisted, and corrupted." He nodded again, studying Toby intently. Toby looked away uncomfortably, mimicking how the traumatised Danny would behave in his shoes.

"I will get your devices back, and then we will talk again. But do not assume that changes anything for you. Because whether you ever leave here? That is a different subject altogether."

Toby shrugged, "I hope to do my job well enough that I'll earn back my freedom." True again.

Ebeid narrowed his eyes, "We will see."

As the camp boss and his posse walked away, Toby looked back down at his neighbour's remains, then back up to see the other prisoners all looking back at him, most of whom had been close enough to hear the entire conversation.

Oh great.

59.

CORPORAL BARANWAL TOOK the SAT phone out of his bergen, powered it on, and waited for a signal to finally arrive. He typed an SMS for his CO's attention;

'Prisoner decap. Sgt Miller inserted. 18 hostiles. Op status?'

He then handed the phone over to Pole, signaled it was his own turn to sleep, gently leaned his rifle onto the dirt wall and shuffled into his corner of their tiny trench.

Pole stretched his neck left and right, then leaned back into his rifle's scope. He really needed to go, but the idea of crapping into a dog poo bag had a miraculous way of getting you properly constipated.

Back at the forward operating base, Lieutenant Linton dialed the number he'd been supplied with, and waited as it rung at the other end.

Mid-ring, a click was heard, "This is Hugo Chalmers."

"Morning Mister Chalmers, my name is Lieutenant Linton, I'm the CO of your man's rapid response unit. I was given this number to call regarding operational updates and questions."

Why are you bothering me? became, "How can I help you, Lieutenant?"

The Lieutenant didn't much like his tone, but shook it off, "Well, I have some updates for you, but I'd like to know our current status first."

"Nothing has changed yet," answered Chalmers, testily, "but I'm expecting ministerial approval very soon."

The Lieutenant shook his head, *Shit! That's what we're waiting for? 'Very soon', my arse.* The Lieutenant was already drifting away, considering alternative options.

"You said you had updates, Lieutenant. Share."

Linton bristled, trying to grasp the man's role; more specifically, if he held sufficient superior status to warrant the attitude. Unsure of anything, he had no option but to answer respectfully, "Yes, I have eyes on the camp. They made a new video this morning, but not the we-have-a-new-arrival kind of video. Your operative has also been confirmed as present within the camp, so my boys need to be cut loose, asap." The last part had been delivered with a comparably testy manner.

"I understand Lieutenant. But you will be informed through appropriate channels once there is any change worthy of sharing." And Chalmers hung up, thinking to himself, *why must everyone insist on babying Miller?*

The Lieutenant looked down at his phone's display in complete disbelief, then dialed a different number.

"Good morning, Lieutenant," answered Warrant Officer McCord.

"Morning, McCord. Look, I just called the number we were given regarding operational planning for this little party we're having over here."

"Yes?" McCord grinned at Linton's terminology.

"And we need a new point of contact, right now. Because whoever that was, they're not looking out for their operative, or my lads. When I asked if he'd got any updates, I was told he's waiting on ministerial approval, given some chain of command crap, and hung up on!" The lieutenant made no effort to hide the irritation in his voice.

"I understand, Lieutenant." McCord was already shaking his head in disgust, none of this should have started without all relevant approvals in place. Cock-ups like this were dangerous and not only was one of his squadrons there, but Sergeant Miller too; a real blast from the past.

"And I need it yesterday, Jim." Linton's volume had ramped up unintentionally.

"Aye, I'm on it."

Debbie's phone beeped twice rapidly, then again, signaling an internal call. She looked down to figure out which extension was calling her. "Yes Lyds, what's up?"

"Ma'am, I just had a call patched through to me, it's an Army Warrant Officer. Says he needs to talk to you urgently?"

Debbie could see no reason for such a senior Army NCO to be calling for her. Sergeant Miller was the first soldier she'd encountered in…

Then it came to her, "Oh, put them through Lydia."

"Yes Ma'am."

The phone's white noise altered slightly, implying she was already through, "This is Debbie Peters."

"Hello there, my name is Jim McCord, I'm a Warrant Officer with the rapid response lads who've been assigned to help Sergeant Toby Miller. An operation I understand you're part of."

"I am, Mister McCord, but in a support role. My department is not very hands on." Debbie's face was contorted in confusion as she awaited his response. "That would fall under the responsibility of Hugo Chalmers, whose information I can give you. Just one second." She started searching for the man's info.

"No, no. I'm calling you to replace Chalmers, Miss, Mrs., or Ms. Peters. Which is best?"

"Anything but Mrs. Just call me Debbie." Her confusion was still apparent.

"Okay then, Debbie it is. Look Debbie, we're an elite regiment, meaning that everything we do is pretty important, it's always rather dangerous, and it's usually quite time sensitive. So, we cannot be stuck with a contact who's happily scratching his arse -while my lads are baking in the hot Syrian sun. Especially not when their hands are tied behind their backs. No offence meant."

The man had elongated the word 'arse' in a manner unique to the northern city of Glasgow, people who weren't known for mincing their words. Debbie didn't want to come across like some petty jobsworth, but equally, she couldn't simply step into Chalmers' operational role -not without some much higher approval.

"If you're worrying about the Headmaster, Debbie -don't," added McCord, "he'll have approved it before you even leave for the night." McCord then chuckled audibly, "That's of course, if… you get to leave tonight."

60.

DANNY SAT ON top of his filthy mattress, squished tightly into the corner of his cell, hugging onto his folded knees. He'd pulled the barred door closed behind him but made sure not to pull hard enough to latch the lock.

After being given a couple of days to acclimatise, the prisoners were all given rotating waves of freedom. Whenever it was their allocated part of the day, they were permitted to come and go between their cells, the exercise area, and the toilets. Danny had only left his cell door on the latch in case need arose for the latter.

After what he'd just witnessed, an unwelcome wave of diarrhea would be the only thing that could lure him from his cell, and with the way he felt, it was a real possibility.

He rubbed at his forehead, trying to obscure his eyes with his hands, hoping to cover up the huge wave of emotion the execution had triggered. He'd seen them before, on the news. He'd even run through the latest batch of executions as professional research before flying out, but they hadn't prepared him for this.

Watching one of those events in a space where you felt safe and relaxed was all out of context.

He saw it in his friends back home who were always so quick to pass judgement on events in the news, and they all felt especially empowered to do so in his presence, because to them, he was their very own fully immersed source. Merely knowing him elevated them, and the validity of their opinion. Seemingly.

But in reality, they were all clueless, some of them seemed barely able to differentiate real news events from carefully crafted TV drama.

In contrast, he saw those news stories up close; he absorbed the heat as he struggled with the sweat, sand, and dirt. He smelled the gunpowder, diesel fumes, rocket fuel, decaying food, animal carcasses, and the overflowing sewage that spewed from damaged infrastructure. He also listened to the agonised wails of both the mortally injured and those who'd witnessed family loss. He found it depressing that he'd even learned how to instantly tell those two sounds apart.

Now he'd watched a fellow professional journalist's barbaric execution, and even he hadn't been prepared for the reality of it. Up until now he'd been as disconnected as his naive friends back home, and he couldn't understand why.

Back home, they all witnessed suffering through a screen, the noise came from the direction of the device's speaker, the images came from that screen positioned right in front of their faces. Even if someone charged the cameraman, and an unexpected face suddenly dominated the screen, it was as meaningless as a movie or a video game.

But in person... Danny shook his head at the memories. In person, those people who ran at the camera in desperation, were on you in an instant. There was no power button, no detachment, and the sounds came at you from every direction, constantly and unpredictably. Explosions, screams, small-arms fire; making you duck, run, or panic. The people -they came at you from the side and from behind, they touched you and screamed at you, sending your blood pressure through the roof. They'd grab at you, beg you, claw at you, and often they'd hurt you too. It was all quite unintentional and only done in the heat of the moment, but you'd leave with scratches and bruises, and that was just on the outside.

He shook with emotion as he thought back; you'd finally be sitting in a car leaving the worst of the mayhem behind you, only to find their blood had stained your clothes and the smell of their sweat had covered you. And he'd coped with all of it, he'd always shown them compassion, he'd shared what little he had to offer them, but he'd coped.

So why hadn't he been better equipped for this? The tears flowed quickly enough that they ran through his fingers; some dripped off his knuckles, some were absorbed by the cuffs off his overalls.

This was the worst point since his arrival. Bullshit; this was the worst point of his whole life, the lowest of the low. His body lurched as he caved under the emotional onslaught. The only thing worse would have been if it were his turn; but that was wrong too, because it implied doubt. There was no 'if' at play, only 'when' it was going to be his turn.

But to know when that would happen, he needed some understanding of why it had been that bloke's turn. What dictated order in this wretched place? The man's beard was Danny's first thought, how long had his beard been? Facial hair was the new measure, it was the camp's version of carbon dating, or rings within a tree trunk. Danny tried so hard to think back, but he could only remember seeing the man once before, and the man's beard? It had been quite long, maybe? Although not much longer than Yannick's. He didn't even know.

Danny winced, wiped the newest wave of tears from his face and squeezed his head between his hands as hard as he could. Maybe some outside pain would beat whatever was going on inside. He squeezed his skull harder, and harder.

Does that mean Yannick is next? Is that how this works? He couldn't imagine coping without his one and only friend, the mere thought made him start shaking uncontrollably. Who had a longer beard? No. Who had the longest?

Danny shook his head angrily, utterly disappointed in his useless powers of observation, he needed to rank the beards in order of length. He needed some idea of order, of schedule. But to do that, he'd need to leave his cell. Danny started rocking himself back and forth, his hands still squeezing his forehead with all his strength.

Inevitably his mind came back to what he'd been trying to suppress; when would it be him who was shoved to his knees in the dirt, and then…

Danny started to sob. Not silent crying, but full-on, violent sobbing, complete with unflattering grunting and snorting noises. It was against his will, but why care? Sure, he'd look weak in front of the other prisoners, but they'd be dead soon enough too, and his shame would die with them.

All gone, no shame.

Eventually he'd have a long beard, and by that point he'd probably be resigned to his fate too, just like they already were, and he'd be the one pitying the pathetic new guy sobbing alone in his cell. That was surely the cycle.

A gentle noise caught his attention; he peered through the tiny gap in his hands, seeing the real world's newest prisoner standing outside his cell door.

"Sorry, mate," Toby offered.

What else could he even say?

Danny kept his knees in tight and his face fully covered. What was this guy's deal? Why wasn't he sobbing in the privacy of his own cell? It didn't make sense, but fuck him, it didn't matter. He was too new to know anything. Danny would keep his head buried. The guy would have to leave in the end.

Oh my God. Danny Ellington was right on the edge. Toby had seen it before; the stress was just too much for him to take. Hopelessness had finally suffocated hope, so what could Toby possibly say to the poor, defeated man?

Toby went to walk away, feeling temporarily defeated, and then it hit him. He turned back and looked back at Danny, "Antonella says…" but he'd started talking too quickly and needed a moment to remember the Italian phrase he'd only heard the once.

And then it came to him, "Baci e abracci." Toby smiled, partly out of relief at having miraculously remembered the alien words.

Danny's hands dropped away from his face; he looked up to see the new guy smiling, genuinely and warmly smiling. *Baci e abracci?* The words took him back and his head suddenly cleared. Stunned, he was able to finally let go of his forehead, "You know Antonella?"

Then other thoughts started whirling around inside his head. Why would she have a stranger say that? And why here? When did she tell the stranger to say that? Danny's eyes flitted from side to side, trying to figure out what the hell was going on.

Toby had underestimated the impact of Kay Catso's words, and of Danny's current state. With his hands finally off his face, Toby could see dark red marks on Danny's forehead, his eyes were red raw, his lower sleeves soaked through. The man was in a bad place. Toby lowered himself to Danny's level, the way you'd lower yourself to appear less threatening to a nervous dog. He stayed outside the unlocked cell and made a point of keeping his hands off Danny's bars.

"Please don't lose hope, Danny." Toby lowered his voice to a whisper, "I promise you; things will get better."

Danny's bloodshot eyes stared back at Toby; his face expressionless.

"Just between you and me though, okay?" Toby smiled a supportive, encouraging smile. Danny nodded his confused response, then Toby raised his index finger and placed it in front of his lips, "Shhh." Then smiled again and left Danny looking a little more confused, but a hell of a lot less traumatised.

Toby paced the exercise yard, waiting for the camp boss to return.

Everything was taking too long: the meetings in the UK had been drawn out and useless, the training was a waste of valuable time, getting here was too slow, and getting kidnapped wasn't much better. Now it was all on him, and he was still operating too damn slow.

He should have already been primed for action, standing in the same exact spot, but with the modified camera in his hands. If he'd done his job properly, he'd be turning on that camera, taking some pictures of the main man, acting it up with them and encouraging their macho rebellious poses. Then he'd turn the camera's on/off switch that last quarter-turn, triggering the display lights for the camera's controls, and simultaneously activating the freshly inserted GPS distress signal.

But he'd failed at everything. He still had no camera, the camp boss had buggered off to somewhere unknown, and his new neighbour was dead.

Toby paced in a more and more regimental manner, and quite unintentionally the horribly intimating glare returned. He looked up to see one of the camp guards looking back at him, and only when the man looked concerned, did Toby realise what he must have been doing.

Toby averted his eyes as fast as possible. It was always hard to hide who you were inside, but sometimes, it was close to impossible. Now what?

Toby strode over to the guard, "Where's the boss?"

The young guard took a step back then yelled at Toby. Toby worked hard to slump, to cower, "When will I talk to the boss again?"

Unintelligible yelling was once again the response, then suddenly Toby took another blow to the back of his head and was grabbed from both sides. He was furious at himself; he'd just let his emotions get a hold of him. Having recognised it so quickly, he made no effort to put up a fight as they dragged him back to his cell.

Lance Corporal Pole leant his rifle on the wall of the trench and typed an update using the SAT phone's SMS feature; 'Miller just beaten. Group leader departed camp +2 guard escort.'

He sighed quietly, put the phone back down on his pack and stretched his neck thoroughly before leaning his head back into his rifle's sights.

Debbie's desk phone rang, she snatched at it without even looking, "Debbie Peters."

"It's your new friend Jim McCord here, Debbie. How are you?"

In spite of the situation, she couldn't help but chuckle, "I'm very good Warrant Officer McCord, I think I've got a newfound appreciation for how good I have it."

"Ay? Well, that's good to hear lass, coz you do, in that nice clean office over there. So anyway, in the interests of inter-departmental relationships, I have an update for you."

Debbie was still smiling, "Go ahead."

"Well, our mutual friend, Sergeant Toby Miller, just took a good beating inside the prisoner camp. And personally, I'm expecting him to signal for the cavalry, pretty damn soon."

Debbie slumped. She still didn't have the news he wanted.

But before she could formulate her response, Jim was going again, "I'll let you in on a secret, Debbie. My lads are not very good at sitting back and watching somebody take a beating. They're a feisty bunch, much better at doing than watching. So, they'll be getting all cranky, if you know what I mean."

"I do, Jim," she sighed, loud enough for him to hear.

"Oh, I notice it's Jim now, rather than Warrant Officer McCord. I don't know how I should take that." Debbie started laughing, just as Jim added, "Doctors pull that shite just before telling you you've got cancer."

Another sigh; she couldn't help but admire what a good job he was doing of cornering her, and so charmingly too. "It's not that, Jim, in fact I just received approval for electronic blocking, which means Toby's face won't appear on the next Zarqawi 'abdi prisoner broadcast."

"Well that's grand, I cannot lie. But have we been let off this damn leash yet, Debbie?"

"I'll beg them again, Jim, and just for the record, that will be my fourth time since our last conversation. They'll stop answering my calls if I'm not careful."

"You do that, Debbie, I appreciate it. And if you get any backlash, tell them Jim McCord says these relationships work both ways. Right now, we need them to do their part, but usually their need for us is far greater. So, don't be shy lass, you remind them of that, coz they know exactly who I am. Okay?"

"Understood, Jim."

Toby had been wrong about one thing. While everything had taken too long from the one perspective, it had been too rushed from another.

If he'd have arrived quicker, then his neighbour might not be getting buried right now, that couldn't be argued. But the flip side was the speed at which their plan had been shaped.

While brainstorming at GCHQ, they'd all been working on the theory that his rapid response team would consist of soldiers, or Royal Marines, from British Forces that happened to be already on the ground. Normal tactics would be to observe the camp from a safe distance, either by tapping into satellite imagery, or by using overhead drones. But neither of those information gathering techniques could guarantee that Toby was where they expected him to be. Hence the need for him to carry a camera that had been modified to send out a GPS signal.

But he wasn't being supported by the closest in-country team. Instead, he was being backed up by the most feared, secretive, and respected regiment in the British Armed Forces, some would say the entire world. The Regiment was the wise old Granddaddy of all 'special' forces.

The point was that the Regiment did things in their own way, and their training was to such a high standard that they took risks viewed as unacceptable by everyone else. Risks like digging in on the doorstep of their targets and watching them from right under their own noses.

The problem was, he didn't know this for sure; he'd heard the stories, everyone in the British Army had heard the stories, and if those stories were true -then they wouldn't necessarily be using drones or satellite images, and he might not need a modified camera to summon help. Any improvised SOS signal would work, whether day or night. Which changed the whole dynamic.

    If… the stories were true.

    And if… the camp was under current observation.

61.

A NOISE STIRRED Toby from his cat nap. What time was it? It was dark, so was it the end of day two in captivity? Or the start of day three?

There was the noise again, a gun shot? His grogginess burned off as the adrenaline started to pump; Toby sprung to his feet. He walked to his cell door and listened more intently.

Another one went off, but louder, dispelling any remaining doubt.

Toby jumped the couple of steps over to his mattress, hauled it to the side and dug frantically at the dirt in the corner. He pulled the stiletto knife from the hole, and the metal gas cylinder. He pocketed the cylinder as he stood up and leaped back over to his cell door.

Another shot, even louder, followed by several in quick succession; the second batch had been much closer.

Toby fed his right arm through the bars of his cell and carefully slide the blade of the knife between the metal door frame and the door's sprung latch, prying back and forth searching for the right spot. Back and forth, back, and forth.

Ting.

He pushed on the door and it moved, so he cautiously stepped outside with his eyes scanning every direction, then gently closed the door behind him. Toby took the gas cylinder from his left pocket, reversed the knife to face blade-down within his right hand,

and started slowly heading away from his cell. He crept past his executed neighbour's empty cell, then on to the next one, noticing another prisoner looking up at him wide-eyed. "Pick your mattress up, and hide behind it, up against the wall." Toby used no more volume than absolutely necessary.

The prisoner was mute in response; whether it was distrust in the newest prisoner for promising to tell Zarqawi 'abdi's story, or I-just-woke-up confusion, was impossible to tell. "Now!" Toby snarled as he continued toward the next cell.

"You too, mattress up, hide behind it, put your back to the wall." The new prisoner translated Toby's orders for his neighbouring cell; and a wave of noise started to spread from cell to cell, each prisoner getting busy and protecting themselves with their mattresses.

The increase in sound made it harder for Toby to differentiate the friendlies from other noises, which were now coming at him from every direction. But something ahead sounded different; within the panicked undertone, he could make out an angry voice.

Toby closed his eyes for a second, trying to home in on specific words. Other than the emotion within the voice, nothing was recognisable, but that in itself was enough information. Toby reopened his eyes and pulled the gas cylinder from his pocket.

He turned to the closest cell's door and slid the cylinder's metal neck into the small gap between the heavy metal door and frame, then flicked his wrist backwards, snapping the cylinder's neck open. Toby took aim at the angry voice and launched the cylinder into the darkness, then quickly pulled his overalls up to cover his mouth and nose.

Gas gas gas.

By now shots were ringing out in every direction. Toby retreated from the gas, already knowing that a face-full of the stuff was about as desirable as detainee survival training.

As Toby neared his own cell, he heard moaning and fast approaching footsteps coming from the direction where he'd just launched the cannister; he backed up flat against the wall with his eyes narrowed, to minimise the effects of the noxious fumes that would inevitably be drifting back toward him.

Prisoners everywhere were coughing, groaning, and crying out, but he knew their suffering would pass. He wasn't immune to the effects himself, just aware of what it entailed and more willing to suck it up than the next man. And suddenly, the next man came blundering right into him, eyes closed, body slamming him hard.

It was dark in the cell block and Toby's eyes were mere slits. But in the gloom, the shape of the person looked reminiscent of the young guard who'd beaten him earlier.

But who it was, was irrelevant. Toby punched the back of the guard's head with the knuckles of his knife wielding hand, heard the man's rifle hit the floor, then spun the same hand upwards ninety degrees, pressing his knife's blade into the skin of the man's throat. Then Toby grabbed the man's left hand and pulled his index finger up hard behind his back, restraining him.

Toby had barely got control of the guard when the exterior doors, just a few feet from his own cell, swung open and two black-clad men strode purposefully through the opening. Both held their weapons at eye level, with ungainly night sights covering their eyes. And in an instant, their aim settled on Toby.

"I'm a prisoner, don't shoot," Toby yelled, as a single shot fired.

The man in Toby's arms suddenly doubled in weight. Toby slowly moved his arms away from the guard, who slumped to the floor, as Toby continued to carefully move his arms upward, in the universal gesture of surrender.

62.

ONE OF THE men frisked Toby's overalls, pulled the knife out from his tight grip and then continued on into the gloom, satisfied that Toby was a harmless prisoner. The man's partner followed him, just a step behind, but it wasn't long until they were both coughing uncontrollably and retreating past Toby, back into the fresh night-time air.

Toby still had no idea what was going on, therefore had no intention of following their direction.

In his younger years, he'd made a couple of spur-of-the-moment decisions like that, ones which leaned toward best-case scenario, only to find it was the wrong call. But with so much experience in the rear-view mirror, Toby was now more inclined to start by preparing for the worst.

He held his overalls over his mouth, then knelt down to the ground and went through the dead guard's pockets, finding a large set of keys. Toby took the keys and the man's keffiyeh, wrapping it around as much of his head as possible and then headed back into the gloom. He stood at the first cell and slid a key into the lock; it fitted, but wouldn't turn. Toby didn't have time to go through this for every cell, so he looked over at the prisoner, who was still hiding behind his mattress as previously instructed.

Toby threw the keys at the back wall. "Let yourself out, then give the keys to your neighbour, do you understand me?"

The man grunted his response.

"No! Bloody promise me, that you're gonna help the others out of their cells." Toby stood, waiting for a response.

"I do, I promise you. I'll make sure we all get out." There was a pause, "But where are you going?"

Mind your business.

Toby continued into the darkness and called out to the other prisoners in a louder voice, "You'll all be fine, it's just CS gas; like tear gas, it'll pass. Your cell keys will be handed to you, one at a time. Just get outside as soon as you can. These men don't seem to wanna shoot prisoners. And don't put water on your face."

He reiterated that point even louder, "Do not put water on your face, you'll only make it worse. The only thing that helps is time and fresh air. So, head straight outside. Right?"

Multiple moans and groans came back at him.

Whoever had stormed the place hadn't identified themselves, not even to Toby, which meant whatever had just happened was outside of Toby's plan. Therefore, he still had work to do, and having the other prisoners continually file out into the night would distract and occupy these armed newcomers, giving him the time he needed.

He peered around the next corner, but the damn gas was making his eyes stream and the sting was agonising, even though he'd left barely a slit exposed through his Keffiyeh.

Toby took a long slow breath through the material of the scarf, and drove on, struggling to ignore the incapacitating effects of the CS gas.

Having found no guard room in the prisoner's block he paused at the exit door, scanning the courtyard in the dark. The new arrivals were all uniformed, but only in that they were wearing the same clothes as each other, it certainly wasn't any army uniform Toby had seen before.

But every one of those new arrivals was now tied up in dealing with the continual stream of exiting prisoners, and as they came out, they were being searched individually, then grouped and guarded.

Toby waited until the newcomers on guard were all facing away from him and sprinted from the prisoner block to the building he'd seen the camp boss head toward earlier in the day.

He reached the doorway and came to a hard stop. Squeezing his body into the shadow of the building, he leaned back out slightly to confirm he'd attracted no attention, and then turned on the door handle, which opened without resistance. It didn't surprise him, after all why would the guards bother locking their own door? Until a moment ago, the prisoners were all safely contained in their cells.

Toby opened the door, but only wide enough for his torso, then slipped in through the small gap and gently pressed it closed again.

Bingo, he'd found the spot. There were ammunition boxes, crates of bottled water, and stolen nick-nacks from prisoners, which had to include his stuff too. Toby scanned the room, knowing time was running out, then saw his bag. He lunged at the bag and yanked at the zip. He pulled the big camera body out and kissed it, "You beauty," then the light level inside the room increased. Toby turned to see one of the uniformed intruders standing in the open doorway, framed by the flood lights which had been turned on outside.

"Fuckers stole my camera, this thing's worth a fortune," offered Toby, then "I don't wanna forget this shit. Say cheese." As he held the camera up to his eye and framed a shot of the incomer.

"Gimme the damn camera you clown and get over there with the others."

But Toby had already turned the button past the on position, illuminating the display lights, and the camera's additional features.

63.

BARANWAL HELD THE SAT phone to his ear. The whole place was in chaos with noise filling the air, allowing him to take a break from being a church mouse. "The camp has just been stormed, not locals, not army; unknowns. They went in hot; prisoners are being pulled out and herded. Multiple casualties, but only terrorists down so far."

"Received," responded his CO, "any sighting of the operative?"

Baranwal grinned, "Someone wearing orange overalls just sprinted from the prisoner block to the control building, but he's being escorted back to the others right now."

"Hold." Baranwal was ordered.

"Correction," the CO's voice was suddenly energized. "The distress signal has been triggered. We're goin' in boys!"

"What are you grinning at?" a particularly large newcomer asked Toby, while everyone else continued coughing away the last effects of the CS gas residue.

"It's just a beautiful night, mate." But that wasn't really the truth; as beautiful as the night was, Toby's smile was merely a reaction at finally being allowed to be himself again. "Don't you think? I mean, I could murder a kebab. Oh no!" He put his hand over his mouth in shame, "Am I allowed to say that? Or is it inappropriate?"

The tall, uniformed guy shook his head at Toby, "Bloody shut it."

"You got a mobile phone I can borrow?" Toby wasn't done, whether the man liked it or not.

"What?" the man asked, amazed the idiot was still talking.

"A phone. Come on, think about it. We've not been able to use a phone since we were taken hostage, which for me has been two whole days, without a phone. And some of these poor buggers have been here for even longer than that, so I want a phone. We all want a phone. Have you got a phone?"

The disbelief was plain to see, "What is wrong with you, pal?"

"Please!" Toby grimaced playfully. "Sorry, I did mean to say 'please'. My Mum was always bollocking me for that when I was a little'un; 'You've got to say your please and thank yous'. No, wait, that wasn't it…"

He opened his mouth in a comically vacant manner, making an act of trying to recall the appropriate phrase, then launched straight back into it, "She used to say, 'Mind your P's and Q's'. Huh? Only now does that make sense!" His Mum really had always been riding him about his P's and Q's but that wasn't why Toby was putting on the show.

"What the hell, John? What is all this noise about?" another man strode towards Toby and his new friend. "Do your fuckin' job, John. Line 'em up and shut 'em up, that's all we need. You ain't gotta make friends with 'em." The new voice was clearly that of the leader. "So, who's making all the noise?"

But Toby had already said, "Who are you?" at the exact same time, so added "Jinx," to wind them up even more.

"What?" asked the new leader.

"See what I mean," added the tall, uniformed man, apparently named John.

"I said 'jinx' coz we both said the same thing at the same time." Toby smiled.

"No, we didn't. I said 'who's making all the..' Stop! It doesn't matter what I said, just shut the fuck up," said the new arrival.

"No. I think you're the one who needs to shut up, mate." Toby stood up slightly menacingly.

"Oh, I am gonna…" the man moved to take a step, then feeling a blade at his throat, stopped dead.

The tall uniform felt a gun barrel press into the back of his head and bit onto his bottom lip as he inhaled slowly, before carefully placing his arms out in front of him.

As he turned to the side, he could see all of his uniformed colleagues were in the same situation, but he'd never seen anything like it before. The people who'd snuck up so effectively wore the camo pattern unique to the British Army on their legs and torsos, yet wore masks and Keffiyehs to fully cover their heads and faces, and there were no insignia, name patches, or ranks to be seen anywhere.

Toby hadn't taken his eyes off the new leader, and now he repeated himself, with a much darker tone evident in his voice, "I asked you who you are."

"PK Corp. We're private contractors," replied the man, not daring to move too much.

"Oh, you boys are so very, very, out of your depth." Toby spoke slowly, "Weapons. On the ground. Now."

Five minutes before, the prisoners had been massed into a huddled group, seated on the dirt floor being lorded over by these private military contractors. Since then, the PMCs had been disarmed and were now seated in their own huddle on the dirt floor, being watched over by a couple of masked Regiment boys.

"Did you see that knife?" tall John whispered to his boss.

"Shut up." The PMC leader was self-consciously looking toward the man who'd wielded the knife.

"That was a Khukuri, a Gurkha knife," the tall man continued.

"Do all of these men look like Gurkhas to you?" The PMC boss was almost whispering.

"No, but?"

"You'll figure it out, John. Eventually." The boss angled his body away from his subordinate.

Lieutenant Linton finally found Toby in the darkness. "I understand you put on a good show there, Sar'nt Miller. Nice job, you helped things along nicely."

"Sir." Toby responded neutrally, "But we're missing at least two prisoners. Permission to take one of your men, Sir?"

The lieutenant whistled to draw in the closest member of his squad. "Baranwal," he spoke quietly, as none of these outsiders needed to know his squad member's names. "Watch Sar'nt Miller's back, please."

"Sir." Baranwal's response was as uniform as Toby's.

"Come on, mate." Toby picked up a rifle from the pile of PMC weapons, then gestured they were heading back to the prison block.

Toby entered the prison block, staring down the barrel of another man's weapon. He moved forward slowly, looking left, then right, but always down the sights of the weapon. His finger nestled on the trigger, so Toby worked to maintain his calmness -as he had no intention of adding an accidental discharge to his surprisingly clean military record.

The noise levels had already reduced back to one more comparable with a normal night in the camp, save for a few lowered voices here and there. One of those voices seemed to be coming from directly ahead. Toby gestured by cupping a hand by his ear, followed by an exaggerated point, indicating that Baranwal should focus on the same sound, the man nodded his understanding and they both continued toward it. The sound quickly became more distinct; they could both hear rapid breaths and a low, panicked voice.

Toby accelerated toward the noise which was coming from inside one of the cells, but in the darkness, he couldn't see anything. Toby gestured that Baranwal should keep watch, and then turned on his stolen rifle's fancy barrel-mounted light -pointing it toward the new noise.

"Please, no," begged Danny Ellington, who quickly shielded another prisoner with his own torso.

"Danny, it's me, Toby, the new bloke. We spoke yesterday, you remember?"

Danny exhaled in relief, then moved his body out of the way, exposing a different prisoner, one whose legs were covered in glistening blood.

"Field dressing!" Toby stepped back to Baranwal. The Gurkha had already pulled it from his pocket and was holding it out for Toby who snatched it off him before laying his rifle down on the floor. Baranwal instinctively took on the role of scanning their perimeter alone.

"Where's the wound?" Toby looked into the bearded man's eyes but he was patchy, going in and out of consciousness. "Hey." Toby gave the guy's face a brisk rub to snap him out of it. "My name's Toby." He rubbed at the guy's face harder. "Can you hear me?"

"He got shot, and it's my bloody fault." Danny was distraught.

"Danny." Toby stared into his eyes.

"Yeah?"

"Shut it. Okay?" Toby's stare held firm.

"Okay." Danny nodded obediently.

"What's your name, mate?" Toby rubbed at the guys face again, trying to stir him into responding as Baranwal continued scanning the immediate area with his own rifle mounted light.

"His name's Yannick," Danny replied for him, then snatched at his own mouth in shame.

"Danny." Toby stared at him again, "I think it's time you went outside," and again Toby sought confirmation, "Okay?"

"Yes, I'm sorry, it's just…" but Corporal Baranwal was already pulling Danny away.

"Okay, let's find this wound, shall we, Yannick?" and Toby set to scanning the blood covered area in the darkness.

"What's going on then, Miller?" asked the Lieutenant.

"Well, Danny Ellington, our secondary objective, panicked when it all kicked off. And instead of sheltering behind his mattress as ordered, he froze in the corner of his cell."

Toby noticed the young officer was looking at him with a confused expression, but carried on with his answer regardless, "When the other prisoner, Yannick, received the keys to open his own cell, he went straight into Ellington's cell next door to help him. But then Yannick took two stray rounds in the thigh. Both wounds are through and through, with no arterial damage. There's a reasonable amount of blood loss but if we can get him to a medic and get some fresh blood in him, he should make it, Sir."

Lieutenant Linton nodded sympathetically. "I meant what's going on, with all this?" The officer gestured at the group of PMCs huddled on the floor.

That was a valid question, and one Toby hadn't yet had time to consider. "Oh, I see." Toby needed a minute to think, so bought himself that time by asking the officer a question, "Where did they come from?"

"Came in from the Northeast but on their approach they walked straight past Peters and Llewellyn's trench, who called it in. That gave me time to mobilise the rest of the troop, which is lucky for you, as otherwise your response team would have just been the closest four guys."

Lord Duggan-Smythe. It was the only possible answer to the officer's previous question. Toby shook his head and ignored Linton's explanation, "Can I borrow your SAT phone, Sir?"

"Uh-huh." Linton nodded as he handed Toby the phone, "For?"

"I need to talk to my handler, to clarify something."

"Mmm." Linton shook his head from side to side. "Not Chalmers though, Miller. My men take on enough risk already, I will not further jeopardise them with a desk jockey back home who cannot, or will not, operate to the same level that we do. So, for the remainder of this operation, I've had all of our support duties switched over to a Debbie Peters. Do you know her?"

Toby had to put the unexpected information about Chalmers to the side, for now. "I do know her, Sir, but I've had no previous reason to memorise her number."

Linton activated the SAT phone's display, scrolled through some options, hit the dial button and handed the phone back to Toby, "That's her mobile."

The phone rang, and rang. And rang. Finally, Debbie's voice answered, although the grogginess made it clear she'd been fast asleep. "Yes," was all she could muster.

"Debbie. Ma'am." Toby didn't really know which version to use, "It's Toby Miller."

Debbie hauled herself up and leaned her back onto her bed's head-board. "Toby?" she answered, looking at the time on her alarm clock, feeling utterly disorientated.

Toby started pacing as he spoke, "I need to talk to Lord Rupert Duggan-Smythe, right now. And yes, I know it's the middle of the night."

Debbie took a breath, waiting for her brain to catch up, as things were moving a little too quickly for her current state. "Give me a few minutes Toby. I'll have him call you on this number as soon as I can get a hold of him. Be ready."

"Yes Ma'am."

Toby walked the camp, finally taking in the scene.

The place had been stormed in the middle of the night. Toby's choice would have been an hour before dawn, but that was just him. In this unexpected attack, the PMCs hadn't killed any prisoners, but that was the only praise they deserved.

They'd taken out every single Zarqawi 'abdi member in the camp. Not a soul had been wounded, every guard had been taken down with two or three clean torso shots, meaning these guys had made a tactical decision that they'd shoot to kill.

That only one man had been caught in the crossfire was an absolute miracle.

Toby was angry, and waiting for the big Rupert to call him back wasn't helping the emotion. On top of that, Charlie Duggan-Smythe was not in the camp. After spending a couple of days on site, Toby had already suspected that, but now, with all the prisoners free, any lingering doubt had been removed.

Another name which fell into the missing category was the camp boss. Also absent was the most vindictive of the guards, the long bearded one with gorgonzola breath who'd hidden his face in order to decapitate with anonymity.

Again, the only positive Toby could find was that nobody else had been killed or injured. Then the phone in his hand finally started to vibrate.

"Hello." Toby made a decision to not identify himself.

"Who am I speaking to?" asked a lady's voice, with a slightly pompous sounding undertone.

"You are speaking to the man on the ground, and I asked to speak to Lord Rupert Duggan-Smythe." Toby knew he was doing a piss-poor job of hiding his annoyance.

Lady Duggan-Smythe was not accustomed to being spoken to in such a manner. "And I demand to know who I am conversing with."

Toby shook his head; his irritation having moved up yet another notch. "You can demand all you want, lady. But I asked to talk to Lord Rupert and I don't have time to waste on this. So, put him on. Now." He growled.

Lady Duggan-Smythe was accustomed to people bowing to her title, something this rough character clearly was not about to do. That caused her a problem though, considering her new role was to absorb as much stress as possible for her husband.

So which route should she take? Because indignant, clearly wouldn't work with the man.

She paused, still trying to pick the best direction, finally settling on a more egalitarian approach for the man who'd already made his inflexibility apparent. "I would like to explain to you that Lord Rupert is still recovering from a heart attack, and my intentions are only to shield my husband from as much stress as I possibly can. So, is this call likely to cause my husband further stress?"

"It is." Toby took a breath, understanding the significance of her altered approach. "Unfortunately, yes."

"Then could we talk amongst ourselves first? My name is Lady Fiona Duggan-Smythe, but you can call me Fiona." She'd never offered that honour to a stranger before, and hopefully the ruffian would understand the significance of the gesture.

"Well Fiona, I'm a member of Her Majesty's Armed Forces and I am in the middle of an operation to recover your son, Charles."

Lady Fiona caught her breath and prepared herself for the worst. But instantly realised nothing could really prepare her for that, especially so soon after nearly losing Rupert.

"Our operation has just been sabotaged by the unexpected arrival of a group of private military contractors, and the reason I am still expecting to talk to Lord Rupert -is to ask if he is behind the arrival of these contractors."

"Let me hand you over to Rupert. One moment."

Oh my God, Toby rubbed at his face with his free hand.

"This is Lord Rupert Duggan-Smythe. I understand you won't identify yourself to my wife?"

You people really are experts at getting hung up on the wrong stuff. "My name is Toby Miller, Lord Rupert. I don't have time for the usual formalities, so I'll get to the point. Did you send in private military contractors to rescue your son, Charles?"

Silence.

Which was as good as a 'yes'.

Arrogant ass. His reticence only made it easier for Toby to get straight to it. "Well, my Lord," the lack of respect within the words was deafening, "Your amateurs just stormed the detainee camp where I'd been carefully inserted as an undercover prisoner."

Chalmers at GCHQ certainly hadn't shared that part of the plan with the Lord, who now gulped and felt the stress surging within.

"And they've killed every single one of the terrorists working within this camp. As a former…" again Toby accentuated the word 'former' to differentiate it from 'currently serving', "…military man, I'm sure you see where that leaves us. Zarqawi 'abdi have between one and three detention camps, and your son was not being held in this one."

Toby let the point settle. "But now, we have no way of discovering the other camp locations, as we have nobody left alive to question; courtesy of your PMCs." His anger flowed through the handset, up into space, and finally back down into the Lord's embarrassed ears.

"So, I have another question for you, my Lord. How did you know the location of this camp? Because nobody outside of our department was privy to that information."

Silence, once again.

"Fine, play it that way. But while I leave you to absorb the significance of that question, and to consider the huge investigation that will inevitably follow this bloody fiasco, I am going to request, very strongly," Toby growled again, "that you order these amateurs to leave this country. Right now."

"I understand Mister Miller. I'll set the wheels in motion as soon as we finish this call."

Finally, some cooperation. Then Toby came up with a trivial way in which he could use the private contractors to his advantage, "And they can undo some of the damage they've done here by escorting the freed prisoners to safety. And in one case, to some urgent bloody medical care."

"Again, consider it done Mister Miller." The Lord really hadn't intended to create such a mess. "Mister Miller?" Lord Rupert asked gingerly.

"Yes, Lord Rupert." The Lord seemed to have stepped off his high horse, so Toby reciprocated with a more respectful tone.

"Is my son still alive?" In the pause his breathing audibly faltered, "Do you think any hope remains?" It's all the Lord cared about; official enquiries be damned. He'd take whatever punishment was due, he just wanted poor young Charlie back.

The words were very effective at reminding Toby of what was still at stake for the big Rupert. "I don't know, Lord Rupert, but if he is, then his only chance lies with us. And we need to be left alone to do our bloody jobs." Then Toby hung up without a farewell and growled one more time -at nobody in particular.

64.

TOBY STRODE BACK to the guard hut, dug around for long enough to find Charlie Duggan Smythe's camera plus his own GCHQ issued camera, which was sitting exactly where he'd left it after triggering its inbuilt distress beacon.

He checked Charlie's camera over, found some damage to the rear of the body but also found that it still had a healthy two bars of battery life left. He popped open the door of the memory card storage area, ejected the first card and then turned the camera back on to confirm the remaining memory card was empty.

Toby then pocketed the removed memory card, picked up both cameras and strode back toward the assembled crowd.

"Sergeant?" Lieutenant Linton addressed him as he strode by.

"One moment, Sir." Toby firmly flashed a flat palm at him and continued on toward Danny Ellington, kneeling down to his level. "Danny."

Danny looked up, still with that traumatised look about him which was part of why Toby had sought him out. "Was your name Toby?" he asked meekly.

"You got it, mate. How are you doing?" Toby smiled that kind smile again.

"I can only think about Yannick, he was protecting me you see."

Toby wiggled his finger to stop him talking. "Danny, he's going to be okay, he'll have a couple of cool scars." It was too early to know that for sure but Toby's gut told him it was the greater likelihood, and he needed to draw Danny back out for his own good. "I need you to do something for me, Danny. Can you do something for me?"

"Um." Danny wasn't sure, just the idea of doing something was overwhelming.

Toby handed him Charlie's big heavy camera and instantly noticed a change in his manner.

"We don't have long, Danny, and we all have a hell of a lot to do, so I need you to be the fastest and most efficient journalist you've ever been." He flashed Danny his best smile again. "This lot," Toby gestured toward the contractors, "Were brought in by a private party, to find and free Charlie."

Danny looked over at the uniformed group of private military contractors.

"And I think we can both see what kind of a job they've done."

There was a new focus evident in Danny's eyes.

"You're free, Danny. You probably haven't had time to absorb that quite yet, but time is pressing. And as you're no longer a hostage, it means you are a journalist again. Personally, I still need to find Charlie, and I won't leave this place until I've done that." Toby stared at Danny with a crazy intensity.

"No, you won't." Somehow Danny just knew.

"So, I need everything you can tell us about the day when you and Charlie got taken. Everything," he reiterated.

"Okay." Danny nodded, visibly energised by his new task.

"And I need you to write the story. You've got a big heavy camera now, and a first-hand account. Nobody's ever had this kind of inside experience to draw on." Toby gestured to the camp around them.

Danny's neurons were firing and he could see Toby was right, this was the professional opportunity of a lifetime.

"With just one condition mate." Toby's eyes were still locked on Danny's. "Okay?"

Danny's suspicion at traps and conditions was obviously returning, which Toby found uplifting.

Toby leaned in closer, "You keep my name out of it. You don't take my photo, or any of my guys. We only get to help people," Toby gestured at his surroundings, "if we maintain our anonymity." He shrugged in a matey kind of way.

Danny nodded.

"Is that fair, Danny?"

"Fair? Yeah, very." Danny nodded confidently as he started to raise himself from the floor.

"It's about time you caught me up, isn't it, Sergeant?" Lieutenant Linton said with a sly grin.

"Yes, Sir. Apologies, Sir." Toby nodded respectfully.

"Just pulling your leg, Miller. Although, having seen you in action, I can see what your old mentor Jim McCord has been talking about." The Lieutenant's smile was sincere. "Do you mind if I call you Staffy? I'm told that's how everyone else knows you."

"Yes, Sir. That's fine, Sir. I don't even know where the stupid name came from." Toby rolled his eyes.

"I'm told it's a comparison to a Staffordshire Bull Terrier." The Lieutenant grinned cheekily.

Toby groaned in embarrassment.

"So? Staffy?"

"Yes, Sir." Toby nodded toward a distant area, implying they should put more distance between themselves and the contractors. The Lieutenant seized the opportunity to turn his back on the PMCs and pull down his shemagh to better breathe the cool night-time air.

"This outfit, I guess they should come first. The only explanation for their presence here was the Lord himself. You know who I mean?"

"Oh, I know, Sergeant."

"It fits that only he'd hire them to get his kid back. No surprise there, but the problem is, there's no reason he should have known where this camp was," Toby gestured at their surroundings. "That is a surprise, which means somebody in-house, over shared."

"Oh, oh dear," the CO's expression soured.

"So, I called him." There was no way to pretty up that information.

"You did what?" The Lieutenant looked like he was struggling to suppress laughter, "You called Lord Duggan-Smythe at…?" the officer looked at his watch.

"Yes, Sir. I did, and I called him out on it too."

Staffordshire Bull Terrier, Linton thought as he shook his head in admiration.

"The summary is that I told him we want these men gone, and not right now, but an hour ago." Another SAT phone started ringing in the middle of the huddled PMCs.

"I also used the opportunity to ask for these freed hostages to be escorted to safety. You know, so we don't have to call in support and lose precious time baby-sitting them while we wait for that support to roll in."

The Lieutenant shook his head at the audacity of his new Sergeant.

"Which included getting some urgent medical help for the French aid worker."

"Okay, Staffy," Linton nodded, grinning.

"So, all that crap is sorted. But," Toby shrugged, "We still need to have a discussion about our primary objective."

65.

MAAH MAHMOUD WAS tired. The journey between the two detention camps was becoming very repetitive, but none of the younger members could be trusted to do anything, not without constant supervision. This included Pashtana, especially Pashtana. Maah looked at his passenger, who was asleep, yet again.

"Wake up, you lazy dog." He elbowed Pashtana's arm hard enough to make the pickup truck weave momentarily until his hand returned to steady the wheel.

Talking to them in their own tongue. The shame of it. Maah would never learn their language -out of pride. They should learn his, if they could manage it. It would be hard for them, and westerners avoided anything hard. They used to be formidable, but they were all too lazy, entitled, and weak to complete anything difficult these days.

But Pashtana's ability to talk their language? It was even worse than the matter of national pride, it was about risk, because what if they got into his weak brain with their slippery words? That's what really angered him every time the prisoners spoke English with Pashtana.

The boy's head was soft; he couldn't be counted on, and Maah hated that he couldn't understand them when they conversed with the foolish boy. It infuriated him that the only logical solution was for him to learn their despised tongue.

Maah opened and closed his tired eyes, trying to blink away the dryness. The sun would be up soon, just in time for him to sleep. Even that concerned him, because with Mister Ebeid in the southern prison camp, Maah was the only one competent enough to run this camp but he desperately needed some sleep in order to do it.

As the camp's silhouette started to appear out of the darkness, Maah could only feel relief. He was exhausted, but sleep would come soon enough. So, who was on guard tonight?

Maah turned as he drove by the outermost man in the darkness, unsure of who it was. And just the one guard? How many times did he have to shout at these incompetents?

He parked the truck by the other camp vehicles and looked back over at Pashtana, but instead of rousing him to get out, he chuckled. *Let the fool stay in the truck, when the sun comes up, that'll wake him; if it doesn't bake him first.*

Maah opened his door quietly, stepped out and closed it with even more care. Then he felt something press into his Adam's apple, something hard and sharp, which didn't make sense…

He squinted in confusion. He just needed a moment to process what was going on.

Maah looked left, then right, and saw a man striding toward him, fast. He watched in disbelief as the man's Keffiyeh was removed to reveal the face of the newest prisoner, whose nostrils flared just before punching him hard enough that pulses of light came and went in Maah's vision.

"I hope you know what you're doing, Miller. I don't want to see this in the news when we get home." Lieutenant Linton looked genuinely concerned.

"It's fine Sir, I won't cause us any problems. You have my word."

Miller's words were surprisingly reassuring, so Linton accepted them and moved on, "So who would you like? As help?"

"Pole. I think I need to make things up with him. I feel bad, you know -about his cheek," Toby grinned. "And your Gurkha, if I can."

Linton nodded his understanding, "Corporal Baranwal."

"Yes Sir, Corp Baranwal, please."

Maah slowly came to, only to find himself seated, and shirtless. He looked down in surprise to find he had no trousers either, although at least they'd left him in his underwear. Next, he looked up in panic, to see a smaller than average man standing directly in front of him.

The man wore an army uniform, but it bore no markings, and he'd seen enough western uniforms to know where to look for markings on these people. The man held a long, curved blade of a type he'd never seen before, but he also wore a rubber mask with big lenses, which made him look like an insect.

Maah caught his breath involuntarily, but he felt no shame, the sight was a little disturbing.

Then Maah composed himself and disguised his real emotion by yelling at them, insisting that whoever was behind this must tell him what was going on. But nobody responded.

After a long pause, the bug-eyed man walked toward Maah and held a map out in front of his face.

"This camp." The man's long knife blade was used to point out their current location on the map.

"Other camp?" the bug-eyed man asked, removing the blade.

Maah couldn't converse with anybody in English, and even if he could, he wouldn't, out of principal. But the bug-eyed man's meaning was obvious -having taken this camp in his absence, now they wanted to destroy the southern camp too.

The idea that he would help them wasn't even worthy of response, so he shook his head slowly with a look of defiance on his face, then settled back into his chair.

"Boss!" the bug-eyed man yelled, with unexpected volume.

Maah's eyes opened wide, wondering what was to come next. Eventually another man came into view, opened the cell door, and entered the room.

Maah immediately recognised the newest prisoner. But he carried himself differently from before, very differently. He had a sense of purpose, he radiated confidence. Anger too. Maah instinctively looked away.

The newest prisoner didn't speak, instead he prodded at Maah's unclothed inner thigh. Maah was furious and started yelling, "How dare you touch me, you deviant," in his mother tongue. Then he looked down to where he'd been touched and noticed two puncture marks about two centimetres apart. Maah's eyes bulged open wide.

He looked back up to see the newest prisoner now held a red and white box, barely an inch in front of Maah's face. It was so close it was hard for him to focus, but one word stood out, 'Antivenom'. The angry prisoner tapped at his watch and left the way he'd come.

Maah tried to control his breathing but struggled. He closed his eyes, thought of the cause, of what he stood for, and his breathing started to calm again, although he couldn't help but wonder exactly which species of local snake they'd manipulated into biting him. This was bad, he'd seen what they could do to a man.

Pashtana sat staring at his naked thigh in disbelief. This isn't how these people did things, they were bound by rules which made them weaker. That's what he'd been told every day since he'd come into the Zarqawi 'abdi group.

He'd been told that westerners couldn't do things like this; that it was completely forbidden for them.

Yet there were the bite marks. And he'd just seen the antivenom.

As he tried understanding the implications of what was going on, his breathing quickened. They wanted to know where the other camp was, but Mister Ebeid was in that camp, and Ebeid would do much worse to him than these westerners ever could.

But the marks on his thigh gave him doubts; Pashtana started to shimmy in his chair.

He looked up, wanting to get a read on the man standing in front of him, but the man wore a black rubber mask with weird goggles built into the face. It was like some horrible childhood tale designed to make you behave, or else.

Pashtana looked away again, still squirming uncomfortably in his chair.

It's a trick!

Maah laughed out loud the moment he realised it. They had him fooled for a while, but they really couldn't do this, which only left the possibility of trickery. No more though, because now he knew.

"Pashtana!" he bellowed as loudly as he could. He needed to warn Pashtana in the safety of his own language, "It is a lie, they are liars. All westerners are liars, don't let them fool you."

He waited for a response, then switched his approach to a different type of warning, "The price will be very high if you betray us. Do you hear me, Pashtana?"

Maah listened intently but still heard no response, which was a little worrying. What if Pashtana was too far away to hear him? Then their trickery might actually work on him.

He had to give them something else to think about, "You worthless scum, you think you are safe here? My men will come and avenge those you have killed. They will find you here and then you know what will happen? I will be your torturer again, but not like before. You will wish for before. Go from this place, while you still can. How long do you think before you are surrounded? This is our land!"

Don't any of them speak Arabic?

"How long does it take, Miller?" asked Linton.

"Well, it's hard to say, Sir. My uncle said it was a few hours, but I don't know for sure."

"A few hours of this noise?" asked the CO.

"Uhh, actually the next stage will be worse than this. Right now, it's just fear, but when the doubt leaves, I think they'll get much louder. Especially the bully."

Linton frowned, "Oh dear."

"Yes Sir. But they've got a saucepan next door. You know, I could rustle up some tea if you're interested."

"I certainly wouldn't say no, Sergeant. Why don't you offer a cuppa to Pole and Baranwal, too? You could always stand in for them while they take a break. After all, the two prison guards already know your face."

"Will do, Sir, I'll be right back."

"Fancy a cuppa, mate?" Toby peeked his head into the cell that Pole was using for Pashtana.

Pole didn't even turn toward Toby, instead maintaining the stare directed at the former camp worker. He knew his eyes were obscured by his mask, but still felt that some sense of his intensity would be felt by the young prison guard.

Toby understood the silence, "Okay, but make sure to keep him well hydrated, we have to follow the rules, even if they don't."

Pole nodded, picking up the energy drink from the floor for the prisoner.

"What about you? Fancy a cup of tea? I can stand in for you while you drink it." Toby was now leaned in, chatting in the same casual way to Baranwal, who nodded without hesitation.

"You wanna tell me where the other camp is yet?" Toby directed the question to the long bearded bully. "Oh yeah, sorry. Bad English, I remember. I meant; Other? Camp?"

"Time is running out. My men are on their way, you would run screaming if you knew what they will do to you…"

But Toby was already on the way out of the cell, "Not a word, mate. I don't understand any of it."

66.

"GO GRAB YOUR tea mate, I've got him for now."

Baranwal exited in silence and Toby moved into his spot, staring directly at Maah, who was surprisingly game for a good old-fashioned staring contest.

Then suddenly a wave of doubt flashed across Maah's face, and he involuntarily broke the deadlock as his eyes widened in fear.

Maah's stomach convulsed, and he doubled up in pain.

"Ahh, so it's starting," said Toby, "It'll only get worse."

Maah was aware the new prisoner was talking but didn't even try to understand his words. Was this real? How could this man do this to him? Was the man not bound by their overly cautious rules?

"Let's face it, you've had this coming, haven't you? Anyway, I'm gonna leave you to it for a while and go see how Pashtana's doing. He's lighter than you, so it's probably more advanced in him."

'Pashtana' was the only word Maah recognised, and he looked up in terror to see the newest prisoner leaving the room.

Toby walked into Pashtana's cell to see him twitching, presumably in response to what was happening inside his body.

Toby tapped Pole's shoulder and pointed at the floor, "Did he drink all of that?"

Pole nodded again.

"Greedy bugger. Okay, I guess you can go to the other cell and keep an eye on him for me."

Pole nodded his understanding while continually staring down the former prison guard, only breaking the deadlock to leave, as ordered.

Toby knelt a couple of feet in front of Pashtana. "Can you hear your colleague from over here?"

Pashtana looked down at Toby, his face unable to hide the fear.

"Because he's losing his arrogance now. Although to be fair, he did stick at it for a long time." Toby sighed and raised his eyebrows. "I know you can speak English, although you seem less cocky without a gun in your hand. It's easier beating a man who's tied up, isn't it?"

No response.

"Or slitting a man's throat who you've abused for years; some poor bugger who can't fight back. Maybe I should use my mate's long knife and…"

Toby leaned in close to Pashtana and whipped his hand from left to right, directly in front of the young guard's skinny neck. Pashtana's muscles contracted in fear. Toby maintained the uncomfortably close quarters and lowered his volume. "Decapitating you; that would be karma, wouldn't it? Do you guys believe in karma?"

Then Toby pulled his head back again and grinned, "But that would be quick. And let's face it, you haven't earned the right to go quickly."

Pashtana looked at Toby with his eyes bulging wide, but it wasn't defiance, and it wasn't anger, unlike Maah. Pashtana looked terrified; he had no fight left. Toby already knew he'd won, now it was only a matter of how long it would take, so he sat his arse down on to the dirt floor and waited.

"He'll kill me!" Pashtana was pleading with Toby, even though his words were those of a simple statement.

People weren't as unique as they liked to think they were. Toby had learned that on previous hostage training courses, even though he'd only previously been trained to survive as a hostage.

Interestingly that same information was now turning out to be useful from the opposing perspective.

In summary, these things took hours or days, but often followed a similar pattern. Stubborn silence was the start, then anger and bravado, followed by the decision to defiantly throw threats back at the captor. Then doubt would start to creep in, which usually ended with an attempt to negotiate a way out. And finally, you reached flat-out begging.

The training course was designed to help you to overcome your natural instincts to follow that pattern. Something Pashtana clearly didn't know.

Toby got absolutely no joy from this. It really would be better for all involved if Pashtana could just give up the information, then this could be over and done with. So, what was the quickest approach?

"But you're gonna die anyway," seemed like the right route.

It was true, and Pashtana knew it. He would either die here now, or at some later point, at Mister Ebeid's hands. He looked down at the floor, wondering, *which will be worse?*

Another violent contraction shot through Pashtana's abdomen, and he looked straight back up at Toby with his eyes begging for something he couldn't bring himself to admit.

"Just for the record, I only have one dose of antivenom." Toby nodded at Pashtana, before looking back down at the floor patiently.

"I can't trust you. How do I know you'll do what you say you're going to do? How do I know I will live? And then what? Ebeid will kill me any way, or Mahmoud."

"I hear you. But you're still not seeing your situation. No matter what, your old life is finished. You will not live here anymore, so your choices are to be a detainee in another country, which seems quite fitting to me, or…" Toby gestured to the chair in which he sat.

Then Toby sighed, "But in neither of those cases can Ebeid, I think that's what you said his name was? Or Mahmoud, do anything to you. So, your options are much more simple than you think."

Pashtana started the fidgeting again. Toby watched the young man's chair, half expecting it to tip-up under such uncontrolled movements. Then Pashtana suffered another violent wave inside his abdomen and his bowels let go momentarily. As the foul fecal smell hit the room, Toby looked back up at him, because still, all he could do was wait.

"Okay, okay, get me the map and the antivenom! Quickly, please!"

67.

"DO I DARE ask how you got these map co-ordinates, Sergeant Miller?" Lieutenant Linton was sitting in the former camp boss's chair.

"I tricked him, Sir, nothing sinister. While they were out, the pair of them were given two pin pricks with the needle from a sewing kit, barely comparable to a mosquito bite. But don't worry, the needle was sterile."

"And how did you sterilise it out here?"

"I think it's better if you don't know the details, Sir."

"Oh dear."

"And inside the bag you brought over for me, I had the empty box for some snake antivenom as requested back at GCHQ. The guards drew their own conclusions, Sir, which were totally inaccurate, for the record."

"And where are they both now…" Linton couldn't help but think the nickname was appropriate for this occasion, "Staffy?"

"They're shitting their guts out, Sir. Sorry, but I don't know how to phrase it nicely."

"All right," it was getting quite hard for the Lieutenant not to laugh, "but connect the dots for me, Miller. You'd mentioned some old conversation with your uncle which inspired you to do this. Care to elaborate for us?" There were four other Regiment NCOs in the room, all hanging on Toby's every word.

"Well, when he turned fifty, his GP told him he had to have a colonoscopy to check for bowel cancer. According to him, it's the world's way of saying 'welcome to middle age, pal.' And he tells this really funny story about how powerful the colonoscopy prep drink is. It's only a laxative, but…"

One of the soldiers burst out laughing, then fought to appropriately contain it with his CO in the room. "I'm very sorry, Sir." The soldier nodded apologetically while still struggling to contain himself.

Toby was also fighting to keep a straight face, "And my Uncle talks about how the shits came on him, so bad and so fast that…"

One of the men now hurried from the room, unable to contain himself any longer.

Toby took a breath, "So fast, that he couldn't stop it from coming out."

"Oh, Miller." The lieutenant winced at the visual.

"I'm sorry, Sir. But apparently, he got caught short." Toby winced theatrically for the entertainment value, sending another soldier scurrying from the room. Although it was immediately apparent that the change of location achieved nothing -considering that all Toby could hear from inside the hut was the two men roaring with laughter outside.

Toby couldn't wipe the smile off his face. "So, he cleaned himself up. And the way he says it, the waves were sudden, painful," He intentionally slowed down the final line, "and it came out of him like a bloody fire hose."

"Eeeurgh!" The Lieutenant finally caved, and laughed out loud too, which was taken as permission for the others to join in.

Toby waited for the hut to settle down and when it finally did, the original pair of NCOs returned to hear the ending. "So, I just poured some… well, a lot actually… of magnesium citrate down their throats while they were both out cold. The rest of it we put in some empty energy drink bottles, that way we could keep topping the wankers up with the stuff. Shit tastes nasty," he grinned mischievously, "just like a cheap energy drink." His audience was enthralled.

"The young guard in particular drunk loads of it, must've thought it was some nutrient rich western concoction. It's really lucky you brought the bag I'd asked Debbie for."

"Are you sure they'll be okay Miller?" the CO asked.

"Absolutely certain, Sir. Once their bowels are empty, they'll be good as new, ready for a colon inspection actually."

More involuntary laughter.

"The only real risk is dehydration, so they're both sitting on the pot in two different parts of the camp, until it passes through them. I never said they'd been bitten, or that they needed antivenom, only that I had antivenom, and just the one bottle. I did say to Pashtana that he'd die, but hell, he might live to seventy before that happens. Anyway, in this place you can get the shits just from drinking water."

Linton thought it through, shaking his head the whole time. "You were that close to the line, Miller." But instead of leaving an illustrative gap between his index finger and thumb, the officer's fingers were pressed together hard.

"I was probably right on the line, Sir, but we've got our location, and they've got plenty of bottles of water at their disposal. Ther're being guarded too, although it's a shit duty."

Too far?

"I really don't know what to say." The Lieutenant could only shake his head.

"I do, Sir. May I?" asked Pole.

"Go ahead, Lance Corporal." The Lieutenant winced, dreading what might come next.

"I bloody love you, Staffy Miller; that's the funniest thing I've seen in my entire life." Pole fist bumped Toby, shaking his head in admiration.

The CO rolled his eyes, "Yes, thank you, Pole. Now could you locate Sar'nt Ross please? As I need a serious meeting with my senior NCOs."

"Sir." Pole saluted his CO and made himself scarce.

"So, this footage is from the memory card that you just removed from Duggan-Smythe's camera." The CO swivelled his armoured laptop toward Toby and Sergeant Ross. Then he clicked play, which started a video showing a rooftop scene.

The footage showed two IC6 males standing on a neighbouring roof, then panned up to a helicopter hovering above, followed by a downward pan showing a third IC6 male standing on the nearby roof. Then the volume became distorted by loud noise as the third man was riddled by large calibre fire, presumably from the overhead helicopter, and finally it panned left to show the original two men taking the whirlybird down with an RPG.

"The two men in the video," the CO had paused it at the appropriate point.

Toby nodded knowingly, "The one who fired the surface-air is sitting on the loo just around the corner, and the smart dressed one giving the orders was my English speaking camp boss."

"Exactly, and considering the helo was an American bird, our cousins are keen to take Maah Mahmoud off our hands, unless you have any objections, Miller?"

Toby shook his head, "That's way above my paygrade, Sir, and it sounds like he'll go exactly where he deserves to go. That's good enough for me."

"No conflict with your operational directives?" the CO was bound to confirm.

"None whatsoever, Sir."

"Good, so let's move on. We have footage here of Mister Laham Ebeid, who we can now identify with certainty as the commander of both camps, and possibly even the head of the entire Zarqawi 'abdi terrorist group." Linton exhaled audibly, knowing what a big catch he'd be. "So, we need to discuss this second detainee camp, which we now know to be the group's only other camp and the current location of their leader, Laham Ebeid. It is also, presumably, the location of our primary and only remaining objective, Charles Duggan-Smythe."

Linton looked over at Toby who seemed lost in thought, then continued on regardless, "So, it appears to me that we have a small window of opportunity, because the only two people from this camp who survived the PMC gatecrashers are both suffering from underestimating Staffy Miller. Therefore, our presence here is still unknown to the remainder of the Zarqawi 'abdi group. So, what are your thoughts on another operation?"

Before Toby could contribute, Sergeant Ross chipped in with an unexpected question, "Will we be green lighted for this one, Sir?"

Toby was momentarily lost, looking from Ross to Linton in complete confusion.

Linton didn't miss the moment, but chose to respond to Ross first, "Good point Sar'nt Ross, we'll need to call in and sort that mess out. Although strictly speaking, we haven't actually run our first operation yet. We arrived at a party too late, without firing a shot, so no rules were actually broken."

Toby stared at his temporary CO, waiting for clarification. Surely, he didn't need to ask?

"Sergeant Miller, it appears that ministerial approval had not yet been received for our involvement as your rapid response unit. Just a glitch, I'm sure." He wasn't at all sure but knew exactly how the update would appear to Miller, so went on, "But as you can see, we deployed anyway."

Toby reeled at the implications, casting his mind back to who'd been involved back at GCHQ, which really didn't help at all. Because while he knew who'd been present, he had no idea which of them was responsible for sourcing ministerial approval. He looked down at the floor, unable to shake the belief that it could only be Chalmers who could handle such a high-reaching request.

"You were about to say something, Miller?" Linton sympathised, but he had another operation to plan, and time was pressing.

Toby looked back up, slowly, "Sorry, Sir. In all the action, I forgot to mention that I was able to learn a little more information from the younger guard, regarding Charlie Duggan-Smythe."

"Then let's hear it, Miller."

Toby slumped, he'd just survived Jihadi prison, but felt no wave of relief.

Quite the contrary.

68.

"I'M CONCERNED ABOUT the implications of what I was told, Sir." Toby was far more concerned about the implications of having been sent into such a high risk operation without the promised help, but was trying desperately to focus instead on the task at hand.

His temporary CO could sense Miller's turmoil, but they had to move forward, and fast. "Okay, Staffy, so let's work through the problem. What have you got?"

It was hard to get past the idea that Chalmers had sent him here, to what? To betray him? To teach him a lesson? What had been his plan? Toby took a breath; this really wasn't the right time. Even more than that, he simply didn't have enough time to figure it out. Not right now.

Toby looked back up and redirected his focus. "The younger guard, Pashtana. Obviously, he spilled the second camp's location and so while he was in a talking mood, I kept pushing."

Linton chuckled again; he couldn't help but think back to Miller's tactics.

Toby didn't allow it to distract him, "Apparently, he was here when Charlie Duggan-Smythe was brought in to the other camp. So, he didn't witness his arrival or meet the locals who'd delivered him."

Linton was listening intently, "Delivered him?"

"Yes Sir. Most of the time it's not hard-core Zarqawi 'abdi who do the kidnapping, it's locals who sympathise with the cause; locals who need cash. The terrorists pay them for new detainees, but only the good desirable ones. They run it like they're trading stolen cattle."

"Understood." Linton nodded away.

"So, rewinding, Danny and Charlie got caught in the middle of a firefight between coalition forces and some Zarqawi 'abdi. The video you just showed us caught the end of that fight. It sounds like a local taxi driver then promised them a ride out of the hot zone, to a safe bar with wi-fi. That way they could write their story, send it in, unwind, all that stuff. But the local driver pegged them as desirables; flashy camera, two man team, all the things they've been told to look out for. So, he skipped the safe part."

"Alright. Makes sense." Linton was leaned back in his chair.

Sergeant Ross, who was sitting on the edge of the desk in front of his CO, now stepped in with his own question, "But how did the two of them get separated?"

"Well for that we've got Danny's first-hand version. Charlie was unwinding, drinking beer, and shoving the word 'God' into conversations with locals." Toby winced at the idea.

"Ooh. Naive." Ross chipped in.

"Yup, especially considering perspectives, meaning it looks like Charlie can only see his own. That's probably fine in the swankiest part of London, but here? Working in the thick of it with Jihadis?" Toby shook his head. "So, when Danny tried reminding him of where they were, Charlie got belligerent, and clocked him in the head. Danny Ellington was not a happy man, and walked."

Sergeant Ross wiggled his head, implying the decision to leave Duggan-Smythe, was still an iffy one.

Toby shrugged, "I agree. But Charlie sounds like an arrogant rich kid, and civvies don't have each other's backs. Not like we do." Toby was thinking specifically about Linton deploying his men to help him, even without the appropriate governmental permission.

"Anyway, after that Danny only knows about his own journey.

But the kid, Pashtana, he filled in some of the gaps for me. He said that Danny was taken by one bunch, then got collected by Mahmoud and ended up in here, while Duggan-Smythe was delivered to the other camp by a different bunch of locals, half a day later."

"So, he is there then?" Linton squinted in confusion.

But Toby wasn't quite ready to answer that yet. "Hang on, it's not that simple. Charlie arrived there in a really bad way; Pashtana did learn that. He'd taken a proper beating, but really bad, not like the little roughing up me and Danny got in here."

Linton couldn't help but grin, as Toby was looking particularly black and blue himself, but he let him continue.

"Charlie had burns on his face, he was missing some frontal hair and his eyebrows. And the worse part was that he wasn't conscious. Pashtana said they have a medic of some sort, who works both camps. But even he couldn't do anything with 'the hairless one', as they were calling him."

Toby was leaning on the wall as he shared the story with Ross and the CO. "Permission to speak openly, Sir?"

"Given." Linton fired back.

In contrast, Toby waited a decent time to slightly adjust his question, "Actually, Sir, can we talk completely off the record?"

Linton nodded, cautiously. Then sighed, "Yes, go ahead, Miller."

"All Pashtana knew beyond that, is that Duggan-Smythe never made it into the main area of the camp." Toby shrugged, "He wasn't sure if Charlie survived that first day. He said Charlie might have already been buried, because the kid saw two new graves there yesterday. But as we know, a grave got dug here today too, and that wasn't for Charlie. So, one and one doesn't always make two. Not in this bloody place."

Linton and Ross were considering the variables. Toby decided to conclude his position on Duggan-Smythe. "The reason I wanted this bit off the record is that I was sent here to bring him home, and so if he's buried in the other camp, then I'm still gonna make sure his body makes it back home to his mum and dad. As unlikable as they are."

"And if Charlie's not in the other camp…" Toby sighed, knowing he had to make this operation a success, with or without assistance. "Then I'll have to figure out where to look next. But you guys were only sent here as my rapid response, for one specific part of my operation."

He sighed again, wearily, "So, you just asked me about planning the next operation, and I'm duty bound to tell you that our primary objective may not even be there and even if he is, we might only be recovering his body. Therefore, it's not exactly the operation you were approved to do here, and strictly speaking, it would also require separate ministerial approval." Toby shrugged, as they all knew what that implied.

"These two should be kept separated. Permanently, if you can." Toby released Pashtana's arm, thereby officially handing him into the custody of a young American soldier.

"They're gonna be separated any ways, we've got special plans for the big dude," replied the soldier as he pulled Pashtana's zip tied hands toward an armoured personnel carrier.

Linton was looking up toward the sky, then around at the horizon in obvious concern. "We're making a lot of noise out here in the open. It's still broad daylight and I don't like it. I don't mean to be rude, but the quicker you guys are gone, the better."

His American counterpart clicked on the large radio that hung from his tunic, "Any movement out there?"

Linton had most of his Regiment men spread about the perimeter, scanning the horizon through their long-range optics, hoping to get advance warning of any unwelcome new attention.

The American officer stood in silence as he listened to his earpiece, then summarised the response, "Nothing goin' on. You have a goat farmer about three-K in that direction, so we'll make sure to head out the opposite way." The officer paused in thought, "Say uhh, do you guys have a bead on Laham Ebeid? We've got a helo crew of four that just got flown Stateside for burial. All his doin."

Linton looked at Toby, who understood exactly what the man was asking, shrugging as he responded. "I only have my primary objective left, Sir, and it's not Ebeid."

Linton had already held the same conversation with his superiors, just after being told he'd finally got ministerial permission to get on with his job. "We may have some idea where he might be."

The US officer nodded, "How about letting us tag along? We could offer you guys some support, then take him off your hands. More guns is always good, you'll get eyes up there too." He nodded upward, presumably to a high altitude drone.

Linton smiled a polite, yet cautious smile before replying, "We don't play well with others, I'm afraid, so I'll have to turn down the offer of you chaps tagging along." *Especially so many of you,* he thought to himself.

His concern was genuine, the Regiment had their own way of doing things, a faster, less support-driven way of achieving their objectives. Extra people would not only slow them down, but potentially cause dangerous misunderstandings.

"The eye in sky is tempting though." He looked at Miller and Ross, who both nodded their agreement.

"Nah, no way man." The American could already see what they were hinting at. "I can't let you play with our toys without us being a part." That would not only be against the rules, but too much of a one-way street.

Both officers knew where this was going, but the American made the suggestion first, "How about you just take one of my guys? Somebody that can communicate with the drone pilot in a nice familiar accent." He grinned to lighten the mood.

"They'd need to be fit to keep up," Sergeant Ross chipped in, "And I mean really, bloody fit."

The officer nodded, he had just the person. "Get Sanchez," he ordered the closest American soldier, "And I mean get Sanchez -to go."

"Sir." the soldier barked extra loud for the sake of all the Keffiyeh wearing Brits standing around.

Toby smiled cheekily at Ross, before turning away and carefully scanning his surroundings, probably out of sheer habit.

"Sanchez reporting for duty, Sir!"

The words were delivered in a higher pitched voice than anticipated, Toby turned back to see where they'd come from.

"PFC Sanchez here, runs half marathons." The American officer winked at Sanchez, then turned to the Brits, beaming proudly.

"But does she do them wearing her bergen?" asked Ross.

"Yes, Sergeant! And my boots." She didn't hesitate to give it back to the Sergeant.

Ross nodded, "Yeah. She'll do."

69.

ANDY LINTON HAD planned this operation with the same set of priorities he used for every other, meaning that operational success and the wellbeing of his men were at the core of the entire decision-making process.

He had sixteen men in-country, plus himself, Sergeant Miller, and now Sanchez, their adopted American. She'd made a good first impression by skillfully using the overhead US drone to guide their route away from any night-time heat signatures. But no traditional infantry soldier was up to the standards of his Regiment, and no matter how efficiently she may have proven herself within her own company, she was still an unknown quantity amongst his.

Additionally, the last thing he needed was to have something bad happen to the coalition soldier he'd been loaned. So, she'd reluctantly agreed to be his 'tail-end Charlie'.

Toby Miller was also an outsider, but Linton viewed him rather differently. Firstly, Miller had been an Army Sergeant prior to his sideways move into the covert work. The earned rank spoke to his experience and his ability to command. Secondly, the fact that he now worked covertly for the government made him a closer relative to Linton's own elite regiment, than to Miller's former Army role. Finally, Linton had just seen Miller at work, and had been quietly impressed with what he'd witnessed.

As a result, Linton had divided his men into four teams. Each team contained four men, with Sergeant Ross leading one team (in which he'd also included Sanchez), Corporal Baranwal would lead the second, Linton would take the third team himself, and (former) Sergeant Miller would lead the fourth.

Linton hadn't been at all convinced by Miller back in Hereford, but the Sergeant had since earned some respect. He had shown himself to be skilled, intelligent, and quite fearless, but he'd also proven to be calm under intense pressure, an invaluable asset in their world. But more than that, he'd had the men laughing out loud. Andy knew his men, he could read their moods without a word being spoken, and he could see that Miller had already won them over, which in turn lifted team morale and steadied everyone's nerves, making Andy's life easier.

On a personal, and more trivial level, Andy Linton had particularly enjoyed the boyish excitement he'd seen on Miller's face when he'd been asked to lead a patrol of elite Regiment soldiers. Mainly because it had been such a surprise to see such a natural and childlike expression of joy on such a composed and disciplined individual.

In terms of the agreed plan, it was straightforward enough; a radio-silent night-time approach from multiple directions simultaneously.

The four teams would all make different vehicular approaches, then each team would further divide, on foot. This would give the Jihadis no time to react, no route to use for escape, and very little opportunity to kill hostages.

Each team would utilise silenced rifles, pistols, and the usual accessories. They'd wear night vision aids which would assist with the choreography of this multi-pronged approach. They'd also wear gas masks to ensure their anonymity was preserved, and to avoid choking on any nasty vapours.

As he ran through the checklist in his head, Lieutenant Andy Linton could see no obvious flaws.

He was seated at the wheel of the lead vehicle, one of four local trucks they'd appropriated from the previous detainee camp -one he now slowed to a crawl, using engine braking only.

To bring it to a complete stop, he dipped the clutch pedal, and pulled gently on the handbrake knowing that bright red brake lights might be visible out here, even a couple of miles out from the camp.

As his vehicle stopped, one of the trucks behind him steered around to the right, and the other two veered left, both taking slightly different courses. Andy watched as they all disappeared quickly into the darkness.

Linton and his patrol opened up their doors, but the vehicle's interior lights had already been disabled, so the surrounding area remained in total darkness. One by one the soldiers checked their kit, and gently pressed on the truck's doors to close them silently.

Andy faced his lads in the dark, carefully confirming that each one was ready to continue. After four separate sets of thumbs up, he indicated their next direction with an outstretched hand, then started a gentle jog toward the final Zarqawi 'abdi detainee camp.

Their gear bounced rythmically as they ran, their boots made gentle noises on the dirt floor, and they could all hear their own breathing; but for now, not a living soul could be seen through their night vision headgear.

Lieutenant Linton signaled his men should pause, then altered the hand signal to indicate a hard stop. The men dropped to the floor and set up splayed positions to ensure their entire surrounding area was covered. Andy had finally caught sight of someone, a single human being smoking a cigarette a little way out from the camp. The cigarette's tip looked like a roaring distress flare through his night vision headgear.

Andy looked down at his watch, it was four in the morning, and sunrise would be at five. He was happy with their arrival time, as any sleeping camp guards would be in the middle of the deepest part of their sleep cycle.

The five-man patrol waited for the guard to extinguish the finished cigarette, then the man turned and started a leisurely stroll back toward the detainee camp. Linton signaled for his men to divide once again, two men instantly headed left, the other two right. Andy was constantly keeping the middle ground between them both, always slightly ahead of his men. Andy Linton took immense pride in being the kind of officer who led from the front.

Andy raised his hand to hold once again, bringing everyone to a pause. Their position was close enough, for now. Andy signaled for everyone to drop down low again, and they waited, everyone continually scanning their allotted direction for potential problems.

To the far right, Andy saw four familiarly outfitted forms move in slowly toward the camp, who paused at a similar distance to his own, before dropping down low too. Then he watched as another of his teams crept in from the far left, with one man signaling for his mates to stop, before continuing ahead on his own.

The sole soldier drew a long knife from somewhere unseen and slowed his pace even further, heading in the direction of the smoker.

Andy looked back to the far right to see two human forms now moving forward, one of them carrying a ladder. Andy made a signal with his right hand to his closest man, then turned left and signaled the man there too. His patrol now started walking in unison, as did all of the other men in the distance, both to his far left and far right. From above, he knew their positions would appear as a perfectly spaced circle, like the spokes of a wheel, with the camp as its hub.

Andy looked ahead again, checking on his kids, that's how it always felt. There was now a human form lying prone on the floor with one of Andy's soldiers kneeling on its lower back. But the man with the curved knife had already disappeared from view, hidden by the camp buildings.

Baranwal's a damn ghost, I'm so glad he's one of my guys. Andy shuddered at the thought of opposing the Gurkha.

Now Andy looked far right; two men were moving very slowly on the roof, which he already knew from Pashtana's information to be the main prisoner building. He had no idea where Miller's team were, but he'd always known they'd be obscured from his view, having approached from the opposite side of the camp.

Andy and his team had now closed the gap to just a few feet from the camp buildings. Everyone knew their exact roles, and so everyone moved to the appropriate position. As Andy looked both ways, he could see all gas masks were in place, and all were looking at him for the final command.

The Lieutenant could feel the adrenaline surging, he took a deep breath, then signaled for everyone to go, and the reaction from his men was immediate.

Only now were there a couple of noises, but not loud ones, nothing that could wake a sleeping person. The tinkle of some breaking glass, the strange expelled-air pop of gas canisters leaving their launchers, the gentle sound of boots running on dirt, a few subdued grunts. A silenced shot here and there, one loud gun shot, and within no time at all, the sounds faded out, leaving the same eerie silence they'd arrived to.

Andy ran to the left where one of his team was kneeling over a man, zip tying the man's hands behind his back. Having pulled the ties taught, he knelt on the man's legs and started the process for his ankles too, then frisked the man's body for hidden weapons. The soldier looked up at Andy, nodding silently, and Andy recognised the movements as those of Peters. He nodded back at Peters, then sighed in relief. *Peters is okay.*

Andy continued heading toward the prisoner area, looking around him the whole time. One of his guys had already taken up a kneeling defensive position, covering the distant approaches to the camp with his rifle, with two partially dressed men already restrained and face down in the dirt right next to him. And again, mask or not, Andy quickly recognised his soldier.

Ahead was an IC6 male, the man was down on the floor, fully dressed, meaning he'd been on guard. And another of Andy's guys was taking the man's weapon, setting it to the side. Another nod to Andy, another recognised soldier.

Andy scanned in every direction and only saw control, discipline, and effectiveness. He inhaled calmly and walked tall; this is why you did this stuff. Nobody would ever know the feeling, nor who they were, nor hear their stories. But the ones present were part of something otherworldly; a tight knit group of people, all thinking, moving, and operating as one.

But Andy couldn't get tied up in those thoughts as some of his kids were still unaccounted for, so he continued his search.

He'd heard the men talking amongst themselves after previous operations about how 'the Gaffer' walked the scene, checking on everyone's work. But that wasn't what he did.

That wasn't the point at all.

He had a list of their names in his head, and he wouldn't stop until all those names were checked off safely. Baranwal? *There he is.* Linton smiled inside his gas mask.

Sanchez strolled past the Lieutenant, hauling a zip tied man twice her size. The lieutenant smiled broadly inside his gas mask, and then saw Miller leading people from a building, all wearing orange overalls.

Miller saw the boss and lifted his mask from his face, having had enough of the sticky air within. "No losses, Sir. My patrol are all accounted for, and we came at them quick enough that the prisoners are all uninjured."

Linton wanted to whoop at the top of his lungs, but suppressed the desire, and peeled the mask from his own face as he approached Miller. "Ebeid?"

"He's right there, Sir." Toby pointed at the smartly dressed camp boss, sitting on the dirt being guarded by Llewellyn.

"And Duggan-Smythe?"

Toby just shook his head.

70.

LORD RUPERT WAS wide awake in his hospital bed; he had been all night. An aching sense of hopelessness had repelled any hope of sleep. But it was more than that, he felt weighed down by recent losses, something he'd repeatedly been told to expect at his age.

The most recent of those losses, a lifelong friend, had caused him the most pain.

At least, so far.

Rupert cast his mind back, shaking his head at distant memories. After being dropped off at the family's preferred boarding school, the very young Rupert had watched his mother and father walk back to their glossy new Jaguar coupe. His small hand had been taken by the new Headmaster with the intention of guiding the new boy into the school, but the young Rupert hadn't allowed it. He'd stood his ground, waiting for his parents to turn and wave goodbye to him.

But they hadn't turned, and they hadn't waved.

The memory was still vivid, and it still smarted.

Even as a young boy, Rupert had worked through physical pain without much drama, he'd fallen from horses he'd been riding, and out of trees he'd been climbing. He'd made a fuss like all children do, but he'd never really struggled with the pain itself. If he was truthful with himself, the only reason he'd even made a fuss was for the increased attention from his mother.

But that first day at the boarding school was the first time he'd ever felt emotional pain, and he was bewildered by its power. He'd stood there that day, still resisting the Headmaster, even as their Jag accelerated away.

And as they finally disappeared from view, he'd felt a new pain, the only kind that would ever really hurt him. As his stomach churned, the young Rupert had felt abandoned, betrayed, and utterly unloved.

In the days after his arrival, he'd cried himself to sleep, night after night; until one day he happened across a like-minded boy. This other abandoned child had quickly become Rupert's closest friend and they'd both survived boarding school by working as a team.

When one boy felt down, the other cheered him up. When one struggled in a subject, the other tutored him through the night. When one was bullied, the other waded in, to even the odds. Rupert had eventually reached a point where he dreaded going back home during the school holidays.

In his young mind, his parents had declared it was a loveless family, so he'd been happy to reciprocate.

But his best pal George could always be counted on. He'd been there when the teenaged Rupert had first met Fiona in a student bar. George had been Rupert's best man when he'd married Fiona -and Rupert had later reciprocated as his. George had even been Godfather to Gemma, Rupert's eldest child.

And now George was gone, taken a year ago by a brain aneurism in the middle of the night. Nobody had seen it coming, so nobody had been given the opportunity to say their farewells.

So, after decades of the most natural male friendship Rupert had ever known, he somehow felt incomplete knowing that dear old George was no longer out there.

Six months later, one of Rupert's golfing pals finally lost his fight with cancer, and just a month ago it was the turn of Rupert's beloved dog. Embarrassingly, the loss of the dog had made him cry more than any human, the silly pup had been his constant shadow.

And now, on top of everything, the idea that Charles was all but gone, was just too much.

Rupert's eyes welled up. He looked across at Fi, who'd taken to sleeping on a camp bed in his hospital room, which they'd been told, "Really shouldn't be allowed". But the nurses who'd initially resisted so strongly had eventually permitted it.

Rupert's breathing quickened as he thought of what a mess he'd made. Calling in a favour with Lucas' private military contractors instead of letting the appropriate people in government do their jobs. *What was I thinking?* That the fool Chalmers had only shared half the relevant information hadn't helped, but still…

If anybody had undermined Rupert like that, sending in private contractors during his period of Army service, he'd have been livid, absolutely spitting fire. There would have been hell to pay for it.

What a reversal, what a disgrace.

Fiona had been disgusted at the undercover operative's manner toward her over the phone, but in Rupert's opinion, the operative had every right to be angry; in fact, the voice on the phone had shown surprising restraint.

No, Rupert didn't blame the operative, or the huge team working in support. He didn't even blame Lucas' PMCs. Lord Rupert only blamed himself, and now he was lost, because he had absolutely no idea what he could do about it.

71.

TOBY HAD BEEN looking over at Ebeid for a while, trying to figure out the right way to extract some final information about Charlie Duggan-Smythe's fate. More specifically, a way that was within the rules for a uniformed soldier.

But he'd got nothing.

He'd considered the symbolic act of removing the uniform and working instead as a sole undercover operative -one with considerably more leeway open to them. But it was a farce, because wearing civvies wouldn't magically alter the situation.

The Regiment boys had immediately locked down the camp's perimeter and Ebeid was now just waiting on the Americans, who would do things their way, in an unknown location.

Toby closed his eyes and ran through the same thoughts all over again, still coming up with no new solution. He'd used up the colonoscopy prep medication, the Americans were only a few miles out, and realistically, Ebeid wouldn't have fallen for that stunt anyway. Ebeid was an arse, but he wasn't a stupid one.

Toby rolled his eyes, knowing he had absolutely nothing left.

He finally caved in and walked over to Ebeid, who was still sitting on the dirt floor with his wrists and ankles zip tied. As Toby approached, the former camp boss looked up at him and glared. "So, will you still write my story?" The sarcasm in his tone was fierce.

But Toby didn't take shit from anyone; he loved, even lived to fight back. "Danny's gonna write it actually, but you might not like his perspecti…"

Although Ebeid had always intended cutting him off, "Just another Western liar," he boomed, then started to recite a short phrase, repeatedly.

"Yeah." Toby nodded. "I am." Now he paused for effect, "But I'd rather be a liar, than what you are. You order dumb impressionable kids to slit the throats of helpless people; noncombatants." Toby intentionally avoided use of the word 'innocent', knowing that believers like Ebeid were incapable of viewing anybody who disagreed with their views as an innocent.

Toby dropped down to his knees again; he didn't need to stand there looking down on the man to make his point. Looking someone in the eye, from up close, was far more his style, "So you're in no position to act morally superior, mate."

Ebeid merely continued to recite the same phrase, his fervour implying it was religious in theme.

Toby set his rifle down. "So, the other journalist who came in, the one with the burned hair. You know who I mean? The poor sod your groupies beat so bad that he never woke up. I'm confused about your position on that. How does that ugly shit help your honourable cause?"

Ebeid paused his chanting and looked up at Toby shaking his head, "Obviously you judge me by your own poor standards."

Toby squinted in confusion, hesitating a moment before replying, "What's that meant to mean?" But instead of replying, Ebeid resumed the repetitive phrase with even more vigour.

"Hey! Dickhead, what did you do with Charlie? Is he here, is he buried here?" Toby growled in frustration, pointing at some freshly dug graves.

Toby waited as Ebeid continued his recital, then he looked around at the other former camp guards before settling his gaze back on the Zarqawi 'abdi leader, and finally, Toby stood up and left him to his recital.

"How are you doing?" Toby now squatted in front of a bearded prisoner wearing orange overalls.

The mere question triggered tears, "Thank you so much." The man flung his arms around Toby, who instinctively snatched at the stock of his rifle, while trying to keep his precarious balance. But it wasn't a trick, the man was sincere. Toby hugged him back, then pulled loose.

"All right, so we travel pretty light, but we've still got a few goodies with us." Toby opened a small camo stuff sack; one he'd previously filled with the best bits from the whole troop's ration packs. "Chocolate." Toby offered, then grinned as the man snatched it from him. "We always have chocolate rations. I bet it's been a while."

The man nodded in response, wiping his eyes dry, "Two years."

Toby's knees dropped to the floor, "Two? Two years?"

"Uh huh." The man's eyes darted up from his chocolate bar to Toby, then away again just as fast. "This is even better than I remembered." He waved the green foil packed choccy bar at Toby.

"Good." Toby grinned, but the smile evaporated as he thought about how long the guy had been held. He had a burning question but some doubts about asking it, eventually deciding it might be a lift for the man rather than a downer, "So do you have family back home?"

The man stopped chewing, looked up at Toby with an innocent, almost confused expression, then Toby watched as the man's eyes filled again. The prisoner slowly raised his hands up to the sides of his head, and stared down at the floor, still tightly gripping his very own chocolate bar.

Toby's eyes bulged. *Oh no, what have I done?*

The prisoner had long-since made himself stop thinking about people back home, It was a source of too much pain, so he'd forced it from his mind as a form of self-protection. But now the memories all came flooding back, "I do."

His wide eyes stared back up at Toby, "Will I… be able, to… see them?"

"Of course you will, mate." Toby affectionately squeezed the man's shoulder with his free hand.

"But." The man's eyes scanned the area containing the restrained guards, although he seemed unable to look directly at them.

"Oh." Toby nodded reassuringly. "Don't worry about them, they're done," then added with real intent, "They'll never have power over anyone again."

"But." The man stopped chewing his chocolate. "What if more come?" he whispered and left his mouth hanging slightly ajar.

Toby took a second to follow his thought process, "Oh. No, no. The only 'more' that's coming is more of us."

He gave the man's shoulder another supportive squeeze. "I'm serious, you're free now, mate." Toby then pointed over to the guards, "And they, are not." He winked at his new friend playfully.

The man's eyes widened and narrowed with his breathing as he finally absorbed this new reality. Then he stood up, ran over to his former captors, and started strutting past them, one at a time, chewing on his chocolate as he finally stared them all down. The balance of power had shifted, and the man's actions broke some of the other prisoners out of their habitual mental isolation.

As Toby's chocolate eating buddy strutted back and forth along the line of camp guards like a self-assured rooster, another prisoner stood up and walked over to join him. Then without warning the second prisoner kicked Ebeid in the stomach with all the strength he could muster.

Toby looked over at Lieutenant Linton, who rolled his eyes and turned away without saying a word. Toby was already on the same page, he knew he had to stop it, but didn't feel any need to rush. Toby got back to his feet and wandered over to the others, then pulled back on the kicker's arm. "Come on, pal, how about some chocolate? I've even got some Garibaldi biscuits if you prefer."

The man swiveled around quickly, and Toby watched as the man's hands lunged toward Toby's rifle. Toby had seen it coming, spinning the gun behind him with his one hand, and seizing the man's dominant hand with the other. Then Toby leaned in close, "I don't wanna zip tie anyone in orange overalls. You fucking hear me?"

72.

TOBY STOOD ALONE, just outside the camp's perimeter.

A hot, dry wind blew uninterrupted across the barren flat land. It was calming, and Toby breathed in the baked air as his shemagh gently flapped behind his head.

Over to his right he could see a familiar looking Regiment member resting on one knee, eyeing the horizon through his rifle's scope. Another was positioned about a hundred feet to his left, performing the same defensive role.

Toby put them both out of his mind and closed his eyes, concentrating only on the way the hot wind pushed at him. He rolled back on his heels then leaned his body forward into the wind, still to the same gentle noise of his shemagh flapping in the breeze.

The last few days had been a whirlwind, stretching his mental capacity to its limit: capture, coping, plotting, reacting, deceiving, defending, and finally attacking. It had all been draining, which he could cope with, but it had left his head overflowing.

He took another deep breath as the wind buffeted him, feeling his mind gradually start to clear. What he needed now was to be selective about which things should reenter his mind.

The desert air was different out in the open. Within the camp walls it had been stale and oppressive, but out here, it seemed to take on a life of its own. Unhampered by humanity's creations, it was free to cut across the land as it had done for millennia. Toby felt his muscles struggle to resist its mischievous course alterations and realised he was nothing, just another inconsequential life form that would come and go in an instant, leaving the same wind to blow over whatever might come next.

He smiled, strangely relieved at how inconsequential he really was in such a place.

With the tension fading, his focus returned, and the questions started to appear. So where was Charlie? Not present in either camp was the only certainty. The learned information was that he'd been badly injured beyond the scope of the prison camp's only medic, had never woken up, and there were two new graves.

Toby had a thought, opened his eyes, and turned around to face the camp.

"Miller." The Lieutenant's proximity startled him.

"Oh, I didn't hear you, Sir." Toby was embarrassed at having flinched in surprise.

"That wind, it only carries the noise in one direction."

Toby nodded; it was true enough.

"That went well." Linton nodded encouragingly. "Just the one fatality, a guard, and he was only taken down after shooting Private Richards. Richards' plate took the hit and so he fired one back, a head shot, just to make sure. But the plate saved Richards' life, he only has bruises to show for it."

Toby sighed to signify his relief.

"You know, Miller, just identifying Ebeid for who he is would have been viewed as a success back home. That we've taken him out of play, too? It's beyond what anybody expected." Linton patted Toby's shoulder encouragingly and smiled.

"That's good to hear, Sir, all of it." Toby returned the smile.

"And the Americans are just a few miles out, so they'll be taking back Sanchez soon."

"She did well, Sir." Toby nodded appreciatively.

"Didn't she? I nearly fell over when I saw the size of the guy she restrained, single handed too. I don't think I could have got him under control!" Linton chuckled at the memory. "They're also taking Ebeid, you know. It's been officially decided that we don't want him, and the Americans do, which earns us some more Brownie points. And they're going to share any and all, intel they gather from him."

"Okay." Toby nodded.

"So, uh, what did Ebeid have to say about Charlie then?"

Toby sighed, "Absolutely nothing, Sir."

"Then what are you going to do, Miller? Do you need some time with him? Alone?"

Toby chuckled, "I'm not torturing him, Sir, or tricking him. I can still find Charlie without his help."

Linton had been watching Miller intently, from the moment they'd first met back in Hereford, and that simple statement was final confirmation of Linton's own conclusions. It was quite liberating to set aside any lingering doubts. "Watch your back, Staffy."

Toby smirked at the seemingly redundant comment. "I always do, Sir."

"Sir?" Linton laughed out loud before playfully punching Toby in the shoulder. "You've called me Sir the whole time, even though you're here as an operator, and not a soldier. McCord was right about you."

Linton finally felt both able and obliged to elaborate, "I didn't mean watch your back here, Staffy. I meant at home."

"What?" Toby turned to look at the Lieutenant, baffled.

He knew he shouldn't, but Linton opened up any way; Miller had earned it. "Look, Miller, when I return to Hereford, I have to give an official evaluation on your performance in the field, and I've been trying to figure out why."

Toby squinted in confusion.

Linton smiled cautiously as he shrugged, "I honestly don't see any reason to doubt you. But as you know, a bad 'eval' here? Well, it could end with demotion for you, Army demotion; if the Army is still your future."

Toby's jaw dropped, and his eyes moved around as he searched his memory, trying to fit this last piece to the messy puzzle he'd been building in there.

"And now, I can supply that eval. One which I'm confident will share the absolute truth."

Toby exhaled cautiously. "Which is?"

"Come on, you know I can't share that, Miller. But let's put it this way; I'll officially sign off with a personal recommendation that you apply for selection. You know, for the Regiment."

The wind went from Toby. In the best possible way.

"As I'm sure you've heard, Regiment selection is grueling. But the lads all think you'd fit in, if you want in, that is. Be aware though, final selection will be brutal, Staffy. Even for you."

Toby was a little overwhelmed, but knowing even that reaction might end up on his eval, he took another breath and chose to ignore the feeling, smiling instead, "That's a hell of a lot to take in, Sir."

And then, rather than adding any more words, Toby put out his hand to formally shake that of his short-term CO, Lieutenant Andy Linton.

73.

CHALMERS PULLED HIS car into one of the better parking spots outside the doughnut shaped building that housed most of Britain's intelligence gathering services. Closer parking was the only perk of such an early arrival time.

But instead of hurriedly gathering his belongings to head in and make a start to the day, he sat behind the wheel of his car, lost in thought. He'd been given no personal updates on the op; his only knowledge was that which had been shared amongst all involved parties. Which in itself was odd, certainly not the usual routine.

An uneasiness had since grabbed a hold of him, one which had apparently stolen his ability to sleep normally.

Chalmers stared out of the windscreen at the gloom which proceeded the sunrise. That was assuming they'd even see any sun -early signs were that it was unlikely. He ran his fingers over his freshly shaven jawline absentmindedly, trying to prepare himself for the day.

What exactly had he told Lord Rupert Duggan-Smythe? Chalmers closed his eyes, realizing that if that was the first thought to come to mind, then it was the cause of his concern.

The GPS coordinates, that's all he'd shared. But he hadn't shared it by text or email, it had been a voice call, to a mobile phone, not even an office extension. Would that help him? The number he'd called could be traced in an instant, but more importantly, the content of the actual conversation couldn't.

He shook his head as he continued rubbing at his jawline. Why would Lord Rupert even share that exchange? There was no possible benefit in doing so. Was there?

Chalmers folded his lower lip between his fingers and pulled at it. There really would be no sense in Lord Rupert sharing that Chalmers had supplied him with the camp location; it would be equally damaging for them both.

He tugged again at his lower lip, a childhood habit he'd broken years ago. Or maybe not. Realising that, he whipped his hand away and grabbed the handle of his leather briefcase.

Enough.

He pushed open his car door, stepped outside and retrieved his overcoat from the back seat, slamming the door shut while shaking his head. "Ridiculous." He chastised himself while pinching the lock button on his key fob.

As he started toward the building, he turned back and took a look at his car, an expensive possession of which he was quite proud. Why had he done that? Because the uneasiness was still there, and as that realisation hit him, he stopped in his tracks.

He could just go home. Call in sick.

The pause extended as he gave the idea proper consideration. Then the rational self took over once more and he resumed his brisk pace.

"Mornin'." The security guard nodded at Chalmers.

"Good morning," Chalmers reciprocated, as he placed his briefcase on the belt that fed the x-ray machine. Chalmers looked back over at the security guard who held his gaze with a blank expression. Chalmers looked up, straight into the lens of the closest CCTV camera, then back at the security guard, who initiated forward movement on the belt that held his briefcase, which quickly disappeared into the scanning machine.

Too late now, is all Chalmers could think as his bag disappeared from view.

"Your badge, Sir?" the security guard gestured toward the electronic card reader.

Chalmers turned around, noticing a second security guard had positioned herself directly behind him, although not especially close. But she was there, nonetheless.

He swallowed and faced forward again.

Chalmers touched at the photo ID card which hung from his neck, and hesitated, turning around a second time to look at the guard behind him. The lady's eyes narrowed and she gestured toward the card reader.

He lifted the lanyard over his head and took the couple of steps toward the reader. On any normal day, he'd have already been inside the lift, but instead he was looking at the card reader, in dread.

"Just hold it up close, Sir." It had been the first guard talking, although Chalmers hadn't looked up, only heard the male voice.

He should have gone home, called in sick. In his gut he already knew that.

"Sir," said the female voice. But again, Chalmers didn't look at her. Only at the card reader.

He'd been told to put Miller's diplomatic immunity operation behind him and get him straight back in the field. And now he couldn't understand why he hadn't just listened and done as he was told. He looked up at the male security guard, apologetically. As the pair held eye contact, the guard's eyes narrowed suspiciously.

"I think you need to come with us, Sir." The guard's manner had hardened. Some of these security guards were former soldiers, and suddenly this guy looked like one.

It's my hesitation, my doubt, that's all this is. Chalmers took a deep breath and committed to normal behaviour; thrusting his ID card at the reader. 'Ehh-eh' it buzzed in response.

Chalmers pulled the card back a few inches, "Um, it's just a bad read, let me try again."

'Ehh-eh' It repeated, now with an accompanying red light flashing above the swipe point.

"Mister Chalmers, is it?" asked the female voice behind him.

But Chalmers just repositioned his card again, then tried it a third time, without saying a word.

Then a fourth.

"It's okay, Mister Chalmers, let's just forget about the card, shall we?" And without warning, the female guard took a hold of his elbow joint with a surprisingly firm grip.

74.

"IT WAS NICE working with you, Sanchez." Toby's smile was huge, partly due to the recent conversation with Linton, but also because he'd been so impressed by the young American. The resultant smile was probably double sized as a result.

"You too, Sarge." His smile was infectious enough to encourage openness from her. "I gotta admit, I really enjoyed it, Sarge. That was so slick! And only one dead Tango? I can't believe we did it, and we made it look so.." She didn't seem to have the words, "…simple."

Toby knew he'd found one earlier, but couldn't remember which pocket it had been in. He fumbled around in the pockets of his borrowed uniform, then found what he'd been looking for. "Here you go, a little souvenir from us." He handed her an embroidered Union Jack flag with a Velcro back.

She beamed with pride, "Oh thanks, Sarge!" She slapped it onto her uniform sleeve without hesitation, then locked eyes on Toby. "So, I know you're special forces, but which one?"

How could he answer that one? He wasn't even a part of the Regiment, just a hanger-on. Toby grinned and played it simple, "I'll catch up with you later, Sanchez."

"What did you give her, Miller?" asked Sergeant Ross.

"A Velcro UJ. I found it in one of the pockets." Toby grinned like a big kid.

"You cheeky bugger!" Ross laughed out loud. "I thought they didn't want our flag anymore! What's the plan, Staffy, bring back the Americans one at a time?"

Toby rocked his head backwards, laughing out loud.

"It was a treat working with you, Staffy." Ross put out his hand to shake Toby's.

"You too, mate, really." Toby shook it back, enthusiastically.

"I'll send Jim McCord your love."

"Please do."

"We're about to head out, and I understand from LL-Cool-A you're not coming with us?"

L L cool A? Only now did Toby learn Lieutenant Linton's daft nickname amongst the men. He chuckled as he shook his head, "No, I can't go home yet, I'm not done. Not without the big Rupert's kid."

Ross nodded approvingly, "Good for you, Staffy. You need anything from us?"

"Yeah actually, I do."

75.

"IS THIS DEBBIE Peters?" asked a particularly well-spoken male voice.

"Speaking. May I ask who's calling?" She already had a strong suspicion, hence her polite phrasing.

"Of course you may, this is Lord Rupert Duggan-Smythe." He reeled off the entire title to maximise the intimidating effect.

Exactly as she'd suspected. She had after all just talked to him in the middle of the night. "How may I help you, Lord Rupert?"

"I'd like to speak with your man in the Middle East, I believe his name was Miller?" The Lord was playing it coy, because at this point he knew Toby Miller's name, address, service history, age, shoe size, taste in music, poor decisions made during his teenage years, etc.

Well, that's not gonna happen, is it? She squeezed her eyes shut, regretting having picked up the call.

Hugo Chalmers was the last person that Lord Rupert had homed in on, and now Chalmers had been placed on leave. Debbie didn't know exactly what had happened there, but the math was simple enough: the detainee camp location had been leaked, Lord Rupert's son was the operation's primary objective, and it looked like Chalmers' career had suddenly been derailed.

Debbie thought fast, all she knew for sure was that Chalmers was out, and the Lord had just called her.

She grimaced. Had the Lord previously gone in heavy-handed

with Chalmers and intimidated him into doing something unwise? It seemed quite likely, which didn't bode well for her, especially considering she appeared to be the newest obstacle in the way of the Lord getting his son back.

She needed to make it through this call without causing any irreparable damage, after which she'd have more time to think. Her first thought was to ensure that she appeared to be of no use to him, so chose a suitably bland starting point. "I'm so sorry, Lord Rupert, but Sergeant Miller is out of contact at this point in time. He's been inserted undercover, meaning he has absolutely no way to communicate with us." She winced as she waited on his response.

"But Sergeant Miller and I have already spoken since his insertion undercover." The Lord sounded thoroughly unimpressed.

My brain can only handle so much. It was time to think it all through again. Toby had called her in the middle of the night, after which she'd managed to persuade the Lord to call Toby back. But she didn't know anything about the subsequent conversation between the two of them.

This really was an unwelcome distraction and a further drain on her already exhausted mental capacity.

A new direction then presented itself, thankfully. "Yes, Lord Rupert, I'm aware of that. But since that first operation, he's gone back into radio silence."

The Lord paused, "So, has he located a second prison camp? Is that why he's radio silent?"

This must be exactly how the Lord had previously handled Chalmers, but she wasn't about to fall for it. "I'm very sorry, Lord Rupert, but I've had no operational support requests from Sergeant Miller, so I really have no idea of his current status."

"Do you expect me to believe that you have no idea of the status, or location, of your own agent?" But as soon as it came out of his mouth, he knew he'd taken the wrong approach. That he'd only done it out of habit wouldn't count for much.

No, I expect you to leave me alone, to get on with my job.

But that wasn't about to happen, so fake sincerity would have to do. "Oh dear, I think there's been a misunderstanding, Lord Rupert. You see, Sergeant Miller is not my agent. He is an operative working for an entirely different department, over which Hugo Chalmers is Departmental Chief. You'd have to direct any specific enquiries directly to Mister Chalmers. So, unless there's anything else, Lord Rupert?" *Then you can find someone else's career to bury.*

For the Lord it was confirmation that he'd gone in like a bull in a fine china shop, yet again.

The Lord did, however, raise his eyebrows in admiration at how well she'd handled him. She'd shown some real skill in redirecting his clumsy approach. He sighed, realising that changing his ways, at his age, wasn't going to be so straightforward.

"Let me backtrack Miss Peters. I apologise, sincerely I do. I'm just desperate to bring my son home and so my heavy handedness isn't without justification, but I do realise it's a clumsy and inappropriate method."

Whoah! Did an English Lord just apologise to her? Debbie reeled in her office chair, then realised she had to reciprocate.

…Or was that yet another ploy?

Safer to assume it was. "I do understand, Lord Duggan-Smythe, but I think all I can offer to do is leave a message with Sergeant Miller's team over there, instructing him to call in as soon as he can. I do hope you understand."

Oh dear. He'd handled the whole thing very poorly. Now she was so intent on watching her own back that she'd remain overly cautious and uncooperative around him. The Lord looked over at Lady Fiona and shook his head, in reality it was at his own mistakes.

How did he continually manage to make the situation worse?

He took another shot, "Miss Peters, I don't know if you have children…"

"I do not," she interrupted, tired of him assuming she was a 'Miss'.

He slumped again, "I only ask…" How should he even phrase

it? The whole thing felt like he was walking on eggshells. "Because if you knew what torture it was to have your child in such danger." And then without warning, the Lord felt himself start to cry. He could hear his own breathing falter, he wiped away a couple of tears with his free hand, and looked back at Lady Fiona, who impatiently wrestled the phone from his grip.

"Please, my darling." She covered the mouthpiece as she rubbed the tears away from the wrinkles below his eyes. "Just try and relax, and let me have a chat with Miss Peters instead." And then, Lady Fiona strode from the room.

"I apologise. This is Fiona." She'd learned from the last phone call to leave her title at the door. "I'm Rupert's wife. I don't know how I should address you?"

Debbie felt the relief at being handed over to somebody a little less formal, "Just call me Debbie."

"Wonderful. Look Debbie, the only reason we called you is because we're scared." The Lady paused to consider how best to continue, before realising that was absolutely perfect, without further embellishment.

Now Debbie felt slightly emotional herself. "I can't imagine, Fiona, really I can't."

"And your Mister Miller seems like our only hope."

He is. Debbie nodded, not quite ready to reply.

"And that's the only reason we've called you. You see we've not lost all hope. Not quite yet."

"I understand, Fiona." Now Debbie felt rotten at her previous approach.

"And all I can ask for, Debbie, is that if you hear anything new, would you please let me know?"

"Of course, as long as it's information I'm permitted to share." Debbie was still aware of the need for her to avoid Chalmers' fate.

"Absolutely, Debbie, I understand your position, and I wouldn't expect anything other than that. Now, let me give you my personal mobile number."

76.

THE FOUR KNACKERED looking trucks were being loaded up with gear by Regiment boys who chatted as they matched their personal kit to the appropriate vehicle. The assumption of a safe return journey wasn't an option, so each man needed his own gear at his side, ready for the next 'oh shit' moment, and those moments never stopped coming. One of them jumped down to approach Toby.

"Here you go, Staffy." Pole handed Toby a SAT phone.

"And you wanted this." Plus a pistol.

"And we managed to rustle up three extra magazines for ya. Seventeen rounds a piece there, plus the mag in the grip and there's already one in the barrel. So, if my maths are any good, you've got sixty nine rounds, total. Honestly Sarge, I think if you need any more than that, you should call us for help!"

Toby rolled his eyes, "Thanks, Pole. It was nice working with you."

"You too, Staffy, and don't forget, you owe me a coupla beers." He twisted his face to showcase the raw wound on his cheek.

"I'm so bloody sorry about that. Honestly."

"Yeah, I know you are." Pole's smile was warm and sincere. "I think I understand old McCord now; I am looking forward to the scar. And it's gonna have some well-fruity memories attached to it."

"It is, isn't it?" Toby was grinning the same way, "Oh, and Lance Corporal."

"Yeah? What's up, Sarge?" Pole understood that Toby's switch from name to rank implied a change to a more official subject.

"You did good, I think you'll fit in here. If you want to officially become Trooper Pole, just keep it up and I think you'll do fine." Toby offered to shake Pole's hand again.

"Nah, come here, you tart." instead Pole wrapped his arms around Toby, giving him a quick squeeze, then let go to properly finish up, "Well, you know where we live now, Staffy, so don't be a stranger." And with that Pole walked back to the closest truck.

"I won't. See ya guys soon." Toby raised his hand to wave them away.

"Course you will, ya dickhead, we've still got your crap car!" Pole flicked him the V's and the trucks peeled out to the sound of laughter, leaving Toby coughing in the middle of a huge cloud of dust and sand.

"You bastards!" Toby yelled out, wiping the dust from his eyes as he laughed and coughed simultaneously.

"You're seriously not gonna tell me what Regiment you're all from?" Sanchez turned around in her seat to grin at Toby again.

Toby sighed and looked out of the Humvee's window, the terrain was becoming more barren again; less trees, and more nothingness.

"I can't." He wasn't even from their regiment, meaning it wasn't his place to share that information. But he couldn't admit to that aspect either, as the next questions would inevitably be about his own role and duties which were just as closely guarded. "We're nobodies, all of us. We don't even exist."

"Eyuh!" She sneered, "Thanks for nothing, Sergeant no-one."

Toby winked at her, as she grinned back at him.

"So, why are you heading off, all on your lonesome?" Sanchez was apparently tenacious in her quest for information.

Toby rolled his eyes, "I'm not gonna be alone, I'm meeting someone. A woman."

"Are you serious? We're driving you out here to get laid?"

"Seriously? Is that the only reason I could be meeting a woman?" Toby shook his head at her, but really it was directed at the armed forces tradition of everybody trying to get a rise out of each other, no matter what flag flew on their arm.

"In my experience, yeah. But maybe that's a comment on the disaster that passes for my fucked-up personal life." Sanchez puckered her lips and shot him a cheeky smile.

"Isn't it, Woods?" She'd involved the truck's driver now.

"Hey! Don't involve me in your fucked-up madness, Sanchez!" Woods knew a trap when he saw one.

"Good for you, mate!" Toby laughed as the vehicle bounced over a particularly rough patch. "That conversation went downhill really quickly though. Did you notice?"

"Didn't it!" Woods was sniggering now too. "Always does around her."

"Alright. It's time to get out, ya damn limey." Sanchez winked back at Toby now.

"Limey? You're the one with the bloody UJ on your uniform!" Toby opened the back door of the Humvee.

"Wait. What's a UJ?" Sanchez squinted in confusion.

"Are you kidding me? You're wearing it on your sleeve, and you don't know what it is? Just look it up will you!" Toby shut the back door and walked around to the front to properly say his goodbyes. "Thanks for the lift, folks."

"You're welcome, bud. Keep your head on a swivel." Woods fist bumped Toby then mimed an exploding fist.

"And ditch that ugly-ass uniform. Quick." Sanchez looked concerned as Toby sauntered around to her side of the truck.

"I'm planning on it." Toby offered her his hand for a fist bump, but she swung open the door, pulled him in and gave him a quick hug. "Seriously, watch your bloody back. Mate." She mocked his accent.

"Keep an eye on her, Woods, she's a good one. Thanks loads

for the help, I'll be in touch." And with that, Toby started heading toward the ridgeline he'd found by studying the aerial reconnaissance images of the local terrain.

A ridgeline that hid a field hospital from view, but only when approached from the east.

77.

"NO, NO. GO! We don't help soldiers here; you have your own medics." The lady was dressed in normal civilian clothing rather than medical scrubs, and barely looked up from her work to dismiss Toby. But he'd anticipated the dismissal.

The stories of these field hospitals and the conditions under which they operated were harrowing. And the fact that their woes were caused by the warmongers on every side ensured it was the only reception he could have expected.

She looked up at him and shooed him away with her arms, as if he were an unwelcome goose that had waddled into her workspace.

"No, wait, I'm sorry. You don't understand, I don't need help." He tried to appear as unthreatening as possible for her, but really did need to lose the new uniform to have any hope of success. "Not the way you think anyway."

"But?" she gestured vaguely toward his face.

He squinted in confusion, then rolled his eyes as the realisation hit him. "Oh. No, I'm fine, honestly." The colour chart of bruises on his face told a different story. "I'm just looking for a friend. I don't need medical help."

The lady wasn't totally convinced about the second part but hadn't planned on offering him help anyway. "Please. I'm so busy, I really don't have time to talk. Can you just leave me to work?" She continued cleaning the nasty looking wounds on an elderly man's face, as a kid moving in Toby's peripheral vision caught his attemtion. The boy was making a game of pushing another bandaged child around in a wheelchair.

Toby looked around the tent, absorbing it all. In the bed next to her current patient, a younger man had a thousand-yard stare and seemed totally oblivious to Toby's presence. There were at least forty or fifty injured people within sight, but he could only see two medics working to help them.

"You're drowning here, aren't you? Can I help? I've fixed people up before." Toby approached her cautiously.

The lady slumped as she looked deep into his eyes for several seconds, trying to get a read on him. He certainly seemed sincere, and she couldn't really afford to turn down help, not anymore. "Fine, we need to clean his wounds, infection is a constant problem. Here…" she pointed to the appropriate supplies, "I assume you know what to use?"

Toby did. He found what he needed and carefully set to cleaning the other side of the man's face. Was it caused by a beating, or shrapnel? He couldn't tell which, only that it was a real mess.

The man's eyes swiveled toward uniformed Toby, who smiled kindly at him. "You're gonna be fine, mate. You'll be playing footy again in the morning."

The lady stopped working for a moment, and looked across at Toby with a slightly bemused expression, "He's seventy-three years old."

Toby shrugged.

He'd only said it to lighten the mood, which it obviously had. It was an Army tactic, an effective one and absolutely necessary. In conflict zones everyone suffered, without exception, and unexpected moments of lightness went a disproportionately long way. "Still looks like a footy player to me."

She rolled her eyes and started chatting with her patient in the appropriate language, presumably sharing Toby's juvenile joke. Then the man started spewing out an unexpectedly long response.

The man became so animated that Toby had to stop cleaning

his wounds, while he patiently waited for the man to settle back down again.

The lady chuckled as the response slowly rolled in. She signalled the old man should stop talking and looked back at Toby, sighing dramatically before starting the translation. "He says he's a Manchester United fan. Also says he was a midfielder but doesn't play so well anymore." Shaking her head at the ridiculousness of the conversation she was now so totally immersed in.

"See!" Toby didn't even hesitate, "I knew it." Making her laugh out loud.

Toby went back to cleaning, now that the man had finally stopped fidgeting. "I'd have guessed he was a right-back though. Can you tell him that, please?"

Now she stopped cleaning, looked at Toby questioningly, shook her head again and continued with her new translator duties. The scrawny old boy turned back to Toby, smiled, and offered Toby his fist, which Toby bumped in a suitably casual style.

"What is all this right-back stuff about?" The lady medic stared at Toby and then at the old man, who was now apparently Toby's new patient.

Toby cleaned as he replied, "Well a right-back, or a left-back, are some of the biggest and strongest players on a football field, so I'm being flattering, to cheer the old boy up."

The lady laughed again, shook her head, and recommenced her work. "Okay, fine." It seemed safe to assume the newcomer was trustworthy enough as she'd never known anyone able to fake that stuff so convincingly. "So, what do you want from me, if it's not medical help? And who are you?"

"His name's Toby and he is looking for a missing journalist. Here, I have a picture." It was a female voice and came from the entrance to the medical tent.

Toby turned to look, and his face lit up at the sight, "Kay!"

Antonella Ferrara walked over to Toby and wrapped her arms

around him, squeezing him tight, before showing the lady medic a phone image of Danny Ellington.

For just the briefest of moments, Toby felt proud of himself at having such good news for her. "No, Antonella. It's okay, Danny's already free, and he's fine."

Antonella's mouth opened as if she were going to swallow Toby whole. "Ma dai!!!! No way! You are serious? Really?" She looked at him doubtfully.

"Don't play with me, Toby Miller," she growled, unconvinced, then the smile was suddenly back, "He is really okay?" Antonella was all over the map, wriggling her hands in the air, and stomping her feet on the ground in excitement. Then she moved in for another hug and tried lifting Toby off the ground.

It quickly became obvious that wasn't going to happen, "You are very 'eavy." She subdued her huge smile for just long enough to supply the customary insult.

"Come here, Kay!" Toby now grabbed her, squeezed her, and lifted her off the floor, and she squealed with joy one more time.

"I'm so sorry, Signora, just give us one moment," and then Antonella led Toby back outside the huge tent. "Tell me everything, mio cazzo bello, including what happened to your face."

"Okay. Right after you tell me what you keep insulting me with." Toby glared with his eyes, but his smile was much more revealing.

"It is hard to translate." Her hands were all over the place, "Cazzo is something like dick, or fuck, I think."

"You are a pain in my arse, Kay." Toby playfully shook his head, as if in disappointment, but the smile betrayed his true feelings.

"Eh, eh." Her hands did all the talking once more.

"I'm so grateful you picked up my call. I didn't know if you'd still be here."

Toby considered how to present the story to her, then considered the added complication of privileged information. But it was all too much, so he just stripped it back to the core, "I got in, as a hostage, the way we'd planned. Then the camp was attacked, but not by my support team, so not as we'd planned."

He raised his index finger in anticipation of the inevitable questions, "But all the hostages are fine, apart from one who got shot in the leg. It was Danny's new friend, actually. But Danny's looking out for him and I think he'll be fine too. Hell, Kay, Danny's even writing a news story about the whole thing. Except for my involvement, or I'll kill him."

Antonella rolled her eyes, grinned, and squeezed him again. "It's too much, it's impossible." She couldn't stop shaking her head. "Thank you, Toby. I'm sorry I didn't trust you, and I'm so sorry for being a bitch."

"You weren't a bitch." She was.

"I was."

"Yeah, alright, you were." Toby grinned, so she punched his shoulder hard. Toby winced momentarily, as she'd just hit one of the souvenirs of his recent kicking from Maah Mahmoud.

"Oh no, are you okay? I feel terrible." She squinted as she properly took in his damaged state. "And you look terrible. So, how did this 'appen?"

"Thanks, Kay." He rolled his eyes for her. "I fell down some stairs."

She went to punch him again but stopped herself just before impact. "You really are a cazzo, you know, but I still like you." She straightened herself to look more businesslike. "So, if we're not here for Danny, why are we here?"

Toby looked back at the medic who was still tied up in cleaning the geriatric midfielder's face. "It's a mess, but I'm still looking for Charlie."

"Ma no!" The lightness evaporated, and her eyes bulged as she threw her hands up to cover her mouth.

"Yup," Toby nodded, knowing it was time to fill her in on Charlie's complicated story.

78.

"THANK YOU FOR helping me, it was a nice gesture." The lady medic smiled at Toby, "I wish you both luck." They shook each other's hands, then the old soccer star offered his hand up too, not wanting to be left out.

"Get well soon, Pirlo." Toby had picked a suitably famous midfield player's name, an Italian one in Antonella's honour. "And thank you for listening." Toby smiled kindly at the lady doctor. "For giving me a chance, too. I appreciate that you're struggling here."

Toby sighed as they turned and walked away, "These places are hard to be in. I really admire her; I don't know how she copes with it."

Antonella looked at Toby in surprise, trying to decide if he understood how odd that was coming from him, in his battered and bruised state -and quickly realised he was absolutely sincere. For him, the medic's job was harder. Antonella smiled and gave Toby's arm a squeeze.

Toby felt the squeeze and looked at Antonella, hoping for some kind of explanation, then shrugged it off as they had other more important things to focus on. "It feels really good to be out of that uniform, it's a bit too conspicuous around here. So, thanks for bringing my overnight bag, and for agreeing to help me again."

Antonella pursed her lips, "As if I wouldn't help."

"Still, thanks, Kay. I really do need someone with the language, coz they're not all gonna know English the way she did. Are you ready to get to work?"

"Of course, andiamo. Let's go." Antonella took the SAT phone from Toby and started dialing numbers from the list she'd compiled. Every conversation involved asking the same question about the young westerner with the missing eyebrows and hair.

After the seventh unsuccessful call, she handed the phone over to Toby, "It's someone for you."

He hadn't even heard it ring. Toby looked at the number displayed, recognised a Cheltenham area code, then set it to his ear.

"Toby?"

He immediately recognised Debbie's voice, "Yes, Ma'am."

"Stop calling me Ma'am, Miller," she snapped, figuring he might finally obey if it was presented as an order.

"Sorry, Mmm… Debbie." Toby scowled like a chastised teenager. His entire adult life had required him to use those formal greetings to anyone in a position of superiority. Letting him continue would be so much easier, why couldn't she just allow it?

"Look, a quick heads up for you. Both Lord and Lady Duggan-Smythe are distraught, and they're calling me because Chalmers has just been placed on enforced leave."

What? So, Chalmers was now in the situation that Toby had been in just a week before? 'In the doghouse', is what his mum would call it. Part of him wanted to laugh, but he still didn't understand what was going on back home and was far more focused on current problems than getting hung up on any of that. "I'm trying to track Charlie down, right now."

"Okay?" Debbie still had no idea of what outcome to expect. "Have you found any additional information since we last talked?"

"Yes." Toby nodded, "But, do you want to know all of it?" Time was pressing and that complicated story seemed like a poor use of it.

"No, no, Toby, Jim McCord let me know the basics. Just let me know what's happened since you separated from your team."

"Okay." Relief. "Well, our American friends secured the camp so they could…" what was the tactful way to put it? He hadn't got time for tact, so it'd have to be the blunt way, "dig up the bodies of the prisoners. They want them all to go home." He swallowed hard, he'd helped them with the work and it had been a disturbing task, "So, I know without any doubt that Duggan-Smythe wasn't buried at that second camp."

"Really?" Debbie sounded energised, "So there's still hope?"

Toby slumped, they were clearly in two very different places, "I don't know about that. There might be a glimmer." Toby forced himself to think back to what had preceded the grave digging. "There was just something about Ebeid, something he said, at the end."

"Uhh, okay, what?" Debbie still felt some excitement at the glimmer of hope.

"Well, I tried baiting him with Charlie being such a helpless prisoner, and how that fitted in with his noble politics. And he said I was judging him by my own low standards, or something like that."

Debbie squinted in thought.

"And I was standing around later, trying to clear my head, and well… I wondered if he'd actually done something good with Charlie. Not bad, as I'd always assumed."

"You mean, like getting him better medical help?"

"That's exactly what I mean."

"Bloody hell, Miller!"

Toby chuckled, "Yeah. But rewind for a sec, is it just Charlie's family that's calling you? Or Danny's too?"

Debbie inhaled sharply, as she had no idea about Danny's family status. Chalmers hadn't shared anything about the Ellingtons, even though it was clearly him who'd talked to the Duggan-Smythes. "Sorry, Toby, I have no idea, we're in a right mess back here, a change of lead mid-operation isn't good for continuity, or clarity. I really don't know who's doing what."

"Uh huh." That much seemed obvious, even his rapid response unit seemed to have been kneecapped by Chalmers.

"Anyway," Toby continued, "Antonella -my new friend," it was no longer sarcasm, "is helping me to talk to the locals, and we're trying to track him down right now. I mean, we still might find he croaked in some field hospital, but…"

"But there's still some hope."

"Yes, ma'am." It had come out on its own, "Ah, I was joking there, I meant Debbie." He heard a faint chuckle. "There is a tiny glimmer, Debbie. But I think it's premature to let our minor royals know that. They're probably already down at the bottom, let's not risk bringing them back up, not yet."

"Got you. And wow, that's far more than I'd expected. Good job, Miller, let me know if I can help."

"Will do, Ma'am." Then Toby chuckled at using the authoritative manner again as he hung up on her.

"Here you go." He lobbed the SAT phone back over to Antonella.

79.

"TOBY!" ANTONELLA SQUEALED for him to come back over to the shady spot she'd been using to work her way down the list of phone numbers.

"Here you go, kiddo." Toby rolled his toes under the soccer ball, hooking it up and flicking it straight into the boy's eagerly waiting hands. The little guy responded with, "Thanks, mate." A phrase Toby had just taught him. Then the little fella went back to playing with the other kids, disappointed at losing the funny foreigner with the black, blue, and yellow face.

"What's up, Kay?" Toby grinned at her, cheekily.

"Toby!" her hands were wildly animated again.

"What?" Cheek was replaced by concern.

"This man!" She grabbed the appropriate stranger's arm and pulled him toward Toby. "He heard about us. The medic lady talked to people. That you're kind, and Charlie, and eyebrows, with no hair. And that you're playing with the kids and helping her clean wounds." She wriggled her neck at Toby.

"Clear…" he nodded for her, "as mud." Still nodding.

She unhanded the man, who couldn't stop his nodding either, or the slightly manic smiling she seemed to have triggered in him. "He. He knows where Charlie is!"

Toby's heart rate soared, but then the caution stepped back in. It had to, it's how he survived. "Can the bloke speak English?"

"No." she grimaced at such a stupid question. *Don't you listen?* "I speak Syriac." She squinted in confusion.

"Good, that way he can't understand me." Toby smiled and nodded back toward the stranger, "Coz what if he's lying?" Toby smiled at Antonella, then at the man again. "And is using our obvious need to lure us into a trap." One last nod for the overly cheerful stranger.

Antonella started again in Syriac, but with her blisteringly fast Italian pace. The man responded just as fast, as did the lady medic who'd joined in, presumably having just connected the two parties. Toby studied the interaction, and he had to admit, there was no obviously troubling vibe from the man.

But did he dare hope?

"Toby, he helps here. He drives supplies from one field hospital to another. There are so many temporary hospitals, and they don't have enough of anything. There are lots of people like him, they're trying to help their country, and hate this war." Her hands waved around frantically, "And the dottoressa backs him up."

Toby looked at the man, studying what he saw. Toby often inadvertently created a barrier when studying somebody, his concentration typically being misinterpreted as an attempt to intimidate, but the man wasn't intimidated.

In fact, he walked up to Toby, grabbed his forearm gently, then nodded as was his way. "Come." He smiled and gestured to a car that couldn't possibly be in running condition.

Toby exhaled cautiously, looked over at the lady doctor, who nodded her approval, and then to Antonella, who was by now frantic in her excitement. What choice did he have? It was just another risk; he needed to minimise it as much as possible, but ultimately, he had to do it.

So, Toby headed over to the poor excuse for a car, as directed.

"He says these men are very dangerous, they are worse than animals." A worryingly tense Antonella spoke to Toby from the front passenger seat without turning back to look at him.

Toby had previously stashed the pistol down the front of his jeans and covered it with his shirt, but now removed it, and rested his trigger finger on the frame. Their small wiry driver was talking the whole time in Syriac, to a fully veiled Antonella.

"Pretend you're in pain, Toby. Right now!" Her voice was panicked, but she still spoke without turning as their car slowed to a crawl.

They were approaching some kind of check point, although very unofficial looking in appearance. Toby groaned, knowing unofficial was always worse. Far worse.

Toby slid his hand underneath his shirt, obscuring the pistol from any outsider's view, but ensuring it was positioned for immediate use. Then he slumped down into his seat and started breathing in a laboured way, opening and closing his eyes as if in a fever, and quietly groaning, just as all of the car's windows rolled down. He'd read about method acting and tried to emulate the way Pashtana had behaved after three bottles of lemon flavoured magnesium citrate.

A young, bearded man approached them and shouted an order at their new driver, who responded respectfully, although the underlying fear was palpable. The young man shouted another abusive sounding instruction and leaned in through the driver's window, looking back towards Toby.

Antonella now offered the armed man her response, but he wasn't looking at her and shook both his head and free hand decisively.

Toby had seen enough to know the self-appointed soldier wasn't buying their story, so as the young man stood up straight in order to grab Toby's door handle, Toby seized the opportunity and stuck two fingers deep into the back of his throat, wiggling them aggressively from side to side.

As the man's face came back into view outside Toby's open window, the inevitable happened, Toby shoved his head and shoulders out of the aperture and started retching, making as much noise as possible, moaning in pain as the contents of his stomach emptied themselves over the car door's paintwork and anything else within range.

The man quickly backed away, his face a picture of disgust and concern. Antonella fired off a sentence of new words at him, at which the man's eyes widened as he frantically waved them through.

As their driver accelerated through the checkpoint, Toby left his head hanging out of the window allowing the remaining fluid to continue dripping from his mouth. Every one of the checkpoint guards instantly backtracked as he passed by.

Antonella exhaled, shaking her head, "I don't know how you understood what he said, but grazie, Toby. That was about to get very, very bad."

Toby pulled his head back in, angling it to use the driver's mirror -so he could study the scene that was gradually disappearing behind them. A rapidly shrinking version of the soldier was shaking his head and looking down at his vomit covered shoes, "You don't need language to know when somebody isn't buying your bullshit. I just made sure to look like the kind of sick you don't wanna catch."

Their new driver now turned and nodded at Toby, his smile finally gone, but his gratitude obvious.

With the immediate threat behind them, Antonella turned around, studying Toby, "You look so bad right now, Toby. You know? Your face? That 'elped."

Toby finally looked at himself in the driver's rear-view mirror, surprised at just how colourful his face was. "Huh. You should see the other guy," he quipped.

Antonella squinted, wondering if there was more to come.

Toby shrugged, "Oh I see. No, the other guy came off far better than me."

Antonella chuckled and shook her head at him.

"Although, he is going to jail. Probably forever, so, you know…"

The driver interrupted Toby's words with more indecipherable information. It seemed like one of those karate movies where the lead character speaks for three minutes straight and the subtitles only translate it down to a single word. So, Toby knew to wait, and wait some more, for an end to finally come.

"The field hospital is just ahead," Antonella finally shared, which was concerning, as the sketchy checkpoint was still barely a mile behind them.

Toby groaned at the dangerous proximity.

80.

TOBY JOGGED BEHIND Antonella, who did the same behind their driver.

Unlike Antonella, who was focused solely on the man in front and his never-ending stream of words, Toby was taking everything else in.

The field hospital was really nothing more than a series of tents. Most were of the same size and design, but periodically their uniformity was punctuated by a larger structure. The tents rolled up and down the sides of a gentle slope, and there seemed to be very little, to no order, whatsoever.

As they continued their jog, Toby scanned left and right, then ahead and behind, and had to work to maintain a professional composure. On the left he noticed a tent that contained what looked like a hundred people, most were packed inside, others wailing and sobbing outside, having spewed out of the open front of the canvas structure. There were so many people that he couldn't see a single bed through the amassed crowd, but he knew they had to be in there.

To the right was an identical tent, with around ten or so beds, all decorated in the style of their occupants, complete with colorful blankets and drawings somehow attached to the fabric walls. As soon as he'd passed the tent, he caught sight of a rifle-carrying Government soldier wandering down the gap between it and the next one.

Toby looked up to the heavens, subconsciously toward the immortal being who may or may not be up there. They'd just passed through an illegal blockade and less than a mile away, here was a symbol of government doing nothing about it. The whole scene was unsettling. Toby was flaring his nostrils, affected by it all in a way he hadn't expected, and didn't much care for.

He spun his head again, keeping an eye on his blind spot to the rear, seeing nothing but aimless wanderers everywhere. As he faced forwards again, he saw that the driver and Antonella were ducking their heads to finally enter one of the tents.

And Toby stopped dead at the sight; three beds in, on the left-hand side, was a fair-haired westerner with missing eyebrows. Toby swallowed hard.

The driver turned to Toby, smiling, nodding, and pointing toward the man's battered form to show he'd been right. Antonella held her hands up to her mouth in disbelief and wiped at moistening eyes, but Toby fought the rising emotion. He had to take stock of the situation, he had to be the calm one. He walked up to the bed and studied the man's face.

Toby looked at the prone form, then exhaled slowly through pursed lips, as a shiver ran down his spine.

Antonella had previously returned the overnight bag containing his personal phone, and only now did he finally use it -unlocking it to compare a government supplied image of Charlie Duggan-Smythe, with what lay on the camp bed before him.

There had to be no remaining doubt before anyone could get too excited.

Toby looked at the photo of a blue-eyed man; young, tanned, and blonde. Then back at the burned, bruised, semi-bald figure laid out on the flimsy bed.

They looked so very different, and the closed eyes didn't help his attempts at recognition, but the nose, the mouth, the jawline; it was him. Toby peered around the subject's head to get an idea of the colour of what hair remained and all doubt disappeared.

Satisfied, he turned to Antonella and nodded his confirmation, she caught her breath, and made the sign of the cross, before bringing her hands straight back up to cover her mouth.

Toby stepped over to the driver and made an effort to show his appreciation for the enormous risk he'd taken by bringing them here. Toby put his arm around the driver's shoulders and hugged him, smiling, "Thank you, Sir. You're a good man."

The driver beamed with pride, as if he'd got the gist of what Toby had said, then nodded as the duo went back to looking at the hairless one.

"è un miracolo." Antonella took her hand away from her mouth, then remembered to use the appropriate language, "It is a miracle."

Toby looked at the details. Charlie's left arm was on an IV drip, and his right was fed by another tube. His eyebrows were both gone and his face was burned, although not seriously enough to leave him permanently disfigured.

He'd obviously been a good looking young man, the old photo showed that. And as Toby studied him more carefully, he noticed that the hair which had been burned away above his forehead was starting to show, like a five-o clock shadow. So, he leaned in closer and saw some evidence of the eyebrows returning too. Charlie's body was apparently regenerating, to some extent.

"Toby." It was Antonella.

If his body was working to repair itself, then that was a good sign.

"Toby!" She repeated with more force.

Toby was still leaned in close, now listening carefully for any noises coming from Charlie. He was breathing, and without artificial assistance, which was a positive.

"Hey cazzo, are you listening?"

Toby turned and nodded for Antonella's benefit, then stood up straight and turned back toward Charlie again. "What did they do to him in here? Can you ask the driver?"

Antonella squinted in confusion but did as asked.

"He says a real doctor helped Charlie, but we can't talk to that doctor as he's disappeared. There was some bombing a couple of nights ago, to the North, another place where the doctor treats patients. And apparently the Jihadis often target the field hospital doctors, so it doesn't look good."

Toby absorbed the depressing information as he continued to stare down at Charlie. Targeting doctors was a new human low for him.

Antonella didn't look impressed with Toby. "What is wrong? I'm sorry about the doctor too, but this is a miracle."

Clearly it was to her, but for Toby, this was another complicated problem to solve. They'd found Charlie, but he was prone, and without a doctor's input it was safer to assume he needed to stay that way. So, he couldn't be taken from here, seated in a vehicle. "Were there any other medics or nurses who worked on Charlie?"

She was clearly irritated, but double checked with the driver. "No, he's absolutely sure, just the one doctor. He says the doctor is a big loss because they never have enough doctors. They need more of them, not less."

Toby knew that without it being spelled out. But he'd been hoping to discover more key facts, like if Charlie's current state had been medically induced. It was obvious that Charlie's injuries were caused by more than just the rooftop explosion, which had probably been the cause of the burned hair.

Danny's story had put them both in a bar shortly afterwards, so Charlie couldn't have been too badly damaged at that point in the timeline.

But Charlie's eyes were now swollen horribly, as was one side of his mouth. His ribs were bandaged up, and so internal breaks had to be assumed. What if the lost doctor had diagnosed brain swelling? Or even brain damage? What if the doctor had chosen to stabilise Charlie, thereby allowing his body to start healing itself?

The other option was that the local thugs had beaten him into the coma.

Toby had done plenty of first aid training, it had enabled him to maintain life under fire, stemming blood flow in fellow soldiers who'd then made it back home okay. But this was something new, it wasn't first aid. That had been previously administered, and so Toby had nothing. Just unanswered questions.

Toby sighed. It was natural to want answers, but he had to make his decision quickly, even if it was based on incomplete facts. And what it all came down to was that Charlie Duggan-Smythe was in a comatose state. So how could Toby get him from point A, to point B?

"Toby?" Antonella was still concerned at Toby's lack of pleasure in having discovered Charlie, alive.

"Just give me a second, Kay." He shot her a half smile, then walked from the tent and took out the SAT phone.

81.

"SO, THIS IS the only contact information you have? Just a phone number?" Toby smiled as he questioned the driver, who'd been true to his word from the very beginning.

Antonella translated and confirmed the driver's affirmative response.

"Can you thank him again please?" Toby placed a hand on the man's shoulder as he waited for Antonella to do her thing. The man smiled enthusiastically as he heard Toby's words. Toby beamed back and patted his shoulder.

"It'll be any moment." Toby looked at Antonella, who already knew not to translate that part. "So, I'm gonna be waiting right outside the tent." Antonella understood his meaning.

Toby closed his eyes and listened for unusual noises, and for a moment he found himself standing back outside the second camp again, enjoying the hot desert wind. Then an ear-splitting whoosh tickled his ears as a jet flew by, so low that you could read its identification numbers, and before he could rub the irritating vibration from his ears, a second aircraft had followed it.

Toby moved out into the most open spot of land, midway between two long rows of tents, and watched as both jets climbed and corkscrewed to the left.

"Well, their altitude is perfect. They're literally right on the deck." The words were mumbled, not being intended for anyone else.

Then the ground shook before the noise of a distant explosion drew every able body out from their tents.

"Get ready, Kay." Toby yelled over as loudly as he could, and watched as their driver and a second volunteer carefully took Charlie's IV bags off their improvised hangers.

Toby was fidgeting, checking his pistol was secure and pacing the spot. "Come on guys, the clock's ticking," he mumbled to himself again; his impatience heightening the tension.

Then as the sound of the explosion subsided, a new noise became audible, an intense beating noise from above. Toby looked up and smiled as an RAF Chinook moved into view, stopping its forward progress to hover right above his head, a stretcher already being winched downwards.

Toby looked over at Antonella, whose mouth was wide open, then he looked back up to see the second whirlybird had arrived, as promised. The support Apache was flying much higher than the tandem-rotored Chinook, and pivoting downward menacingly, its guns at the ready.

But Toby knew the risk to both choppers was minimal. All of the local rebels and terrorists, at that exact moment, were heading in the opposite direction out toward their detainee camp, blissfully unaware of the last few day's events. Foolishly they'd only be focused on taking the fight to whoever had just launched the unexpected aerial attack on their camp.

Toby ran over to the stretcher and steadied it, as a helmeted airman descended from a second parallel winch. "Are you Miller?" he bellowed quite effectively, clearly accustomed to making himself heard over the thunderous noise.

Toby nodded, then gestured toward the tent. "He's in here, come on." Then the pair of them unclipped the stretcher and jogged it into the tent, where Antonella and the two locals helped them to lift Charlie Duggan-Smythe into place.

Both Toby and the airman cautiously scanned their surroundings as they carried Charlie out into the light of the day, and then the airman reattached the device to the pulley system, before attaching himself to steady Charlie's ascending stretcher.

Having pulled Charlie's stretcher into the aircraft's fuselage, the winch reversed direction and the airman signaled down to Toby, who shouted to Antonella, "We're next. You ready?"

"Si!" she squealed over the double beat coming from the huge object hovering above. Antonella turned to hug the driver who'd made it all possible and was taken aback by how many people had come out to watch the scene unfold.

The size of the crowd woke Antonella to the importance of the event, so as the helicopter hovered overhead, she pulled her camera from her backpack, held her hair out of her eyes and started shooting images of the scene, of the crowd, of the helicopters above, of the tent, and then of Toby, whose hand was covering her lens.

She looked out from behind the viewfinder to see Toby shaking his head at her, sternly. "If my face gets out there, I'll never be able to do this again. Do you want that?"

Antonella now shook her head back at him, as the two empty harnesses swung into reach.

82.

TOBY WAS THE last one to get pulled in through the open door of the hovering helicopter, and looked around the inside of the aircraft as he did so. Charlie Duggan-Smythe was already secured, with his IV bags elevated and an RAF medic checking him over. Meanwhile, Antonella was being strapped into her seat by another airman.

The airman who'd descended by winch to help with the stretcher, now unclipped Toby's harness allowing him to step inward from the open door. As Toby moved further into the aircraft, he noticed an additional person seated directly opposite Antonella.

Toby suddenly felt exhausted, and had little interest in who the stranger was, only in taking his own seat. He looked over at Charlie Duggan-Smythe and decided that was where he should be, choosing the closest spot possible.

Toby settled his bum into the fabric seat, took a deep breath, looked down at the unpainted floor and let the air escape his lungs, adding "Can't believe we did it," for the benefit of nobody in particular. The medic turned and grinned at him, having a pretty good idea of how that felt.

Only now, did Toby finally allow himself to appreciate the situation.

He looked around the aircraft smiling as the helicopter's altitude increased. Antonella was beaming back at him; the closest airman offered him a thumbs up and then he caught sight of the stranger again.

She was about his age, well groomed, wearing civilian clothing and looking more than a little out of place, given the scenario.

Toby looked back down at the aircraft floor and smiled to himself again, suddenly feeling utterly exhausted, then as he looked back up, he saw the stranger was waving over at him.

She wasn't allowed to get up and move around, those were the rules. But as a serviceman he'd automatically be given more leeway, so he sighed, hauled himself back to his feet and walked over to her, taking a seat, one empty spot away from hers.

As he sat down, the noise level increased dramatically, the bird's nose lowered, and everyone could feel the pace of the huge helicopter suddenly increase.

"We're really moving now, we'll be in safe airspace pretty soon." He found a weary smile for the un-uniformed stranger, still unsure of who she was.

But she knew exactly who Toby was, right down to the personal stuff. She also knew what he'd just been through; although looking at his facial damage, she suspected that she'd underestimated the severity of it. "You're Toby Miller, correct?" she struggled to make herself heard.

Toby smiled back and nodded his response.

The lady leaned over and wrapped her arms around him, "Thank you so much for saving my brother."

What? You're another Duggan-Smythe? He hadn't expected that. Then he realised he should have; they were probably the only people with enough clout to get a family member on board a military aircraft crossing hostile air space.

"No worries." He smiled politely.

"You're quite mad. Really. I don't get why you'd do this." The wave of relief at seeing her brother alive was intense, and it helped her to lose some of the typical Duggan-Smythe family restraint.

"Don't get me wrong," she continued, "right now, I love you

dearly for all of the risks you've taken, but I can't understand why you'd do it?"

"Does it matter?" Toby needed a subject change; he was ready to drop.

She thought it through, realising he was probably fobbing her off, which she wasn't ready for.

What she'd already said about loving him for saving Charlie boy was true, but she'd also been sent by her father with an expectation of gleaning some very particular information from the operative.

And being the eldest, she knew how to follow family orders. "Of course it matters. You could have died out here, so why would you volunteer? Knowing that risk?"

Volunteer? Is that how it happened? Toby sighed, knowing he was far too drained for this rapidly deteriorating conversation. "Why does that bloke volunteer to get lowered on a steel cable, into war zones?" Toby pointed over to the airman who'd been winched down with the stretcher.

"The same goes for the pilot who waited for us, hovering on the spot, knowing what an easy target this big bird is. Why do any of us do this stuff? I'm no different from any of them. I'm sure my answer's the same."

She couldn't possibly take that standardised response back home to Daddy, it wasn't anywhere near insightful enough -he'd made that crystal clear to her before departure. But unlike her father, she'd learned that pushing harder wasn't always the most appropriate technique.

"My name's Gemma." Her smile was noticeably less forced than her questions.

"I'm Toby, which you knew before you boarded." His smile was much more guarded.

"I did, but only because I'm so very interested in the man who saved my dear Charlie boy." Her smile still beat his.

"I didn't save him, I just found him. Have you seen the mess he's in?" His smile now disappeared completely. *Why did I change seats?*

Gemma squinted in thought. She'd been told to return with an understanding of his motivations, but now the fellow had genuinely caught her interest.

Lord Rupert had shared everything he knew with her; the operative had been sent in undercover, been terribly mistreated and still calmly earned the trust of Charlie's newspaper colleague.

He'd then kept the prisoners safe while under attack, after which he'd forced her father to admit blame for such a poorly judged decision, which in itself thoroughly impressed her. She couldn't remember Daddy ever having been wrong before. Never.

Then instead of giving up, the operative had ascertained the location of another prison camp, and mounted an attack with some secret unit. They'd freed all of those poor devils too, yet still found no Charlie boy. But again, the operative had kept at it. Beyond that point in time she was in the dark, but Charlie was right there with her, alive. It was a resounding success. Yet the operative's only focus seemed to be feelings of guilt at Charlie's poor state.

Gemma pursed her lips, and chose another approach, "What would you do Toby, if you couldn't do this anymore?"

What? He glared at her for asking such a weighted question. Since this thing began, he'd been feeling cornered, observed, and judged, and now this, right when he was at his most vulnerable?

He was way too tired, too hungry and too angry to be questioned like this, so maybe some brutal truth would make her back off. "I dunno? I'd probably be stealing the nice car your Daddy bought for you for some joyriding fun." Toby then stood up and left.

As Miller took a seat next to Charlie's medic, Gemma leant her head backwards, re-running what had just happened. She'd only hoped to understand why the operative was willing to do what he did, but his reaction implied he'd been insulted, even threatened by her last question.

It was obvious she needed to give the operative some time to simmer down, as she'd probably underestimated his exhaustion and stress levels. But the flight was a short one, meaning that her time alone with him was very limited. So, Gemma broke the rules, unbuckled, and walked over to the Italian journalist -who'd apparently assisted in the operation to free Charlie boy.

"Hi, my name's Gemma, I'm Charlie's sister." Gemma smiled as she buckled up next to the Italian.

"And then what happened?" Gemma's smile was becoming rather more forced and less natural, with every new question.

The unconvincing smile didn't go unnoticed by the Italian lady. She responded, but the doubts were forming in her head. "He helped the doctor by cleaning the old man's wounds. Then while I called around the local field hospitals, he played calcio. You know, soccer, with the local kids. He taught them some silly English phrases too. Lui e molto caro."

He is very sweet. Holidays on the Amalfi coast meant that Gemma understood the Italian phrase. She nodded and smiled again, "But I understand you didn't like him so much when you first met?"

Antonella's trust evaporated in an instant, suddenly feeling like she'd been cornered. Tricked even. "No, and I was wrong. Toby e un caro amico; I don't like what you're trying to do to him. Basta, enough! You can go away now," Antonella's hands waved toward the seat Gemma had previously used, "Or I will."

Gemma sighed and relocated back to her original seat. Daddy's task wasn't making her any friends, which was odd, as Toby seemed to be surrounded by them.

Toby had watched as Antonella became irritated toward Gemma Duggan-Smythe, an odd interaction, which had ended in them separating.

What would you do if you couldn't do this anymore? That's what she'd asked him. Toby shook his head, truly feeling overwhelmed.

He needed to sleep, but right now he had no choice but to deal with this newest problem -yet another dosing of stress. He had to think it through, but his brain was beyond fried.

He closed his eyes and listened to the beat of the rotors, knowing the rhythm would calm his mind. So, what had happened first? That was easy enough -Chalmers initiated everything with his ultimatum about the rescue operation. Then the cavalry had been sitting on a red light, with him imprisoned, again courtesy of Chalmers. Now, Chalmers had been totally pulled from the operation. That all seemed to flow in the right direction.

But prior to that, Linton had been ordered to evaluate Toby's operational performance in the field. And now he was being grilled by the big Rupert's daughter -with oblique questions about career changes? No flow there, just turbulence.

Toby slammed his balled-up fists down onto his legs, then slumped and dropped his head into his open hands.

It was all over.

He'd been so naive. He'd believed in the absoluteness of the official report that had cleared him of misconduct in bringing Madyson Lutz back to the UK. He'd assumed the suits in government had believed his stated version of events, i.e. that he'd travelled to the US with the sole objective of persuading her to return. The second assumption was that they'd forgiven it being unsanctioned because the outcome had been to everyone's satisfaction. How utterly naive. He shook his head, knowing he was screwed.

But how screwed?

Would an Army return still be an option? It would certainly help if he resigned from his covert role before they could kick him out. But he'd have to move quickly, and who would he offer the resignation to? Chalmers had been placed on leave, so Debbie? Toby squinted in confusion.

And then what?

Anything but civvy life.

Captain Bowyer wanted him back, and Lieutenant Linton had just encouraged him to apply for his regiment of elite forces. So, uniform it would be, one way or another; he had no problem with that, he loved being a soldier.

Assuming they weren't going to close that door on him too.

"How are you doing, Sarge? You need anything?" The medic had been briefed enough to already know Toby's military rank, and rank was always the go-to greeting for anybody in service.

Toby looked over at the guy and smiled, it was only fair; he wasn't part of Toby's problem, quite the opposite. "Nah, I'm good, mate. Thanks for the ride though, I dunno how we'd have got him out otherwise. How does he look to you?"

"Oh, he looks rough," then a grin appeared, "Not much worse than you though."

Toby chuckled.

The medic sat up straight, and lost the smirk, "But his vitals are solid enough, I see nothing that worries me there. I think he's probably got a broken rib or two, so we'll have to be careful about how we move him, but regarding this," the medic gestured toward his sleeping form, "This was induced and I'd say this was done because he'd got brain swelling from the damage sustained. But he'll need an MRI and some expert eyes to confirm that."

Toby allowed that information to soak in, then finally felt a wave of relaxation pass over him. "Fingers crossed then."

"Absolutely," the medic nodded. "I've got a question for you too."

"Fire away."

"How did you manage to get the American jets to fly over like that? Our pilots said their bombing run bought us the time we needed to get in and out clean."

Toby shrugged, "We handed some terrorists over to the Americans, terrorists who'd just shot down one of their whirlybirds."

Toby really wasn't thinking as clearly as usual. "Sorry, mate, that was a bit tactless. I'm beat and not thinking straight."

"Don't, it's what we all do, you know that." The medic nodded encouragingly.

"These Jihadis took out their whole crew, so we handed them over. The yanks were really appreciative actually. Anyway, they told me they don't like leaving those camps standing, even after they've been cleared out. So, I just asked them if they could delay their bomb run until it was a good time for me."

The medic grinned at Toby's slippery plan, "They really were appreciative!"

"Yeah, I guess you're right. I even asked if they could run their approach low enough to piss off the remaining Jihadis. I knew it'd draw them away from where we'd found Charlie, and sure enough they took off like a dog chasing a ball. That's how it turned into this coordinated rescue."

"Then thanks, Sergeant, from the whole aircrew. Today we felt a bit less vulnerable. I wish everybody found ways to minimise the shit that comes flying up at us."

"No worries. I'm just relieved it worked."

The medic looked down, laughed, paused, then looked back up at Toby. "So, they lost a crew, and you found the bastards who'd brought their bird down. Then the Yanks showed their appreciation with that fly-by and bomb run, which probably saved our skins. So, who do we pay it forward to?"

Toby scratched at his head, still feeling slightly dim witted, "No bloody idea!" he laughed in embarrassment, "Maybe you start a new cycle?'

The medic laughed back, "I like your thinking, Sarge, will do. Oh, and you can relax now, a few minutes ago our Apache escort peeled off, which means we're already heading over the Mediterranean."

Toby rubbed at his dry eyes, "I think I'll get some shut eye then, thanks, pal."

83.

THE CHANGE IN noise was enough to wake Toby, meaning that cat napping was apparently still where he was at. "What's happening?" he asked the medic.

"We're dropping off your Italian friend and topping off the fuel."

As the vague sensation of a floating horizon was replaced by the predictability of solid ground under the helicopter, those present unbuckled and set about their practiced duties.

"Don't go far," the medic told Toby, "We wanna get airborne again, as soon as. We need to get him home." He nodded toward the younger of the two Duggan-Smythes.

At the same point, the more senior of the two Duggan-Smythes approached Toby.

"Look, I'm exhausted. I don't have the patience to be grilled like this. Just reach out to my handler if there's anything else you need." Toby turned his back on her and walked down the rear ramp to catch a last breath of warm Italian air.

"Ciao bello." Antonella had followed him down the ramp and wrapped her arms around Toby, giving him a tight hug. He reciprocated with a hearty squeeze.

"Thanks, Kay, for everything. And I'm truly sorry that I was snappy with you when we first met." He let her go to better look at her.

"It is nothing, Toby, we were both wrong. But now I think you should call the lady with the photo on your phone, no?" She shimmied her hips playfully.

Toby nodded and grinned, "You were right about that." Toby looked acutely embarrassed, lowering his voice to continue, "maybe about all of it, I don't know yet, but maybe."

Antonella's hands went wild, as they'd done so many other times, "Oh, I must meet her, I'm so happy for you, Toby."

He shot her a cheeky grin, "You know what? I might even suggest we meet up in Italy for a few days, I wanna see more of the place."

"Oh no! Then we will meet up, her and me, we will be great friends, what was her name again? No! Don't tell me, it was Mary-Ann, a very American name. Is she American. No! Don't tell me, I will see when we all meet. You must have a big Italian family dinner with us, it will take hours and it will be beautiful. Maybe we can invite Danny! Oh Toby, I am so happy for Danny! Thank you so much, for… for being you!" She tugged on his hands as she spoke.

"Oh, uhh. Yeah, you're welcome. And I'd love to! All of it. Just be patient with us, we don't know any Italian yet." He shrugged, hoping to imply that might change.

She leaned into his ear, "A secret for you caro, if you make an effort, everyone will love you. Okay?" Then the pair hugged once more.

"Baci e abbracci." Toby whispered as they hugged.

"Esatto! Just like that!" Antonella kissed him on both cheeks, then smiled one last time.

"Ciao ciao ciao," she called as she threw her bag onto her back and strode toward the private arrivals entrance.

Gemma sat down next to Toby, who'd chosen his seat with the sole aim of being left alone by her.

He raised himself to leave.

"No, please! Don't go, Toby. Just give me a moment of your time."

He threw his hands up in protest, sighed, then dropped back into the seat, utterly exhausted.

"If my father could give you anything or do anything for you, to say thank you, what would it be?" Gemma's expression was finally more real, less intense, less practiced.

Toby took a long breath. "A better car," he sighed.

"Okay!" She snapped efficiently.

But he hadn't finished. "For the man in Syria who drives supplies from one field hospital to the next. Coz without him, Charlie wouldn't be here."

Gemma nodded; he certainly knew how to throw a curve ball.

"But it can't be some brand new shiny thing, or it'll get him killed. Something perfect mechanically, but not attention grabbing. That's really important."

"Got it."

"And instead of sending in private military contractors to do the work of soldiers, who are more than capable of doing their own bloody jobs, maybe your dad could station some PMCs in those field hospitals to help the poor bloody locals. Do you have any idea how bad they have it?" Toby glared at Gemma, which wasn't really fair as the glare was aimed at the situation itself.

Again, his response was not at all what she'd expected. But oddly, it was exactly what she'd been hoping to learn. She paused, as while the answers had been uplifting and selfless, she was still waiting on an answer to the question of how the family could show their appreciation to Toby, personally.

She considered touching his arm, the way the Italian woman had when she'd interacted with him. But Gemma knew she'd blown the opportunity to make that kind of connection with him. "But Toby, what could we do for you?"

Toby could have yelled at her in frustration, but instead forced himself to express his feelings at a more respectful volume, "I don't want anything. I just want to do my job, this job. It's the only thing I'm good at. It's all I've got." Then he stood up and left, again.

Although, this time Gemma wasn't insulted, quite the opposite as now she finally understood Toby Miller's motivations, which was all she'd been sent to do.

84.

DANNY WATCHED AS the other passengers stood up row by row, manhandling their various bags and cases out from the tight overhead lockers.

"Après vous." The man in the row behind Danny's seat gestured politely for Danny to exit first.

"Merci boucoup, but I'm waiting for a wheelchair." Danny smiled sincerely at the civilised offer.

A month ago, he'd been done with everybody.

One day he'd be at work in a conflict zone, watching as people's lives were ripped from them: homes, loved ones, everything they valued. The next day, he'd return to his own home to find himself surrounded by people whose perspectives were alien to him; complaining about internet speed or a neighbour's parking, as if these trivialities warranted sympathy and equal news coverage.

This incompatibility was due to his work, there was no doubt. He had other colleagues who worked on the domestic news desk, they'd always be looking for the next thing to run with; find something obscure that a few people were worked up about and run with it until they'd got the entire nation talking about the same subject. Sheep, masquerading as leaders, that's how he saw most of them.

Real or digital made little difference either. On the one hand you had people trying to ruin a restaurant's business because their Tikka Masala had come out lukewarm, while on the other hand you had online beheadings happening in the country he was about to visit.

But he'd just come close to being the star of one of those videos, and now the world seemed like a different place. Although it was him that had really changed.

Danny had been shocked and ashamed at his own inability to cope under pressure, but full of awe and admiration at his cell neighbour's ability to manage well enough for two.

Danny looked down at Yannick, and grinned. Here was a man he'd just met, relatively speaking, but he already knew they'd be friends till the day they died. "There's just two rows left to exit, Yannick. Then we'll have enough space to get you out of there."

Yannick's reaction was simply to smile, a huge beaming smile.

"Oh, here we go. Someone just came in through the back door with a chair. It's nearly time!" Danny's smile grew to a comparable size.

Yannick took a deep breath and bit on his lower lip. He wasn't ready to talk yet, he was genuinely concerned that if he let his emotions out, they'd overrun him.

As the airline employee rolled the folding wheelchair into position, Danny and Yannick worked together to get Yannick's legs over the fixed armrest and into position. "Are we good?" Danny checked with his friend.

Yannick looked down at the bandages covering the bullet wounds on his leg, and seeing no evidence of blood seepage, he nodded away, still grinning like a kid who'd been gifted a puppy.

"Let's go then, shall we?" Danny threw his backpack over his shoulder, the one containing Charlie Duggan-Smythe's camera, and started pushing Yannick toward the aircraft's large front door.

Danny hung-up to end the call with his parents. They'd been disappointed that he wasn't coming straight home, but their joy at hearing his voice was uplifting, and they understood the reason for the diversion. They'd even encouraged it, after hearing the summary of recent events.

Danny looked down at Yannick, "Ready?"

The smile was still there, but some nerves seemed to have crept in too. Yannick shrugged in response.

"You'll be fine, mate, as long as I've got your back!" And both Danny and Yannick laughed out loud at the in-joke, having forged a brotherly bond that few other people would ever comprehend.

Danny took a deep breath, feeling sympathy nerves for his friend, but this time he was committed to being confident and upbeat enough for the pair of them.

"Come on then. Let's do it." and Danny Ellington pushed Yannick's wheelchair out of the secure area and into the arrivals hall of Paris' Charles de Gaulle airport.

As he rolled forward, Yannick struggled to keep his eyes in any spot for more than a split second. It didn't help that his perspective was lower than he was used to, because from the wheelchair he couldn't see beyond the people closest to him inside the packed arrivals hall.

Still, it wasn't to be permanent. He'd been very lucky.

Danny knew exactly who Yannick was searching for, but his unfamiliarity with the person's appearance meant he couldn't really help. So instead of scanning the crowd, Danny just concentrated on Yannick's face.

And then it came.

When the change in expression happened, Danny could have cried.

Yannick immediately did start crying.

And as Danny searched the crowd for what Yannick had already seen, one person stood out.

That the lady was also crying made the job much easier, but what Danny hadn't expected was for the lady to be pushing a chair of her own, containing what looked like a newborn.

Yannick went to pieces, "Ce n'est pas possible? Je suis un pere?"

He tried lifting himself from the wheelchair, but Danny wasn't having it. "Absolutely not! After everything we've been through, you think I'll let you pop your stitches and bleed out the second you land on home soil? I think not!"

But Yannick wasn't listening, just feeling. The tears flooded from his eyes at the sight. "Am I really a daddy? Why didn't anyone tell me?" He looked up at Danny for the briefest of moments. "You organised this? You talked to her? But when? While I was being operated on? Why did you not say?"

Danny winced, doubting his decision, then playfully sung, "Surprise!"

Yannick's head was spinning.

She'd given him a memorable night of adult fun before his departure all those months ago. It was their custom, one essential ingredient in keeping the marriage healthy. But since then, he'd lived with so many doubts: maybe she'd assumed him dead and met someone else, or she'd gone through so much pain after his disappearance that she'd held him responsible and hated him for it, or she'd travelled through Syria and Iraq on her own looking for him and met a fate worse than his own.

But this? Nearly three hundred days in captivity and this was the only option he hadn't considered!

The lady stopped for a moment and held her head in her hands, clearly in a comparable state of shock, then she put them straight back on to the handles of the push chair and started sprinting toward the two men.

It was just too much. As the lady's pace increased, Danny finally admitted defeat and allowed some tears of his own to release themselves, "Congratulations, my dear, dear friend, and welcome home."

85.

TOBY WATCHED AS Charlie's stretcher was carried from the Chinook helicopter. Thankfully, Gemma remained glued to Charlie's side, as Toby couldn't handle any more reminders that his current career was so irreparably screwed.

He lingered inside the helicopter and continued to observe as the two young Duggan-Smythes were greeted by an elderly man on crutches, a lady who was dressed rather like former Prime Minister Margaret Thatcher, and three rapidly moving people who seemed to be there in some kind of service role.

Toby took in the situation, fully aware that his only way out took him straight past them all. He growled to himself and headed toward the huge rear door.

"Be safe, Sarge." The medic patted his shoulder as he walked by.

"You too, mate, and thanks again." Toby smiled without stopping.

"Are you Sergeant Miller?" asked a new voice from behind.

Toby turned to reply, "I am," then added "Ma'am," due to the pilot's rank.

"We really appreciated you creating the distraction back there." She offered him her hand.

Toby accepted it and shook it, "And I appreciate the ride home, Ma'am." Then they both looked down toward the blue-blooded family gathered at the bottom of the exit ramp.

"Good luck with that, Sergeant." She chuckled, then left Toby in order to finish her duties on board the helicopter.

Toby straightened his posture and resolved to maintain his professionalism and civility, even if they weren't going to reciprocate. Then he finally started down the shallow ramp.

"That's him, Dad." Gemma nodded toward the operative.

Lord Rupert looked at Woodcock, who understood what was required.

As Toby reached the bottom of the ramp, a suited man nodded his head deferentially. "Sergeant Miller?" he asked.

"I am." Toby responded neutrally.

"Lord Rupert Duggan-Smythe would like to meet you." The man directed an open palm in the direction of the elderly man on crutches.

Toby huffed and led the way toward the Lord.

"Mister Miller?" Lord Duggan-Smythe locked his eyes on Toby's.

Toby held his stare, initially hung up on why he'd been greeted as Mister Miller, rather than Sergeant Miller. Because with this crowd, it seemed that nothing was without meaning.

"Lord Rupert," he responded without emotion, once more.

"I wanted to thank you, in person, for bringing my dear boy home."

Toby hadn't expected such sincerity from the Lord and was a little taken aback, "You're welcome." However, Toby also felt the opportunity to make an important point couldn't be missed, so added, "But I never had any intention of returning without him."

Lord Rupert looked into the eyes of the operative, looking for some glimpse into what lay inside, but the man had a true poker face, and so the Lord saw nothing. "Again, your work is sincerely appreciated, and I am forever in your debt."

Toby held the Lord's stare but didn't know quite what to do with that last comment. As the pause became uncomfortable, Toby decided to just take his leave, "You're welcome, Lord Rupert. I was just doing my job."

And Toby walked away with his head held high and parade ground perfect posture.

86.

"MS. PETERS IS READY to see you, Sergeant Miller." The young man opened the door to yet another new meeting room.

At the head of the table, Debbie Peters sat alone. "Toby!" she greeted him warmly and beckoned for him to sit next to her, rather than at the far end, as a subordinate would typically do.

Toby liked Debbie, so this was going to be hard. He opened his mouth to greet her as 'Debbie', but the occasion demanded formal, not familiar, so instead chose, "Ma'am," accompanied by a respectful nod.

Oh dear, she understood the significance, which suggested the Lord's conclusions were correct.

"I wanted to formally offer you my resig…"

"No!" she snapped. "No, Toby." Her glare showed she meant business, so Toby waited in silence, as his rank required him to do.

"You are scheduled to sit before various departmental heads in," she checked her watch, "six, or seven minutes time. So, I will only accept whatever it is you're about to offer me after this scheduled assembly. Is that understood, Sergeant Miller?"

"Yes Ma'am." Toby nodded again.

"Now, before heading in, I'm going to allow you to take a look at this, because I'd hate for you to make a rash decision based on incomplete information." Debbie slid a Ministry of Defence document folder across the table.

Toby opened the manila folder and looked at the first page of the two-page document contained within.

Re: Sergeant Toby Miller

Field Assessment Type: Undercover attached operative

Operation: Trojan Horse

Observing Officer: Lieutenant Andy Linton

Summary: In the field Sgt Miller's performance was exemplary.

Sgt Miller exhibited an uncommon ability to rapidly adapt to liquid situations, unhampered by hesitation or doubt. Miller's ability to utilise lateral thinking while under intense pressure resulted in him creating unexpected solutions, which were not only effective in terms of achieving the required objectives, but also in terms of minimising the associated risks for his rapid response unit.

As objectives altered, Miller's role was required to adapt from that of a solo undercover operative to that of a team member within a highly disciplined and tightly-knit elite regiment of HMAF.

Even within these challenging changes of structure, Sgt Miller always acted upon orders given by superiors without question or hesitation. Sgt Miller commanded his 'adopted' subordinates utilising a 'lead by example' approach, which earned him the respect of, and inspired loyalty within the men. Sgt Miller was calm and fearless in the face of extreme danger, but always remained on the right side of the line, never showing any signs of venturing into the reckless. His communication was first class and his ability to both bond and empathise with civilians, even while under extreme duress -was a source of inspiration for those around him.

This section is left blank for observing officer's personal notes:

I remain unaware of the reasons for this behavioural assessment/operational evaluation but feel bound to conclude by stating that if Sgt Miller were to be deemed no longer able to serve within his current intelligence role, I would have no hesitation in encouraging him to apply for SAS selection. I feel bound to end by stating that should he apply for regimental selection, the men he recently served with have openly discussed their approval of Sgt Miller and stated that they have no doubt he would pass selection with flying colours.

Signed: Lt, A. Linton C.O.

Toby scanned the following page, then closed the cover and slid the file back over to Debbie. Before looking over at her, he needed a moment to savour the uplifting words contained within the eval document. All he could hope for now was that the following panel of suits would not close that door to him.

"Thank you, Ma'am." He made sure to maintain the professional, emotionless manner.

Debbie smiled such a warm sincere smile that Toby felt a rise in emotions. He swallowed hard, realising he wasn't ready to leave this world behind him. But he resolved to take it on the chin with dignity, so stood up and followed Debbie Peters, as ordered.

87.

DEBBIE OPENED THE door for Toby, who walked into a room which seemed designed for intimidation. In the centre was a single chair, basic in construction, and around the walls were several more of these chairs, all unoccupied, save for one which contained Lord Rupert Duggan-Smythe.

Toby looked at the front of the room, where there were seven people, all seated behind a long polished wooden table.

Debbie had entered the room with Toby and now gestured for him to sit in the sole central chair. As he sat down in the flimsy folding seat, he sighed, feeling a court martial coming on. Still, he had to maintain who he was, or at least who he'd become since enlisting -as he couldn't face being the old Toby anymore.

Toby took a deep breath and raised his head to look at the panel assembled before him. Some of the faces were new to him, but a couple were familiar. One was the Chief of the Defence Staff, and another was the Foreign Secretary, Rupinder Garcha. Everyone knew her face -she was on the news often enough.

Some old instinct within Toby wanted to slouch, to remain defiant toward their authority over him, but that part of him was now so small, as to almost not exist. So, Toby sat up straight and nodded toward the panel as a dutiful greeting.

"Sergeant Miller." The centrally seated speaker was studying various documents on the table in front of her.

"Or is it Mister Miller?" She looked over the top of her reading glasses toward Toby.

"I'm not sure I know myself, Ma'am." Toby responded respectfully, then heard a chuckle from Debbie who'd sat a couple of seats down from the big Rupert.

The spectacled lady looked across at her colleagues, both to the left and right, seemingly amused by Toby's response, finally answering him with, "That's a valid answer."

"So," she continued, "I have here in front of me, various documents about your time in service of our country." She huffed and looked up from the paper mountain, "Far too many documents, in all honesty." She peered back over her glasses at Toby. "Do you know why you are here?"

He didn't. Of course he had his suspicions, but not really knowing for sure was a cruel form of torture -one that seemed far worse than the waterboarding Pole had recently tried on him. "I do not, Ma'am."

Only now did Toby take in the name plates positioned in front of each person at the head table, from which he learned the speaker was the Director of GCHQ.

She nodded, "Having already studied this," she looked back down at the paper mountain before her, "huge pile of documents which pertain to your service, I've learned that you were sterling in your work for Her Majesty's Armed Forces, which led to your move into the world of…" she hesitated, trying to select the appropriate terminology, "bigger problems. Our world. Where you've also impressed."

Toby sighed; he knew a big 'but' was on the way.

"And then I read the file about the US diplomat's wife. A Mrs. Madyson Lutz."

Toby's stomach felt like it had dropped out from under him.

"Which is the first time in your record where opinions become divided on your service to our country." She locked her beady eyes on Toby once more.

"Yes Ma'am." He was no longer intimidated, just calmly resigned to his fate. *What did they wear in prison these days? It used to be a smart collared uniform, like in the old 'Italian Job' film, now it was probably some ugly shapeless sweat suit, which would be fitting for the scrote he really was.*

"I learned that the victim of that horrific incident was in fact your nephew."

"Yes Ma'am." It still hurt deeply to think about poor young Luke, who'd been taken from them far too early. Toby swallowed hard, then inhaled deeply.

"And the greater feeling I get when reading this information is shame. Absolute shame at the whole thing."

You don't need to lay it on so thick. I'd do it again. Toby's nostril's flared defiantly.

"I am utterly ashamed," her volume had increased considerably, and Toby looked down toward the floor, never a fan of speeches drawn out solely for the speaker's own entertainment.

What was the point anymore? The rank, structure and discipline was all over. There were probably a pair of red-capped MPs already waiting for him in the hallway.

"That we didn't sanction the operation ahead of time, thereby avoiding these negative perceptions which have hindered you…"

What?

Did he hear her right?

"…in your exhaustive efforts to rescue the youngest son of Lord Rupert Duggan-Smythe."

Toby's mouth dropped open as his head rotated from her to the big Rupert, and then back again.

"That one of our own departmental chiefs took it upon himself to punish you, based on nothing more than his own personal judgement of your actions. And after we'd so calculatingly declared you free of all culpability."

It was the truth. The committee's concerns at how the Lutz operation was initiated, were more than outweighed by the perfectly packaged end result, which had even been praised behind closed doors by the Prime Minister himself.

For Toby, the room started spinning.

"That on top of this, one of our own saw fit to order a performance evaluation, without consulting anybody within GCHQ? It is simply staggering. So, Mister Miller… or would you prefer I refer to you as Sergeant Miller?"

Toby had to get his shit together, fast. "Uh, Toby, Ma'am."

She chuckled, which further hit him where he didn't expect it.

"I can only apologise to you." She leaned forward and nodded respectfully toward Toby now. "Because we aspire to create a professional environment where our best operatives feel sufficiently empowered to share their opinions and expertise. An area in which we quite clearly failed." She slammed shut the open file.

"I should also add that this unofficially ordered performance eval has only served to confirm your professionalism in the field. In fact, upon reading the evaluation, which was supplied by the Commanding Officer of one of our most elite regiments, we decided to take matters one step further."

This didn't sound good. Toby couldn't keep up with the direction changes.

"So, we interviewed every single person you came into contact with during this last operation, including all relevant US soldiers. And, to a person, their support of you, and their respect for you, is unwavering."

Oh! Toby's face twitched and contorted under the weight of the emotions which ran through him. The irony was that he hadn't felt such strong emotions since the day when Lutz had run over his poor nephew, which is what had kicked this whole damned thing off.

"Therefore, it has been decided that the entire file regarding your actions in bringing Mrs. Madyson Lutz back to face British justice will be permanently sealed, so that this travesty may never happen to you again."

Toby looked up to the heavens, back down, then took a breath and tried to settle himself. "Thank you, Ma'am." He could feel his lower lip quivering.

"No. Thank you, Sergeant Miller, for serving your country so very ably." The other members of the table now contributed their own versions of agreement.

"Which leaves us with just one more item of business; your future."

Toby looked back up at the Director of GCHQ, and his confident smile returned.

I have a future?

The smile grew.

"I understand that your original unit would like you back. But I also have this eval, offering you an alternative route." She locked her eyes on Toby, "Which is high praise indeed, however…"

Toby leaned forward, to be closer when the words were spoken.

"We have a third option." The speaker frowned in concentration, but Toby was all ears.

"Your actions," she hesitated for word selection again, "and your approach to solving problems; they are atypical."

He winced, *Is that the good kind of different?*

"You've shown an unusual willingness, and ability to adapt in the moment. You are also, it seems, very down to earth and willing to muck in. We have been informed by our American cousins that you insisted on picking up a spade to help them dig, in spite of your own exhaustion and injuries."

Toby was starting to feel embarrassed at all the attention.

"You've also managed to bring together two branches that don't always play so well together; our armed forces and governmental departments united in their prioritising of the common goal."

She chuckled, "Realistically we have two entirely separate operations that would have both been allocated a far higher percentage probability of failure, than success. But look at these results."

She took a breath before peering over her specs with a new

intensity. "Your actions with the Lutz case really should have been sanctioned ahead of time. And let me be crystal clear -there will be no more solitary planning Sergeant Miller. But this will be the very last mention of that old case."

He was overjoyed to hear it. "Yes, Ma'am. I understand."

"Therefore, to better utilise you, we feel you should be in a new type of role. One where you would have been given the opportunity to pitch that operation to your superiors, ahead of time."

Toby caught his breath; he liked the sound of this.

"Might that interest you, Toby?"

"Yes Ma'am," he spat back. Rather too quickly.

"Having thoroughly studied the recent Zarqawi 'abdi operation, we've decided that any new role should have you positioned alongside Debbie Peters, as you two appear to have worked particularly well together."

"I absolutely agree, Ma'am." Toby turned to smile at Debbie, who shot an equally large one back at him.

"Which I think ties things up for now. But before you run off, there's the small matter of a start date."

"Yes, Ma'am." Toby settled back into his rickety chair.

"It has been decided that after surviving such a brutal and challenging operation, you will take the coming week off for some leave, because you look like you've been through hell." She gestured towards his face, totally oblivious to his hidden bruises, which were equally extensive.

"Then you can report for your new duties, all healed up, the following Monday. Bright and early." And with that, the Director stood up and started gathering her papers.

Toby sat in his seat for a moment, absorbing it all. The exposed chair had previously resembled the place of a tortured man, but now it was one onto which a spotlight shone.

The thought of which made Toby jump straight up and off the thing.

"Thank you, Ma'am." He shot over to shake the Director's hand, then worked his way down the table repeating the action.

As they started to head out of the doorway, Toby turned to see Debbie and the big Rupert had remained seated, so headed over to them.

"Lord Rupert." Toby offered the Lord his hand, and a grateful smile.

But Lord Rupert was still fragile, so tugged on Toby's hand and let out a gentle grunt as he pushed upwards with his legs.

Toby looked into the Lord's eyes, finally seeing the fragile elderly man behind the title. "Come on, mate, let's get you back up, I understand you've been through hell."

Lord Rupert got to his feet and started shaking Toby's hand, chuckling the whole time. "I think we've both had a challenging week, Sergeant!" The Lord's smile was suddenly infectious. "Exactly as I stated at our last meeting, Sergeant Miller; I am truly in your debt."

Toby was still reeling, trying to take it all in, but it didn't require much imagination to see that the Lord had played some part in this, meaning that any perceived sense of debt had already been paid.

"How is Charles, Lord Rupert?"

The Lord chuckled again, "Gemma was absolutely right about you."

Toby didn't look convinced, "Actually, Lord Rupert, I think I owe her an apology, I wasn't…" now Toby struggled to find the appropriate words, "…very gracious to your daughter."

"Tsh! You'd been to hell and back man! She's not fragile, she understands. And now I understand what everyone else was saying; that you instinctively set it all aside, to prioritise being a decent human being. Quite the conundrum you are, Sergeant Miller."

Toby finally let the Lord see a genuine, warm Toby smile, "And umm, Charlie?" Toby chuckled at having to ask him twice.

"They're preparing to bring him out of his coma, Sergeant Miller."

Toby's smile grew.

"Do please remember, Sergeant, you will always have friends, and allies in our family."

Toby's smile was constant as he listened to the elderly gentleman, "And I appreciate that, Sir."

"Well," the Lord shuffled himself upright, and into the type of posture which belonged to a former soldier. "Lady Fi sends her thanks to you, Gemma too. Oh, and Woodcock would like the information for the driver in Syria in order to supply the man with a better vehicle for his invaluable work. So be sure to seek him out."

"I will, Sir, you have my word." Toby nodded as he spoke.

"And very reassuring that is. Now, I am going to try and heal alongside my son, so all the best to you, Sergeant Miller." Woodcock, who'd arrived from nowhere, stepped in and helped the Lord from the room.

Debbie waited for Lord Rupert to take his exit before starting her own conversation with Toby. "The Lord has some questions of his own to answer to. Chalmers supplied him with a classified location; then, as you know better than any of us, the private military contractors bolloxed the whole thing up."

Toby grinned at Debbie's unexpectedly fruity language.

"So, while the Lord hired them, which implies culpability, he'll probably still escape consequences because he didn't plan their operation. I think that in the end, his status will be enough for him to come out smelling of roses."

Toby was home, the operation had been a success, and at that exact point in time, he had no issue with the Lord's privileged position.

"So, I'll be seeing you in eight days, Toby."

"Yes Ma'am." Toby grinned.

"Ha! Gotcha! I won't be your superior, Toby. 'Alongside', that was the term they used. So, it would be very inappropriate for you to continue calling me Ma'am. Suck it up and start using my name."

"Yes Ma'am. In eight day's time."

And Debbie took her exit, shaking her head and chuckling as she disappeared through the open doorway.

Ring… ring…

"Hello? Is it really you?"

Toby smiled the biggest one yet. "Sure is. Didn't expect you to pick up though, you're always in mid-flight."

She chuckled, "That's good coming from you! You've been absent without explanation, for?" She paused, as she considered how many days it had been.

"Yeah, I'm sorry. That's why I'm calling."

Mary-Ann suddenly felt a wave of doubt, so held fire.

"Oh no, nothing bad," Toby reassured her. They were right, he'd been to hell and back, and now it was time for him to be equally committed to making his private life a success, as his professional one. The first step was honesty -at least more than she'd had up until now.

"My work. There's so much I can't tell you."

"I know, sweety, and that's fine. I don't need you to."

"But I'm going to start being open, wherever I can."

"I don't expect anything you're not willing to give."

Toby paused, it was a truly terrifying idea to put himself out there. "I know, which is one of the things I think I love about you."

"What?" she stammered.

Toby clammed up, realising he'd made a horrific mistake. How was she going to respond now? With a 'Thanks'? Or an, 'I know'?

What had he done?

"I love you, Toby Miller, and you just made my day, my week, no, my…"

Toby laughed so loud that it cut her off, then he stopped himself as he wasn't quite done yet. "Sorry, I wanted to tell you that, so you could survive the next part."

Gulp.

"I was going to end it Mary-Ann. Not because I'm unhappy, but coz," he took a deep breath, "my work is so bloody risky. At any point I might be the one who doesn't make it home, this last one made that real clear. And I didn't think that was fair on you."

She remained silent as she thought it through from his perspective. She'd always sensed some turmoil within him but hadn't understood the cause, and without that clarity she'd never known how to help.

This was a blessing; he'd opened up, finally allowing her to give that help. "That's a horrible thought. It makes me feel sick in my stomach, but we're not going to lose this. Not for something that might never happen."

He liked that logic.

"I accept the risk, Toby. I admire what you do, it's honourable and you should never miss out on a good home life because of such a noble commitment."

He was so glad he'd told her. "So, how's your schedule?"

It was a sudden subject change, which automatically piqued her interest. "I dunno, loose. Why?"

"How does a few days in Italy sound?"

"Seriously?" He could hear the excitement in her voice.

"We've got some locals we can hang out with. After that, maybe we hop back to England, you know, meet some of my friends and…"

Toby pulled the phone away from his ear as the squealing started.

And family… I was going to add, family.

A NEW KIND OF GREY

TOBY SAT IN the back of the rideshare, trying to figure out what the smell was, eventually deciding the previous day's rubbish from a fast food joint would smell similar, but considerably better.

He really needed his own car back, warts and all. Maybe he should've been greedy when Gemma Duggan-Smythe had been in such a generous mood.

The rideshare pulled into his sister's street, which meant Toby was just seconds away from taking a deep lungful of fresh air. But her street was busy, with far more parked cars than normal. "Where you want me drop you?"

"Here." Toby would rather walk the remaining distance than sit in that car any longer, especially with the rear window switches child locked.

"No boss, I cannot make your walking."

But the moment the driver stopped, Toby exited the car. He inhaled deeply, carefully studying the congestion which surrounded his sister's house, then car horns went off everywhere, making him jump out of his skin. He assumed a defensive posture with his legs bent and his fists in front of him. Then the voices started.

"Surprise!" yelled his sister's voice, accompanied by the same greeting from various others.

"What you gonna do, Staffy? Punch my car?" yelled another familiar voice.

"Oh dear, Toby." That one was his mum.

"Sorry, Tobe, but you're impossible to surprise." His sister Tracey ran up, wrapped her arms around him and they gave each other a long squeeze. "So, this was the best way; we had to get you before you could recognise who owned all the cars."

"Uhh," he growled, "you got me."

"We got him!" she called out to everyone. "But what happened to your face?"

"What?" He'd already put the bruises out of his mind, but he couldn't really share how they'd arrived, so went with, "Nothing."

Tracey just laughed, "Happy birthday, bruv."

"But it's not my birthday, that was…" He squinted as he tried to work out how many days ago it had been, "A week ago?"

Toby's mum joined him and Tracey. "What happened to your face, Toby Miller?" she asked, accusingly.

Full name, already? "Nothing mum."

But Tracey was still going, "Yeah, it was a week ago. But you'd disappeared, you weren't even answering your phone."

"I couldn't." *I was a prisoner.*

"I can't even talk to my own son, on his birthday? Really." His mum pursed her lips and shook her head.

"Alright, Tobe?" Now Damien, Tracey's husband, joined them, "What happened to your face, Tobe?"

"Nothing!" his eyes bulged in annoyance.

"Alright, alright. Happy birthday, mate." Damien looked hurt, so Toby gave his shoulder an affectionate squeeze.

"Hello, Mister Sergeant Miller, Sir." It was one of his dead nephew's school friends. "What happened to your face, Sergeant Sir?"

"Nothing lad, and it's just Sergeant." *Would this never end?*

"Alright Mister Sergeant Occifer Miller, Sir."

That's just taking the bloody piss, Toby turned toward the voice, ready to blow a gasket, then stepped back, "Pole?" He couldn't believe his eyes. "No bloody way! What the hell are you doin' here?"

"Your sister invited me when I dropped your car off. Me and

the lads fixed the window for you. And you owe me some beers anyway, so I said 'yeah, why not?' But what happened to your face, Sergeant Sir?"

"I'm gonna bloody nut you, Pole. Seriously!" Toby grinned and growled simultaneously.

"So how do you two know each other?" his mum asked politely.

"The pub," responded Toby.

But at the exact same time, Pole had answered with, "From the football, Missus Miller."

"So, it's from work then." It was a statement, rather than a question.

"No," from Toby.

And "Yes," from Pole, who quickly reinvented his answer as a "No."

"Well even if I'm not in on the official secrets act, it's always very nice to meet one of Toby's work friends."

"Oh, we're not friends, Missus Miller, he did this to my face." Pole pointed at his scarred cheek.

"Pole, she'll bloody kill me." Toby squirmed awkwardly, "He's just joking, mum."

"Well did you, or did you not, do that to him, Toby Miller? He seems like a very nice young man to me."

"But he's not a nice young man…" *he's a trained killer.* Toby sighed, "You're right, he is a nice young man. I'm sorry, Pole, about what I did to your face.

Pole was struggling desperately to suppress the laughter.

"Now don't you feel better for doing that, Toby Miller?" His mum was glaring.

"Really, mum?" he slumped. "Toby will do just fine. I can remember my own last name, you know."

"Oh, that boy. So help me God." And his mum walked off, growling in a manner not unlike her son.

"You're welcome, Staffy!" Pole was crying with laughter, "You wait until I tell the other lads in Hereford."

"Oh, you…" Toby snarled. Then a smile took its place, "Beers are in the house, they always are. Now go fuck off and get a drink."

Tracey took her brother's hand and gave it a tight squeeze. Toby smiled at his big sister's unwavering support, then his smile faded, and it took him a moment to ask, "When's she gonna forgive me Trace? For being such a shit kid, I mean."

Tracey's eyes welled up and she wrapped her arms around him tightly, "I don't know, Toby." She sighed, "I think in some ways she already has, it's just…" but Tracey had no answer, so squeezed him hard again, "I don't know, bruv, I'm sorry, she is proud of you though, I know it."

"Happy birthday, Miller." Somebody tapped at his shoulder.

Tracey released her grip and Toby turned around to see it was WPC Lucy Bell, the only cop he'd ever step up and help, if ever required.

"Oh my God!" she staggered backwards. "What happened to your bloody face?"

Toby threw his hands up in protest, smiled at his sis, then took Lucy's hand. "Come with me, please," and led Lucy into his sister's house, which was now filled with people.

"Alright, Staffy?" said a young voice.

"Hello Mister Miller, Sir." said another.

"What happened to your face?" a third.

Toby breezed past them all and dug through Tracey's kitchen drawer. At the bottom were still the paper stickers they'd used the last time her house had been filled with kids. He took a fat black marker pen and wrote, 'Nothing happened to my face' then peeled it from the sheet and stuck it onto his t-shirt.

"Seriously though." Lucy had patiently waited for him as he worked on his comical solution, "What the hell happened to you?"

Toby bent at the waist and let his upper body go all the way down to the countertop, which he butted gently with his forehead. He took a breath, then stood up straight. "Work."

"Oh." Lucy nodded knowingly, then looked around the room

trying to find the bloke Toby had just been talking to. "And who was that?"

Toby cleared his head of the other stuff, then thought back to who she could mean, and the choices were Pole, or the local teenagers, so he made an educated guess, "A soldier friend."

"Oh." Lucy flashed her eyes in that certain way.

"He's a really good guy, come on," then he led her toward Pole, who'd already found a beer and was talking to Toby's brother-in-law, Damien.

But he'd only got halfway there, when, "What happened to your …"

Toby flat-handed the kid, then pointed at his new paper t-shirt badge.

"Oh. Okay." the kid shrugged and smiled.

Toby continued on toward Pole and Damien.

"Alright, Staffy." Toby paused to turn, having recognised that particular voice. "Whoah, who fucked you up?" It was Jay, the incompetent mugger.

"You," Toby glared, "Don't move a single bloody inch," He glared hard at the kid to hammer home the order.

"Pole!" Toby caught Pole's attention.

"Yeah?" Pole turned.

"This is Lucy, she's a mate, and she's cool." Toby gestured to her.

"And Lucy, this is Pole. He's got a scar on his cheek. It's dead sexy." and Toby left them to it.

"Jay?" Toby returned to continue his conversation with Jay the teenage mugger, as promised.

"Did it hurt?" Jay couldn't take his eyes off the bruising.

"No." Toby leaned in close, "I didn't even notice when it happened."

"You really do look like a MMA fighter now. Or a boxer I suppose. Like I always said, but now…" the girl gestured her hand in a circle which contained the mess on Toby's face. "it's way worse. Nice house though, but it's not yours, is it? It's your sister's, I mean

I already know, coz Jay told me. Ain't you got your own gaff? That's a bit saddo."

What was her name? "Kayleigh! You guys got together?"

"Well, that's a bit previous innit? I mean, we're hanging out a bit; but maybe, you might be right. We'll see, eh?" she wiggled her head as she spoke.

Toby chuckled at the cheeky nipper and grinned at Jay. Then he lost the grin, "You. You respect this bloody house. Don't forget, I know what you're like."

"No, Staffy, that's not fair. I've changed." Jay seemed truly insulted.

"He has. I mean I didn't like, know him before, but I know he has. You know?" Kayleigh tried so hard to act like somebody twice her age.

"Okay, sorry." Toby put his arms out in defence. "So how exactly have you changed then, Jay?"

Jay had proof, so he filled his chest with air and stood up straighter, "I joined up, Staffy."

Toby's eyes bulged, he grinned and mulled it over for a moment. Then finally he chuckled, "I'm not laughing at you, Jay. Only at how we got here." Toby nodded his approval, "Good for you, kid." Then Toby offered to shake his hand.

Jay shook Toby's hand like a proper young man, then Toby unexpectedly yanked him in close, "Now you listen to me, kid."

Jay swallowed hard.

"Your two sisters are dead smart, I remember them."

"Yes, Staffy."

"But unlike you, they weren't scared to show it."

"I'm not scared." Jay sneered.

"Then prove it, kid." Toby still had him pulled in uncomfortably close. "This crap, this normal life stuff, it's gonna seem irrelevant to you really soon. So, you're gonna need to make new habits."

"Okay, Staffy." Jay was getting interested in where this was going.

"Acting dumb only works when you're a teenager who's got nothing else going on in life, and I think you've got some smarts in there." Toby rapped on Jay's skull with his free hand, "So start showing them to the world, especially to the Army. Okay?"

Jay's eyes moved around in thought, then he looked back at Toby, "Yeah. Okay, Staffy."

"Coz I know you've got the willpower to do it. But you gotta stop playing it dumb. Coz you're not." Then Toby released Jay's hand and ruffled up his perfectly manicured hair. "Now I'm gonna leave you kids to it, coz I've gotta go talk to my sis."

"Alright, Staffy, see ya later." Jay had a newfound confidence about him. Kayleigh merely pouted and looked around the room at all the adult saddos.

"Hey sis, how are you doin?" Toby wrapped his arm around Tracey's slim shoulders.

She smiled, it was cautious, but a real one. "I'm getting there."

"Thanks for doing this." Toby gestured to the crowd.

She just grinned and shrugged.

"Luke would love this, and I mean love it." Toby looked deeply into her eyes and nodded, to reinforce his own words.

"I know." Her uncertain smile held firm.

"What happened to your…" a passerby started to ask.

"Don't." Toby pointed to his badge.

The passerby accelerated away.

"How are you doing, love?" Toby's mum had joined them, and was checking on Tracey, really out of habit.

Tracey smiled warmly and nodded; her brother was home.

"And you Toby, when am I going to meet this lady friend of yours?"

Toby inhaled slowly, maybe this would do some bridge building? "How about next week, mum?"

His mum's eyes narrowed, "Yeah right. I'll believe it when I see it."

"Toby!" Damien's voice yelled across the living room.

"What?" Toby looked over to see his brother-in-law cutting through the crowd carrying a huge bottle, gift wrapped with an abundance of colourful foil ribbons. "What the hell?"

Damien reached Toby and thrust the bottle toward him. "Some driver just delivered it, for a Sergeant Toby Miller."

Toby took the enormous champagne bottle from Damien, as his mum ripped the card off the side then opened it, without even asking for permission. Toby sighed, utterly powerless against her.

"Who are the Duggan-Smythes?" She locked her eyes on Toby suspiciously.

"Seriously?" Toby pulled at the card, eventually winning the tug of war with his mum. The only written words were 'From the Duggan-Smythe family, in sincere thanks.'

Toby shook his head, then laughed out loud. "Pole!" He bellowed across the room, "This is for you too." He waved the huge bottle in the air.

Meanwhile Tracey had ignored the ruckus to pull up a news page on her phone. She'd read a story about Syria earlier in the day, and that double-barreled last name had just triggered some vague sense of recognition.

Her suspicions confirmed, she placed her mobile phone back down on to the kitchen counter, and looked over at Toby proudly, "My baby bruv."

ABOUT THE AUTHOR

An internationally published writer and photographer for magazines, newspapers, non-fiction books, commercial clients and television; Simon Green now brings those professional writing skills to storytelling.

    Rescue & Redemption is the follow up to Green's highly rated fiction debut Hit & Split, whose central character Toby Miller was described by Kirkus Reviews magazine as "a surprisingly endearing hero" amongst many other superlatives in their glowing review.

`www.shotbysimon.com`

Printed in Great Britain
by Amazon